The Girl From Pit Lane

Gracie Hart was born in Leeds and raised on the family farm in the Yorkshire Dales. Though starting out as a glass engraver, and then raising her family, Gracie has now written several family sagas.

Gracie and her husband still live in the Yorkshire Dales and they have two children and four grandchildren.

GRACIE HART

The Girl From Pit Lane

EBURY
PRESS

This edition published by Ebury Press in 2018
First published by Ebury Press in 2018

1 3 5 7 9 10 8 6 4 2

Ebury Press, an imprint of Ebury Publishing
20 Vauxhall Bridge Road,
London SW1V 2SA

Ebury Press is part of the Penguin Random House group of companies
whose addresses can be found at global.penguinrandomhouse.com

Penguin
Random House
UK

www.penguin.co.uk

A CIP catalogue record for this book is available from the British Library

ISBN 9781785038075

Printed and bound in Great Britain by Clays Ltd, Elcograf S.p.A.

Penguin Random House is committed to a sustainable future for our business, our readers and our planet. This book is made from Forest Steward-
ship Council® certified paper.

MIX
Paper from
responsible sources
FSC
www.fsc.org   FSC® C018179

One

'Stop your bloody brat from gawping at me,' Bill Parker snarled at his wife, Sarah, as her daughter Mary-Anne watched her stepfather greedily eat the stew that had been gently bubbling over the coal fire for most of the day. The gravy was running down his chin, making tracks on his black coal-dusted skin.

'Mary-Anne, go and help your sister with the water for your father's bath.' Sarah gave a warning glance to her oldest daughter, knowing that Bill was in no mood to be challenged. He'd been drinking since the end of his shift down the pit, and was now the worse for wear. A time the whole family knew to be wary of him, as drink did nothing for the usually mild-mannered man.

'Yes, Mother.' Mary-Anne needed no further prompting as she made for the back door of the small two-bedroom miner's cottage to their wash house that adjoined the terraced house and was the refuge from their stepfather's wrath.

She knew better than to say, 'he's not my father.' In truth she'd only been staring at her stepfather as she'd been wishing that there

1

would be enough stew left over for her and her sister as another supper of just bread crusts would be unbearable. But when Bill had come in leery with drink, and in a mood as black as the coal dust that covered him, she knew better than to ask for even a taste of the stew that had tantalised her taste buds for the most of the day.

'Mind you and Eliza make sure the water is warm enough and let your father eat his meal in peace.' Sarah looked at her daughter, knowing that she understood to make herself and her sister scarce in order to protect them from their stepfather's anger.

'Yes, Mother.' Mary-Anne closed the door behind her and sighed as she stepped into the dark, freezing backyard, making her way to the attached wash house where her younger sister was tending to the copper boiler, full of water to fill the tin bath for her stepfather to have his daily bath in.

'Bill's back.' Mary-Anne sighed and sat down heavily on the stool that was her usual hiding place when needed.

'I take it he's the worse for drink, else you wouldn't be here with me.' Eliza poked the burning embers underneath the huge copper boiler, which took up most of one of the corners in the wash house, and wiped her brow free from the sweat that was trickling down her flushed face.

'Aye, there will be no reasoning with him; you've just to look at him tonight. I don't know why old Lewis the landlord at the Boot and Shoe doesn't tell him to get himself home earlier. He knows what he's like when he's had too much.' Mary-Anne looked at her sister and was thankful that they were both in the relative safety of the wash house, but she feared for their mother who was left behind appeasing her drunken husband.

'Lewis is just a greedy bastard and Bill is easily led. He can't walk past the doors without feeling he's got to go in.'

Mary-Anne sat down next to her sister and waited. Their stepfather would either appear for a wash in the tin bath that was next to them or he'd hopefully be so drunk and dozy that he would go to bed after his supper.

'Eliza, our real father would have belted you for saying words like that and Mother still would if she heard you saying it.' Mary-Anne looked shocked at her younger sister.

'You can't deny I'm right, though. And as for our true father, I sometimes worry that I can't even remember his sweet face, it has been so long since he died and our lives have changed so much.' Eliza put her head in her hands and fought back tears.

'You were only young; I'm surprised you can remember him at all. I barely can and I'm two years older than you.'

Mary-Anne had been nine, and Eliza just seven, when their father had died and their whole world had fallen apart. Their father had been a miner like Bill but a rock fall at Rose Pit had cost him his life over ten years hence.

'Well, I do, and I curse the day our mother met Bill Parker. He's nothing but a drunken bully.' Eliza lifted her head and spat out her words of hate against their stepfather.

'He's a drunken bully who took us all in when he could have sent us to the workhouse. At least we're still with Ma and have a roof over our heads.' Mary-Anne went quiet as raised voices could be heard from inside the cottage.

'I don't know why she doesn't leave him,' Eliza whispered. 'I couldn't put up with his ways.'

Bill's voice could be heard shouting at their mother and both sisters looked at one another, not daring to go and help their mother, as they knew it would only make matters worse for all of them. A crash of breaking china followed and Bill's voice bellowed from within.

*

'Don't you bloody tell me to go to bed, woman! Who do you think you are? You're nothing but a penniless whore with two useless bitches tied to your apron strings.'

Inside the small cottage, Bill clenched his fist close to his wife's face as the other held her tight by the neck pinned to the whitewashed kitchen wall.

Sarah struggled for breath as Bill leered at her, his breath smelling of stale beer as he breathed heavily on her. She put her hands on his arms and tried to pull them off her.

'Bill, let me go. This is no good for anyone.' Sarah gasped as he released his grasp slightly. 'You've just had too much to drink. Go and sleep it off.'

'Shut your mouth!' Bill swung his fist into Sarah's face making her head spin, and she felt a trickle of blood run down from her burst lip. Then she felt her feet give way beneath her, as Bill pummelled her head against the wall leaving her unconscious and crumpled on the floor.

Bill looked at his wife lying still and lifeless on the flagstones and then looked around at the plates he had thrown at her and the upturned chairs. He grunted to himself and then stumbled backwards, making his way to the stairs where he stopped unsteadily in his tracks, satisfied that he had vented his feelings on his wife but wondering if he should check she was still breathing.

As unsteady on his feet as he was, he decided against it and crawled his way up to his bed as Sarah had told him to do previously. Sprawling out on the clean sheets in his coal-dusted clothes and with his boots still on, he smiled to himself as he fell asleep. He'd taught that whining bitch a lesson, for sure; she'd not tell him to go to bed in a hurry again.

*

In the warm gloom of the wash house, Eliza and Mary-Anne whispered quietly to one another. Waiting – once the shouting had finished – to hear their stepfather's footsteps visiting the bottom of the yard privy before coming for his bath.

'He's not coming. He must have gone to bed. But where's Mother? She usually comes to tell us that the coast is clear.' Eliza shot Mary-Anne a worried glance; her stomach was churning and she felt sick.

The racket from within the red brick terraced cottage had been so bad. She knew that Bert and Ada Simms, their next-door neighbours, would have been able to hear the night's traumas. That once again it would have given Ada something to gossip about, and reason to pry into their affairs. But most of all she was worried for her mother's safety.

'I'll go. Stay here. Something must be wrong, else mother would have come out here.' Mary-Anne stood up and looked down at her cowering sibling. 'Put the fire out, Eliza, but don't empty the copper boiler. We'll use the water for washing the clothes tomorrow.' Mary-Anne breathed in deeply; as the eldest she felt it her duty to protect her younger sister. Even though Eliza spoke harsh words, deep down she knew she was petrified of Bill when he was in his cups. They both were.

'No, we'll both go.' Their father always bathed daily, getting rid of the dirt and grime of the coalface only leaving Sunday free for the girls and their mother to indulge in their weekly ablution. Eliza reached for the jug that their mother usually filled with water to rinse their stepfather off in his bath and filled it with hot water from the copper boiler, pouring it on the fire that still burned underneath. Watching the steam rise as the fire spat and fought for its life she held her hand out for her sister and clenched it tightly as they made their way out of the wash house, and into the house.

'Mother!' Both girls rushed to their mother's side where she lay, head propped against the kitchen wall with a trail of red blood from her matted hair streaked down the whitewashed wall.

Sarah groaned and opened her eyes, trying to focus on her two daughters.

'I'll go and get help. I'll get Mrs Simms from next door.' Eliza looked at her mother. This time her stepfather had gone too far.

'No, no, Eliza, don't,' Sarah whispered as she came around. 'She can't do anything for me that you can't ... Besides we don't want the neighbours to know our business. Although no doubt she will have heard everything tonight, the way your father was ranting. Help me up, Mary-Anne. I'll be all right once I'm up on my feet and I've got a cup of tea in me.'

Both Mary-Anne and Eliza helped Sarah to her feet. Mary-Anne set one of the upturned kitchen chairs right, then sat her down gently. She sent Eliza to the wash house to fetch hot water, eyeing her mother warily while her sister was gone.

'We can't go on like this, Ma. You've survived this time, but next time he might kill you.'

When her sister returned with the water, Mary-Anne bathed her mother's battered head, dabbing her matted blonde hair gently with a clean tea towel and then patting the split lip that had poured blood down the front of her mother's high-necked white blouse. 'You've got to leave him. We'd survive somehow.'

'No, I can't leave him. It's only when he's been drinking and doesn't know what he's doing. Tomorrow he'll be full of remorse, like he usually is, and won't touch a drop for a while.' Sarah sipped the tea that Eliza gave her and winced as the hot drink scorched her cut lip.

'Well, he's made a nice mess of the kitchen.' Mary-Anne looked around at the smashed dinner plates and the stew that she had longed for now spilt over the flagstones. 'Looks like we're going to bed hungry yet again.'

Sarah reached for Mary-Anne's arm. 'He's a good man is your stepfather. He puts up with a lot, and not many men would have taken us all on when your father died.'

Eliza picked up the broom from behind the kitchen door and started sweeping the broken pieces of crockery up from off the floor, stopping at the bottom stairs to listen to the snores coming from the upstairs bedroom. 'He's snoring like a stuffed pig now. I wish he was dead, like my proper father. He wouldn't have done anything like this.'

'Eliza, don't say things like that, you should never wish anyone dead. My girls, we have to endure what life throws at us and us women are at the mercy of the men we wed, always remember that.' Sarah held her arms out to embrace her daughters, holding them tight as she stared into the dying embers of the fire. If she could turn back time and change her lot in life she would, but she had made her bed and now she must lie in it, with her drunken brute of a husband.

All she could do was pray for a better life for both her girls, that they would marry good men and be more contented in life than she was. She would continue to do what she had to do to keep her girls safe and a roof over their heads, no matter what she had to put up with.

Two

Ada Simms had scrubbed and donkey-stoned her front steps so much that they were now whiter than the bleached whale jaw-bones that arched over the gateway to Fenton House in nearby Rothwell. The traded donkey stone from the rag-and-bone man made of bleach and sandstone was nearly at the end of its life after so much scrubbing. But she was determined to catch and speak to her next-door neighbour after hearing all the racket the night before as she and her Bert had sat around the fire after enjoying their supper.

Bert had told her to mind her own business, but Sarah was her friend and a neighbour – it *was* her business. And besides, her friend May Atkins had hinted that all was not as it seemed next door when she had joined her for tea the previous week. She'd watched from behind her lace curtains as Bert had knocked for Bill Parker to join him on the walk to their work at the pit, but if she'd been hoping for some signs of last night's trouble she'd been disappointed. She'd watched them walk to work together in the light of the dim gas lamps as usual, just as if nothing had happened. What she'd expected she didn't know, but now she had to wait for Sarah to appear, just to put her mind at rest that she was all right.

Ada's senses twitched as she heard the handle of the door being turned at number one, Pit Lane, and she got ready to catch her prey like a cat with a mouse. She stood with scrubbing brush in hand and leaned on the adjoining garden wall. No matter that the weather was freezing and the cold wind was making her hands sore, she was determined to make next-door's business her business.

'Good morning, girls.' Ada sounded deflated; she had been hoping that it was Sarah that was leaving the house.

'Morning, Mrs Simms.' Eliza and Mary-Anne chimed together.

'Everything all right at your house? How's your mother?' Ada enquired, making it quite obvious that she had heard the previous night's goings on.

'She's fine, thank you. Busy washing some sheets.' Mary-Anne smiled at her nosy neighbour. She wasn't even lying – after her stepfather had walked out to work without saying a word to any of them, her mother had stripped the bed he'd layed on and was busy scrubbing the bedding free of coal dust.

'I'm sorry if we were a bit noisy last night. I dropped some of my mother's best china and my stepfather lost his temper with me. 'Eliza jutted her chin out a little as she embroidered the story, almost daring her neighbour to challenge her lies. 'I'm such a clumsy devil. I swear I'm not be trusted with anything.'

'Oh, I didn't hear anything my dears. Bert and I are oblivious to the world around us once we're settled in front of our fire of an evening.' Ada blushed and looked at the two brazen-faced young women. 'Are you off into town?'

'Aye, we are off to the market in Leeds to see what clothes we can pick up and then we might be doing a bit of knocking and begging on rich folk's doors if there's nothing that's of worth on the market.' Mary-Anne closed the garden gate quickly behind her and Eliza, eager to leave their inquisitive neighbour.

Ada watched as the two young women walked down the rough track of Pit Lane. Strange, Sarah was doing her sheets on a Thursday; Monday was her wash day along with the rest of the street, she thought.

No matter what had gone on next door, they were covering their tracks, and no matter what they said, she knew full well it was more than just dropping a few plates.

Eliza had to wait for her sister several times as she hobbled along the towpath of the Leeds-to-Liverpool canal that flowed on the outskirts of Woodlesford on its way to service the many mills and factories before it reached the Irish Sea.

'I don't know about second-hand clothes … I could do with a new pair of boots.' Mary-Anne sat down at the edge of the canal and looked at the hole in her boots that was making her foot sore. She watched as one of the open barges known locally as 'Tom Puddings' passed them, loaded with coal from the pits on its way to feed the factories of Leeds or the ports of Liverpool and those along the banks of the Humber. Her skirts edged up around her knees as she sat on the bank, making the man steering the barge shout out an offer of making some quick money.

'Now, that's a pretty sight. Penny for a quick 'en?'

'You keep your hand on the tiller,' Mary-Anne shouted back, 'it's the biggest thing you'll hold all day, and more stiff.'

The cheek of the man; she wasn't a prick-pincher like the women and girls that strutted down Canal Street. He'd have to seek his relief there.

She pulled down her skirts and pushed the piece of cardboard that had been filling the hole in the bottom of her boot back into place and quickly laced her boot back up. In the distance the growing city of Leeds lay in front of them, blanketed in the smoke of the busy industries that were making Leeds one of the largest manufacturers of wool and textiles in the country. But while the factory and mill owners were thriving, building their fancy houses on the outskirts in Roundhay Park and Chapel Allerton, the ordinary factory workers suffered at their hands, living in back-to-back houses with open sewers running down the streets, overcrowded and starving.

'Hurry up, Mary, and stop encouraging the bargemen; they don't need a lot. And you know that Ma would give you a clout if she heard you being saucy. We'll miss the best buys on the market. You know old Mrs Fletcher will not hold on to her best stuff for long before she sells it on to someone else.' Eliza was eager to go and rummage on the Fletchers' rag-and-bone cart to find clothes that she and Mary-Anne could wash, repair and then sell on in their little lean-to shop in the centre of their village.

The clothes made them a small profit, which helped to boost the family income. They had an understanding with the rag-and-bone man's wife that they had first choice of her best clothes providing they were there before seven in the morning. Otherwise they took their chances with everyone else rummaging through the cart, and this morning, after checking their mother was all right after the previous night's skirmish, they were late. The prospect of knocking on doors asking for any old rags through the back streets of Leeds, like they sometimes had to, did not fill Eliza with joy. Too many times they had been shouted at – 'no hawkers' or worse. Once a dog had been set on her.

Mary-Anne finally rose to her feet and stretched. 'I know, I'm coming. I don't know about you but I'm tired. I tossed and turned all night thinking about things.'

'So did I, and I don't think Ma went to bed at all. She slept in the chair next to the fire, rather than disturb our stepfather. He hadn't a lot to say to us this morning, I noticed. ' Eliza urged her sister to walk faster, as they ambled along the cobbled towpath. 'He ate his porridge, grabbed his snap box and then left. I hope he's regretting his night's work and that he's got a sore head this morning. Because I'm sure Mother will have one after his battering. Let's hope he doesn't come home in a state like that for a while now. I hate him when he's in such a bad way.'

'Heaven knows what next door thought,' Mary-Anne replied. 'Ada Simms was doing her best to find out what the noise was all about, and did you see her Bert's face, when Bill went out of the house as black as he had returned to us last night? I'd like to be a fly on the wall next door tonight when he arrives home; I bet Ada never lets up.' Mary-Anne strode out and smiled at her sister, knowing that Eliza was thinking the exact same thing. Eliza and she were so close; there was a bond between them that could never be severed. They had relied on one another for support since their true father had died, and now they were nearly both full-grown women, independent but the best of friends.

Making their way out of Leeds docks, Eliza and Mary-Anne arrived into a city that was bustling with life of all sorts, and the two sisters hurriedly made their way up to the market at Briggate. They passed by men who were surveying the site for the new building that was going to be the corn exchange, which in coming years would be busy, filled with local merchants bidding on and buying corn and maze. The smell of the tannery and slaughterhouse nearby wafted down, while street traders called out, making everyone aware of the wares they were selling.

The city was alive with street urchins, ducking and diving between the merchants and their customers, picking a pocket here and there, and the less bold or nimble begged on street corners for a farthing to keep them fed for the day.

The constant noise from factories spinning wool and cotton filled the air, along with the smells of the city, open sewers, smoking chimneys and cooking food from the stalls that were tempting people as they went about their business.

Eliza and Mary-Anne weaved and picked their way through the crowds, avoiding the worst of the dirt and horse manure on the busy street, arriving at the wide avenue filled with market traders called Briggate.

The spire of Holy Trinity Church rose above them as they walked up the rows of shops and traders that lined the route. Outside the printers' shop they spotted Mrs Fletcher with her flat cart filled with rags and second-hand goods, bought and traded from the well-to-do houses around the Headingley and Kirkstall districts of Leeds, where the higher echelons of Victorian society lived.

'Morning, lasses, I thought you were going to miss your chance this morning. I was just about to empty your sack onto my cart, thinking you weren't going to show.' Mrs Fletcher was as round as she was tall, tendrils of her long straggling grey hair were escaping from under a dirty white milk-maid's cap and her dress was of a rough woven wool and was just as filthy. She grinned a toothless grin at her two best customers and wiped her running nose along her sleeve. 'Got some good things for you today. My old man went up Roundhay; there's a lot of well-off gents up that way and they have to keep their women suitably attired. What do you think of these then?' She emptied her sack, uncovering an array of cast-off dresses, shawls and skirts all in need of washing, mending and a bit of care before being re-sold by Mary-Anne and Eliza.

'How much do you want for this one?' Mary-Anne lifted up a green brocade dress with a tear where the skirt was attached. It had in its time been a stunning dress and must have cost a pretty penny when first made.

'Sixpence?' Ma Fletcher put her head on one side; her cheeks were ruddy with small veins that came from making her living so long outside in all weathers. She reminded Mary-Anne of a cheeky garden robin as she waited while both sisters inspected the garment.

'Threepence? It will take me a long time to repair this and then it's a bit fine for some of the ladies that come to our shop in the village.' Part of the game was to haggle and all three knew it was what was expected.

'Four pence and we have a deal.' Ma Fletcher waited and watched as both sisters looked at one another.

'Yes, go on, and all the rest from out of your sack for a sixpence?' Mary-Anne watched Eliza holding up various items of clothing, inspecting them for the amount of wear and tear.

'A silver sixpence and you can take the lot. It's a fair price, there's some good stuff. You'll soon sell it in your shop in Woodlesford.' The old woman waited.

'A sixpence if you'll include those boots.' Mary-Anne pointed to pair of lace-up boots on the cart that looked to be about her size. They looked scuffed and dirty but they didn't appear to have any holes in, unlike the ones she had on her feet.

'Aye, you girls will be the death of me with your hard bargaining. But, go on, we've a deal.' Ma Fletcher spit on her hand and held it out for either Eliza or Mary-Anne to shake.

Mary-Anne shook it hesitantly and found a sixpence from out of her coat pocket while Eliza pushed the traded clothes back into the hessian sack that they had come from.

'What are you girls going to do now you've robbed me blind?' Ma Fletcher watched as Mary-Anne picked up the boots by their laces and smiled, knowing that they had made a good deal.

Mary-Anne looked at her sister who was having a second look through what was left on the cart. 'We might just go and see our aunt, now we've done our business. Do you think we should, Eliza?'

'Yes, if you want, we have the time now.' Eliza stopped rummaging and put the sack with contents over her back. She quite liked her Aunt Patsy and was keen to visit her as she was never welcome in their home. Their stepfather Bill would not allow her in his house because he thought her to be immoral; it was common knowledge that she helped young women in trouble with unwanted pregnancies with her herbal concoctions and potions. Patsy knew her plants, herbs and their properties well, and their mother often commented that if she had been born a century or two earlier her sister would probably have been branded a witch.

'You give her my best wishes now, won't you? She stopped me from nearly killing my old man when he had the toothache. I swear another day of him moaning and bellyaching around the house would have driven me to seeing him off. That oil of cloves soon put a stop to it; she's a canny woman is your Aunt Patsy.'

'I'll tell her you were speaking highly of her. She'll be glad to hear that she was able to help. Good day, Mrs Fletcher, we will be back to see you next week.' Mary-Anne smiled; they may have been late to the market but so far it had been a good day.

*

'We can't let our stepfather know we've called in on Aunt Patsy. He'd only threaten us with a belting.' Eliza stopped for a second to catch her breath as she reached Pounders Court, a small, enclosed square of old squat weaving houses where their aunt lived. It was in one of the poorer areas of Leeds. The gutters ran open with excrement from both humans and animals, and in the corner of the square was a midden piled high with waste from all the houses. Eliza pinched her nose, trying not to breathe in the stench.

'I know, I wish Aunt Patsy lived somewhere a little better, but she never will, not until Uncle Mick finds work. You know what our mother thinks of him; she calls him a lazy Irish Paddy and doesn't know what Aunt Patsy sees in him.' Mary-Anne looked at her younger sister as they knocked on the door of their aunt's house.

'That's my mother calling the kettle black,' Eliza whispered as she heard footsteps from the other side of the door. 'She isn't exactly married to the most upstanding man in society.'

'Come in, my dears, it's lovely to see you. How's that sister of mine and what brings you knocking on my door?' Patsy was open with her welcome as she ushered them into her humble two-room home. The bigger of the two rooms was full of drying herbs and plants that hung from the low dark beams and filled the many jars that lined the small badly lit room. After the stench of the courtyard, Aunt Patsy's aromatic home was always a pleasant relief and the girls felt almost heady from the scents that filled it.

'Ma is as well as to be expected and we've just come on a short visit after doing some business with Mrs Fletcher, who, by the way, asks to be remembered.' Mary-Anne sat down at the scrubbed clean wooden table across from Eliza and her aunt.

'Ah, she's an old devil – would take the clothes off your back if you let her. You just take care when it comes to her.' Their aunt nodded in the direction of the sack at Eliza's feet, and smiled. 'Looks like you've bought some stock. I hope she didn't fleece you. Now tell me . . . your mother, you say she's as well as to be expected. She's not ill, is she? Or is it that good-for-nothing man that she married after losing your father? Too fond of his drink is that one.' Patsy looked across at her nieces; they seldom visited unless there was a reason, and the reason was usually their stepfather. 'He's been hitting her again, I take it? That brute of a man. Say what you like about my Mick but he'd never hit a woman, it's a coward that does that, especially in drink.'

'We found her on the kitchen floor last night, he'd hit her head against the wall before going to bed. She'd made us stay in the wash house knowing he was the worse for drink.' Eliza hung her head.

'But she's all right now?' Patsy looked at both the girls, concerned. 'Else you wouldn't be here.'

'Yes, we left her washing the linen and our stepfather's gone to work down the pit.' Mary-Anne sighed and looked at her aunt.

'She should never have married him,' Patsy whispered low. 'How he keeps his job at the mine, I don't know. Some days he must still be drunk when he's at the seam. It's your mother I feel sorry for, she's always having to put right his wrongs.'

'Well, he does keep his job, and for that we should be grateful. He's not a bad man when he's sober.' Mary-Anne knew Bill had taken them all in when he didn't have to. Whatever his faults he had put a roof over their heads.

Eliza shook her head; she never gave her stepfather any credit and had little time for him. 'No, he's just a drunken bully and I hate him.'

'Now, hate is a strong word, Eliza, you should use it sparingly. Although I do tend to agree with you.' Patsy sat back in her chair and looked at her two nieces, wishing there was something she could do for them. 'Lawks! Can you hear that baby next door? All it does is screech. That's Ruth Watt's youngest, poor hungry little beggar. Ten kids already and her Davey out of work the best part of this year. There will be heartache at that house before long; they can't continue living like they do. It would have been better if she'd got rid of it, than get attached.' Patsy sighed, she was very matter of fact when it came to children, never having been blessed with them herself. 'It will waken my Mick up if it doesn't shut its mouth.' Patsy glanced at the door to the back room, waiting for her husband to stir from his bed after having his usual mid-morning nap.

'Is Uncle Mick all right?' Mary-Anne asked her aunt.

'Aye, he's fine. Still a martyr to his bad back and he can't seem to get a job because of it, but we are not starving unlike the ones next door.' The girls knew that their aunt often got paid, or paid in kind for her remedies. 'Mick has got an old friend of his coming to stay with us for a while, from Ireland. A man called John Vasey.'

Mary-Anne looked around the small house curiously, wondering where any visitor could possibly stay. Her aunt saw her expression and answered accordingly: 'He's going to be renting the cellar from us, so his bit of extra money will help keep the wolf from the door. I've just made him a bed up and put him a chair to sit on down there. It's not much but I don't suppose he's expecting a lot after the famine in Ireland. Which is good because we haven't got a lot.'

The sisters looked at one another. Their aunt was keeping her family afloat as both they and their mother had tried to do, but her solution had given them Bill to deal with also.

'We'll get back and make sure our ma is all right, and get these clothes washed before Bill comes home and needs his bath filling. I'll just change my boots, these I've got on have got more holes than leather.' Mary-Anne bent down and started to un-lace her old boots.

Patsy looked at her niece swapping her boots around, picking up the old boots and looking at the hole in the bottom of their soles. 'What are you doing with them? Can I have them?'

'Yes, they're worth nowt to me. Have them if you think you can use them. They let the water in and you can see one's got a huge hole in it.' Mary-Anne stood up in her new boots and tried them for size while watching her aunt examine her old ones.

'I'll give them to Ruth. Mick will re-sole them for her. It's better than having no boots at all, providing they fit.' Patsy smiled at her nieces.

'She's got no boots?' Eliza exclaimed. 'She's got nothing on her feet?'

'She's got nothing, lass, apart from a lot of hungry mouths to feed. So you be thankful for what you've got because your lot in life could be a lot worse than it is.' Patsy put the boots down and reached for a small jar from one of her shelves. 'Here, girls, could you give this to your mother? She will probably have run out of the last bottle she asked from me. Tell her it's a bit stronger than usual and to take it with care. Make sure your father doesn't see you give it to her. You know what he thinks of my potion-making.'

Eliza took the bottle and thanked her aunt. Her mother had always a bottle in her bedroom drawer. Her mother had called it her pick-me-up when Eliza had asked her one day what it was for and had quickly re-hidden it out of the way of her stepfather.

'Give my love to your mother and keep out of the way of your stepfather.' Patsy opened her door and watched the two girls leave her home. They were good girls but compared to her life in the city they didn't know how lucky they were. She closed the door behind her and sat down at the table looking at the boots with a hole in them. Her Mick would fix them and make sure they got a good home next door. She put her hands over her ears to stop the noise of the baby wailing, it should never have been born, its father needed gelding. She bet that there was probably another one on the way already, he was that irresponsible. She gazed out of the grimy windows and sighed, feeling a moment of despair. You were born and you died; that was life full stop.

Mary-Anne and Eliza made their way home in relative silence, both thinking that their lives were perhaps not so bad and that they shouldn't have gone moaning to their Aunt Patsy with their worries.

'Mary, don't let me ever marry a useless man like Mick and Bill or Davey Watts and have children I can't afford.' Eliza stopped on the dockside and looked around at the barges being loaded and unloaded with goods. Men were shouting, ponies were being whipped into action as they pulled heavy carts laden with goods for the city and women were selling themselves along the dockside for a few pence.

'Let's make a pact between ourselves that we both will find a wealthy man that will keep us in a suitable fashion. I don't want to live like my aunt Patsy nor be used like our mother.' Mary-Anne linked her arm into her sister's.

'Yes, let's set our sights high; I don't want to just make do. We will wait until the right man comes along and not be rushed into marriage.' Eliza looked back at the disappearing docklands and then turned around to face the unfolding countryside where they lived. She hoped that she would never lead a life like the one they had just left behind. She and Mary-Anne were worth more than that – of that she was sure.

Three

Highfield House

'Father would like us all to go to luncheon tomorrow.' Catherine Ellershaw looked at her husband across the breakfast table as she shooed the servant away from offering her another portion of poached eggs.

'Aye, well, I haven't the time nor the inclination to be having luncheon with your father.' Edmund Ellershaw owner of Rose Pit answered his wife from the relative safety of behind the morning's paper, the *Leeds Intelligencer*.

'He said he was looking forward to talking to you as he wanted to know how the colliery was doing now that coal is being transported by rail and canal.' Catherine bit into her toast and placed her knife down sharply on her plate to gain her husband's attention. 'You know we owe father a lot. We wouldn't be living here at Highfield House if it wasn't for him. The least you could do is to be sociable with him.'

Edmund sighed and put his paper down. 'Your bloody father, it's all I get in my ear from morning to night. He might own nearly every woollen mill in Leeds but he forgets I've a living to make and a mine to run and I just can't drop everything on his request of luncheon. Take our William: he'll keep him amused and it will keep him out of my way. As it is he just gets under my feet at the moment; he doesn't seem to be interested in getting his hands dirty, learning his trade. Which sets him at a disadvantage when he one day becomes the owner of the coal mine. Take our Grace with you as well, she always sweet talks her grandfather, being the apple of his eye.'

'Perhaps our William will find his feet in textiles; someone has to take the reins from my father and it certainly won't be you, as you've no knowledge of the industry. I will take him with me and hint to my father that he would do well to encourage him into the running of the mills. It could be the making of him.' Catherine Ellershaw smiled thinking of her precious eldest son who had just turned twenty and was back from Cambridge after finding it not to his liking, and being unable to settle into his studies.

'Aye, let your father take him under his wing. So he can spoil him even more than he is already. When I was his age, I'd been a miner for at least five years, knew my job inside out and was gaining the respect of my fellow workers. I wasn't swanning about with a poetry book under my arm, too precious to get my fine clothes dirty.' Edmund Ellershaw was disappointed in his son; he wasn't the tough manly figure he had hoped him to be, as the rightful successor to the pit at Rothwell. The pit that Edmund had bought when his old employer had struggled with its upkeep and had lost interest in. Ellershaw was a self-made man – at least where the mine was concerned – and he never let anyone forget it.

'Not everyone is interested in mining, although it seems that it is the only thing talked about in this house. Have you thought any more about my proposal of taking a house in Roundhay? It would be so much more civilised there. Better for Grace, William and baby George. We could employ a proper nanny for him then, not just a local girl, plus we would have the Whittakers as neighbours.'

'We want nowt with moving to Roundhay; Highfield is a good enough house and we are away from the rabble in Leeds. Besides, you'd never be away from the Whittakers, you'd be playing cards with them all day.' Edmund threw his napkin down, he'd had enough of his breakfast and enough of hearing his wife and the notion that she had got of moving to Roundhay. A notion put into her head by her empty-headed friend Rosaline Whittaker, whose husband gave her anything she wanted just to keep her quiet. 'I'll be away to the pit now; time's money and I can't afford to be losing either.'

'It seems to me you never have time for discussing our family and our needs, Edmund. And it isn't as if we lack funds, Father would never see us short.' Catherine looked up at her husband whose face belied the anger that he was feeling inside.

'I'm away, say good morning to the boys and Grace when they eventually decide to get out of their beds and join you for breakfast. I'll be back in time for dinner tonight.' Edmund pulled his chair away from the table not giving his wife or servant a second glance as he walked through the dining room into the hallway, picking his hat and riding crop up from the hall stand. He stood for a minute and looked at himself in the full-length mirror in the hall, and wondered where all the years had gone.

He had once been a handsome young man full of ambition and a desire for life. Now he was middle-aged, grey haired with a podge of a belly and a wife who never gave him a moment's rest. No wonder he made the colliery and his office there his refuge from her nagging voice and his unbelievably spoilt children.

It was his own greed that was to blame, he thought, as he looked around the grand hall of Highfield. He already had his mine when he met the Ellershaws. If he hadn't had his head turned by the thought of Catherine's money – or rather her father's money – he would have been happy with a local lass from Woodlesford or Rothwell, one that would have been happy with just a roof over her head and bairns to care for. Not always wanting something bigger and better. He opened the front door and hesitated as he pulled it to. What was wrong with the house they were in? It was the biggest one along Princes Street; its six bedrooms were big enough for their family and guests when they entertained. His wife had a cook and several maids for all the work. He, himself, refused a valet but there was a groom to tend to the coach and horses and a stable lad besides the gardener.

Their house stood proud on the corner of the street, in its own grounds and the fluted columns at the doorway hinted at the wealth that lay within. Nay, they wouldn't be moving to Roundhay, she'd have to be bloody satisfied with her lot. Edmund loosened the reins of his already saddled horse from the tethering ring in the garden wall and mounted. Time to get to his office and to wait for a visitor he knew would show their face today, a face that always gave him pleasure, albeit entirely one-sided.

Four

Sarah Parker closed the door behind her and set off up Pit Lane, following in her husband's footsteps, and those of all the miners who headed to the pit every morning.

Her stomach churned with the thought of what she was about to do and her legs felt weak underneath her. She looked ahead of her, watching the pithead wheel that dominated the skyline turn, as men were lowered to their work deep down in the bowels of the earth. They were in search of the black gold that powered the wheels of the industrial revolution that was spreading like wildfire throughout the country.

Coal fed everything – the new steam engines that powered their way along the North Midland Railway; the engines that turned the spinning mules in the many mills around Leeds – and industries just could not get enough of it.

She hurried on; sooner she got it over and done with, the better. Her skirts brushed the side of the frost-covered grass and she pulled her shawl tighter around her as the early morning sun took its time to warm the sparkling white countryside. She looked up at the sign above her head and walked in through the open gates of Rose Pit, glancing around the yard to make sure her Bill was not there and that he was out of the way, down below at the seam head.

The yard was full of pithead ponies waiting for the precious coal to be brought up from the earth below, their handlers too busy to see or care about the desperate woman that quickly made her way to the office of Edmund Ellershaw, the mine owner. Even if they had given her any notice they would have recognised her as a regular visitor and all of them knew why she had come. Her with her husband down below, risking his life every day for her and her lasses, while she satisfied old Ellershaw as his mistress, the dirty old bugger.

Sarah stopped in her tracks as Tom Thackeray the mine supervisor pulled the office door open, blushing as he paid his respects, knowing full well why she was there.

'Morning, Mrs Parker. Not a bad day for November.' He touched his cap as he stepped down the steps allowing her to the office door. 'Is Eliza well, Mrs Parker?' He had to ask her, even if he didn't like to be seen with the woman that everybody knew to be Ellershaw's whore. Eliza, her youngest daughter, had caught his eye and he was sweet on her.

'Very well, thank you, Tom. I'll tell her you asked after her.' Sarah smiled at the young man as he walked away and then quickly entered into the office of the man she absolutely loathed, who had treated her no better than a dog. He owned her, just like he owned the colliery, the house she lived in and half the houses in Woodlesford and Rothwell, and there was nothing she could do.

'I thought I'd be seeing you today, Sarah. The state your man was in yesterday morning, I should have sacked him on the spot and thrown you out of that house once and for all.' Edmund looked at the creature before him. Despite two children and a world of care, she was still a handsome woman and she was his for the taking. 'So, he's drunk the rent money away yet again and given you a good hiding into the bargain by the looks of that lip.'

Edmund got up from his comfortable office chair and rubbed his finger around Sarah's trembling cut lip. His face inches away from hers as he pulled her towards him.

'Well, you know what I want, don't you, Sarah?' His spare hand fumbled with his breeches buttons as he watched Sarah's heaving breasts and ran his tongue as far as he could go down her bodice, licking between them and biting as he aroused himself. 'Payment will be made and accepted with interest.' He turned Sarah around, splaying her hands out across his desk and lifting her skirts up as far as they could go, exposing her naked buttocks. He ran his fingers between her legs and Sarah winced as no care was shown to her private parts. 'That's it, you just can't get enough of me, can you, my dear little whore?' He widened her legs with his knees and entered her with a force so hard that Sarah's eyes filled with tears as he satisfied himself. She'd lost count of the number of times that she had put herself through the degrading act of making herself available for Ellershaw's sexual desires in order to protect her family. She hated him with every inch of her body, but worse still she hated herself for letting him use her like a whore. She closed her eyes until his thrusting had come to an end and he withdrew, buttoning his trousers up quickly as he hid his shame.

Sarah breathed in deeply, pulled her skirts down and turned around to look at her assailant. 'We are square? The rent's paid for this month?' She shook as she pulled her skirts straight and looked at the man she hated. One day she'd get even with him, but until then she was under his control.

'Aye, we are square, until the next time.' Edmund wiped his saliva-covered chin and slumped down in his chair. 'Now best get off before somebody comes in; we don't want the husband finding out about our little arrangement now, do we?'

Sarah held her head up high and stepped out of the red-bricked office, breathing in the sharp frost-filled air of the morning. Her legs shook as she sneaked out of the yard, noticing one of Bill's friends looking at her as he spat a mouthful of saliva out onto the coal-dusted yard. He went about his work and didn't acknowledge her, knowing full well her business with old Ellershaw – all the colliery workers did. That was everybody, except Bill.

Sarah made good her escape, hoping nothing would be said to her husband about her visit and that he would stop drinking, praying hopefully that there wouldn't be a next time, when she had to degrade herself to Ellershaw's perversions – a prayer she knew would never be answered, not while the landlord at the Boot and Shoe enticed Bill with his ale and he drank himself to oblivion.

Five

'Go on then, get it opened and read. You won't know what's in it if you don't.' Mary-Anne watched the excitement on her younger sister's face as she looked at the handwritten note that they had found pushed underneath the battered door of their small workshop when they arrived that morning.

Eliza looked up with a beaming smile at her older sister; they both had a good idea who the note was from. He'd been making his presence known to Eliza for some time now, since he had moved to the village, and now it would seem that the handsome but shy Tom Thackeray had decided to put pen to paper. She carefully unfolded the cream parchment, her hand shaking as she read the words aloud.

Dear Eliza,

I would be most honoured if you would walk out with me this coming Sunday. Could we perhaps meet after chapel and take a short stroll around Woodlesford together?

If I hear nothing to the contrary, I will wait for you outside the chapel gates at twelve.

Yours faithfully
Tom (Thackeray)

'Well, he gets straight to the point: short and sweet.' Mary-Anne laughed and smiled at her younger sister, whose cheeks had turned rose-bud pink. 'Are you going to meet him?'

Eliza quickly folded the note away into her apron pocket and composed herself. 'I might, I don't know. After all, he's the supervisor at the Rose, he's at least got a good job. Please, don't tell Ma, I want this to be a secret, and besides, she will only want you to escort me.' Eliza reached for Mary-Anne's hand and squeezed it tight. 'Promise me you won't tell her, because if Stepfather finds out he'll not agree to it. You know how he hates anything to do with the management at the Rose.'

'I'll not say anything, you lucky devil.' Mary-Anne grinned at her younger sister. 'Just be careful what you get up to, as you don't know the first thing about Tom Thackeray apart from where he works and that he lives on Wood Lane at Rothwell with his mother. You know he's new to the village, he could be a right wrong 'un. Don't you get led astray!'

'I don't know what you mean, our Mary! We will just take a gentle stroll around Woodlesford as he suggests.' Eliza felt the letter in her pocket and went to sit at her usual seat in front of the shop's window, picking up a garment to mend as she thought about the handsome blond-haired man that had caught her eye over a year ago and was now asking to walk out with her. A feeling of warmth and excitement fluttered within her; Sunday could not come fast enough.

Mary-Anne looked up from her sewing and sighed, she could sense the excitement that her younger sister was feeling over her meeting with Tom and had meant every word she had said when she had called her a 'lucky devil'. How come Eliza was the one with a sweetheart demanding her attentions? Everyone always commented that she was the one with the looks, Eliza didn't have her striking long auburn hair or her green eyes, which she had inherited from their father; instead Eliza was blonde with blue eyes, taking after their mother, and was, in Mary-Anne's eyes, a little plain.

A pang of jealousy filled her as she accidently stabbed herself with the needle and thread that seemed to have developed a life of its own. She sucked on her injured finger, tasting the iron-rich blood that clotted on her finger end and looked over at her sister, thinking that served her right for being so jealous. Eliza didn't bear any grudges against anybody and was the more open of the two of them. If the boot was on the other foot, Eliza would be glad that her sister had a suitor. She looked down at her finger, making sure it had stopped bleeding before carrying on with her handiwork, concentrating on repairing the green organza dress that they had bought and washed earlier in the week, burying the jealousy she felt. After all, it was only Tom Thackeray, and he was just a mine supervisor, of little importance.

'Are you not coming to chapel today, Mother?' Mary-Anne pulled on her best bonnet and waited with Eliza in the kitchen of their house on Pit Lane. Eliza scowled at her sister, not wanting Mary-Anne to encourage their mother to join them, else her meeting with Tom would be noticed.

'No, my love. I'm going to miss it. I don't feel myself this morning and I'll stop and keep an eye on this piece of brisket that's simmering on the fire for Sunday dinner.' Sarah looked at her two daughters in their Sunday finery and smiled; any mother would be proud of such good-looking girls as hers. 'Besides, Bill has gone rabbiting with that friend of his and he will want them skinning and gutting as soon as he returns home. He might be good at catching them, but making them fit for the pot is another thing with him.' She brushed a lock of hair away from her brow and reached above to the stone mantelpiece for the small cash box that held the household's change. 'Here, put a penny in the collection and say a prayer for me. A good word with our maker is never wasted and the Lord knows I could do with him on our side at the moment.'

Sarah sighed and fought back the tears as she ushered them out of the warmth of the kitchen into the crisp air of the late November morning. She needed to be on her own for as long as possible this morning and she needed to keep her nerve as she started to feel the gripping pains low within her stomach as Patsy's herbal potion started to take effect. 'Go on, girls, Minister Hamilton will be waiting. You know he likes to talk to everyone before they enter his chapel.' She kissed her girls on their cheeks and then leaned on the kitchen door as she closed it behind them.

Once the girls had disappeared out of sight, she made her way down the garden path and into the outside privy, thankful that, unlike some of the pit houses, each of the cottages on Pit Lane had its own private privy, which meant she was able to keep her predicament within its walls.

Pain rippled through her body. Patsy's concoctions had never acted this quickly before, she thought, as she reached for the door latch and pulled the door to her, pulling her skirts up and sitting down on the wooden bench that acted as an earth closet. Sweat dripped down her brow as pain ripped across her, making her nauseous and weak as she waited for the deadly potion to do its worst.

'God forgive me,' she whispered as the poisons took hold, her pain doubled her up and her head spun. Blood poured from her, down her legs and into the earth closet below, as her body rejected Edmund Ellershaw's bastard child.

In the darkness of the outside lavvy, Sarah cried; it wasn't the first time she had sought to get rid of a baby but this time it was different: she was weak and the blood wouldn't stop flowing. She felt giddy as her head felt lighter and lighter, and she leaned back against the cold whitewashed walls of the outside toilet.

The condensation from her breath trickled down the walls and she tried to concentrate on the race that the droplets of water were having with one another to overcome the pain. She closed her eyes and prayed for the pain to stop, trying to keep herself awake, but was too fearful to leave the safety of the outside lavvy in case the neighbours saw what was happening to her. She sobbed as she saw in the dim light her skirts and legs covered in her own blood, realising that something was very wrong. But before she could even think to cry for help, another spasm took hold and she fought back a scream of pain, then lost consciousness as the darkness came, her life dripping and ebbing away with the tiny dead soul that lay in the earth closet below, alone and in shame.

'I don't know why you're making you'sel look so smart. She's nowt special this lass you've set your cap on. Her mother's the talk of Woodlesford the way she goes behind her man's back with Edmund Ellershaw.' Madge Thackeray looked at her son as he preened himself in the hallway mirror.

'I wish I'd never told you about Eliza, Mother, because you've never let it rest since I mentioned her name.' Tom put on his hat at a jaunty angle and picked up the change from the hallway table for the chapel's collection. 'I'm only having a quick walk out with her, I'll be back in time for my dinner.'

'Well, make sure you are. You can do a lot better than that'en. I brought you up to set your sights higher than a common lass from Pit Lane.' Madge sighed and looked down at her knitting, putting it to one side with disinterest as he closed the front door behind him, as she watched him pass the kitchen window, whistling like a cock robin on his way to walk out with Eliza Wild – her, whose mother was nothing more than a trollop and her stepfather a drunk. She'd wanted so much better for her lad. Why wouldn't he listen to her? He always had been stubborn, even as a young'un, she thought. There was never any telling him anything and invariably it always ended in tears. Just like this would, with this young hussy. Never mind, she'd be here for him, no matter what; that's what mothers did. You learned by your mistakes and this lass was definitely that! She picked up her knitting and gazed into the fire. Tom was all she had in the world since her husband had died and they'd moved here. She knew it to be selfish, her wanting him to stay at home with her, but he was all she had. Nothing else mattered.

The chapel service seemed to last forever as the preacher yelled out his warnings of hell and brimstone and paused with long looks at some of his known fallen within his congregation. Mary-Anne and Eliza wriggled in their hard wooden pew, wishing for the service to come to an end and for Mary-Anne to go back to home comforts, while Eliza kept glancing over at Tom, who shot quick looks in her direction, not wanting anyone to notice his stares.

'Well, I thought the minister was never going to shut up.' Mary-Anne pulled on her gloves and looked at her younger sister, who was fidgeting and looking flushed as she watched the chapel goers shake the hand of the preacher before disappearing to their homes. 'Go on then, he's waiting for you. I'll give Mother your excuses and tell her you're helping out the less fortunate or something or other. It depends how hard she questions me to what I say, but you're all right, I'll not tell her you are with your sweetheart.' Mary-Anne laughed and dug her blushing sister in the ribs with her elbow. She looked over to the yew tree that stood next to the chapel gates and the young handsome man that stood underneath it, looking down at his shoes. 'Get gone and enjoy your time together.'

'Thanks for covering for me, our Mary. You know I'd do the same for you.' Eliza smiled at her older sister before nearly running to where Tom stood.

Mary-Anne watched as the young man offered his arm to Eliza and noted the huge beam on her face as she turned to mouth her thanks yet again. She'd never seen her sister look so happy and radiant, she thought, as she watched the young couple walk in the direction of Pottery Lane. Another slight twang of jealousy swept over her and she held her head up high as she felt a tear well up in her eye. She checked herself quickly as the voice of her neighbour brought her to her senses.

'It was a good sermon, don't you think, Mary-Anne? Full of the warnings of the sins that can tempt us, and the good Lord knows there's plenty of them.' Ada Simms gazed up and down at Mary-Anne and looked into the distance as Eliza and her beau disappeared nearly out of sight. 'Was that your sister I saw, walking out with Tom Thackeray? Now don't they make a lovely couple? I didn't realise that they were sweet on each other.' Ada Simms folded her arms underneath her ample bosom and waited for a response.

'They are just going for a Sunday stroll together. There's nothing between them.' Mary-Anne looked darkly at the local gossip.

'Sure, isn't that how it starts? I remember when Bert used to wait for me after chapel, and look at us now. Married for the last thirty years and still as happy as the day we set eyes on one another.' Ada smiled to herself as she thought back to the years she had spent blissfully married to the man she had met all those years ago.

'Then, I'm glad for you Mrs Simms. I hope your happiness continues. Now, if you'll excuse me, I'll have to make my way home; Mother will be waiting of me.' Mary-Anne wanted to walk back home on her own, not wanting to make idle conversation with Ada Simms as they walked the same route.

'I'll walk with you. I usually visit Miss Beaumont at Applegarth House, but her arthritis is making her so unagreeable of late. I really don't know why I should give her the benefit of my company. She can be so sharp in her comments when she is that way inclined.' Ada set off on her walk down the street, in the direction of their home.

'Did I not hear that Miss Beaumont has found herself a suitor? Perhaps that is why she is not so agreeable. I'm sure I heard that Mr Todd has been calling on her ... perhaps she didn't want you to find out her secret, hence her sharpness.' Mary-Anne smiled at the old gossip, knowing full well that her neighbour wouldn't be able to resist the temptation of finding out if what she said was true.

'The silly old fool. Why would she want a man at her age, especially Mr Todd? He's no spring chick either. They always say there is no fool like an old fool.' Ada Simms stopped in her tracks and looked at Mary-Anne. 'Perhaps I should show a more caring side and visit Miss Beaumont; after all, she is being a martyr to her pain.'

Ada looked up into the face of Mary-Anne and smiled. 'Forgive me my dear, I'll let you walk home alone and I'll just make my way to Applegarth, after all it would not be very Christian of me to neglect a friend in need of friendship.'

'I quite understand, Mrs Simms. Please wish Miss Beaumont my warmest wishes and that I hope that her arthritis is not too painful.' Mary-Anne sniggered as she watched as the old busybody turn around on herself and made her way past the chapel to the track that led to Applegarth House. She'd fallen for her tasty morsel of gossip, hook, line and sinker, just as she knew she would.

Eliza shivered as the cold wind bit through her best coat.

'Are you cold?' Tom pulled her close to him.

'Just a little. It's my own fault, I should have put my shawl on but I wanted to look my best for you.' Eliza linked her arm tight into his as they stood on the bridge overlooking the Midland railway.

'Aye, it's that wind is biting. Perhaps it wasn't the best idea I've had to walk out on a grey November morning, but I couldn't wait to ask you any longer.' Tom looked at the lass he'd adored from afar for so long and couldn't believe that she was there, standing arm in arm with him. 'Besides, it'll be Christmas before long and I wanted you to know how I felt about you before the other fellas made their advances to you at the Christmas dances that you are sure to be attending.' Tom blushed as she turned and looked at him.

'I wouldn't have wanted for you to wait another minute, Tom. I don't mind that it's cold, honestly; I'm glad that you asked me to walk with you this morning. Anyway, tell me, how do you feel about me, Tom Thackeray?' Eliza hugged Tom's arm and grinned up at the bashful lad.

Tom went red, and spluttered. 'I think you are so bonny, Eliza, and have done for some time. I didn't think you'd have even read my letter, let alone be waiting of me this morning. I didn't even think you knew I existed.'

'Now you are being silly. You must have noticed me looking at you when I come to the colliery on errands for my father,' Eliza confessed. 'I always accepted them, for the chance that I may catch a glimpse of you while there.'

'You did! It's a wonder you could make me out under all the muck and coal dust. It's a mucky job being a miner, but you'll know that with your father being a miner.' Tom looked at Eliza and saw her shivering.

'He's not my father, he's my stepfather,' Eliza quickly said. 'We are not related, nor do I want to be.'

'I'm sorry.' Tom bowed his head. 'You obviously don't get on with one another.'

'No, we don't. I miss my father, he was twice the man Bill Parker is. Even my mother will say that most days, she knows she made a bad decision the day she got re-married to him.' Eliza rubbed her hands together to warm them and looked at Tom.

'You're freezing. Come on, we'll walk to the end of your lane and get you home. My mother will be wanting to serve Sunday dinner anyway. Heaven knows how much moaning she will do if I'm later than one o'clock.' Tom sighed and put his arm around Eliza as they turned from the top of the railway bridge down into Woodlesford.

'You are like me, aren't you? You've no father?' She walked quickly by the side of Tom trying to keep warm.

'Aye, I lost my father last year when there was an explosion at the Midland Pit. It was a bad day, my mother's never got over it.' Tom glanced at Eliza. 'Trouble is, she depends on me too much and thinks I should be by her side when I'm not at work.'

'It's early days yet. Your father hasn't been dead long, it'll take her time to adjust. She's lucky she's got you. Our mother tried to make a living after father died, but struggled, and then when Bill turned up one day he was the easiest way out of our situation, or so she thought. I can't blame her for marrying him, but she could have done a lot better, of that I'm sure.' Eliza and Tom stopped walking at the bottom of Pit Lane and looked at one another.

'Can I walk you to your door?' Tom asked.

Eliza looked up at Tom. 'My mother and Bill don't know I'm with you, so we had better say our goodbyes here.'

'All right, I understand. Can we meet again, same place next week?' Tom looked into the blue eyes of Eliza and hoped that the answer would be yes.

'I'd like that. And next time I'll wear something warmer instead of my pride getting in the way.' Eliza grinned.

'In my eyes you'd look beautiful in anything that you wear,' Tom said as she walked away from him. 'See you next week!' he shouted as he watched her set off to run to the small terrace of miner's cottages at the bottom of Pit Lane. 'You don't need fine clothes to impress me, my Eliza,' he whispered as she turned to wave him goodbye.

'Mother, Mother, where are you?' Mary-Anne yelled, as she rescued the pan of burning brisket from the fire. The pan had filled the kitchen with the smell of burning meat and rancid smoke, which caught in the back of Mary-Anne's throat as she opened the back door to let the smoke drift out into the sharp midday air. She coughed and spluttered and caught her breath as she placed the boiling hot pan down onto the frosted cobbles of the backyard before going back into the kitchen. 'Mother, are you up there?' Mary-Anne stood at the bottom of the stairs and called up them, deciding to climb up just in case her mother was lying ill on her bed. But there was not a sign of her as she searched in each room.

Mary-Anne stood with her hands on her hips and glanced out of her parents' bedroom window, which overlooked the yard and the earth closet at the end of the yard, wondering why the house was empty and where her mother could be. It was then she noticed the redness of the heavy white frost next to the earth closet door. It looked like blood seeping into the frost, creeping across the yard with long fingers. 'Mother!' she yelled and ran with skirts pulled up down the stairs into the cold frosty air to open the earth closet's door to discover her mother still bent double, soaked in blood, dead.

'No, no, you can't be!' She bent down in the pool of blood that surrounded her and cradled her mother's head. 'What have you done, what has become of you?' Mary-Anne sobbed. 'Don't leave me, please don't leave us. Both Eliza and I need you.' She hugged the blonde-haired head of her mother and smelt the familiar scent of her mother's clothes. She looked around at the blood surrounding them both and she knew her mother had gone and that no amount of pleading and begging would bring her back to life. She was old enough to know what had happened – her mother was dead along with the sister or brother she had been carrying who was now lying in the excrement below.

She sobbed and cried in the empty cold of the earth closet and wished she was like the dead baby, unknowing and untouched by the harsh world around them. Life was going to be harder now, more than ever without a mother to protect them. Her and Eliza had nobody except Bill Parker and now her mother had gone he was not beholden to them. Her thoughts flit to Eliza and how happy she had looked linking arms with Tom Thackeray. It was a day she should have filled with good memories; now it would be one of the worst days of her life. Poor Eliza ... what news to come home to. How was she going to tell her? Mary-Anne let out another sob as she realised that her loving mother had gone forever and that their lives would never be the same. God have mercy on their souls.

Six

'Bloody hypocrite,' Bill Parker mumbled as he stood at his wife's graveside.

'Now, Bill, that's no way to talk about the Minister Hamilton. He was only giving you some advice in your grief.' David Bowers patted his work colleague on his back and shook his head as he turned and watched Eliza and Mary-Anne leave their mother's grave, comforted by their next-door neighbour Mrs Simms.

'He knows nowt about me; the bugger isn't even wed. How would he know about my grief? And I'll handle it in my own way.' Bill looked down at the coffin of his beloved Sarah and looked up at the gravedigger, who was wanting to fill the grave in before dusk fell on the frosted graveyard. 'Aye, get her covered, you bugger. She's not here anymore, anyway. She'll either be rotting in hell, or up in paradise according to that sanctimonious bugger of a preacher.' Bill spat out a mouthful of saliva and turned away from the graveside, catching sight of his stepdaughters as they left without letting him know their departure. 'Aye, you get your arses home as well, because you'll not have any tears for me,' Bill shouted after them.

The two girls and Mrs Simms didn't look back as they left the chapel yard, Bill wasn't worth wasting their breath on when he was in such a way.

'Bill, it's their mother that they've just lost. They are as broken-hearted as you, if not more so.' David was taken aback by his friend's self-pity in his own grief and wanted to shake him out of the dark hole he had dug himself in since the death of his wife three days ago.

'And what am I supposed to do with them two?' Bill growled. 'They are not my blood and they've never taken to me. I never replaced their precious father and am not about to now.'

'You look after them, Bill. That's what your Sarah would have wanted. And besides, you need someone to run the house and both of them are fine lasses. They'll soon be finding husbands of their own and then they'll be off your hands. And you keep off the drink like the preacher says, because you might not like what we're saying but it does nowt for you, when you get so drunk.' David knew Bill would either take his advice in the spirit it was given or take against him too. He hoped it would be the former and that it would make him think.

'I know you mean well, David, but I'll not get through the day without a gill or two today. I swear, this'll be the last time you see me worse for wear in the Boot and Shoe, but today I've got to drink to my old lass.' Bill patted the only friend that had stood by him through thick and thin on the back, and then urged that he walk with him to the Boot and Shoe to help him drown his sorrows. He hoped that the landlord had already set up a gill on the bar for him; his thirst was so bad.

*

'Now, will you girls be all right? Your father seemed to be in a bit of state with himself.' Ada Simms looked at the two girls who were bearing their mother's death with dignity.

'He's not our father!' Eliza retorted.

'Aye, I keep forgetting, he was your mother's second husband, poor soul. You haven't had blessed lives, have you, you two?' Ada Simms watched as Mary-Anne stoked the fire and put the kettle on to boil. 'You've lost both your parents, through no fault of your own. Life can be cruel sometimes.'

'We will be fine, thank you, Mrs Simms, we've got one another.' Mary-Anne smiled at her younger sister. 'Thank you for being there for us today, your presence gave us strength.'

'Aye, well, she wasn't a bad woman, your mother. If I'd only known she was losing a baby out there in the backyard I'd have been there for her. I feel so guilty when I think of her and what there was of a baby lying dead in the earth closet. Thank heavens Bill had it in his heart to bury it with her. The poor woman.' Ada drew her lace-trimmed handkerchief from up her sleeve and patted her dampening eyes. 'And you poor dears then had to see to her and tend to her until he came home after checking his snares. You poor, poor dears.'

Mary-Anne looked at her younger sister who sat shaking in the chair next to the fire, clearly remembering how her day had turned from being full of joy into the worst of her life. 'We'll have to bear what life has thrown at us, Mrs Simms. Now, if you don't mind, Eliza and myself need some time on our own to gather our thoughts; it's been a hard few days.' Mary-Anne walked to the hallway and opened the front door to usher their well-intentioned next-door neighbour on her way. The sisters needed time together before their stepfather returned.

'Well, you know where I am if you need me. Bert and I will help in all that we can. Not that we're ones for interfering into other people's lives, but sometimes it is good to know you've got someone there for you. If you need them.' Ada sniffed into her hanky and picked up her black skirts as she made her way down the garden path to her home, looking back at Mary-Anne as she closed the wooden garden gate behind her. 'Remember, just give a shout if you need anything.'

Mary-Anne closed the front door and sighed as she leaned back against it before going into the kitchen. 'I thought she was never going to go!' Mary-Anne looked across at Eliza and watched her as she sniffed hard, stifling another onset of tears.

'I nearly asked if we could stay with her tonight because I'm that afraid what mood Bill will come back in, and now we have no mother to protect us.' Eliza breathed in heavily and glanced with tearful eyes at her older sister.

'Hush now, Eliza, we will be all right. We'll go to our room before he returns and bolt the door. Just like we used to do when our mother was alive. He can't break the door down, and, if he tries, next door will hear and come around to see what all the noise is about.' Mary-Anne knelt down and cradled her younger sister's head. 'We will be all right, I'll look after you, I swear.'

Eliza kissed her sister on the cheek. 'We will look after one another, and I will always be here for you; on that I promise.'

'Get yourself home Bill. Them lasses will be wondering where you are and you can barely stand up, you've drunk that much.' Derek Lewis, the landlord of the Boot and Shoe, picked up the grieving miner's empty tankard and shook his head as Bill and the hardened drinkers from the Rose Pit continued their efforts to sup his barrels dry.

'I'll go when I'm bloody well ready. Fill 'em up again, tha'll not say no to my money.' Bill felt into his waistcoat pocket and pulled out his last few coins and put them down on the oak counter for the landlord to take.

'You've had enough, lad, and I'm closing the bar.' Derek Lewis looked at the burly miner who was lost in grief and regretted his decision as he scanned the drunken mob that was looking like they were going to lynch him for his refusal of another gill.

'Nay, you know better than to refuse us. We'll just help ourselves!' Jack Langstaff yelled and slammed his tankard down and laughed at the meek-mannered landlord.

Derek looked at the six-foot tall miner, who had a reputation as a good fighter and had the respect of all the miners after he had single-handedly lifted a pit prop on his shoulders for one of his colleagues to be saved after a rock fall. He had muscles on him like a prize fighter and he'd have been an unwise man to go against him in drink. 'Just another gill and then you are all on your way; some of us need our sleep.' Derek sighed and went back on his decision for fear of his life.

A cheer went up and Jack got slapped hard on the back.

'Here, take your brass.' Bill pushed the coins towards Derek and looked up at him with bloodshot eyes.

'You can have this one on me, in respect of your loss.' Derek looked at the mess of a man and for a brief moment felt sorry for him.

'God bless Sarah, she was a good woman. Or should I say, a good lay, so I've heard old Ellershaw brag!' Jack raised his empty tankard in the air and said what everyone had been thinking all night.

Bill sat up from his chair and it toppled backwards onto the stone-flagged floor as he walked over to the hefty Jack who was grinning from ear to ear, oblivious to the response from his friends around him. Bill's mood had changed as he grabbed Jack's neck, forgetting that his target was nearly twice the size of him and young enough to be his son.

'What did you bloody well say about my wife?' Bill snarled and held him tight but Jack brushed him away like a fly as he toppled, too drunk to stand.

'What?!' Jack looked around at the astonished faces of the drinkers. 'I only said that old Ellershaw was having his way with her, like everyone else knows that's here. She was never away from his office, we all know that she paid him in kind for the rent when you were working your guts out at the pit face. But if you want to make something of it, come on you bugger.' Jack took a swig out of his tankard and then threw it down onto the stone floor before rolling his sleeves up in readiness for the fight he knew was going to come.

The rest of the group looked at one another, not believing that Jack had come out with what everyone knew to be true but was not spoken about. It was common knowledge how Sarah Parker paid the rent when her Bill had drunk away his wages. 'Hold your tongue, Jack, you know nowt. Anyway, you don't speak ill of the dead.' David Bowers looked at Bill who was still sat on his backside wondering quite what to do with himself.

'I'm nob'but telling the truth, that she was Ellershaw's whore. It's probably his baby that they've buried with her.' Jack wiped his mouth and looked around at the brooding miners and knew he'd said too much.

'Get yourself home, Jack, while you can. You're not welcome any longer in this establishment.' Derek stood between Jack and the deflated Bill, even though he knew he took his own life in his hands by doing so. 'All of you get away to your beds and be thankful you've homes and wives to go to.' He looked at David Bowers, the most sober of the bunch, for support and watched as the mob, led by Jack, left the Boot and Shoe, brought to their senses by the words uttered by the only sober man in the room.

'Aye, get yourselves home, lads,' David shouted after the mob and looked down at Bill, holding out his hand for him to grab, to help himself off the floor. 'Take no notice of Jack, his mouth runs away with him in drink.' David looked at the dumbstruck Bill and heaved him to his feet.

'Nay, David, I know he's right. I just used to turn a blind eye. I was never good enough for her or those stuck-up lasses of hers. She wanted better.' Bill stood up, unsteady on his feet, and propped himself up next to the bar.

'You'll get him home, David?' Derek started to clear up the knocked-over tankards and looked at the two crestfallen friends.

'Aye, I'll see him back home. After that he'll have to look after himself. He slung Bill's arm around his shoulder and staggered with him out of the inn. 'You've got to stop getting into such a state, Bill, one day you'll not make it home.'

'What home, I haven't got a home, nor a job, cause I'm not going back to that hellhole after tonight,' Bill mumbled.

'It'll look different in the morrow, lad, get yourself a good night's sleep and things will look a lot clearer in the morning.' David went quiet and concentrated on getting his broken-hearted friend home, knowing nothing would look better in the morning. To be honest things would look worse in the cold light of day, when he realised everyone had known so much about his beloved Sarah's dalliances with the owner of the Rose Pit.

*

'I think I heard David Bowers' voice. He must have brought Bill back home,' Mary-Anne whispered to Eliza who lay next to her. Both hardly dared to move as they heard the drunken men climb the stairs and enter their parents' bedroom.

They lay still as they heard Bill relieve himself in the chamber pot and then the springs on their parents' bed squeak with the weight of their stepfather being put upon it, followed by footsteps going down the stairs and the front door slamming after David Bowers' safe delivery of his charge. 'He'll not give us any bother tonight, Eliza, he'll be asleep as soon as he hits the pillow. Go to sleep and don't worry; we can rest easy tonight.' Mary-Anne hugged her fretting sister in the bed that they shared and sighed and stared into the darkness, worrying what the days ahead would bring. No matter what was thrown at them she was going to have to be strong for her and Eliza.

Seven

Bill lay in his bed. His head was thumping and his mouth was dry and he felt full of the excesses of the previous night's drinking. He lay looking out of the small window of the bedroom, watching the clouds scuttle across the sky and remembering the words Jack Langstaff had uttered while off his head on drink. He knew them to be true, even though he'd never tackled Sarah about it.

If she had not been Ellershaw's mistress he would surely have been dismissed from his position at the pit before now and have lost the roof over his head. God knew he had abused his position there plenty of times when the worse for drink. But he'd never had the sense to put his house in order; perhaps if he had done his Sarah would still be with him. He listened for any signs of life in the house, but it was silent; not even a peep from the usually busy kitchen.

He reached for his pocket watch from out of his waistcoat and sat up in the bed. Ten o'clock – his shift at the pit would have started four hours ago and his absence would have been noted by his fellow workers and, no doubt, by management. His colleagues would understand the situation but Ellershaw and his sidekick Tom Thackeray would not have been so forgiving. What the hell, he thought, he'd no intention of going back there anyway. He'd nothing to keep him at Woodlesford or to keep his job at Rose Pit. It was time to go back up to the north east, back to Sea Houses, where he belonged. Sarah and their bairn was dead, and her lasses hated him, so they must learn to look after themselves.

He caught his reflection in the swing mirror that stood on the washstand and thought how rough he looked. Where was the good-looking young man that had looked back at him ten years ago? Sitting on the edge of the bed, still dressed in his previous day's clothes, was an angry shell of a man with greying hair, a man who was not him, he thought, as he watched himself run his fingers through his thinning hair.

He stood up and made his way to the washstand. He poured the jug of water into the bowl before refreshing his face with scoopfuls of the ice cold water. He patted his face dry with a washcloth, reaching out for the handle on the washstand to steady himself from the dizziness that he was feeling from his night of drinking. He then took down the carpetbag from the top of the wardrobe and grabbed the few shirts he possessed from the wardrobe, placing them in the bag.

Still overcome with emotion and drink, he opened what he thought to be his drawer for his shirt collars, handkerchiefs and socks to take with him. His hand lingered as he realised he'd opened the wrong drawer and inside was what was left of Sarah. Hung over as he was, he couldn't fail to spot the small bottle, tucked away between Sarah's hair grips and everyday things that had meant so much to her. He recognised the faint handwriting immediately; while it was barely readable he knew it to be from her sister, Patsy.

He opened the cork stopper to smell the small amount of potion that was left in the bottle. The pungent smell made him feel sick as he quickly put the stopper back in place. His mind raced wildly putting two and two together quickly. So that was it: Sarah's death was Patsy's doing. Her and her ways to help women out of trouble ... she'd killed her own sister with her wicked potions.

Bill looked at the bottle and felt his hands shake with the anger he felt towards his sister-in-law and the fact that Jack Langstaff's words might be true when it came to the baby that Sarah had tried to get rid of. It probably hadn't been his baby she had lost after all – she'd tried to get rid of Ellenshaw's bastard. He raised his hand and threw the bottle against the wall, watching what was left of the potion trickle down onto the floor amongst the broken glass pieces. That cemented his decision to leave, but before he did there was someone he had to pay a visit to ... a visit that was long overdue.

The five miles walk into Leeds from Rothwell was if it had never taken place as Bill entered into the industrial smoke-covered city. His temper had spurred him on and his only thoughts were to give Patsy a piece of his mind. He wasn't afeared of her husband, Mick. He was just a lazy paddy and would probably not even leave his bed if he raised his hand in violence to his wife. By God, the woman would pay for her evil deeds. How many other unborn babies had she caused the death of? No wonder she wasn't a mother herself, she didn't deserve to be.

He pushed his way through the crowds up Briggate, his carpetbag slung over his shoulder as he pushed and barged his way up through the busy centre and up to the back streets that lead to Pounders Court. He stopped a few yards from the corner of the entrance to the court and took a moment to make clear his thoughts on what he was about to do. He immediately regretted his stop as the stench from the nearby tannery filled the air and a rat, fat from feeding on the waste from the skins, scuttled across the cobbled street almost over his feet.

The slums of Leeds were not for him; he might not have lived in a palace but at least he hadn't lived like the low-life that lived in these back streets. Even the rat probably had a better home than half of the poor wretches that lived here, he thought, as he looked around at the squalor that surrounded him.

With his thoughts still set on giving Patsy a pasting, he turned the corner into Pounders Court. He walked past the young lad that was playing with an old tin can, amusing himself by hitting it around the yard with a stick. Bill noticed that he looked as if he had never been washed since the day he was born, his clothes were in tatters and his feet were bare. He made for the closed door of Patsy and Mick's house and banged his fist on the crackled paintwork of the rotting door.

Patsy opened the door and was surprised to see her brother-in-law on her step.

'Bill, what brings you to these parts?'

'You should bloody well know ... after all it's your doing that she's left us.' Bill slammed the door behind him, dropping his carpetbag back on the floor and walked towards Patsy.

'Left you? What do you mean, left you? Has she run off with another fella? I've heard nowt from our Sarah, nor her lasses for over a week or more. I wouldn't blame her for that; you never were good enough for our lass.' Patsy saw the anger on his face and knew that through necessity she was going to have to stand her ground with the man that her sister had married.

'You fucking bitch.' Bill lunged at Patsy and pinned her to the wall. 'She's dead, killed by one of your witch's potions. You evil bitch!' Bill looked around the dark room filled with herbs and bottles of potions. 'How many other folk have you killed with the bloody rubbish you brew?' he snarled as he slapped Patsy across her face.

'Mick, Mick!' Patsy shouted as Bill slapped her again.

'Shout of him all you like, I can take him on any day. The lazy Irish bastard.' Bill banged Patsy again the wall again and again. 'No wonder you didn't show your face at the funeral, you murdered your own sister and her baby.'

'I didn't know, nobody told me.' Patsy screamed, tears falling down her cheeks.

'You didn't bloody care. You wizened-up excuse of a woman. Just because you are barren, you think everyone else should be.' Bill's hands grabbed at Patsy's throat.

'I think that's enough now. You can put Patsy down and get out of my house,' Mick said loudly as he emerged from the cellar, grabbing Bill by the shoulder. 'Feck off and leave us be. We are sorry to hear of your loss, but I'm not prepared for you to bray my Patsy to pulp just because she helped your Sarah get rid of a baby she didn't want. Happen you should look at yourself, you are as much to blame.'

Bill turned around and swung a fist at Mick, who dodged it smartly. 'I'll floor you, you bloody paddy. I'm not to blame for my Sarah's death!'

Bill lunged at Mick and then stopped short as he saw another man, the new lodger, come up from the cellar.

'Aye, you do right to stop your ranting. John Vasey here is Mayo's prize fighter. You wouldn't stand a chance if he sets into you.' Mick grinned as his close friend rolled up his sleeves to lay into the man that was causing so much distress to the best home he'd had since his eviction from his croft in Ireland. 'He'd knock your block off in a second and think nothin' of it.' Mick looked up admiringly at the tall, muscular, dark-haired man that stood silent, awaiting of instructions. 'Now, pick your bloody bag up and leave us be. And don't bother coming back. With Sarah gone, you are no longer welcome here.' Mick looked at his wife who was covered in blood and crying, curled up in a heap on the floor.

'She killed my Sarah, I hope she can't live with herself when she lies in bed and thinks of what she's done.' Bill swiped his hand along the table that was covered with bottles filled and about to be filled with Patsy's remedies. Smashing glass and liquids onto the flagged floor as he looked across with hate at the weeping woman.

John Vasey stepped forward ready to hit Bill.

'Leave him, John. He's not worth it. Besides, he's leaving now, aren't you, Bill? Before anybody else gets hurt!' Mick knew that Bill liked to pick on women but wasn't man enough to fight either him or John. Besides he couldn't help but feel a bit of pity for him, after losing his wife.

'Aye, I'm off. You'll not see me ever again. I'm off back where I belong, leaving you and yours in this muck-midden you call your home. She should hang for what she's done!' Bill pointed his finger at Patsy as he picked his bag up and opened the door.

'I am sorry for your loss, Bill. Despite our differences you didn't deserve to lose Sarah. Patsy was there for her when she asked for help, she's as heartbroken as you – you can see that.' Mick looked across at his sobbing wife and watched as Bill dropped his head and slammed the door behind him. He breathed out heavily as he watched him leave through the small window.

'Are you all right, Patsy?' Mick went over to his wife and knelt down next to her.

'I'll take myself back downstairs.' John Vasey looked at the grieving couple and thought it best if he made himself scarce.

'Aye, all right, Thanks, John.' Mick looked up at his quiet, well-meaning friend as he helped Patsy to her feet. 'Are you all right, lass? I'm sorry I never heard him come until it was too late to save you from his blows.' Mick put his arm around her waist and sat her down on a chair next to the table covered with smashed bottles and dripping medicines.

'I'm all right, nothing that time won't heal. But our Sarah, Mick! Have I really killed her? I asked Mary-Anne and Eliza to tell her that it was a strong mixture and to be careful with it. She must not have headed my words or they forgot to tell her.' Patsy sobbed and wiped her eyes with her apron as she looked around her at the chaos that Bill had brought them. 'She should have known how much to take.' Patsy gripped Micks arm.

'Aye, Patsy, perhaps you shouldn't dabble in what nature intends for us all.' Mick looked at his wife and wiped the blood away from her nose with the end of her apron.

'And let women like my sister keep having bairns that they can't afford nor love, like her next door? Besides Sarah knew it wasn't Bill's she was carrying and that wasn't the first time. If that useless bastard didn't drink so much she wouldn't have gone and had to bargain and plead with her body to keep a roof over their heads and him in work.'

'You mean, she had another man in her life?' Mick sat back and waited for his wife to tell her secrets.

'Aye, she'd an arrangement with Ellershaw that owns the Rose. It's his baby she was carrying. She'd tried to get rid of it a month earlier, but it didn't work. That's why I was so glad to see her girls on my doorstep when they came by out of the blue. Else she would have had to have gone full-term with the baby if she'd left it any later. I'm not a murderer; leave it too late and I'll not do owt about it, as it's a baby by then.' Patsy's hands shook as she looked at her Mick with tears in her eyes. 'I should have written a note to go with the bottle, but I didn't want the girls to read it, so I just asked them to tell her it was strong. Oh, Mick, what have I done? I have killed my sister! Bill is right, I am responsible for her death. And those poor lasses ... what are they going to do without their mother? I can't say they'll be sad to see the back of Bill, but they'll have to look after one another now. I've even missed the funeral, because I didn't know.' Patsy sobbed. 'Happen he's right ... happen I am a bitter, old, twisted and wizened woman and I should be hanged.'

'Now, Patsy, you know that's not true. You thought you were helping; you weren't to know she'd take too much ...' Mick put his arm around his wife and felt her body shudder in convulsions of grief. He didn't quite know what to say; it was his wife's domain and best he didn't know too much about the workings of women. But what he did know was that it was a tragedy and an event that was going to change all their worlds.

Mary-Anne and Eliza walked home from their busy day at work in the sewing room to a house that was in darkness and silent as the grave.

'He must have got his arse out of bed and gone to work, he'll be back after his shift,' Mary-Jane said to her relieved sister as they made their way in darkness to the kitchen. 'Here, you light the gaslights and I'll get the fire going.' Mary-Anne reached for the packet of vestas above the fireplace, and struck one to set alight the fire she'd laid in the grate that morning. As the fire flickered and burnt and the dim light from the gaslights grew stronger, they realised that things were not right in the kitchen. Chairs were tipped up and the money box from the top of the fireplace was on the kitchen table with its contents missing.

'We've been robbed, our Mary! Somebody's been in our house! '
Eliza looked around her.

'Here, come with me ... they might still be in the house. Grab
Mother's rolling pin ... we might need it.' Mary-Anne lit a candle
and looked fearfully at her sister as she sheltered the flame with
her hand and walked down the passage, lighting the gaslights in the
hallway and parlour as the both glanced around, hoping not to find
the thief still inside. 'Well, all is all right in here, nothing's been
touched. But I'd better check upstairs. You stay downstairs, just in
case I disturb somebody and then you can catch them when they
make their break for it. Just hit them over the head with the rolling
pin.' Mary-Anne lit the oil lamp that sat in the centre of the oak
table that her mother had polished with love and care nearly every
day. It had been the one decent piece of furniture that she'd been
able to keep from her first marriage, bequeathed to her by a distant
relative. Mary-Anne gave a quick glance at her sister as she left her
shaking at the bottom of the stairs.

Eliza watched as the shadow of her sister was distorted on the wall
as she climbed up the stairs to their bedrooms and feared for both
their lives as she watched her disappear into her parents' bedroom.

'Eliza, Eliza, come quickly!' Mary-Anne shouted downstairs.

Eliza quickly made her way upstairs and stood at the entrance to
her parents' room. She gasped as she saw the near-empty wardrobe
and the contents of her mother's drawers scattered all over the floor.
They could see that their stepfather's drawer had been emptied. But
it was when Mary-Anne pointed out the shattered remains of the
bottle that they recognised as the one they had brought from their
Aunt Patsy's that they both realised what had happened.

'He's gone, hasn't he? He's left us.' Eliza sat down on the unmade
bed and looked around her.

'It looks like it, Eliza. He could at least have left the bit of money that there was in the cash box downstairs. And he's made a good mess up here by breaking Aunt Patsy's tonic.'

'He always hated Aunt Patsy. That's why she never visits. She won't even know that we've lost our mother. We were both in such a state we didn't dare mention to Bill that she should be told. What are we going to do, Mary-Anne? We are on our own ... how are we going to survive?' Eliza held her head in her hands.

Mary-Anne looked at the shattered glass and gasped. 'Did you tell Mother that the mixture was stronger than usual? Because I never thought about it when I saw you give it to her.' Mary-Anne looked at Eliza and waited.

'No, I never said anything ... I was too busy thinking about the bargains we had made that day. I just forgot.' Eliza went quiet. 'You don't think ...?' Eliza looked at her sister and didn't even want to comprehend what they were both thinking. 'It was just a tonic, she said.'

'I know Aunt Patsy told us it was just a tonic, but she wouldn't tell us the truth, now would she, if it was one of her potent concoctions.' Mary-Anne reached for her sister's hand.

'Oh, Mary-Anne we've killed our mother. We should have remembered to tell her that the tonic was strong. The baby's dead and so is she, and now Bill has walked out on us. We've no money. Our clothes shop will only just keep us fed, let alone pay the rent. Thank God father left us that on his death and that mother never made us sell it, no matter how tough the times were. At least we have that. Not that the dilapidated place is worth anything much.' Eliza started to cry.

Mary-Anne put her arm around her shaking sister. 'We'll manage, we'll have to, and something will turn up. And at least we can sleep easy in our bed tonight, now Bill's gone.' She looked around at the shattered glass and the empty wardrobe. She knew she spoke brave words to her sister, brave words that she couldn't justify. Just how were they going to survive, she didn't know, but survive they must.

Eight

'This doesn't feel right.' Eliza looked at her parents' bed with the array of her mother's clothes and possessions on it that they were planning to sell in their shop.

'It'll make us a bit of money and keep us fed, Eliza. Mother wouldn't have minded, she'd understand. Besides, they are no good to anybody just hanging there unworn, and we will keep back something to remind us both of her. I thought Mrs Simms next door might like this little brooch with the bluebird on it. It's not worth anything but it's pretty and Mother loved it. And Mrs Simms has been so good with us since Mother died. Now, what would you like to keep of hers? I'd like this hair slide. Can you remember how she used to always wear it at Christmas when we had friends and relations over at our old home? Father used to always admire her with this in her hair.' Mary-Anne picked up the hair slide that was set with paste diamonds and smiled, remembering the good times before her father had died and before Bill Parker had made his way into their lives, as she popped the slide into her pocket.

'I'd like the locket please. It's got a lock of our father's hair in, and so we shouldn't sell that.' Eliza picked the locket up from the few pieces of jewellery that her mother had possessed and held it tenderly in her hand. 'I just can't believe she's gone; I miss her so much.'

'We both do, but we've got to be practical. It's no good clinging to the past; we've got to look to our future. If we can sell most of this in the shop, and that green organza dress, we should be able to keep our heads above water until after Christmas. After that I don't know … we will have to play it by ear. I'm just worried that now Bill no longer works at the pit Ellershaw will want his cottage back; I pray not. Perhaps I'll have to get a job in one of the mills in Leeds and leave just you to look after the shop, you could nearly live there on your own and I'd just have to seek a room to rent. Or perhaps we could both manage to live in the shop if we had to?' Mary-Anne sighed, the last thing she wanted was to walk the five miles to Leeds and back every day to work like a slave in one of the many woollen mills that were springing up or to live there in one of the many doss houses. 'Besides, you may soon become Mrs Thackeray the way that Tom looks at you. It's a pity you couldn't meet him last Sunday, but I'm sure he understood when you told him you couldn't when he attended Mother's funeral. It would have not been respectable for you to do so, not yet.'

'He won't look twice at me anyway, dressed in these mourning clothes, nobody will. I expected him to call around now we are on our own. He's sure to know that Bill has left us, with him not going to work.' Eliza's face said it all. Life had just started to look rosy for her until her mother had been found dead. Now, with Bill leaving and rumours rife about their mother's demise, she and Mary-Anne were the centre of gossip and avoided like the plague.

'Nonsense, of course he will. Give him a little time and he will make himself known again. He's being respectful of our grief.' Mary-Anne felt sorry for her sister and remembered her smiling face when she had walked out with Tom on that fateful Sunday morning.

'I doubt it. His mother hated me before all this, so she definitely will now.' Eliza sighed. 'I'll make us a cup of tea, I think we can just afford it. Perhaps we should ask for tick next time we go into Farrar's shop, although Mother always said she'd rather do without than owe anybody anything. You don't honestly think old Ellershaw will throw us both out, do you?'

'I don't know, as long as he gets the rent he might be happy. We'll manage, Eliza, something will turn up. While you put the kettle on, I'll go around to see Ada Simms and give her this brooch. She may be a nosy old biddy but you must admit she's been good to us once she found out Bill had left, bringing around that tasty hotpot last night and watching out for both of us.' Mary-Anne followed her sister downstairs and opened the front door to visit her neighbour.

Eliza looked at her sister. 'Don't tell her any of our business though, Mary.'

'I don't think there's anything left to tell, Eliza; everybody knows our plight and what they don't know they are making up. I'll be back in a short while.' Mary-Anne stepped out of the house and went around next door to knock on the door of number two, Pit Lane.

Ada Simms answered the knock and stood in her hallway and looked at the young woman who looked slightly haggard, after the events that had shook the family.

'Mary-Anne, is everything all right?'

'Yes, I'm fine, thank you, Mrs Simms. I've just popped my head around to give you this, I thought you might like something to remember our mother by and you've been so good to both of us these last days.' Mary-Anne reached into her pocket and passed over the small silver brooch. 'We are clearing her clothes and possessions out, we thought we could sell them in the shop.'

'Aye, lass, that's kind of you. Your mother often wore this on her high-collared blouse. Are you sure neither of you two lasses want it?' Ada Simms felt her eyes fill with tears and she fought them back as she picked up the brooch from Mary-Anne. 'Anyway, what am I thinking about? Come in out of the cold. Come and have a drink of tea with us and tell me how you are both doing. I'd just put the kettle on to boil before your knock on the door.'

'No, you're fine, Mrs Simms. I must get back to Eliza, she doesn't like to be on her own at the moment.' Mary-Anne knew once in the house she would struggle to escape from the bombardment of questions that she would be subjected to.

'I understand. Poor Eliza ... she will miss her mother. And then for Bill to up sticks and leave you both ... I always thought he was an uncaring man. Now, Bert and me have been talking and I know that you'll not both feel like celebrating Christmas but we'd like you to come for dinner here; it's the least we can do. It'll not be anything fancy, mind, just a piece of pork and a tattie or two, but it will be better than you two sitting on your own. I couldn't have you doing that, now could I?' Ada reached for Mary-Anne's hand in reassurance and waited for her to answer.

'Oh, I don't know. We'd be imposing on your Christmas and as you say it's the last thing on our minds at the moment.' Mary-Anne hadn't given Christmas a second thought, apart from mending the green dress that was now in the shop window in the hope that someone would buy it for the party season.

'I won't take no for an answer. Else I wouldn't be much of a Christian soul, now would I? I'm sure Eliza will be all right with it; anywhere is better than sitting feeling sorry for yourselves, because Christmas is the time we miss our loved ones. And with your mother's death being so fresh, it will be hard this year.' Ada smiled at Mary-Anne and she knew it was futile to decline the invite.

'Very well, it's very kind of you to think of us. We will look forward to it.' Mary-Anne smiled at her neighbour and then bade her farewell.

As she closed the garden gate, her face dropped. The last thing she wanted was to sit around the Christmas table with Ada and Bert Simms but this year they would be fools to decline, else it would probably mean at best a dinner of bacon and egg, and at worst bread and dripping. A piece of roast pork would be most welcome, no matter what Eliza said about the invite.

'Oh, Mary-Anne, how could you? How can you expect us both to sit with them two and enjoy our food? Ada Simms is such gossip, and Bert looks at me like I'm a piece of dirt on his shoe. I'd rather be eating bread and dripping than watching every word I say and besides, I'd rather forget about Christmas this year.' Eliza sighed.

'Just for once we'll have full bellies that day. I'm beginning to forget what one of them feels like since Mother passed. If we'd not had the charity from next door, we'd have been starving by now. We've got to take the opportunities that are sent our way, and I can just taste that pork with apple sauce. So just, for once, smile and enjoy your day.' Mary-Anne spoke sharply at her younger sister; she could be so ungrateful sometimes.

'I'll hate every minute and so will you if you are truthful.' Eliza looked at her sister as she wrapped her mother's clothes up in readiness for the shop.

'I know, but we have to do these things to survive. And after all it will be Christmas in a fortnight, whether we like it or not. The rent on the cottage will be due, we need some oil for the lamps and some coal. We've always taken that for granted with Bill working at the pit, now we'll have to buy it.' Mary-Anne could have cried but she had to look strong for Eliza's sake.

Nine

Grace Ellershaw looked at her brother and grinned at him as he picked up his swagger stick from the hallstand.

'Mother,' she called up to the nursery above, 'William and I are just going to take a stroll up Woodlesford. We thought that we might do a little Christmas shopping, if there's anything to buy in this godforsaken village.' She was overjoyed that her brother had returned from Cambridge as she had missed his company so much. Now she was going to be selfish and have a day with him all by herself.

'I really don't know why you are doing this, Grace, when we could have taken our coach into the centre of Leeds, where there is choice beyond belief.' William Ellershaw tipped his hat and offered his sister his arm as they closed the door of Highfield behind them both, neither waiting for their mother to reply.

'I'm doing it, dear brother, to get some time with you on your own and to save me from boredom. Besides, Leeds is so busy at this time of year, although I am going to have to pay a visit to Grandpapa to remind him what I would dearly like for Christmas. I'm sure you did that when you visited him the other week. You'd be a fool if you didn't.'

'I couldn't get a word in edgeways for Mamma trying to convince Grandpapa that he needed me to help buy his ever-expanding empire. However, he didn't look impressed and I didn't push myself forward as I don't know the first thing about wool.' William scowled. It was getting to be a little tedious, the way his life was expected to fold out before his eyes, on the whim of parents and grandparents. He had reached an age in his life where he no longer needed to be told to wipe his nose or not speak until spoken too, but his parents still insisted on treating him as a child, just like his younger brother George.

'What are you going to do, William? You just can't waste your life in reading your books and staying in your room out of the way of father. He is really angry with you for leaving university and then for not showing an interest in the mine.' Grace looked up at her brother, whom she loved dearly, and smiled at him. 'Mamma might be right, Grandpapa could give you a good position in life, and after all he is one of the richest men in West Riding.'

'Don't you worry your head about me, Grace, I'll show more interest in things this coming spring. I just need some time to myself. I've a lot to think about since I left Cambridge; there are things back there I regret leaving and it is taking me time to get over the loss.' William looked at his caring sister; she was as pretty as a picture in her dark purple bonnet and purple mantle to match. Her black hair was carefully pinned up in a bun underneath her hat and her dark eyes sparkled with wit. Many of his friends showed interest in her but none seemed to be able to match her wisdom and love of learning. She too enjoyed her books and had a better business head on her than his father, he often thought. Along with her kind heart, she would make some-one the perfect wife.

Grace stopped in her tracks and looked up at her handsome brother. He had not been himself since his return and she had often noticed him of late looking glum as he tried to go about making a place for himself at home again.

'What do you mean you regret leaving something behind?' she asked. 'And are getting over your loss? Oh, William! Was a woman the reason you left Cambridge? Did she break your heart?'

'You ask too much, my little sister. But yes, it was a woman. She was called Amelia and I was smitten and all was going well until she decided my friend Samuel was a better option for her. Better connected, you see; I'm just a miner's son, from up north. Father might be well off but for certain people we'll never be good enough. Samuel is the godson of the Earl of Leicester, much better suited for a millionaire's daughter. Mother knows, but she didn't tell Father; you know he'd have no time for matters of the heart. Women don't rank high in his life, and I feel he always looks down on the fairer sex. Anyway, he'd never understand that I had to leave because I was broken-hearted, so it's best he never gets told.' William bowed his head, remembering his love of Amelia and how flippant she had been with his affections, especially when she had laughed at the ring that he had thought was worthy of her hand in marriage. Which had led her to telling him that Samuel, his best friend, or so he had thought, had been courting her behind his back and it was his hand in marriage she intended to take.

'Oh, William, I knew there was something wrong. Why didn't you tell me earlier? You know I'd wouldn't say anything to Father.' Grace squeezed her brother's hand tight.

'I'll get over it, and it will be good to be home for Christmas. Mother was glad to see me even if father wasn't. And baby George seems to have taken to me. Besides, there's plenty more fish in the sea, so they say. I'll live.' William shrugged his shoulders and smiled wanly at Grace.

'Was she really a millionaire's daughter? What was she like?' Grace questioned her brother. 'How could she court your best friend? He must be nothing more than a cad, to go behind your back like that. I hope that Samuel Westbury never comes near our home again.'

'Yes, her father has lots of money. He'd made his fortune in sugar and rum from the Jamaicas and yes, she is very, very beautiful. And I'm trying desperately to forget her, so stop your questions, Grace, before I make a fool of myself. I not only lost her but also my dearest friend, who I had shared all my deepest confidences with. I've been such a fool, I should be hard like our father.'

'I'm sorry, I didn't mean to hurt you. I just knew there was something wrong.' Grace took her brother's arm as they walked along Aberford Road towards the heart of the village.

'I'll forgive you. Now, let's look at the amazing display of gifts that are available in Woodlesford compared to Leeds,' William said sarcastically, while glancing in the butcher's window at his display of poultry and pigs trotters that adorned the window next to the workshop of Eliza and Mary-Anne. 'Besides, is it not time you found yourself a husband? Or is no one good enough for my little sister?'

'I'm not ready for a man in my life; in fact, I don't think I will ever get married. From what I've seen, women are better off without them.' Grace went and hastily stepped next to the little dress shop that had caught her eye. 'You may joke, William Ellershaw, but to be quite honest I don't think I've ever seen a more beautiful dress than this one in this window.' Grace pressed her nose up to the glass of the little lean-to that had seen better days, and gazed at the green organza dress displayed there. 'I've got to have it, it's perfect for the Eshald House dance. You know how we ladies have to look our best for that event, whether we are in the market for a man or not.'

'Don't be daft, this is clearly a second-hand shop. The girl back there probably got it given from her mistress ... a hand-me-down, is that what you want to be seen in?' William gazed through the window and watched as Eliza concentrated on her sewing.

'I don't care where it came from, I've got to have it!' Grace opened the paint-worn door and entered into the small wooden lean-to that was Mary-Anne's and Eliza's workshop.

Mary-Anne looked up from her sewing and knew instantly who her customer was. She was Edmund Ellershaw's daughter, Grace – spoilt, headstrong and wealthy – and behind her stood her brother William, who everyone knew to be a disappointment to his father, but would one day be very wealthy when he inherited his father's pit and the woollen mills in Leeds owned by his grandfather. She smiled and quickly glanced at Eliza before standing up from her sewing.

'May I help you?' She walked towards the couple, noticing that William looked uncomfortable in the shabby surroundings.

'Yes, I couldn't help but notice the beautiful dress in the window. May I have a closer look?' Grace looked at the older of the two sisters and couldn't help but admire her clear complexion and vibrant auburn hair, and had a fleeting thought that, with her colouring, the dress would suit the shop girl even better than it suited her.

'Of course, miss. Is it for yourself? It is quite special.' Mary-Anne walked over to the window and took the dress from the display, draping the many folds of organza over her arm and showing Grace the intricate stitching on the tight bodice. 'You'll notice how the neckline would show off your beautiful slim neck beautifully and I believe the waist will fit you perfectly once laced up.'

'It's beautiful.' Grace smiled at Mary-Anne. 'Did you make it?' Her eyes could not hide her love of the dress as she held it against her and smiled at her reflection in the old mirror at the back of the cabin.

'My sister, Eliza.' Mary-Anne turned to her young sister. 'She is the seamstress of the two us; I'm proficient in mending but Eliza can make anything from nothing and make the most beautiful garments.' Mary-Anne looked over at Eliza and gave her a long stare, hoping that she'd go along with the lie.

'So, it's not second-hand? You've sewn it from scratch?' William felt the quality of the material and looked at his sister's face who was truly enamoured by the dress, holding it next to her and looking at herself again and again in the aged full-length mirror that stood on the wall.

'It's a new line that we are trying. It cost quite a bit to make but it is something we thought worthwhile doing, and I enjoy designing my own dresses.' Mary-Anne got up from her work desk and smiled at William and his sister.

'Well, you are to be congratulated. It is so beautiful, don't you think, William?' Grace turned to her brother who was busy looking around the workshop.

'Indeed, my dear. Are you going to buy it? Is it your size?' William smiled at his sister and looked at Mary-Anne who was smiling at him unashamedly.

'You suit it perfectly, miss, and if it doesn't fit when you take it home, Eliza can always alter it, but I think it will fit like a glove and that it has just been waiting for you to come along.' Mary-Anne looked at Grace and knew that she had made a sale.

Grace looked for a price on the dress. 'How much is it?'

'A guinea, miss. We couldn't let it go for any less. We barely make anything as it is.' Eliza smiled at the pair and noticed they did not flinch at the price.

'That's quite reasonable, isn't it, William? In fact I will take it and please accept an extra sixpence for you to deliver it to my home at Highfield.' Grace rummaged in her posy bag for payment. 'Oh, dear, I've forgotten to pick up the money from my bureau! William, may I ask you to pay for the garment? I feel such a fool.'

'Really, Grace, you would forget your head some days.' William reached into his inner pocket and pulled out his wallet, handing the guinea over to Mary-Anne. 'There's no need to deliver the dress; we'll take it now.' His hand lingered with the payment as he looked into Mary-Anne's emerald-green eyes.

'Thank you, sir.' Mary-Anne passed the dress and the money to Eliza who started to wrap the dress up in brown paper, her face betraying the fact that William had put stop to an extra sixpence.

'Don't be so miserly, William, give the girls the sixpence anyway. They've probably earned it and I would have paid double the price for the dress in Leeds.' Grace smiled and looked around the shop. 'Would you make me further dresses and outfits if I asked?' She ran her hand down the skirt of one of their mothers dresses that the two sisters had just placed on the old tailor's dummy they'd found discarded outside one of the fashion shops in Leeds and turned to smile at Eliza. 'It would save me travelling into Leeds and Father always says we should support local industry.'

'Of course, miss, we could take your measurements and then we could fit the perfect dress.' Eliza drew a sharp breath in, hoping that she could fulfil her request. Little white lies about the dress she had remade were one thing but promising a young lady new designs without knowing where the material to do so was going to appear from was quite another.

'Then you will be seeing me again shortly.' Grace smiled at the two sisters as William placed the parcelled dress under his arm after scowling at his sister for making him give an extra sixpence for nothing. 'I will return if the dress does not fit, but I'm sure it will be perfect.'

'Thank you, miss ... sir.' Both Eliza and Mary-Anne curtsied and smiled as the couple made their way out of the shop. They watched as they walked down the road together smiling, Grace Ellershaw linking her arm into her brother's as he carried the package and his swagger stick under the other arm.

'Hell's bells, Mary, you were cheeky! A guinea and she made him pay the extra sixpence!' Eliza grinned from ear to ear as she looked at the money on her sewing desk.

'Aye, and what about you and your new line of dresses?' Mary-Anne laughed at her sister. 'I bet she'll be back. She fell for that dress, hook, line and sinker, she didn't care that we might not have sewn it ourselves – the devil might have done for all she cared – and she had to have it.' Mary-Anne laughed. 'At least we'll not go hungry this week and I can pay the rent when the tallyman comes at the end of the month.'

'And what about if she comes back for something else? I know I can sew, but we won't be able to buy the material that she will expect her dress to made of, nor perhaps style it the way she wants.' Eliza looked at her sister and could have sworn at her for being so confident in her skills.

'You can sew anything and you know you can, and as for material, when it's needed we will ask her for money up front. She won't think anything of it, she's a spoilt rich girl.' Mary-Anne grinned. 'We'll go and see Ma Fletcher at the start of next week and see what she's got in and go and see Aunt Patsy, I feel guilty at not letting her know that our mother died. We were too caught up on our own grief . . . Besides, Bill wanted to keep her death within our direct family, I think he was ashamed of how she died.' Mary-Anne looked at the money that could never replace their mother but at the same time eased the situation.

'We couldn't have done anything else, Mary. Bill wouldn't allow us to tell her and he made it clear he'd not have let he come to the funeral. You know he hated her.' Eliza hung her head. 'Besides I keep thinking about when we found in mother's bedroom. I really do think she took it on purpose and that it was more than a tonic. After all, that's what Aunt Patsy is known for.'

'I know, but why would she do that?' Mary-Anne looked at her sister. 'We might not have loved Bill, but she did and I'd have thought she'd have wanted his baby.'

'She knew she couldn't really afford another mouth to feed. Because, let's face it, Bill was not to be relied upon. We should have done more to bring the money in.' Eliza sighed.

'We did all we could. As it is let's greet tomorrow with a bit more hope, we can't bring mother back but we can make her be proud of us.' Mary-Anne smiled and pocketed the coins. 'William Ellershaw is a bit handsome, isn't he?'

'He is, but he's not daft, he knew that dress wasn't new.' Eliza grinned.

'Doesn't matter, our Eliza, we still got his brass and that's all that matters. And we'll have more of it if we are canny with his sister.'

Mary-Anne felt for the comfort of the money in her pocket and thought about the business Grace Ellershaw could pass their way. She and Eliza would survive even though they may have to lie through their teeth to do so.

Ten

'What do you think, Father? Is it not perfect?' Grace Ellershaw flaunted her new dress in front of her father as he sat next to the fire in the parlour of Highfield.

Edmund looked up and looked at his radiant daughter in a new dress yet again.

'Aye, it's all right. Have you been spending my brass again?'

'No, she's been spending mine,' William quickly added.

'Well, then I'm right, it is mine you've been spending.' Edmund folded his paper and looked at Grace. 'Where did you get that from then?'

'I found it in Woodlesford, would you believe? At that little shed-like thing next to the butcher's. It was in the window and I just couldn't leave it.' Grace sat down next to her father, making sure the green organza was shown off to its best as she titivated the many layers of the dress.

'You mean you bought it off Sarah Parker's two lasses? I can't see them two having anything as good as this in their window, they usually sell second-hand tat from Leeds market. They'd take the clothes of your back as soon as look at you, them two.' Edmund grunted. 'I hope you didn't pay a lot for it.'

'A guinea, which I thought was a fair price.' Grace looked down at herself with pride.

'Aye, and they probably bought it for tuppence and did their best to make it look new. You've been robbed!' Edmund knew the sisters by sight and reputation. The youngest had been a regular visitor to the pit when she brought Bill his snap that he often forgot. But the elder he'd hardly knew, and hadn't seen her for a while.

'That's what I thought, Father,' William spouted. 'I told her she was being conned, that they wouldn't have made it from new.'

'Then you should have stopped her from buying it, you useless bugger. As it is the money will only come back into my pocket anyway; they'll need to pay the rent on their cottage end of this week, else they are out. I can't afford to have them sitting in one of my cottages, now their mother's dead and their stepfather's buggered off. He always was a useless devil.'

'Well, I think you are both wrong; this dress I was assured was hand-made and I'm actually thinking of employing them to make me another. And how could you be so heartless, Father, if that has happened to them both, just before Christmas as well. You could at least wait to see if they manage to pay you.'

'If you do go back, Grace,' William said, 'perhaps I'll come with you. I wouldn't mind another glance of the older sister, she's a pretty thing with that long auburn hair and pale skin.'

'Tha wants nowt to do with either of them. Their mother was a whore and their father a drunk, and if they are anything like either they'd eat you up and spit you out lad,' Edmund said sharply – he didn't want his son to have anything to do with the pair, let alone Grace with her hair-brained ideas of employing them to make her dresses. 'And you keep away from them, our Grace. Get yourself into Leeds and to a proper dressmaker, and stop spending my brass on some trollops.'

'Whatever you say, Father, but she is beautiful.' William bowed his head and noticed the smile that his sister gave him as she recognised a new interest in a woman after his heartbreak, even if she was entirely unsuitable. He also noticed that she did not reply to her father, which meant her head was set on giving the two sisters another visit.

'Aye, well, beauty is only skin deep; remember that, both of you,' Edmund growled.

'You prefer money, don't you, my dear?' Catherine Ellershaw looked up from her sewing. 'After all, is that not what you married me for?' She watched as her husband thought of something biting to say in front of his two children.

'I married thee for thy money *and* thy looks; I got the best of both worlds.' Edmund gave a withering smile to his wife. 'That's what you two want to do. Brass and beauty, you can't go wrong with both.' Edmund went back to his paper.

'I'd say, children, that you marry for love, although good connections and breeding come into play in our polite society and nobody wants a donkey on their arm. Do they, William? A pretty little thing is to be preferred.' Catherine smiled at both her children.

'Well, the Parker sisters are certainly not donkeys, they are both quite beautiful and gifted.' Grace beamed at her brother. 'Our William, I think, is quite besotted with them, I can tell.' She chuckled and tenderly touched her dress as she looked coyly at her brother who was turning a bright shade of red in fear of what his sister was going to say next.

'You keep away from them, do you hear? They'll bring nowt but heartache to you, my lad. If you are that desperate go down to the quayside in Leeds and get what a red-blooded male at your age needs – a good time with a woman who knows exactly what to do – instead of wasting your money on second-hand dresses from trollops. The prick-pinchers will satisfy you and not make demands on you. At least tha knows it's a fair bargain then.' Edmund's face turned a deep shade of purple and red as his voice rose in anger at his son and scandalised daughter. 'No son of mine will be associated with those two bitches so get that into your head.' Edmund threw his paper down and stood next to the fireplace scowling down on his family group.

'Edmund, I don't think there is any need for such vulgar talk in our home, especially in front of Grace and me. In fact a decent family man would not know of such things, let alone suggest his son go and ask for their services. I feel quite faint thinking about what you have just said. William, for once you don't heed your father's advice, and Grace, try to forget what your father has just said.' Catherine Ellershaw composed herself and looked at her husband, regretting once again the day she had married him.

All three looked up at the man, who seemed to have got upset over nothing more than a second-hand dress and where it had come from. They knew their father spoke as he liked, but never as rudely as this before.

'Bugger it. All of you can do what you want, you always do anyway. If you want to waste your money on trollops and their tat then do so. But no good will come of it, mark my words.' Edmund stormed out of the room, leaving his family gazing after him.

'Take no notice, my dears, I fear your father is in a mood; he will have calmed down by the end of the day. He must be having a few problems at the pit.' Catherine Ellershaw resumed her sewing as Grace and William glanced at one another. They would both be returning to the girls their father disliked so much, just to prove a point if nothing else. The more he forbade it, the more they would want to return.

Eleven

'Oh my poor dears, I wish I'd known about your mother … but I didn't find out until it was too late and she was already cold in the ground.' Patsy hugged her nieces when they appeared on her doorstep with their usual bag of second-hand goods.

Eliza wiped back the tears, hugging her aunty as they entered her home, but Mary-Anne held back.

'We didn't realise you even knew our mother had died. We couldn't get a message to you and Bill didn't want you at the funeral.' Mary-Anne felt reserved towards her aunt, still in doubt that she was perhaps the cause of her mother's death.

'I didn't know, not until that bastard Bill Parker came and tried to knock seven bells out of me, blaming me for our Sarah's death. The man's mad. Has he calmed down any?' Patsy looked at both of her nieces and felt a pang of guilt over the death of their mother, knowing something must have gone wrong when she had drunk her potion and knowing that Bill was probably right in his accusations.

'He's left,' Eliza said quietly. 'We don't know where to, but he's gone. Leaving us on our own.'

'Are you all right, coping on your own? When he was here he said he was clearing off, but I didn't think he was really going.' Patsy looked at the two girls who both looked pale and worried.

'Yes, we are fine, better without Bill, although we are having to pay our own way in the world as he even took every bit of coin we had in the house. He never did give a damn about us two.' Mary-Anne sighed, her heart thawing towards her aunt. 'We didn't realise he'd been here; I hope he didn't hurt you too much, Aunt Patsy.'

'He was a bastard, was Bill Parker. It's a pity it isn't him that's in the ground, not your mother.' From the darkest corner of the cramped cottage, Mick spoke up as he puffed on his clay pipe. 'Your mother was a grand woman, she thought the world of you two. It was a bad day when she married him. It's him that's to blame for her demise, at the end of the day.'

Patsy glanced nervously at her husband before turning to the sisters. 'Now sit yourselves down, girls, I'll make you a bite to eat. We've enough bread and cheese for all of us. Mick, give John a yell, tell him to come up from the cellar and meet Eliza and Mary-Anne, it'll give him someone fresh to talk to.' Patsy put the kettle on the fire and went to the cupboard for a fresh loaf of bread and the cheese, placing both in the centre of the table. 'He's a good man is John. He's no bother, you two could do with a lodger like him. It would bring some extra money in your hands.'

'John, get yourself up here, for a bite to eat and to meet our nieces.' Mick stood at the top of the cellar steps and bellowed down to where John Vasey was living, before pulling up a chair at the table. 'He'll not be with us long, that's the problem. He's only here for a year or so, until he's made enough money for passage to New York and America. He's turned his back on the old country and he knows England's not for the likes of him.' Mick looked at the two lasses as they watched for John Vasey to appear from the cellar.

'Aye, sit with us, John. Make yourself comfortable. This is Eliza and that's Mary-Anne. These are the two dear girls who I was telling you have just lost their mother, God rest her soul.' Patsy leaned over the tall and broad John as she poured everyone a cup of tea. 'Help yourselves, girls. Sorry I've not enough plates for everyone,' she apologised as she placed the bread, butter and cheese in the middle of the table with only four plates to share between them.

Mary-Anne looked up at the dark-haired man as he pulled back a chair and sat across from her.

'My condolences on losing your mother. You must be missing her.' John's Irish accent was as broad as he was but Mary-Anne couldn't help but notice the bright blue of his eyes. With his dark black hair and charming manner, he was quite a handsome man.

'We are, she was very precious to us both,' Mary-Anne replied as she squeezed Eliza's hand tightly, noticing a single tear run down her sister's face.

'No doubt it will take a time to get over your grief, that's to be expected. I lost most of my family in the famine and those that I haven't lost have fled. Ireland is no place to be at the moment. So I know your grief.' John helped himself to piece of cheese and bread, and broke into it on the table. 'Good piece of cheese this, Patsy, I thank you.'

'I'm sorry, that must have been terrible to have lived through. Your loss must be worse than ours.' Mary-Anne looked at the man across from her and saw the hurt in his eyes.

'Aye, well, you make the most of your life to honour the ones you've lost. They are always with you, looking down and watching over you, so don't ever forget that, girls.' John bit into his bread and went quiet.

'I was telling them that you are off to America, John, once you've got your passage money.' Patsy sat down at the head of the table and looked at her lodger.

'That I am. America's the place to make money, if you are prepared to work. Plenty of opportunities if you are willing to take them.' John looked up from his dinner and winked at Eliza as she dried her eyes and listened to his soft Irish lilt.

'What are you doing now, Mr Vasey, to earn your passage?' Mary-Anne asked, interested in how the Irish man was making his living while staying with her aunt and uncle.

'I've got work when they want me down in the canal basin, unloading and loading goods.' He smiled broadly. 'And there's that much stuff comes on and off those barges that perhaps they don't notice the odd bottle or two or the odd round of cheese going missing. Eh. Patsy!' He grinned across at his landlady mischievously as he enjoyed his mouthful of stolen cheese and shared a knowing nod. Mary-Ann laughed, fully aware of how most people she knew had to take their chances when they came.

'You just take care, John Vasey, else it will not be America you go to, it'll be Australia they'll be sending you to, for thieving, if they catch you.' Mick looked across at his friend with a smile, 'And don't you be turning these young heads with your tales and schemes.'

'Does any material come your way? Mary-Anne suddenly asked, causing her sister to look up sharply.

'By the roll, what are you after?' John looked over at the young lasses that up to then he'd thought as innocent as the day was long.

'Anything, just as long as you don't get caught,' Mary-Anne said, turning to Eliza.

'Though the posher the better, some silk, organza or taffeta anything; don't worry I'll put it to use,' Eliza chimed in, realising what her sister intended and thinking this might be the opportunity to get their hands on the material they needed. 'We'll pay you for it.'

'Leave it with me. And don't worry about payment, what the eye doesn't see the heart doesn't grieve about, or so folk tell me.' John grinned. 'Just put the kettle on for me when I come knocking on your door, that'll be enough.' He smiled at Mary-Anne and instantly she knew they had a new friend in John Vasey.

Tom Thackery stood at the bottom of Pit Lane and breathed in deeply. He'd left home with his mother's hard words ringing in his ears. Once again she'd chastised him for wanting to visit Eliza, even harder this time as it had become common knowledge how Eliza's mother had died and speculation was rife on the parentage of the dead baby. He'd told her it was partly on the request of his employer, Edmund Ellershaw, but she'd looked at him if he was lying, despite showing her the note to Mary-Anne written in Ellershaw's hand for him to deliver. He reached for the note within his coat pocket and wondered what business Edmund Ellershaw had with Mary-Anne, and why he'd asked him to deliver the letter when he could have sent it with his tallyman if it was to do with the rent. He reached the cottage on Pit Lane and stood on the doorstep, his heart pounding as he waited for either Eliza or Mary-Anne to open the door. He couldn't help it; to deny he had no feelings for Eliza would only mean him being a fool to himself.

However, it was Mary-Anne who opened the door. 'Tom, it's good to see you, Eliza will be so glad that you've called by. She's been worrying that she would not see you again, seeing as she couldn't walk out with you the past Sunday. Come in.' Mary-Anne showed him down the gaslighted passageway to the back kitchen.

Tom took his cap off and followed Mary-Anne.

'I hope I haven't called at a bad time,' he said, as he walked. 'But Mr Ellershaw asked me to deliver you this note, so I thought it would be a good opportunity to ask how Eliza and yourself are coping.' Just then they entered the kitchen where Eliza was sat.

'Tom, I thought I heard your voice.' Eliza stood up and smiled at him, she had missed him these past weeks.

'I've just come to deliver this note from Ellershaw and I wanted to make sure you were both all right,' Tom repeated, beaming at Eliza, thinking how bonny she looked in the glow of the kitchen fire, even in mourning black. He reached into his inside pocket and passed Mary-Anne the note and then stood not knowing quite what to do as the girls looked at him.

'Sit down, Tom, next to the fire, and warm yourself. The night's so cold.' Eliza made her visitor welcome as Mary-Anne read the note.

'What does Edmund Ellershaw want? Is he throwing us out of our cottage?' Eliza asked, fearing the worst.

'No, that's what I thought when Tom said he'd a note from him. It's a miner's cottage after all … But no, he says he has some money that's owing to us after Bill disappeared without giving notice and he's asking me to call into Rose Pit and collect it.' Mary-Anne sat down next to the table and watched as Eliza fussed around Tom.

'That's good news. But it's not like Bill to not know that he's got money owing to him, perhaps he didn't want to show his face at the pit to collect it before doing a runner.' Eliza smiled across at Tom as she watched his every move and expression.

'I didn't think the pit owed him anything.' Tom looked puzzled. 'I was sure when I looked at the wages he was paid up to the day he left. But then again I could be wrong.'

'Well, we won't say no to an extra bit of cash will we, Eliza? Every penny helps at the moment. I'll walk up and see Ellershaw tomorrow; the money will make up for what Bill took from the cash tin, when he left us with nothing apart from the few pence Eliza and I had between us. Perhaps he's being kind and taking pity on us both.' Mary-Anne folded the note and placed it behind the biscuit barrel on the sideboard.

'You are both all right for money now, are you? You are not short of anything?' Tom looked around the kitchen that looked a bit sparse compared to his home.

'Thank you, Tom; we are managing. We sold a dress in the shop the other day and make a good profit, which will see us fed and a roof over our head for the next few weeks. With whatever Ellershaw has waiting for us will help us out ever more, thankfully,' Eliza assured him. 'It was his daughter who bought the dress, so it would seem we are beholden to the Ellershaws for our welfare this Christmas. '

'I shouldn't say this but this generosity surprises me. You don't want to be in their pockets; Edmund Ellershaw is not the upstanding businessman that he would have everyone believe. Some of his ways leave a lot to be desired.' Tom thought back to the numerous occasions when he had seen Sarah Parker's comings and goings from the pit's offices after her dalliance with his boss, and realised that her daughters knew nothing of the sordid affair that had been going on.

'We don't live in anyone's pockets, but I will go and collect Bill's wages; after all they must owe him them.' Mary-Anne looked across at Tom. It was usual for workers to have little sympathy for their bosses.

They had heard Bill speak of the hard toil he had undertaken at the pit, for little or no recognition from Edmund Ellershaw, so Tom's comments did not surprise her.

'What are you doing for Christmas, Tom?' Eliza changed the subject.

'I'll be at home with mother. It is our first Christmas in this area and we don't hardly know anybody else. Besides, that's what she wants. Ever since we lost my father, she's been a bit out of sorts. What are you two girls doing? You won't feel much like Christmas this year, I suspect; it's been a cruel time for you both.' Tom hung his head and felt sorry for the two young girls, knowing what it was like to lose a parent.

'Mary-Anne in her wisdom accepted an invitation to join next door for Christmas dinner. I just know I'm going to hate every minute of it! The endless questions of Ada Simms ... I just know she will never shut up. It will not be the same without Mother – it never mattered before that we didn't have much on Christmas morning. We had each another and now there is just us two.' Eliza felt a pang of sorrow at the memory of Christmases past and knew that things would never be the same.

'I'll come around and see you in the evening, that is if I'm invited?' Tom leaned over and took Eliza's hands, giving Mary-Anne a quick glance for permission.

'Yes, you must. Make our Eliza's day and give her something to look forward to.' Mary-Anne smiled at Tom, he was clearly besotted by her sister, and any fool could see that. And she was happy that at least one of them might have some enjoyment at Christmas.

'I'll look forward to that, Tom.' Eliza blushed. 'As long as your mother can spare you for a short while.'

'She will. She's got to realise I have my own life no matter how much she wants me to herself.' Tom rose from his chair and put his cap back on his head. 'I'll be away now. If you want me for anything, just come to the Rose and let me know. I'll do what I can to help.' He looked at Eliza and wanted to give her a kiss, but thought better of it. Perhaps another time, when they were alone, because he knew that there would be another time – he'd make sure of that.

'Goodbye, Tom. Thank you for calling and delivering the note.' Mary-Anne walked ahead to the front door, leaving the couple alone for a few seconds. Smiling to herself as Eliza reached for Tom's hand and whispered her farewells to him tenderly. At least Eliza had someone in her life, someone who seemed to care. Now all Mary-Anne needed was a sweetheart of her own.

The north wind cut like a knife through Mary-Anne's thin dress and shawl as she made her way to Rose Pit. She pulled her shawl closer around her as she got to the huge iron gates. She looked across at the huge pit wheel that carried the miners up and down, and to and from the bowels of the earth. It was a place that she had hardly visited, but now she entered the yard to the pithead, passing the pit-ponies and miners busy shovelling coal and manning the pit wheel. She quickly glanced around her as coal-dusted men watched her knock on the office door of Edmund Ellershaw, some almost with a look of shock on their faces that there was a young woman in the yard.

'Enter,' a voice called from behind the scabby wooden office door.

Mary-Anne opened the door and walked in.

'Yes, what do you want?' The middle-aged greying haired man who she knew to be Edmund Ellershaw didn't even bother to lift his head up from the ledger in which he was engrossed in writing.

'I'm Mary-Anne, sir. Bill Parker's my stepfather. I received your note saying that you owed us some money from when he left his job.' Mary-Anne stood feeling awkward as Edmund finally raised his head.

'I'm sorry Miss err ... Parker.' Edmund Ellershaw looked at the young woman that stood in front of him and realised what his son had said about her beauty was no exaggeration.

'It's Wild sir, my surname is Wild. My sister and I never took our stepfather's surname after my mother got married.' Mary-Anne looked at the man that nobody ever had a good word for and felt slightly nervous knowing that he could ruin her life in one fatal swipe, if he decided to take away their cottage from them.

'Aye, that's right. I asked you to come, didn't I? Take a seat, Miss Wild, while I look through our wage book on how much back pay is owing to you.' Edmund watched as Mary-Anne sat down hesitantly and nervously looked around her. He reached over for the red leather-bound wages book that was on the bookcase behind his desk, and studied the figure-laden pages.

'Well, damn me, I'm going to have to apologise, Miss Wild, because it seems I've made a mistake. We don't owe your stepfather a penny. In fact he owes us, as he asked for a week's wages in-hand so that he could pay for your mother's funeral before he buggered off, and he only worked three days of that week. So it would seem that you owe us three shillings and four-pence for the days he didn't work.' Edmund Ellershaw looked gravely at Mary-Anne, watching as a look of panic crossed her face.

'We can't be held responsible for his debts!' Mary-Anne protested and scowled at Edmund Ellershaw.

'And yet you were willing to take his wages?' Ellershaw gave a big sigh. 'Well, maybe out of the goodness of my heart I won't pursue you through the courts for it ... But you and your sister are still living in one of my cottages as well. Next you will be telling me that you can't afford the rent. Now, while I feel sorry for you in such a delicate situation after your mother dying and your stepfather leaving you and your sister, I have to look after my business. I think I'm being more than generous to let you remain in one of my houses; after all, you are not doing owt for my pit.' Edmund Ellershaw got up from his chair and looked across his yard at the men coming up from the mine after their morning shift.

'You'll get your rent money, sir.' Mary-Anne looked down at her hands and could nearly have cried. One day she had enough to make life comfortable and the next it had slipped through her fingers like dry sand.

'My dear, don't get upset. I'm sure we could come to some arrangement; payment doesn't always have to be made in money. Perhaps you could secure the rent on your cottage in a different way if you know what I mean and, if you decide to do so, perhaps I could overlook the money owed by Bill Parker. After all, as you say, it does seem to be a little unfair on you.' Edmund walked over to the chair that Mary-Anne sat in and ran his hand over her long auburn hair.

'I don't know what you mean,' Mary-Anne said indignantly, though fully aware of what he was implying. 'Please don't touch me.'

'Think about it, my dear. Come visit me twice a month and you would not have the worry of how the rent was to be paid. I'd even supply your home with free coal, so that you are kept warm. No one need know about our little arrangement.' Edmund ran his finger around Mary-Anne's worried face and grinned at her. He breathed in deeply, recognising the scent as the same soap her mother had used. 'Perhaps you'd like some time to think about it; after all I don't want to force you.' Edmund went to sit back down in his chair and glanced over at the daughter of his old lover. She was far more beautiful than Sarah had ever been and so young and ripe for the plucking. He'd have to treat her better than he had her mother, perhaps use one of the rooms at his gentleman's club in Leeds to do his entertaining.

'I'm not a common prick-pincher, I don't sell my body to anyone.' Mary-Anne stood up, shocked by Edmund's conduct and lecherous suggestion. How could he even think that of her? She could think of nothing worse.

'I'm not suggesting that you are either common or a prostitute, my dear, but without the rent money you will lose everything and that little second-hand dress shop in the middle of Woodlesford will not keep you and your sister fed and a roof over your heads. Indeed, I will recommend that my daughter reclaims her money back as she was sold the dress from you that she showed me as new, when we both know it was second-hand from one of your, let's say, dubious suppliers.' Edmund grinned, knowing that without the money his daughter had given them the two sisters had not a penny to their name. 'Perhaps you need time to think about it?' Edmund repeated as he sat back in his chair and looked at the horror on Mary-Anne's face as she knew not what to say. 'Should we say, after Christmas, so that you can enjoy the festive period in peace?'

Mary-Anne reached for the door. 'I'd say good day, sir, but you are no gentleman and you don't deserve to be called sir. I will return after Christmas, but with the rent money in my hand and not to be yours just for the taking.' Mary-Anne spat her words at him. 'I will not be bought.' Closing the door behind her, she pulled her shawl around her and put her head down, not looking up as she quickly made her exit from the pithead. How could that dirty old man even think of such a suggestion to her? She had to keep her respectability, but how to make the amount of money she needed in order for her and Eliza to survive? Especially if Grace Ellershaw returned the dress as her father had threatened. Just what she was going to say to Eliza she didn't quite know, but she must never know about Edmund Ellershaw's filthy suggestion.

Twelve

Eliza looked at her sister's horrified face. She'd only done what she thought was right, as she had thought that Mary-Anne was going to return with enough money to pay for the extravagance.

'You should have waited, instead of banking on me returning with money.' Mary-Anne looked at the array of sausages, bacon and faggots that Eliza had decided to buy while Mary-Anne was at the pit. But that was not all she had bought, for, along with the meat, there was a selection of Christmas presents for their next-door neighbours, a token thank-you Eliza had thought for their invitation to the Christmas dinner – albeit, just an ounce of tobacco for Bert and a handkerchief for Ada, but it was money spent that they could now ill afford.

'I thought that you'd be returning with Bill's wages. I should have known that Tom would be right and that Edmund Ellershaw had got it wrong.' Eliza realised that she had spent too much of the guinea that was to have given them security for the next month.

'Well, he gave us nothing. He'd looked at his books wrongly.' Mary-Anne sat with her hands in her head and breathed in deeply. She hadn't told Eliza everything; it was pointless to make her worry,

96

but Eliza's good heartedness had caused Mary-Anne more worry than she would ever realise.

'I'm sorry, Mary-Anne. I only thought that for once we could eat decent for a day or two – after all it is Christmas.' Eliza knew she had done wrong.

'I wouldn't mind but you don't even like Ada and Bert Simms, you were the first to complain about having to go around to them. And then you go and spend our hard-earned money on them. They would have understood if we had brought them nothing.' Mary-Anne looked across at her sister and could have cried.

'I'll try and make it up to you, Mary-Anne. In fact, while you were at the pit, Grace Ellershaw paid us another visit. She looked around the shop and said she would be back.' Eliza tried to cheer her sister up but was more worried when the mention of Grace upset her even more.

'What did she say? Did she mention the dress we sold her?' Mary-Anne could only think one thing: that she had called in to see if her father was right and to return the dress post-haste.

'No, she just wanted to know if we could make her a dress soon. I told her that we hoped to have a new stock of material in, into the new year, and she seemed quite happy. I couldn't really talk to her long as Minnie Armstrong was waiting to see if our mother's skirt was her size.' Eliza watched her sister's face go ashen. 'I was polite; she will be back.' She tried to reassure her older sister. 'She liked that dress so much.'

'Did Minnie buy Mother's skirt?' Mary-Anne hoped that perhaps some of the lost money had been recouped.

'No, but she did buy a string of beads that were our mother's for a penny. I'm sorry, Mary-Anne; I should have waited for you to come back with the money in your hand.' Eliza felt so guilty. 'I could take the handkerchief back, if that would help?'

'No, that would only get folk talking. What's done is done now. We are just going to have to make the most of what we've got. It isn't your fault, Eliza, it is that bloody Edmund Ellershaw. He made both our hopes rise and I don't blame you for buying what you did. I'll look forward to the sausages, they'll be a real treat.' Mary-Anne smiled at Eliza but deep down inside she could have wept. Edmund Ellershaw's words echoed in her ears and the thought of having to go back to him once Christmas was over and let him have his way with her was beginning to look like the only way out of financial ruin for her and Eliza.

Christmas morning dawned cold and frosty and both Mary-Anne and Eliza woke up to see the intricate patterns of fern leaves made in ice crystals on the window panes of their home.

'I don't want to get out of bed, Eliza. It's so cold,' Mary-Anne said as they huddled together for warmth.

'I don't want to get up yet either, you kept me awake most of the night, tossing and turning. Why didn't you sleep last night? Were you worrying about money?' Eliza turned to her sister and stroked her long auburn hair while waiting for an answer.

'I used to like Christmas when I was younger, everything was magical and it was the one time of the year we were all together and no matter how little we had, our mother always had a full table and had managed to either make or buy a present for us both. Now I realise how much it must have cost her in more ways than one. But just for that one day she must have forgotten all her worries and enjoyed the day. Even after Father died and she married Bill, Christmas was different to the rest of the year. He usually didn't get too drunk and he even used to play blind man's buff with us and enjoy his dinner. Those days have gone, haven't they, Eliza? We only have one another, and then I moan at you for buying a pound of pork sausage and a few cheap presents. I'm sorry, my dear sister.' Mary-Anne hugged her sister tight. 'You know I'd do anything for you.'

'I know, Mary-Anne, and I will always be there for you. Things will get better in time; I just know they will.' Eliza kissed her sister on the cheek and noticed that she was nearly crying. 'Let's make the most of today, just like we used to do. Old Mrs Simms will have a good spread; she and Bert don't seem to go without.'

'Mmm … at least we will come home with our bellies full.' Mary-Anne turned away from her sister and gazed across at the frosted window. She would make herself enjoy today no matter what was to become of her in the future, because now she had decided what she was to do and it was nothing to feel proud of.

'Come in my dears, happy Christmas!' Ada Simms welcomed her neighbours in to her home and showed them into her parlour.

Bert was sat next to the blazing fire, contentedly smoking his pipe with his legs resting on the fire's brass fender, warming his feet.

'Now then, lasses, happy Christmas. Come and make yourselves warm. It's a bit parky out there today.' The ageing miner smiled at both girls as they sat down on the settee that nearly took up all the room in the small parlour. He'd always wanted children of his own, but him and Ada had never been blessed.

Eliza looked around her; she'd never been in the Simms' parlour before, and she was amazed at the opulence in it compared to theirs. The wallpaper was a rich red and Staffordshire pottery adorned every nook and cranny. Two large lions with their mouths open in a roar particularly took her eye, and she looked at them thinking how hideous they looked, almost looking as if they were grinning at her.

'Ada, get our guests a drop of your ginger cordial; that will warm the cockles of their hearts up.'

'Would you like some help, Mrs Simms?' Mary-Anne looked at their neighbour, dressed in her Sunday finery.

'No, dear. You sit back and enjoy the warmth. The pork is in the oven, along with the potatoes, and I've swede and carrots on the boil. Along of course with a plum pudding. You've just got to have a plum pudding at Christmas.' Ada shuffled off to the kitchen to get the drinks, leaving the two girls with Bert who went quiet as he puffed on his pipe.

'We are grateful for your invite today, Mr Simms,' Mary-Anne said, breaking the silence. 'And Eliza and myself have brought you this small present.' Mary-Anne stood up and passed the ounce of Kendal Twist tobacco, wrapped in Christmas wrapping, to Bert.

'Aye lasses, you shouldn't have got us anything, we didn't expect anything from you both. Money will be tight enough at your house this year. And with your mother dying and Bill buggering off, dinner was the least we could do.' Bert held the present in his hand and felt a sorrow for the two lasses sat across from him. No matter what kindness they were able to show their neighbours, it could never make up for their loss. 'Look what these two have given me, our lass. I told them they shouldn't have wasted their brass.' Bert showed Ada the ounce of tobacco that he had unwrapped and smiled at them both while they thanked her for the small glass of ginger cordial.

'Oh, my word, they shouldn't have given you anything. If we can't have you two at Christmas after the year you've both had, we don't deserve all the good things the good Lord has given us. Besides, we have no family of our own, so it will make a pleasant change.' Ada sat down in a chair opposite the two girls and sipped her glass of cordial.

'We've got you this as well, Mrs Simms. Just a small thank you.' Eliza passed Ada her parcelled handkerchief, and watched as she fought back a tear.

'You shouldn't have, really we didn't expect anything.' Ada opened the parcel and looked at the embroidered handkerchief. 'That's lovely, my dears, but as I say you really shouldn't have. Now let's go through to the kitchen and enjoy our dinner. The smell of the pork cooking is filling the house and I can't wait another minute.'

'Nay, I can't either, and I bet these two have been thinking of it since they woke up this morning.' Bert grinned at both of the girls and rose from his seat. 'Come and fill your bellies, lasses, and then, before you go, Ada will put a basket of bits for you to take home. She's been baking all day yesterday; there's enough to fill an army in our kitchen and pantry. She'll not see you go hungry.'

'We can't thank you enough,' Mary-Anne told the elderly couple. 'I don't think either Eliza or myself were looking forward to today, now we have no family. And we both woke up this morning not wanting to face the day.'

'Well, you can count on us being here for you. Bill was a law unto himself and we used to often worry about you two and your mother when we heard him coming home from the pub. But we didn't like to interfere. And now he's gone and your mother, God rest her soul, isn't here to look after you both ... you knock on our door if you need anything. It's the least I can do for your late father. Now he was a good man. It was a bad day when he got killed at the pit.' Bert had put up with Bill but knew he hadn't been half the man that their true father was and had always felt sorry for the plight his neighbours were in, ignoring the gossip he used to hear about Sarah and her so-called relationship with Edmund Ellershaw, rumours he had never shared with his wife.

'Thank you, Mr Simms, we will appreciate that.' Mary-Anne smiled at the grey-haired, amicable old man.

'Now, come on, sit down around our table and try and forget for an hour or two the year's happenings, I promise you'll not go home hungry.' Ada Simms ushered Mary-Anne and Eliza into the kitchen and sat them down at the round table that she had laid out with her best china and cutlery. The kitchen was warm and homely, with the smell of pork roasting in the fireside oven and the kitchen window white from the steam that was rising from the cooking swede and simmering plum pudding. Eliza and Mary-Anne looked at one another and knew that they had misjudged the Simms. They weren't nosy, they were more caring than anything and today they were grateful for the care and attention that the couple were lavishing on them. Eliza's mouth watered as Bert carved the pork, its skin shone with pearls of juice and the roast potatoes that accompanied it were lovely – crisp and brown on the outside but soft and creamy on the inside. It had been a long time since both girls had enjoyed such a feast and for that they were truly grateful. Silence fell around the Christmas table while they all enjoyed every mouthful.

'I'm so full, I'm fit to bursting!' Eliza slumped in the chair next to the newly stoked fire in the kitchen back home.

'How big a portion did she give us of plum pudding? And that sherry sauce … I didn't expect that with her being a Methodist. I didn't think they would be as bigger hypocrites as us.' Mary-Anne began putting away the basket of baking, cold sliced meats and pickles that their neighbours had given them.

'They both surprised me a lot. Our mother always accused them of being nosy, but perhaps if she'd got to know them better, she might have been surprised.' Eliza sat back and patted her stomach.

'I think it's Bill that they didn't like, even though he walked to work with old Bert every morning. Nobody liked him from what I can make out, he'd no respect from anyone. Do you think we should visit Mother's grave tomorrow? I feel guilty at not showing her our respects today.' Mary-Anne carried the gifted goods to the pantry and then sat in a chair opposite Eliza.

'I suppose we could, and our father's. But we've no flowers to put on them.' Eliza looked into the flickering flames and wished her sister had not brought her back to reality.

'I don't think that will matter. They'd both understand, and, anyway, they wouldn't last long with this frost, and where would we get them at this time of year? We'll go tomorrow afternoon, then.' Mary-Anne closed her eyes and felt the fire's warmth, trying not to think too hard of what was to be in the future and to forget the past in the warm glow of the fire and the flickering of the oil lamp's glow, sleep overtaking her as Ada's dinner made her feel content.

'You should have woke me up!' Mary-Anne stirred and sleepily exclaimed as she heard her sister answer the door and a male voice join her as the visitor and Eliza came down the passage to the kitchen.

'You looked content for the first time in days, I didn't have the heart.' Eliza smiled at her sister. 'Look who's come to visit.' Eliza turned and beamed at Tom standing behind her.

'Merry Christmas, Tom!' Mary-Anne asked as she shook herself awake, 'Have you had a good day?'

'Yes, thank you.' Tom smiled at the sleepy Mary-Anne. 'And you?'

'Too good. Mrs Simms next door has fed us until we are nearly bursting – I've never known myself to go to sleep in front of the fire before.' Mary-Anne stood up and looked at her younger sister who was placing the kettle on the fire.

'I just thought I would call in; my mother thinks I'm taking a walk after our dinner. Which I am, it's just your house is on my route and it would be rude not to call in and wish you a happy Christmas.' Tom stood by the side of the table and watched Eliza's every move as she quickly made him a cup of tea.

'Do sit down, Tom, it will only take you a minute or two to drink your tea.' Eliza pulled Tom a chair out from the table and urged him to sit down. She wanted him to stay as long as he possibly could; he'd made her Christmas just by calling around.

'I can't stay long, but this cup of tea is most welcome, a warm up before I return home.' Tom gazed across the table at Eliza and blushed as their eyes met.

'I'll make myself scarce and leave you two for a minute or two while I go and brush my hair, I must look a terrible fright after waking up so quickly. Mary-Anne made her excuses and looked at the pair of love-birds in front of her. She knew when she was not wanted, and if she had been Eliza she wouldn't have wanted her sister to sit like a gooseberry between them. She left the kitchen and walked upstairs, listening to the young couple laughing and enjoying one another's company. Eliza was lucky, she couldn't help but think, as she climbed the stairs. She had a good-looking young man with good prospects interested in her, whereas she had nobody, and the future looked nothing but bleak to her.

She sat in front of the bedroom mirror and idly brushed her long auburn hair, re-arranging the ribbon that tied it, and looked at herself. What had she done to deserve to be in such a terrible position? No parents, no money and, worst of all, the threat of Edmund Ellershaw. What the coming year held for her, she didn't dare think, but at the moment it looked like nothing but hardship and degradation in the hands of Ellershaw, but she had no option when it came to him – they had to survive.

Eliza shouted up from the bottom of the stairs, bringing her back from her dark thoughts. 'I'm just walking out with Tom to the end of the lane, Mary-Anne.'

'All right, Eliza. Take your shawl, it's cold out there,' Mary-Anne shouted back, and looked again at her reflection as she heard the front door close. 'Take care, my little sister, and enjoy life while you can,' Mary-Anne whispered as she fought back the tears. At least one of them was happy.

'It must be so cold and dark down there,' Eliza said to Mary-Anne, as she looked down on the frost-covered grave of their mother and lost baby. 'We don't even know if the baby Mother lost was a girl or a boy, it was just bundled up in a sheet and put in with her.'

'I try not to think about it. Mother clearly hadn't known either. And that's the baby that killed her.' Mary-Anne looked down at the cold grave and shivered. 'She was getting too old to be bothered with another child, and, besides, we struggled without having another mouth to feed.'

'You think she got rid of it, don't you? That she drunk the potion that Aunt Patsy sent her, in order to lose the baby.' Eliza put her arm around her sister as they both looked down on the grave.

'I do, but I can't blame her. I just wish she was still with us. We'd have managed somehow. It might have done Bill good to have a child of his own, made him more responsible.' Mary-Anne walked away across the graveyard to where her father lay. She crouched down, running her fingers over the frosted grass. 'Happy Christmas, Father. We miss you,' she whispered.

'You were always close to Father. I was my mother's child; you were Father's. I was always jealous of the love he showed you.' Eliza stood by her sister and watched as she lovingly stroked the simple headstone under which their father lay.

'He loved us both, Eliza; he had no favourites. But most of all he loved our mother. He would have hated the way she was treated by Bill and for her to do away with the baby she was carrying.' Mary-Anne held her hand out for her sister to take.

'We've got one another, Mary-Anne. I'll always be here for you. Don't despair, you have been so sad and quiet over Christmas.' Eliza linked her arm through her sister's as they both left the graveyard. 'Things will take a turn about, of that I'm sure.' Eliza swallowed hard as they closed the iron gates of the cemetery behind them. She knew in her heart that things would not get better, that life was going to be a struggle and that she had to do the most to keep Mary-Anne's spirits up and to help both of them survive.

Thirteen

The Boxing Day ball was in full swing at Eshald House. The gravelled driveway of the grand house was busy with guests arriving, alighting from their carriages. The servants were busy welcoming the visiting dignitaries and gentry of the district.

The large, square-set Georgian house with its grand fluted columns sat in its own grounds with the brewery buildings set behind. Eshald Well Springs Brewery was one of the main employers in the area and the smell from the maltings filled the air of the surrounding district most days, while the gasometer that also stood in the grounds supplied light to most of Woodlesford and warmth to the only hot-house in the district, which was Timothy Bentley's main indulgence. His money might be new but he had settled into the finer things of life very easily and he liked to supply flowers all year around to his house and the chapel in Woodlesford.

Edmund Ellershaw and his family were guests of the Bentleys. Grace had especially looked forward to attending the ball, and she was smiling and laughing as the footman helped her down from the family's carriage.

'Oh, Father, just listen to the music and look at the people here!' Grace turned around and smiled at both her parents and her brother William as they entered into the grand hall, the butler offering the family glasses of champagne.

'Aye, Bentley knows how to put on a show all right.' Edmund glowered at the young maid who took his cloak.

'Remember, Grace, don't drink too much, and William, you take heed too.' Catherine Ellershaw looked at both her children and checked herself in the long hallway mirror before walking into the main ballroom by the side of her husband.

'Well, that's telling us.' William lifted his glass and grinned at his sister. 'I don't know about you, but I aim to make the most of this night and I'm sure my father will. He always says, "don't look a gift horse in the mouth", and this gift horse is going to be one I make the most of.' William raised his glass and then walked to where a line of his friends were watching the frivolities of the evening.

'Grace, how beautiful you look. Where did you get that dress; it looks absolutely divine!' Jessica Bentley, the oldest daughter of the Bentleys, swanned over to Grace and glanced up and down at the green dress that had been bought from Eliza and Mary-Anne.

'Well, Jessica, I don't know if I should tell you this, but I bought it not a quarter of a mile away from here. In a little shop in the middle of Woodlesford. I knew when I saw it in the window, I just had to have it, regardless of the shop it was in.' Grace sipped her drink.

'Really! Did it not come from Leeds or Manchester? You must tell me more about this little shop, or even take me to it. I love the cut, the colour and the style just suits you to the ground.' Jessica urged some more of her friends to come and admire Grace's outfit, and soon the whole group was admiring the green dress that had started life on the back of Ma Fletcher's rag-and-bone cart.

'They are just starting out. They are two sisters who run the shop, and it was the youngest one who I think made this. I would recommend that you pay them a visit, once Christmas is over. At the moment they don't have any material in as they have just lost their mother and I think they are perhaps not as wealthy as they make you believe. My father was extremely annoyed that I had given them my trade. But if they supply quality clothing like this, why shouldn't I?' Grace took a sip from her champagne flute and smiled at the group who all knew her as being a young woman who knew her own mind and they were all devout followers of where she led.

'Indeed so, my darling Grace. The poor girls will need our support. I'm sure we can all pay them a visit once they are back upon their feet and Christmas is over.' Jessica looked around at the group of young women who all nodded in agreement.

'They would welcome that, I'm sure. I myself am going to go back shortly, to ask for another dress similar to this design but in a different colour, I would like a new dress for my birthday in March, probably in red. I look best in red, my mother says.' Grace looked around her.

'Then I will come with you when you do, Grace, and perhaps order a dress myself. Give them my support. Father always says we must support our community and that, as we are one of the largest employers in the area, people are reliant on our money.'

Grace sat back with her friends around her and sipped her drink, confident that she had established customers for the small shop that had taken her eye and the two girls who she had felt so sorry for, especially after her father had not shown them an ounce of compassion. He was different altogether to Jessica's father, who, though he came from similar humble beginnings, had the time of day for everyone and put his money back into the surrounding area. She would return to the little lean-to and she would not be alone.

Sarah Marsden, meanwhile, sat back, looking perplexed at her friend's new dress, and finally decided when Grace was left alone for a few minutes to comment upon it. 'I think I've seen Winnie Oversby in a dress very much like that one, perhaps two seasons ago. It was at Temple Newsholme when it was her cousin's wedding. I remember it because she had a white rose corsage around the neckline and I thought how stunning she looked.'

'Oh, Sarah, you must be mistaken. I assure you this is brand new and the neckline would not look right with a corsage around it; it is too high. Perhaps it is of similar material?' Grace smiled and carried on watching the gathering; her friend was surely mistaken.

'Mmmm ... perhaps you are right, but I could have sworn it was the same dress.' Sarah decided not to pursue the conversation when their chattering friends returned, but she knew she was right, even if there was no longer a rose corsage in sight.

Fourteen

The new year had been ushered into Mary-Anne and Eliza's home by Bert Simms being the traditional first footer as he crossed the threshold after the stroke of midnight with a piece of coal in one hand and a penny in the other, a tradition that had for centuries been upheld in northern England and Scotland. The coal symbolised warmth in the home, and the money symbolised wealth in the home for the coming new year. Bert had stood laughing on the doorstep and tried to assure the girls that once the grey hair that was now on the top of his head had been jet black, thus upholding the other part of the tradition that a dark-haired man was the most desired to bring good luck into the home.

Now, on the second day of January, Mary-Anne stood outside the gates of Rose Pit and knew that, no matter how much good luck was wished on them both by their neighbours, it was up to her to make things happen and gain security for both her and Eliza.

Her stomach churned over as she knew what she had to do and as she thought about Edmund Ellershaw waiting of her and what he would demand of her. She breathed a sigh of relief as she saw Tom enter the pit's cage and get lowered by the winding engine man, Joseph Jackson, down the two yards below to the main mine shaft.

She had just time to slip unnoticed into the office and hopefully go about the unsavoury business transaction that she was dreading to undertake. She breathed in deeply, dreading the moment that Edmund Ellershaw's hands were to touch her. She had no experience of such things; she was a good girl and was waiting for the man she had one day hoped to marry. Despite her being worldly-wise and able to give anyone a mouthful of cheek, she had kept herself pure and was proud of the fact. Now all was going to be lost to a dirty letch. She knocked quietly on the bleached wooden door and waited.

'Enter.' Edmund's voice came from within, and Mary-Anne felt her legs turn to jelly as she stepped across the threshold and into the office of the man that now controlled her life.

'Ah, you've returned. Have you given my suggestion some thought? Even though you seemed to be sure that you could live without my charity. Because, believe me, it is charity; I could get what I need anywhere along the docks and they'd be a lot more experienced than a slip of a lass.' Edmund looked up at the ashen-faced girl.

'Well, if you've changed your mind, I'll go and leave you free to the prick-pinchers on Canal Street. Perhaps they are better suited to you with all the disease that they carry.' Mary-Anne breathed in deeply, controlling her nerves and feeling angry at the man sat across from her for insulting her by asking her to degrade her body and being not even remotely thankful for what he was asking of her. 'Can we just get on with it, and then we are straight for a month, and I don't have to think of coming back here for a while?' Mary-Anne stood in front of him and waited for the lustful Edmund to get up from his seat and carry out the act that she had lain awake thinking about and dreading ever since Christmas Eve.

'What! You thought I'd take you in here, for all my workers to know what I'm getting up to?' Edmund sat back and sniggered. 'I'm not that common, my dear. Tonight, wait for me at the end of Pit Lane and my carriage will pick you up. Eight o'clock, and come in something decent; I'm taking you to my gentleman's club at Holbeck, where I've got a private room. Now go, before anybody sees you.' Edmund put his head down and watched as Mary-Anne sighed.

Unlike her mother, he had decided that Mary-Anne was worth showing off on his arm at his club, and, besides, Tom and his other workers had let him know just how disgusted they were with his arrangement with her mother. Their mumbled words and dark stares had left him in no doubt after Sarah's funeral that they had figured out just what his relationship with her had been. And who the father of Sarah's dead baby was. They would be up in arms if they suspected him of taking advantage of the situation again with her daughter.

'What if I don't want to go to your club? I just can't leave my sister without any explanation,' Mary-Anne asked the disinterested Ellershaw.

'Then our understanding is off, and I will serve notice on your cottage by the end of the month, my dear.' Edmund leered.

Mary-Anne stood for a moment and then made for the door. She closed it behind her and walked out of the pit yard. How was she going to explain her time away from home to Eliza? Holbeck was only a few miles down the road, it shouldn't take that long to get there and back. But what would be expected of her once at the men's club? How long would she be expected to stay there? Surely

Edmund Ellershaw would have to return home to his wife? Mary-Anne worried about her plight all the way home and was thankful that the house was empty when she returned to her refuge. She sat down in the kitchen and hugged herself, rocking back and forth to give herself comfort, her mind racing, wondering what would be required of her at the club. What if Edmund Ellershaw invited some of his friends to join in his sport? She just couldn't bear to think about it.

'Eliza, I've decided to start sleeping in our mother's room. I haven't been sleeping of late and I know I disturb your sleep.' Mary-Anne looked at her sister as she ate her potato hash that she had made for her sister's return from the shop. 'I've moved my things out of our room this afternoon, and I am airing it now with a copper bed warmer.' She poked her dinner around the plate, and didn't feel like eating anything, worried that she was lying to her sister and that the evening's agenda with Edmund was not as clear as she would have liked it to be.

'You're not that bad, besides, we keep one another warm when we sleep together.' Eliza did not raise her head and just kept eating her dinner.

'I'll not be in tonight either. I've decided to attend the talk on spiritualism in the village hall. It's something I've been thinking about for some time and they always have a meeting once a week so I thought, with it being a new year, I'd show some interest.' Mary-Anne couldn't look at her sister as she lied through her teeth, making up her excuse for not being at home that evening.

'Spiritualism! Isn't that when folk talk to the dead? What's made you want to do that? It won't bring our mother back, you know. It's all fake.' Eliza couldn't believe her ears and lifted her head to look at her sister.

114

'I know, but it seems to be all the rage at the moment. I just wanted to see what it was all about.' Mary-Anne cleared her plate away and breathed in deeply. 'Have you sold anything at the shop today? I suppose it will have been quiet.'

'Minnie came back for that skirt, she asked if I could add a piece into the waist so that it would fit her. I've started on it this afternoon and she's coming back with the money tomorrow, so at least we will have a bit in the cash box.' Eliza looked at her sister who seemed to be acting strangely to her. 'What's up, our Mary? You seem to be really unsettled with yourself.'

'There's nothing wrong with me, apart from missing Mother.' Mary-Anne smiled at her sister wanly.

'That's what this spiritualist nonsense is about ... I'm right, aren't I? Well, you go if you think it will help you. But I'm not setting foot in the place, so don't ask me to come with you.' Eliza sat back in her chair and pushed away her empty plate.

'No, you're fine. I don't expect you to. I'll go on my own.' Mary-Anne knew she was safe with lying about the meeting. Eliza had always made clear her thoughts about the afterlife and her disbelief in such like. 'I don't know how long it goes on for, so don't lock the door on me if you go to bed.'

'Get yourself back before the witching hour, else the bogeyman will get you.' Eliza laughed and pulled a face at her sister.

'You'll stay like that if the wind changes.' Mary-Anne grinned but in her head she was thinking that the bogeyman had already got her and she was to meet him that evening.

Mary-Anne stood at the end of Pit Lane and shivered in the cold of the winter's evening. Her stomach was churning as she hid in the shadows, not wanting anyone to see her loitering and waiting for the carriage of

Edmund Ellershaw. She'd snuck out of the house, trying to avoid the questioning looks that she knew Eliza would have given her if she had caught her in her best clothes. She was sure to have questioned her dressing so fine, just for a spiritualist meeting. She hadn't liked lying to her sister, but it had to be done.

The night's silence was broken by the sound of horse's hooves and a carriage being pulled at speed along the rough surface of Abberford Road, and it pulled up for her to climb into the dark interior.

'So, you've not changed your mind then.' Edmund Ellershaw sat across from Mary-Anne as she hid herself in the darkness of the interior. He reached over and ran his hand up her leg under her skirts and breathed in heavily as she closed her legs together trapping his hand between her knees. 'No matter, you won't be doing that when I get you alone in my room,' he whispered, and withdrew his hand from between her legs, aware that his groom could hear the conversation from within the carriage. 'You'll do as I want and you won't complain, else it will be the worse for you,' he snarled.

Mary-Anne sat back and said nothing; if she could have left the carriage without harming herself she would have. But the carriage was moving at speed as they drove into the village of Holbeck on the very edge of the sprawling Leeds city, and all too soon they had arrived.

'Good evening, Mr Ellershaw, sir.' The doorman of the gentleman's club opened the carriage door and unfolded the steps out for Edmund to alight.

'Evening, Jones. It's a bit parky tonight.' Edmund stood next to the doorman and watched as Mary-Anne took his hand and was helped down out of the carriage.

'Good evening, miss.' Jones looked at the frightened young thing that was joining the biggest lecher in the club and couldn't help but feel sorry for her. 'Mind your skirt as you climb the stairs, miss,' Jones commented, as he watched Edmund put his arm through hers and take her through the revolving doors into the brightly lit hallway of the club.

Mary-Anne turned around and gave a faint smile.

'Dirty old bugger, he's old enough to be her father,' Jones said to the groom that was driving the coach.

'Aye,' the groom replied, 'he's a bastard when it comes to using women and she's too pretty to be used by him. I wouldn't mind a go myself, but then again I don't have the money that he does. That's what attracts them.'

'I'd like to tell his wife, that'd make him think. She's the one with the real money, not him.' Jones closed the carriage door and went back to stand in the doorway as the groom went around the back of the club to stable the horses. Both knew Edmund Ellershaw for what he was.

Mary-Anne felt as if all eyes were upon her as she stood in the grand hallway of the gentleman's club. The air was filled with cigar smoke and pompous businessmen all sipping their brandy and discussing business. But she could also see them stop and glance at her on the arm of Ellershaw. It was a million miles from anything that Mary-Anne had previously experienced and she felt vulnerable to their stares. They were men her parents had always told her to respect, but now she realised that they were no better than anyone else; all had their vices.

'Now Ellershaw, this is a pretty filly you've got on your arm.' Bernard Hargreaves, owner of the Fleet Mill, looked Mary-Anne up and down and patted Edmund on his back.

'Aye, she's my entertainment for the night.' Edmund patted the old codger back as he picked up his room keys from the reception while keeping an eye on the quaking Mary-Anne. 'Come on, follow me up the stairs and say nothing to nobody.' Edmund linked his arm through hers and half pulled her up the stairs, past paintings of the great and good patrons that had at one time been part of the club.

'You wouldn't be willing to share, I suppose, Ellershaw? Make an old man happy,' Bernard Hargreaves shouted up the stairs making Edmund stop in his tracks and Mary-Anne show the shock she was feeling of being discussed like a piece of property by two elderly men. Her stomach turned and she felt sick as she was bartered over.

'What do you think? ' Edmund shouted back and pulled on Mary-Anne's arm to get her to the top of the stairs.

'I thought not,' Hargreaves muttered to himself as he walked into the main smoke-filled room to join his colleagues.

'I'm not a prostitute to do with what you want,' Mary-Anne said as he closed the bedroom door behind them. 'I'm only doing this to keep a roof over mine and Eliza's heads.'

'But that is exactly what you are … a common little prick-pincher. Being paid for services rendered; that's why nobody is blinking an eye at you joining me in my private room.' Edmund threw off his cloak and jacket and undid the collar on his shirt before grabbing Mary-Anne by her arms and throwing her on the bed. 'Time for payment, my dear,' he whispered in her ear as he lay down on top of her, pulling her skirts up and bloomers down and then fumbled with his trousers.

'Get off me,' she shouted and pushed against him. But he was too strong as he pushed her down into the bed and pulled his manhood out.

'That's it! This is what you want and what I expect from you, my little pretty bitch.' Edmund Ellersaw grinned as he watched her panic.

Mary-Anne wanted to scream as he entered her, fighting him and pushing at his shoulders as he took his satisfaction. This wasn't how she had wanted it, she should never have agreed to this. She grimaced as he tried to kiss her, his breath making her feel sick as he licked her face and breasts, ripping her bodice to see more of her flesh, thrusting into her until he looked down upon her with satisfaction. 'You make a better ride than your mother.' He laughed and caught his breath, taking pleasure at the look of horror on Mary-Anne's face. 'You mean you didn't know your mother was a whore too? Dear me, she must have overlooked that story when she tucked you both into bed. I'm so glad it's been my pleasure to have told you.' Edmund Ellershaw looked down at the distraught girl that had given him so much pleasure, and knew he had to also break her spirit.

'You are lying. My mother would never do anything like this,' Mary-Anne cried, pulling her skirts down and noticing the smattering of blood on what was her perfectly pristine blue dress, and the rip down her bodice. While she held back her tears, she was not going to let him know that he had taken her pride as well as her virginity, and now also the warm memories of her mother.

'She was, my dear; how else do you think that useless excuse of a man kept his job and your mother keep a roof over your heads? Regular as clockwork she was at least twice a month, just like you will be.' Edmund sniggered as he buttoned up his trousers and ran his finger down Mary-Anne's flushed breasts.

'That's where you are wrong. I don't believe you, and this is the first and last time you are ever going to touch me.' Mary-Anne stood shakily at the side of the bed and stared at the man she now hated.

Making her way to the bedroom door, she stopped for a second. 'You'll get your rent, or we will find somewhere else to go. You are not the only landlord in Woodlesford.'

'Perhaps you should join your aunt in the gutter in Leeds. You'll be back, you've no option as I'll make sure my daughter will not be giving you any more trade, so you can forget her money.' Edmund sat on the bed and laughed as he watched Mary-Anne slam the door, not even waiting to be taken home. She'd be back, he thought. She had no choice.

Mary-Anne ran down the stairs, nearly knocking the doorman over in a bid to escape from the den of iniquity, flying out of the revolving doors, down the steps and into the night.

'You all right, miss?' The doorman shouted after her as he straightened himself up and watched as she fled, but he received no reply.

Mary-Anne cried and tumbled her way along the rutted road out of Holbeck and over the high steep hill that lead her back home, only looking back when she could see the safety of the outskirts of Woodlesford. Her legs shook; not only had she walked nearly six miles in the dark but she had done so after she had been raped, although other people would not see it that way. After all, she had gone into the club willingly on Edmund Ellershaw's arm. All that she held dear had been taken from her in that sordid room by a dirty, controlling uncaring bastard.

She looked back at the dim lights of Leeds and caught her breath, sitting down on the edge of the road that lead to Wakefield, in the darkness. Tears flowed all too easy and she sobbed in the cloak of the night, not holding back the fear and the hurt that was ripping her in two. Had he been telling the truth about her mother? If not, then how did he know about her Aunt Patsy in Leeds, and could the dead baby that her mother had been carrying have possibly been his? So many questions, the answers to which she did not want to hear. But one thing she knew for sure, and that was that she would never lower herself again to give in to Edmund Ellershaw's lusting ways. It would not happen to her again, she vowed, even as she was beginning to realise that she was not the first in her family to be bought this way.

Fifteen

Eliza lay in the darkness wrapped in her bedding, uneasy at the thought that Mary-Anne had not yet returned. She'd tried to sleep, but without her sister's body next to her and worrying about how strange Mary-Anne had acted before she left for her so-called meeting, she'd failed to do so. Perhaps it was a man she was meeting, and wanted to keep it a secret. Whatever it was it definitely was not a spiritualist meeting, not if it kept her out to this time. It must be all of two or three o'clock in the morning by now, as she had gone to bed at eleven and since then she had tossed and turned for at least a few hours.

She was just about to get out of her bed and go downstairs when she heard the front door open and shut, and the bolt on the back of it being closed. She listened as she heard Mary-Anne climb the stairs and enter into their parents' old bedroom. Even before the sobbing started, Eliza had guessed that something was wrong, but Mary-Anne's cries and tears clawed at her heart until she could stand it no more. She climbed out of bed, shivering in the cold, pale moonlight shining though her curtainless window, before walking to her sister's room.

'Mary-Anne, are you all right?' She stopped outside the bedroom door, knocked quietly and listened as her sister stopped her sobs for a second.

'Yes, I'm sorry if I woke you, Eliza.' Mary-Anne blew her nose and composed herself. 'Go back to bed, I'm fine.' She didn't want her sister to see her in such a state.

'I don't think you are all right, dear sister. I've heard you crying and you have returned so late.' Eliza put her hand on the latch of her sister's door and entered into her bedroom. 'Mary-Anne, what's wrong? Where have you been tonight, and don't give me that rubbish tale of a spiritualist meeting, because I don't believe it for a minute.' She looked at her sister sitting on the edge of their parents' bed, half undressed and, even in the light of the candle that burned by Mary-Anne's bedside, Eliza's could see the pain and anguish on her face.

'I can't tell you; it's nothing to be proud of. I wish I had never done it.' Mary-Anne started sobbing.

'You can tell me anything; I'll not be shocked. Even if ... oh, Mary-Anne, you've not ... offered yourself to anybody, have you? Is that what you've been doing to this time of the night, like the girls on Canal Street? They make most of their money after dark. We aren't that destitute yet.' Eliza took her sister's hand and squeezed it tight as she sat down on the bed next to her. Mary-Anne started sobbing again.

'Oh, Eliza, I've been a fool! I have worried so much over this Christmas – I didn't know what else to do and he made it sound like there was no other way out and then you had spent some of the money we didn't get. I could see no other way out of our predicament.' Mary-Anne looked at her sister in the faint candlelight, debating whether to tell her the whole story.

'Who? Mary-Anne, who have you been with?' Eliza looked into her sister's eyes.

'Edmund Ellershaw. He knew we couldn't afford the rent or the coal to keep us warm from his colliery, so we came to an arrangement.' Mary-Anne breathed in deeply.

'You mean he exploited and forced you into giving him your body? Is that where you've been until this time? With him?' Eliza hugged her sister.

Mary-Anne nodded her head and sobbed.

'Oh! Mary, he's a contriving bastard. You shouldn't have gone, he'll always have one over on you now. Are you sure you're all right? Did he hurt you? Where did he take you?' Eliza quickly checked her sister for any injury and then hugged her tight, swaying back and forth with her as she sobbed louder.

'He took me to his club at Holbeck, Eliza, and then he forced me. I hate him, Eliza, he didn't give a damn about me or my feelings, and he just wanted his wicked way. I felt such a fool as I ran out of his club.' Mary-Anne sobbed.

'Holbeck? Have you walked all the way back from Holbeck?! He didn't even have the decency to bring you back home?'

'I wasn't going to wait. I was frightened that he'd want me again, or worse still that some of his cronies would join him in his so-called sport. So I fled.' Mary-Anne shook but thought better than to tell Eliza the full story of the evening. It was better her younger sister kept her memory of their mother unsullied, as perfect as they had always thought her to be.

'My dear sister, don't do this again. Even if we are out on the streets, it would be better than you trading yourself to such a wicked man. Something will come along to save us, of that I'm sure. Now why don't you come back into our room and let's get some sleep and you try to put the horrible experience behind you.' Eliza stood up and supported her shaking sister, walking her back into the bedroom they had shared all of their lives. 'It's late now but tomorrow is another day and we can sit down and talk about things together. I don't want you to feel you are the only one responsible for our welfare. I'm not a child anymore, you can tell me your worries. They're better shared.' Eliza watched as her sister took her clothes off and climbed into bed, still upset by her night of shame. Eliza didn't know what she was going to do, but one way or other Edmund Ellershaw was going to pay for this night.

Both girls watched as the coalman from Rose Pit delivered four sacks of coal, emptying them down the coal shoot in the outhouse.

'Well, at least he's honoured part of our bargain,' Mary-Anne said bitterly as the coalman tipped his cap at them, before striding off to his horse and cart, waiting for him outside on the lane, then urging his horse onto his next drop-off point. 'At least we won't freeze; perhaps my night of shame was worth it for that.'

'Nothing was worth that and you know it. After we've used this coal up, we'll put an order in with the Nibble and Clink pit. We'll get away with not paying for it for a month or two and hopefully things will have turned the corner by then. We'll also have a wander around Rothwell and Woodlesford tomorrow and see if we can see anything cheaper we fancy to rent that doesn't belong to Ellershaw. We can always do a moonlight flit, it would serve him right to be left with this cottage empty.' Eliza had decided that neither of them were going to be beholden to the controlling pit owner who had ruined Mary-Anne's life.

'But I like living here, and now Bert and Ada Simms have shown their true nature and are looking after us since mother died and Bill left, I even like our neighbours.' Mary-Anne sighed.

'A house is just four walls with a few knick-knacks in it, we can soon make somewhere else our home as long as we have one another.' Eliza was determined that no one was going to have control over them ever again. 'We've enough money to get us to the end of January if we're careful, and I'd like to see the tallyman try and throw us out anyway. I'd go and thump on that bloody Ellershaw's door and tell his wife just what he gets up to when her back is turned.' Eliza was angry at the abuse Mary-Anne had taken and she, being the feisty one, was not going to put up with it. 'The bastard.'

'Eliza, Mother will be turning in her grave, what with my actions and your language. You'll not say anything, even if we do get evicted.' Mary-Anne thought back to Edmund Ellershaw scoffing at the easy conquest of their mother and went quiet as she listened to Eliza venting her plans for vengeance on her assailant. Perhaps Eliza was right to want to fight back, for the sake of their mother if nothing else. Edmund did deserve a taste of his own medicine, but at the same time she did not want their family's dirty linen made public. There had to be a better way to hit back at him and time would reveal it.

The day passed slowly in the lean-to shop. Mary-Anne finally sold Minnie Armstrong her mother's altered skirt, looking at the few pence that she paid for it and thinking that it would keep them in food for a few more days. Eliza made herself busy repairing and stitching garments that Ma Fletcher had sold them the last time they had visited, and she watched as her sister re-arranged the shop window.

'It's a pity we haven't got another green dress like the one Grace Ellershaw bought.' Eliza looked up at her sister's attempt at making a garment like those they had repaired and remade. It now looked interesting enough to catch a passing shopper's eyes. 'She hasn't been back yet; I don't know if that's a good thing or bad, given the circumstances.'

'That was the other thing Edmund Ellershaw said, that he'd be making sure Grace had nothing more to do with us. I'm just glad that so far she has not returned the dress that she purchased. Knowing Edmund Ellershaw, he could have demanded that she got her money back, and that would have been a disaster seeing we have spent quite a bit of time and money on it. I worried when you said she had returned and looked around the shop.' Mary-Anne sighed.

'She couldn't do that, and, besides, she'd have brought it back by now if she had listened to her father. Her brother seems to be more like him; perhaps hopefully she takes after her mother. Though her brother is quite handsome, don't you think?' Eliza smiled at her sister.

'I can't find the son of Edmund Ellershaw handsome! Besides, I think he has an air of arrogance about him.' Mary-Anne looked at her sister and couldn't quite believe what she was hearing after the night she had endured. 'You shouldn't even be looking at him. What about Tom – I thought he was the love of your life?'

'He might be, but he doesn't have much money and I think his mother has a lot of say in his life. Anyway, there's no harm in looking, and William Ellershaw is good-looking, but he does have an air of superiority about him, you are quite right. He wouldn't look twice at either of us anyway, you can tell that he thinks we're not worthy of his attentions.' Eliza looked up from her sewing and saw Mary-Anne staring out of the window, a piece of mending in her hands. 'Are you all right?'

'Yes, just thinking that there is no justice in the world and that the more money people have the more they seem to want, and they don't give a damn about people's feelings. I feel so dirty after Edmund

Ellershaw's unwanted attentions, I sometimes think I can't live with the shame.' Mary-Anne dropped her head and looked at the garment that had seen better days in her hand. Her life was like the garment, in tatters, and she didn't know if she could mend it.

'Who's that knocking on the door at this time of night?' Eliza got up from her chair next to the fire and walked along the passage to the front door.

Mary-Anne looked up from her sewing and heard a man's voice talking to Eliza at the front door, recognising the soft Irish lilt of John Vasey's tones immediately. She quickly put her sewing down and checked her hair as best she could in the reflection of the copper kettle before Eliza brought him into the kitchen.

'Mr Vasey, how good to see you. What brings you out at this time of night?' She couldn't help but admire his dark hair and chiselled chin as he stood in the doorway of the kitchen – as well as the heavy sack he was carrying on his back.

'This does, my young ladies, as well as your lovely company. I could hardly bring you stolen goods in broad daylight, now, could I?' John Vasey grinned at the two girls as he heaved the heavy sack onto the table. 'You said you wanted material, Eliza? Well, here you are, straight out of the docks of Liverpool, slipped away from a barge that I unloaded last night.' John Vasey grinned as he pulled several lengths of brand-new silks, cottons and taffetas out of the grubby sack. 'No questions asked but payment is going to cost you dearly.' John smiled as he saw a glimmer of alarm cross Eliza's face. He chuckled. 'A pot of tea and something to eat and a roof over my head for the night. That's the payment I demand ... And then I'll take myself home again on a Tom Pud as soon as it's light.'

John smiled as he noticed the excitement in Eliza's face. She picked up each covered board of material clearly imagining the clothes she and Mary-Anne could make.

'I don't think that you ask enough in payment, Mr Vasey,' Mary-Anne interjected quietly. 'There's a small fortune in material here in front of us.' Mary-Anne felt the quality of the materials on their kitchen table and looked up at their most welcome late-night visitor. 'Will it not be missed and get you into trouble?'

'Nay, it'll not be missed. Besides, a few boards of material mean nothing to the wealthy retailers in Leeds. I thought you two could put it to better use.' John stood next to the fire and warmed his hands.

'Please sit down and warm yourself and I'll make you some supper.' Mary-Anne pulled the Windsor chair that was her usual seat closer to the fire and urged John to make himself comfortable as Eliza showed her appreciation of the fine materials being delivered by putting the kettle on to boil.

'So, what sort of a Christmas did you girls have? It would be a queer sort for you both with you just losing your mother.' John sat back and watched both the girls as Eliza took the material from off the kitchen table and into the parlour, and Mary-Anne sliced some bread and brought a slice or two of ham and some cheese for him to eat.

'It has been strange; heartbreaking, in fact. We both miss our mother so much and if I was truthful even Bill in a strange way. He might have been a bastard, but he was always here and was alright when he was sober.' Mary-Anne sat across from John as Eliza brewed his tea and watched as he took his first sip.

'That brute ... I didn't think a lot of him. If I hadn't been there that day when he called in at your Aunt Patsy's, I think he would have killed her, for sure.'

'He did have a temper on him, especially in drink. We used to fear for our mother when he was in his cups.' Mary-Anne looked at the soft-spoken man who was enjoying his supper.

'I've no time for a man that lifts his hand to a woman, drink or no drink. They can't call themselves a man in any shape or form.' John looked across at Mary-Anne, who had caught his eye when he had first seen her at his new lodgings. He couldn't help but notice that some of the bloom had left her cheeks and that she looked a little drawn. 'You are better off without him if you couldn't trust him in drink.'

'I hated him; he wasn't anything like our true father.' Eliza looked at their guest and poured him another cup of tea, making him feel welcome in their home; it was the least she could do as she was so thankful for the material that he had brought. Tomorrow she would sit down and work out some designs, and between Mary-Anne and herself they would create and sew the most desirable dresses that anyone could possibly imagine.

'Your Aunt Patsy said your da was a good man; tragic that he lost his life down the pit, and that your mother was left to fend and look after you two without any help. She must have had it hard, and then for her to marry a bastard like Bill. The poor woman.' John shook his head and looked into the fire.

Mary-Anne swallowed hard and tried to control her feelings, holding back her knowledge of just how far her mother had gone to protect their family and keep them all fed and warm. 'How are Aunt Patsy and Uncle Mike? We usually see them over Christmas but didn't get into Leeds this time.'

'They are doing grand. She's a good woman, is your aunt. Makes me feel at home and treats me like one of the family. I'm grateful for her for giving me a roof over my head while I earn my passage.' John

130

smiled at the two sisters and noticed Eliza yawning. 'Are you tired, girl? Don't stop up on my account. I'll make myself comfortable in this chair next to the fire and will let myself out in the morning.'

'I am slightly, but, no, you must sleep in our parents' room; the bed is already made up and aired.' Eliza stood up and yawned again.

'Get yourself to bed, and thank you for the offer of your parents' bed, but it wouldn't be proper, me sleeping upstairs; you hardly know me. I'll be all right down here. I appreciate you letting me stay.'

'I think it is us that should show our appreciation, Mr Vasey. I can't thank you enough for the material that you have brought us tonight, and it will make all the difference to us keeping a roof over our heads.' Mary-Anne cleared his mug and plate away and smiled. 'You are more than welcome to sleep upstairs; it is the least we can offer you.'

'Nay, I'll stop down here. I'll just visit your necessary before I make myself comfortable. That is unless you would like to sit with me a while, Mary-Anne? I can see Eliza is ready for her bed but perhaps ...' John stood up and waited for a reply.

'The privy is out in the yard.' Mary-Anne opened the back door and showed him the lavvy at the bottom of the yard. 'Yes, I'll stop up with you for a while – just a while, mind. We have a busy day in the morning.' Mary-Anne smiled at their guest and gave a glance to Eliza.

'Aye, you will now you've something to work with ... There's more where that came from, so don't you worry lasses, I'll keep you supplied. I'll bid you goodnight, Eliza. Get yourself to bed, I'll not keep your sister too long. And you can trust me with her, I promise,' he said reassuringly, as he walked out of the back door and up the flagged path to the lavvy, guided only by the light from the oil lamps in the kitchen.

'Goodnight, John, and thank you again for the cloth,' Eliza shouted up the yard. 'Will you be all right left with him?' she whispered to Mary-Anne as soon as he was out of sight and inside the lavvy. 'Do you trust him on your own?'

'I'll be all right, don't worry. He's not exactly like Edmund Ellershaw, he's even concerned that he is sleeping here under the same roof as us two. Besides, he's a friend of Uncle Mick, and he wouldn't have anything to do with him if he thought he was a wrong 'un.'

'Well, if you're sure ... you can always shout if he tries anything on.' Eliza kissed Mary-Anne on her cheek.

'I will, now get yourself to bed. Not that you'll sleep, you'll be too busy thinking about what you can do with the material. I think John Vasey is the answer to our prayers, yours especially!' Mary-Anne hugged her sister and then watched as she made her way down the passage to climb the stairs to bed. She then added another coal or two to the dying embers of the fire, prodding it into action with the poker before sitting in the chair across from where John Vasey had previously made himself comfortable.

'Now don't be putting too much on that fire. We'll not be staying up that late, you've your work and I'll have to be leaving at first light.' John smiled and sat across from Mary-Anne.

'No, I've just added a bit to keep the chill at bay.' Mary-Anne smiled back at him.

'Eliza made for her bed then? I hope I'm not keeping you up. I'm more of a night person myself, especially since moving to here from Ireland. My thoughts won't let me sleep, I dream of all the atrocities and things that happened over there.' John sighed and went quiet.

'Eliza likes her bed, but I'm a bit like you – I'm a night owl, I don't need much sleep. Tell me about Ireland, if it doesn't make you too sad … I know you left because of the famine but other than that I don't know much. It might as well be the other side of the world to me, here in Woodlesford.' Mary-Anne sat back in her chair and looked at the sorrow on John's face.

'I don't mind talking about it at all. I love my country but how do I tell you of a place that's so close to my heart but is dying with every breath it takes? And a country that has taken all of the people that I love.' John looked at her and breathed in heavily.

'I'm sorry, perhaps it is better that you don't talk about it.' Mary-Anne realised that the man across from her was as heartbroken as her and waited for his reply.

'Nay, it's something that should be told and it is the reason why I aim to go and look for a better life in America. I'll tell you about my family and I'm sorry if it upsets you.' John paused briefly. 'Our family – my mother and father and my brother and two sisters – farmed on our small croft in County Mayo. It wasn't the biggest of farms, just six acres, but it kept us fed, with our main crop being potatoes and a few hens scratting about in the yard. Our landlord had cut our acreage down in previous years for him to raise cattle on to send back over to England, where he came from. We could not protest as it was happening to a lot of the farmers around us and no one argued with the English landowners. It would have fallen on deaf ears anyway and he'd not have thought twice to have demanded all his land back. Then when I was ten, the worst thing that could have happened did and I still remember walking through our fields full of potatoes and my father nearly sobbing as he touched the potato leaves that were blackened and wizened with blight. They were to have fed us all year around, the only way to keep us fed on such a small portion of land. With nothing on the table, and no means of income, it was decided that my older brother would leave home and go across the water to America to make his living. My mother cried when he went with next to nothing in his pocket to board the ship at Bray but little did she know she was going to cry more in the following years. John stopped for a moment and looked across at Mary-Anne who gazed at him with sympathetic interest.

'Go on, please tell me more.' Mary-Anne listened intently.

'The prime minister Peel did what he could for us all, purchasing tons of Indian corn from America but it arrived late March, leaving us with empty bellies all winter. My sister was the first to go – she always had been a sickly lass and the lack of food left her so weak, she died the week before the corn came. Later in the spring our spirits rose as the few potatoes that we had planted looked healthy and we hoped that the coming autumn things would be back to normal, but it wasn't to be. For five years the blight hit our crops, I lost my father, mother and my youngest sister. The workhouses were full and along the roadside people begged and died while walking to what they hoped to be salvation, but in truth there was nowhere to go and nobody wanted us. With all my family bar myself dead, the landlord evicted me and set fire to our croft, leaving me with nowhere to rest my head. I remember watching and crying behind the hedge as the bailiff's men set the thatch on my beloved home alight. I was cold, hungry and alone and I thought the good Lord had forsaken me. The whole of Ireland was starving and dying, and nobody looked to be doing anything except the Quakers and the poor houses that couldn't cope with demand. It was then I found Mick for the first time. I'd made my way to Ballina because I'd heard there was a soup kitchen there. You were fed only so long as you were prepared to work, building the roads that the English government had decided that we could build for them to earn our daily crust. We met while building the road and decided to have an easier life and find work in the north; it hadn't been hit with the famine that year as bad as the west and east coast where we were. Mick was a bit older than me, a bit wiser and crafty with it, I soon found out as we walked and begged our way to Belfast, nearly dying on our journey but determined to survive after so much hardship. We've been friends now for the last twelve years. He found work in the shipyards at Belfast and then in Liverpool, before marrying your Aunt Patsy, and I stayed in Belfast working on the docks. How we survived those years I don't know. Has Mick never mentioned them to you?' John warmed his hands by the fire's flames as he waited for Mary-Anne to reply.

'No, he never talks of it. To be honest we weren't allowed to associate with Uncle Mick; Bill didn't like him nor my aunt Patsy. You've had a terrible time of it,' Mary-Anne whispered. 'I'm so sorry for your loss and your hard life; it makes me feel quite humble.'

'Nay, you've nothing to feel sorry for, it's none of your doing. You can't change the past, and, besides, I'm happy with my lot in life at the moment. I'm saving up for my fare to finally join my brother in New York and then we will be together again at last. He's making a name for himself over there buying land and has gone into the construction business, so some good has come out of life's trials.' John smiled at the beautiful lass sat across from him. 'If it hadn't have been for Mick taking me under his wing, I don't think I'd have made it. I owe him a lot. So when Eliza asked for some material, I thought nothing of it. A bit of material taken from under the noses of those who can more than afford it is my way of payment for his kindness, and, besides, I'd like to be there to help you, from one who knows what it's like to be down and out.'

'Well, we really do appreciate it and you're welcome to visit us anytime you wish. Eliza's face lit up when you showed her the material, it will keep her out of mischief for days.' Mary-Anne smiled as she rose from her seat and yawned.

'Get yourself to bed, Mary-Anne. Don't sit up any longer with me, you look tired.' John rose and poked the fire. 'I'll say goodbye now as I'll be gone before you wake in the morning.'

'I am tired, life's been hard since we lost my mother, but how can I complain after what you have told me?' Mary-Anne smiled and touched his arm lightly.

'If you need anything, you'll let me know. I'll always be there for you if you think I can help.' John smiled back at the young woman and thought how bonny she was.

'Thank you, John, that means a lot. I'll go to bed now, but if there's anything you want, just help yourself. You never know, one of us might be awake in the morning to say goodbye.' Mary-Anne made her way to bed.

John sat in front of the fire and looked around him at the sparse kitchen; it was a pity he had made his mind up to go to America, as he could have felt quite at home here with Mary-Anne by his side.

'Aye, our Ada, those lasses are going to end up in bother.' Bert looked out of his bedroom window as he pulled the bedroom curtains open, letting the early morning light into the room.

'What do you mean, Bert?' Ada came to the window and looked down to the next-door's gateway. Both gasped as they watched Eliza give the dark-haired man a parting kiss on his cheek. 'The hussy, he must have stayed the night!'

'We should have known what they'd be like if they were left to their own doing, their mother was no better, Ada.' Bert moved away from the window. 'I hope it's just a one-off and that men aren't going to be calling day and night.'

'Oh! Bert, we can't have that, not next door! I'll have to say something.'

Sixteen

Eliza and Mary-Anne looked at the reams of material laid out on their cutting table that, between them, they had managed to carry all the way to their little shop.

'Well, you said you wanted material.' Mary-Anne looked at the smile on Eliza's face.

'I know, isn't it exciting? I don't think I've ever seen as much material in my life. Just look at this blue brocade; I'm just imagining the dress I could make with this! I'll have to get a move on, though, and have a play around with a pattern or two. See if we can entice our Miss Grace back, if no one else.' Eliza ran her hand lovingly over the brocade that she aimed to make the most of.

'What did John say when you said goodbye to him this morning? I felt awful that I wasn't up in time to see him on his way, but I was so tired ... I haven't been sleeping well of late.' Mary-Anne had left her sister to give her thanks and farewells to their welcome visitor but now she was wishing she'd stirred herself from her bed.

'He didn't say a lot. I think he was embarrassed that I gave him a kiss on the cheek to show my gratitude. He mumbled something that I couldn't make out and then sloped off to the canal. I bet he'd have shown more interest if it had been you. I think he likes you, Mary-Anne, I kept seeing him looking at you last night. I wasn't really tired, I thought I'd leave you to get better acquainted. However, I was a little worried that I had left you with a man we hardly know, so I lay in my bed and listened to you both talking. I just wanted you to be safe after your terrible experience with Edmund Ellershaw.'

'Eliza! How could you be so forward? What would he think of you? You can't just kiss him! As you say, we don't really know him and he might have misunderstood your intentions.' Mary-Anne shook her head. 'However, I think he's harmless. John told me about his past last night. He's really had a hard life and only has a brother left alive and he's over in America. That's why he's so determined to go there.' Mary-Anne made herself busy, not wanting her sister to know that she had enjoyed her evening with the dark-haired Irish man.

'Well, I think he is quite good-looking; no money though, which is a bit of disappointment. I suppose it's rare to get both and if you do there's always a downside – like Grace Ellershaw's brother. He's got the social skills of a gnat – the way he acts he must take after his father,' Eliza said unthinkingly with a laugh, as she unrolled the material.

'Do you have to mention that man? I'm trying to put him out of my mind. I am hoping that we'd both be too busy for me to dwell on that night, what with your idea to make your own clothes, and if I continue trading with Ma Fletcher and making something out of nothing we will be able to pay our way in the world. The less I hear about Edmund Ellershaw and his son the better.' Mary-Anne wiped a tear away from her eye and concentrated on organising the drawer that held their supplies of bobbins and lace without even looking up at Eliza.

'I'm sorry, Mary-Anne. Me and my big mouth. I didn't think. I didn't mean to cause you any pain.' Eliza put down the material and hugged her sister tight. 'Now, you're right, let's keep busy – I can get a move on making our first dress from scratch and you can deal with the second-hand side, that will work well.'

'I'm sorry,' Mary-Anne sobbed. 'It's just I can't get that horrible night out of my head and I am so worried that I will be forced to do the same again at the end of the month!'

'You will not have to go through that again! I will make sure of that, I promise. Now pass me the cutting shears and let us make a start with our new venture.' Eliza smiled 'The sooner we get a new dress in the window the better. We might not want to see Edmund Ellershaw or his snobby son, but we do need his daughter Grace to call upon us.'

Seventeen

'Your William is so handsome, does he not have a beau?' Priscilla Eavesham giggled and smiled at her friend, Grace, as her brother gave the group of ladies his apologies for not accepting their invitation to join them for tea.

'No, he's quite the bachelor. Although what you see in him, Prissy, I do not know. He can be the most trying of brothers some days, just like he is today, skulking around, like a bear with a sore head. In fact, I'll let you into a secret but you must not say anything to him ...' Grace whispered low to the group of four young women who were gathered around the table in the parlour at Highfield House. 'But then again perhaps I should not. If he found out that I'd betrayed his secrets he'd be most vexed.' She quickly re-thought the confidences that he had told her in a moment of weakness.

'Oh, Grace! You've got to tell us now that you've started. Else you are just a tease,' Prissy gasped.

'I really shouldn't say.' Grace looked at her friends and knew that she had their attention, as they all leaned in like a witch's coven to hear the words they knew she could not keep to herself. 'He's returned from Cambridge with a broken heart ...'

The three young women breathed in sharply at the same time and looked at one another waiting for the next sentence.

'Even my father doesn't know about it, he just thinks William has given up on his studies. All he does is mope about the house, lost in his poetry. Although he did show some signs of his old self when I went to that little shop I was telling you about and a girl with red hair caught his eye. He even sent me in the other week to see if she was there, but alas I had to tell him it was only the younger sister that was serving that day.'

'The shop where you got your beautiful green dress from?' Jessica Bentley asked.

'Yes, he even told Father how good-looking she was. So there are signs that he's recovering from his heartbreak, if a pretty girl can attract his attentions.' Grace sat back in her chair and sipped her tea.

'A common shop girl? What has she got that we haven't?' Priscilla said crossly. 'It's clearly not money or position!' Priscilla Eavesham thought of herself as one of the finest catches of the district, what with her father owning Leventhorpe Hall and, while her father might be from new money, it was only a matter of time she thought before she landed herself a suitable husband.

Jessica Bentley looked at Priscilla. 'Men may want a girl with a sizable fortune, Priscilla, but they don't always want marriage. The girl is obviously pretty, else he wouldn't be showing interest in her. Why don't we pay the shop a visit, and see this auburn-haired beauty for ourselves? She obviously has more than us ladies can offer William, else he would be here enjoying our company.'

'Yes, we'll do that and perhaps purchase something, especially if they have dresses as beautiful as the one you wore to the ball, Grace,' Sarah Marsden, the quiet one of the group, added.

'I should say that neither of the girls have done anything to encourage my brother's interest,' Grace said swiftly, her delight at being the centre of attention giving way to her kind heart. 'Though I do believe they could do with our custom, ladies. My father said they had both lost their mother recently and that their stepfather had deserted them; he was only a miner who worked for my father.' Grace looked around at the horror on her friends' faces.

'Then we will pay them a visit. See what our rivals look like and purchase whatever takes our fancy. It is our duty, ladies, to give to those less fortunate than ourselves. Especially if what we purchase there is as fine as the dress you were wearing, my dear Grace.'

'Next week, ladies? It will soon be the spring ball, and I don't know about all of you, but I have nothing at all to wear in my wardrobe.' Grace looked around at her friends and hoped that they would not say anything to their parents about their organised visit.

'Yes, and then we can have coffee in that sweet little place on the corner; perhaps your William would like to join us then?' Priscilla looked at Grace expectantly.

'I'll ask him, but I wouldn't count on my brother. May I ask you to keep this between ourselves? My father thinks that I have lost my senses shopping in Woodlesford instead of Leeds and he seems to have a great dislike of the girls that run my little find. But what does he know about fashion? Besides the more he protests the more I am determined to shop there. I know my own mind, ladies, as do you, my dear friends.' Grace sat back and felt satisfied with herself; the little dress shop was going to be her charity project, something to justify her wealth and privilege, and if she could get her friends to help then so much the better.

*

'Eliza Wild, what do you think you were doing this morning at the break of dawn? We both saw you, and I can tell you we will have none of that in the house next to us. No matter how tight the money is at your house. You should have more pride!' Ada Simms had waited all day for the Wild girls to return home and the more she had thought about it the more she had got worked up about the sight she and her husband had witnessed out of their window. She'd watched for their return from behind her lace curtains and had raced to tackle them before she entered into their home.

'I'm sorry ... what do you mean?' Eliza looked at her red-faced neighbour and didn't understand what she was insinuating.

'You know full well, Eliza Wild! I saw that man you were kissing on the doorstep this morning. He'd obviously stayed the night. I thought you girls had been brought up better than that. No good will come of it, you know.' Ada was flustered as she felt awkward tackling them both.

'Mrs Simms, I think you are thinking the worst of my sister and me with no just cause. Mr Vasey is a friend of my uncle's. He came late last night with a gift of material for us, and, yes, he did stay the night ... downstairs in a chair next to the fire. Eliza got up early to thank him and say our goodbyes – that must be what you saw when you were looking out of the window.' Mary-Anne unlocked the front door as she watched the old woman look sternly at them both.

'It's no good, Mary-Anne, she's made her mind up that I had a man in my bed last night. Just look at her face,' Eliza snapped. 'Don't you dare judge me because I've done nothing that I'm ashamed of.' Eliza pushed her way past Mary-Anne, the basket on her arm creaking as she squeezed past the doorway and Mary-Anne.

'I'm sorry, Mrs Simms, but, believe me, you are mistaken. It is as I have said. Eliza is blameless ... as am I.' Mary-Anne looked at her irate neighbour.

'Well, perhaps I got it wrong, but my eyes don't usually deceive me.' Ada Simms took a step back, regretting that she had said something and that Eliza was now in such a foul mood with her.

'Well, Mr Vasey is a very honourable man and it was he who insisted he slept downstairs, away from both of us. I dare say he could imagine how idle gossip could arise ...' She gave Ada a pointed look and was relieved to see her words had struck a nerve. 'He came to help us, not to take advantage of either of us. Now if you'll excuse me I have things to do.' Mary-Anne left Ada on the doorstep and closed her door behind her.

'The old bitch! What does she think I am?' Eliza growled as she lit the kindling to get the fire going. 'She's just a nosy old cow looking out of her bedroom first thing this morning. '

'It'd be her Bert going to work, he always gets up early.' Mary-Anne spoke quietly, thinking that if Ada Simms knew the truth about her own recent experiences she'd wash her hands of both of them.

'Our mother was right: she's best kept at arm's-length if she thinks like that. No wonder she never bothered with her.' Eliza stood up near the fire and looked at her sister who had started to busy herself in the kitchen.

'Just forget it, Eliza; you know you did nothing wrong. It's up to her what she believes.' Mary-Anne sighed.

'She's a nosy old cow!' Eliza said with spite again and, taking her shoes off, she slumped in her chair, still muttering to herself as Mary-Anne set the table for supper. 'I never have liked her! And how can she judge me just by seeing me give John a peck on his cheek?

Though I know he was embarrassed by it, I regret even getting up to say goodbye now.'

'Well, it's done now. And she was wrong. Now let's have something to eat and forget it.' Mary-Anne bit her tongue. She could easily have lost her temper with her sister, who seemed to forget her night of shame. Eliza had done nothing wrong so she had nothing to worry about, unlike herself.

The following Monday, Mary-Anne awoke early and started off on her own along the canal to Leeds. It felt strange doing the walk alone; for the last few years she'd always gone with Eliza and she missed her company. The towpath along the canal was slippery with a hard hoar frost covering everything, making the hedges and grasses along the canal bank shimmer and sparkle with the early rising sun. She walked carefully over the crackling pools of frozen water and made her way down towards the canal basin and then on as usual to Ma Fletcher and her cart. She was cold to the bone when she reached Hunslet on the outskirts of Leeds and wished she had asked Eliza to come instead of her. But at the same time she knew Eliza was better with a needle and thread and would be busy in the shop attending to the new dress she was making. It was already taking shape and was looking good, with a deep neckline and a full skirt with perfect pleating, wide enough for any fashion conscious lady to fit a horse hair-padded crinoline underneath to make her the height of society's fashion. Even though Eliza knew it looked good, she kept finding fault with her own handy work, doubting her every stitch, unsure of her own newfound skills of designing a dress from scratch.

Mary-Anne made her way through the village of Hunslet through to the bustling city of Leeds, passing Clarence Dock where the smell of the malting hops and barley from the Tetley Brewery filled the air, making her hungry with their sweet heavy smell. The canal and dockside alongside the huge towering warehouses were busy with barges full of coal, wool, fruit and vegetables, cotton and any other commodity that helped keep the busy city of Leeds functioning. Dock workers were like ants, busily unloading cargo from barges to horses and carts or stocking it into the tall, red brick warehouses. Though they were busy in their work, the dockhands still took time to admire a pretty girl, shouting a rude comment or two in her direction, more in keeping for the prick-pinchers of Calls Walk. Mary-Anne didn't give them a second glance as she weaved in and out of the busy canal side and made her way along Calls Wharf.

'Mary … Mary-Anne!' a voice shouted out above the hum of the noise, over managers and foremen shouting their orders as goods were hauled and winched into place. 'Wait, Mary-Anne.'

Mary-Anne turned and saw the now-familiar figure of John Vasey pushing his way through the workers. He had a flat cap on and a checked muffler around his neck and she could just see a striped shirt underneath his dark jacket and waistcoat. Mary-Anne walked back to him and he smiled at her.

'I thought you weren't going to stop, that you couldn't hear me above this din.' John grinned. 'What are you doing down here at this time of the morning?'

'It's good to see you, John. I'm on my way the market at upper Briggate. We have an understanding with a woman with a stall there, her husband is the rag-and-bone man and she keeps back the best clothes for us. Are you at work?' Mary-Anne smiled at John as some of his work colleagues jeered at him talking to her.

'I am, with a load of scoundrels who don't know how to treat a woman and are only jealous.' He raised his voice, loud enough for them all to hear. 'I'll walk with you to the start of lower Briggate; they can manage without me for a while.' John walked alongside Mary-Anne, smiling at her as she tried to think of something to say.

John finally broke their companionable silence. 'I enjoyed our time together, I hope I didn't bore you with my tales of home.'

'No, not at all. I just thought how hard your life must have been and it put our situation in a different light. Ma always used to say there's always someone worse off than you. It's easy to get wrapped up in your own troubles.' Mary-Anne had thought a lot about the conversation that they'd had the previous evening and had been surprised by her growing affection for the dark-haired man by her side. In fact she had to admit a pang of jealousy towards Eliza, given that she'd been the one who had dared to kiss him goodbye, even if it had been just a quick kiss on his cheek.

'How long will you be up at Briggate? Will you have time to join me for a warm-up around the brazier in the warehouse before you return home?' John stopped as they neared the busy, wide street of upper Briggate. 'Or if you don't want the attention, would you prefer a quick drink in the Adelphi? One of the men will cover for me.'

'No, no, not the Adelphi. It's far too posh. The Tetley Brewery has spent a small fortune on making it their flagship and they won't want the likes of us sitting in their snug. I'd only feel uncomfortable in there.' Mary-Anne blushed and looked down at her feet. 'A warm would be fine, if you are sure that it will not get you into trouble. I've had my fair share of catcalls from dock workers in my time, they don't bother me.'

'To be sure, Mary-Anne, you would look a lady no matter where we went together. Don't you realise how blessed you are? You'd turn any man's head. And more fool the Adelphi if they don't appreciate our trade. But a drink of tea it is and I'll make sure my mates hold their noise. They're used to gawping at all the girls on Calls Walk, and have no manners when it comes to a proper lady.' John touched her arm gently and smiled as she was obviously embarrassed by his flattery.

'I won't be long – half-a-hour at the most.' Mary-Anne looked at the soft-spoken man, giving him one last smile before turning to walk quickly up through the busy street, smiling to herself at the words said by her newfound friend. He was a good-looking man, not in the first flush of youth but perhaps that was a good thing from what she had seen of him. He seemed genuine and caring and she knew she could do worse, but perhaps her dreams of a life with John Vasey as a companion were running ahead of themselves; after all it was only a cup of tea and a warm up they were sharing, nothing more.

'Now then, Mary-Anne, no Eliza with you today? Where is she? Is she too busy making money to come and see an old woman with her wares that are nearly given away to you two?' Ma Fletcher stood with her hands on her hips and grinned, showing her decaying teeth to the world.

'She's in the shop, busy sewing, so I've come by myself today.' Mary-Anne quickly glanced over the cart, already starting to handle the rags and shoes that had seen better days as she answered the old woman.

'You want nowt with this, I've your usual here … a few good bits and a few not so good, but better than what's on top here. My old man says it will be better pickings this coming week or two; a lot of the so-called ladies of society are re-arranging their wardrobes ahead of the spring party season and throwing their offcasts out.' Ma Fletcher pulled up her usual bag of garments that she'd put to one side and placed it in front of Mary-Anne. 'I was sorry to hear of your troubles

– your poor ma … And I hear that Bill's buggered off. How are you both coping? You'll be missing your mother, no doubt.' Ma Fletcher watched as Mary-Anne shook out a dress or two that she'd put to one side and noticed how pale she looked.

'We're managing. We both miss our mother but we can't say the same of Bill. He never took the place of our father.' Mary-Anne sighed and held up the clothes from the bag that she'd been presented with. 'I'll take these, how much do you want for them?'

'Three pence and that's a bargain! I thought neither of you would be losing tears over Bill he was a wrong 'un and no mistake. God knows why your mother married him.' It wasn't often Ma Fletcher undercharged for her wares but just this once she was willing to show a little charity to two girls she knew were having a hard time of it of late. She watched as Mary-Anne clearly thought about questioning her sudden generosity and then thought better of it.

'That's good, I hadn't much more on me. Thank you. I'll take the lot.' Mary-Anne pushed the heap of clothing back into the hessian sack, stood back and looked around her. 'I think my mother thought she was securing a good life for us all when she married Bill, but she got more than she bargained for. We didn't know how much he liked his ale … and what might happen when he drank too much.' Mary-Anne looked at Ma Fletcher and sighed.

Ma Fletcher beckoned her closer. 'My mother said to me that you never know a man until you live with him, and then it's too late when you've a ring on your finger. Better to live over the brush and just put up with the gossip than not to be your own woman. That's what me and my old man have done for the last thirty years; everybody thinks we are wed, but we never got around to it.' She paused, looking to see if she'd scandalised the younger woman, but Mary-Anne was amused if anything, prompting her to continue. 'Besides, it makes no difference, it's only a bit of gold and a few words that are never taken any notice of, if truth was told. Better that you can up-sticks and move on if he treats you bad and he'll respect you more for knowing that. Never get tied down, lass, else you'll regret it all your life.' Ma Fletcher watched as Mary-Anne felt in her bag for the money she owed her.

'Both Eliza and myself have vowed the men we marry have got to be able to provide for us well. We won't settle for less,' Mary-Anne assured the old woman, picking up her bag and hoisting it on her back.

'It ain't just money, you want, lass. It's love and respect – that's what's gold in a relationship and don't you forget it. Money doesn't make a man, you've just to look at some of the snobs around here that look at you and me like we're dirt. Look for someone with a good heart, not a big wallet; he'll make you more than happy and tell your Eliza the same. Just you two listen to Ma Fletcher, she'll be straight with you. Now, same time next week? And I'll hope to have a few more bits for you next time but, fair warning, I'll be back to my usual prices. I'm not a charity after all.' Ma Fletcher took Mary-Anne's money and looked at her with her ice-blue eyes that looked as if they were reading your soul.

'Thank you for your concern, I'm sure we will both know when the right man comes along, not that we are looking for one especially at the moment. Yes, I'll be back next week and I thought you had charged me light today.' Mary-Anne managed a grin.

'Aye, I'm a soft touch really, but everyone needs a bit of help occasionally. You take care, Mary-Anne, and just you heed the words of an old woman, I might be long in the tooth now, but once I was young and pretty just like you. Time goes so quickly and you look in the mirror and realise all too soon that you've turned into an ugly old woman. Enjoy yourself while you can.' Ma Fletcher watched as Mary-Anne made her way through the crowds. She shook her head and sighed. A girl like Mary-Anne would need all the luck in the world to find a man with money in his pocket willing to marry a common lass like her, no matter how good looking she was.

John glanced up at Mary-Anne who was warming her hands around the brazier. Her cheeks were flushed with the warmth and she looked even more beautiful than before. 'Did you get some good bargains at the market?' he asked as she sat down on a crate, her bag by her side.

'I did actually, Ma Fletcher was kind to me today – she gave her sympathies on the loss of our mother. She also tried to give me some guidance when it came to living my life.' Mary-Anne looked around her at the huge bales of wool that were piled high, waiting to be dispatched to the many woollen mills in Leeds.

'She must think you're in need of a steady hand now your mother is no longer with us. She'd probably not be impressed with you sharing your time with an Irishman whose only a wharf-man at that – and one that you hardly know.' John rubbed his hands together and held them near the flames as he gazed over at Mary-Anne.

'But, I do know you; you told me all about yourself the other evening. And whether you're Irish or English makes no difference to me. You showed what sort a man you were by helping Eliza and me out. Besides, what does Ma Fletcher know really? A rag-and-bone man's supposed wife who has never left Leeds … she is hardly one to give me advice, no matter how well intentioned. I didn't tell her I was meeting you, only because it was none of her business. I can do what I like in any case. Anyway, we're friends, I hope. And this is just a friendly chat over a cup of tea.' Mary-Anne looked across at John and watched as he smiled.

'No matter what she'd have said, you'd have done what you had wanted; I can see you that you're a stubborn woman, Mary-Anne. A woman with a mind of her own.' John grinned and turned to answer a work colleague who shouted at him to get his courting done as the gaffer was on his way.

'I'll go, I've appreciated the warmth. Perhaps we will see you again, you are most welcome to visit us, John Varney. Eliza would be delighted to see you, it would seem she has a soft spot for you.' Mary-Anne thought back to Eliza's kiss and found herself feeling jealous again.

'Ah, Eliza likes me for the material I bring her – cupboard love, I think it's called. Now I would hope you would just like me for my company, Miss Mary-Anne Wild, and that I keep you entertained with my stories.' John's eyes danced with excitement as he waited for her reply.

'Indeed you do and, as I say, please visit us again; there will always be a welcome for you in Pit Lane.' Mary-Anne lifted her bag of clothing over her shoulder and walked past the wharf-side workers with John by her side.

'You'll be seeing me again, Mary-Anne and not just for Eliza's sake,' John replied, watching as she turned around and smiled before weaving her way through off-loaded cargo, disappearing amongst the workers along the canal side.

'You will be seeing a lot more of me, my auburn beauty, of that you can be sure,' he whispered to himself. Mary-Anne was the woman he had been waiting for, of that he was certain.

Eighteen

Eliza and Mary-Anne stepped back onto the cobbled road and looked at their handiwork that they had just put on display in their shop window.

'It works well, Eliza, whatever made you think of putting the dolly tub under the skirt to make it look like a crinoline?' Mary-Anne folded her arms and looked at the first finished dress in the prize position of the shop window, the long billowing skirts cascading from the tight bodice, which was displayed on the dolly tub and the posser from their scullery, which was acting as arms and a neck on the display.

'Well, neither of us have such a thing as a crinoline and I wasn't going to attempt to make one.' Her sister paused. 'I guess I could have used metal hoops from a barrel for the width. Anyway, crinolines are definitely not for the likes of us, and just why anyone would want to wear one I will never know, you wouldn't be able to move and they look that dangerous to me. I'd pity the poor man who was walking next to me if I had a crinoline on; he couldn't get near to me for the hoops. Also, Anne Cookman told me that they can spring open and cut into your legs if you are not careful. She is really wary of standing next to ladies that wear them because of that.'

'Aye, you can tell they are not for us working lasses, only the toffs are wearing these, those with nothing to do but to look pretty, but that's who we need to sell this dress to so let's hope we catch the eye of Grace Ellershaw or her friends.' Mary-Anne shivered in the cold wind that blew along the cobbled street. 'Let's go in Eliza, it's bitter out here and just listen to that poor beast making that noise in the slaughter house behind the butchers, it knows it is about to meet its death. I can't abide thinking that its throat is about to be slit and its body cut up for sale in the shop.'

'You'll not be saying that when you are eating your stew later in the week. But aye, I'll be glad when it's been stopped from bellowing, even though the drain that runs in front of our shop will run red with its blood for a while. I hate the sight of that. I wish we could afford a better property; let's face it, this is just a glorified shed that our father once built for all his bits, not the most attractive property on the row of shops that it stands on, but it will have to do for now.' Eliza picked up her skirts and walked up the three shallow steps to the doorway and opened the weather-worn door that led into the wooden lean-to that they had converted to their workshop a few years after their father's death. They had been trying to make a living mending and re-selling clothes from the market since both had learned to sew, kept warm by a small paraffin stove that filled the room with the smell of the burning oil through winter. In the summer, the wooden boards creaked in the warmth of the sun.

'Well, we will just have to make the best of it, because it is all we have and we can't do anything about it. I still worry that we can't afford to live on Pit Lane, let alone look for a new shop. This month's rent is not yet covered, so let's pray that your new dress will bring wealthier customers in. I don't fancy hiding from the tallyman or having to give myself again to Edmund Ellershaw.' Mary-Anne sighed as she closed the door behind her.

'Dear Mary-Anne, stop thinking about Ellershaw; you will not be going there again. Things will take a turn and we will be able to pay the rent when my dress sells, and it will sell, believe me. I've also enough material for at least one more. I only hope that John Vasey can return with more fabric. He's been a godsend for us both in more ways than one if the way you spoke about the meeting with him the other day is anything to go by. Besides, you also got some really good bargains from Ma Fletcher the other day. I still can't believe she did us a good turn over those, she must have had a pang of guilt for all the times she's haggled with us over a farthing or so.' Eliza knew her older sister was still worrying about how to pay the rent and the hold that Edmund Ellershaw had over her. But she had recognised a glimmer of the old Mary-Anne when she had told her about her chance encounter with John Vasey.

'I don't know what you mean about John.' Mary-Anne blushed. 'Though I agree he has been a godsend to both of us with his supply of material but it's nothing more than that.' Mary-Anne made herself busy making tidy the bobbin drawer and averted her eyes from her teasing sister.

'I saw the gleam in your eyes and the blush in your cheeks when you talked of him. I might have been the one caught kissing him but I think it should have been you, my dear sister. However, I'm sure he will return and hopefully he'll bring me some material as his excuse for paying a visit.' Eliza grinned as she warmed her hands at the paraffin stove. 'So much for us both wishing for a man with money: John Vasey has set his cap at you, an Irish man with not even his own roof over his head, and my Tom lives with his mother and daren't stand up to her when it comes to visiting me. We truly are foolish.

Was it not just more than a few weeks ago we said a man without money was no good to either of us?'

'I know, but so much has changed in such a short time. Losing Mother has made me look at things in a different light. I still don't wish for us both to scrimp and save all our lives like Mother did, but I realise that happiness is perhaps more important.' Mary-Anne gazed out of the window and then quickly hurried to her sister's side. 'Grace Ellershaw is walking up the street with a group of her friends, they are heading this way. Do you think that they'll like the dress and call in, or will she have been told not to visit us again?' Mary-Anne felt her heart thumping and felt stupid for getting into such a fluster over a group of well-to-do young women. But in truth she couldn't help but think whose daughter Grace was and that was giving her a sense of justice at the price that the two sisters were going to demand for their work if she showed interest in the dress.

'Shush! Look busy, they are coming up the steps; they've seen the dress. Did you hear them gasp? What a racket, just listen at them giggling ...' Eliza sat down and made a show of looking busy, picking up her sewing of a new dress as Mary-Anne reached for her mending and tried not to look so interested as the party of young women entered the shop.

Eliza smiled at the noisy foursome and stood up to greet them as she would any customer. 'Good afternoon, ladies. What may we do for you today?'

'Good afternoon Miss ... err ...' Grace waited and looked at Eliza, realising that she didn't know if the sisters had taken their stepfather's name.

'It's Wild, miss. I'm Eliza Wild and this is my sister Mary-Anne.' Eliza smiled.

'This is Miss Priscilla Eavesham, Miss Jessica Bentley and Miss Sarah Marsden.' Grace introduced her friends who all stood gazing at both Eliza and Mary-Anne between glancing around the small wooden room. It was clear the young ladies felt out of place in such humble surroundings. Mary-Anne knew that Miss Priscilla's father owned Leventhorpe Hall and the other girls were from similar well-to-do families. Even so, Grace smiled and continued, 'My friends so admired the green dress that I bought from you for the Christmas season that I convinced them all to pay you a visit. And we can see that we will not be disappointed by the looks of the garment in the window.' Grace turned and smiled at her group of giggling friends who by now were looking at the array of bonnets, gloves, shawls and second-hand wares that were placed around the shop.

'Have you just finished it? We couldn't help but admire your design. The colour is exquisite and the fact that the skirt is large enough to put a crinoline beneath it is absolutely marvellous. Even though our good Queen Victoria has been heard saying that she thinks the fashion to be degrading, dangerous and disgusting and she desires for us womenfolk to abandon it, we all think it makes us look more appealing. Don't we, ladies?' Grace turned to her companions and waited for their support.

'Oh, yes, Grace. I love wearing mine, even though my grandmother does not approve either. I do want to follow the latest fashions, although I must confess sometimes a crinoline is not practical especially on windy days or when I have to travel in the carriage. In fact in can be quiet embarrassing.' Sarah Marsden blushed as she watched Priscilla and Jessica feel the blue brocade of the dress in the window.

'They are perhaps not practical for everyday wear, but I would not think to attend this year's spring balls without one. This dress look would magnificent on me, I think. How quaint that you have placed it over a barrel, I notice. Did you not have a crinoline cage spare?' Priscilla Eavesham looked across at Mary-Anne and down her nose at her, remembering that this was the common girl who, much to her disdain, had caught the eye of William Ellershaw.

'I'm afraid mine has one of the steel hoops broken and Mary-Anne prefers not to wear one, as it prohibits her in her work. We thought it looked quite fitting over the dolly tub ... err ... barrel, as it was only to display our work.' Eliza answered quickly. 'Would you like me to take it down from the window for you to see more clearly?'

'Yes, I'm afraid, just like you ladies today, I prefer not be quite so restricted when at work but the style of a crinoline is so extravagant and the gentlemen do look twice at a lady who wears one, of that there is no doubt,' Mary-Anne said as she rose from her seat and joined Eliza at the window to reach for the admired dress. 'We have only just put it into the window, so you are the first ladies to have seen it.' Mary-Anne looked across at Eliza as they pulled the bodice away from the posser, showing off the lace around the sleeves and collar and listening to the four girls comment about the delicate stitching and the beautiful design.

'The skirt has several yards of material in it; as you can recognise there are many layers and folds, it does take some considerable time to create, but of course each of our dresses is tailored to fit if you are all interested. Our stock of material is over here if you care to look and we have a new delivery arriving shortly.' Eliza noticed the delight on each young woman's face as they tittered and gasped between them. 'I can take your measurements now or if you prefer to have your measurements taken in your own home you could perhaps ask your lady's maid to take them for you. I can give you a list of measurements required. That is if you are interested in commissioning a gown.'

'I want this blue dress; it will suit me perfectly. Can you adjust it for me if I find that it does not fit?' Priscilla Eavesham held the bodice to her, and looked triumphantly at her three friends who wished they had got there first.

'Yes, of course, and we will deliver and bill it to Leventhorpe Hall, if you wish. It will suit you perfectly. I should make you aware that the price is a guinea.' Eliza held her breath.

'The price is of no consequence to me, my papa will be paying for it, as long as it makes me happy he will not question the price.' Priscilla looked admiringly at the dress; she'd known she wanted as soon as she'd seen it in the window. The shabby shop belied the mastery of the seamstresses, and both her and Grace had recognised that immediately.

'Oh, Prissy, I wanted it.' Grace wailed. 'After all it was I who brought you here!'

'We have a lovely red brocade fabric that would suit you more, Miss Ellershaw; it would go so well with your dark hair and we could soon put it together for you in a trice, once we have your measurements. Red is a little daring; it would make your sweetheart think you were mysterious and passionate.' Eliza smiled as Priscilla's face dropped, thinking that perhaps she should have looked at the option of a different colour.

'Yes, I see. I don't yet have a sweetheart but if it would make me stand out more during the season ... But I wouldn't want to look too provocative. Well, only to a certain gentleman in my life.' Grace giggled and looked at her friends as she blushed at the thought of James Bland, the man she had had her eye on for some time. 'Could I possibly order myself one and send my size to you with my maid, although the previous dress I purchased/from you fit like a glove if you can remember the measurements.'

'Certainly, whatever you wish, and thank you for your custom once again, it is appreciated.' Eliza smiled and glanced across at Mary-Anne who had returned to her work of mending one of the dresses she had bought from Ma Fletcher and had Jessica and Sarah watching her. 'Can we tempt one of you ladies with a new gown?'

'No, I don't think so at this moment in time.' Jessica turned around and gave Eliza a thin smile before addressing Mary-Anne. 'Is that somebody's offcast that you are mending? I seem to recognise the gown, I'm sure it is the dress that Gertrude Barker was wearing at last year's hunt ball. I remember it because I admired the lace work on the cuffs and that is what you are sewing now.'

Mary-Anne stood up. 'It is indeed, miss. Miss Barker had kindly given it to her maid to throw out or do with as she liked, and I am repairing it for her because, like you, her maid Tilly thought it to be a shame to lay waste such a lovely dress. We also do repairs and mending, though of course most of our work involves Eliza designing and making garments, like the one Miss Eavesham has just purchased.' Mary-Anne knew if they suspected that anything was bought and sold second-hand they would lose their new customers, so covered her tracks with a straight lie, in the hope that not one of the ladies would know the name of Gertrude Barker's maid.

'I see that accounts for the less desirable garments that you have on display on your ... shop. I take it they will eventually be collected by their owners, repaired as good as new?' Jessica gazed around her.

Mary-Anne nodded.

'It is a good service you have for the less fortunate than ourselves. I will tell some of our staff of your services, but I myself will not purchase anything today.' Jessica had an air of arrogance as she looked around the small poky shop and she didn't quite understand what Grace and Priscilla saw in the dresses that they had been so quick to buy. They were pretty enough but she could not overlook her shabby surroundings. Besides, now that she had met Mary-Anne, the common girl who had attracted William Ellershaw's eye, she was not happy. To offer her custom was a step too far.

'Thank you, we will be more than happy to do any mending and alterations that you can send our way, miss,' Mary-Anne said politely, even as she noted Jessica Bentley's cool demeanour towards her.

'Well, I would like to buy these new gloves and I promise to return once I am in need of something.' Sarah Marsden passed Eliza a pair of white crocheted gloves, which their mother had made just before she had died. 'How much are they? I have a little change on me, so there is no need for you to bill me.' Sarah delved into her purse and waited for a reply as Eliza wrapped the gloves up in brown paper and string.

'They are four pence, Miss Marsden, and thank you for your custom.' Eliza smiled and, having wrapped the gloves in brown paper, passed them to the quiet woman who had patiently waited her turn.

'Here, take this sixpence; I'm sure I would have paid all of that if I had bought them in Leeds and they are so beautifully crafted.' Sarah thrust the sixpence into Eliza's hands – Eliza had already upped the price she would have accepted for the gloves but she wasn't about to say no to selling the gloves at almost twice the price.

'Why, thank you miss, that is very much appreciated and we will both look forward to your return.' Eliza smiled at Sarah, not quite believing that she would be willing to pay so much more than the gloves were worth. Apart from the hoity-toity Jessica Bentley, the ladies seemed very willing to overlook the shabby interior of their little shop. Money didn't seem to have any value in these young women's eyes and she didn't feel one bit guilty at charging a guinea for a dress that had cost but a few pence to make. Eliza realised that in an instance their fortunes had changed, these young ladies with their fripperies had put food on the table and saved Mary-Anne from Edmund Bentley, which was all that mattered.

'Yes, we thank you for your patronage, ladies.' Mary-Anne shared a look of relief with her sister. 'If there is anything we can do for you, please let us know. The dress will be delivered to your home, Miss Eavesham, and we will await your maid's instructions, Miss Ellershaw.'

Mary-Anne held the door open ready for the party to leave. As she did the stench from the slaughterhouse hit her nostrils and the sight of the drain running with blood onto the cobbled road from the slaughtered beast made her ashamed of the premises that they were in. She decided, in this instance, that honesty was the best policy.

'I'm sorry, the butcher next door has just slaughtered a cow and I'm afraid we share the same open drain as him. Please take care of your dresses as you leave the shop and avert your eyes from the drain.' Mary-Anne and Eliza watched as the group of well-to-do ladies tried not to show their disgust as they left the shop, holding their dresses well above their ankles and at the same time trying to keep from breathing in the stench from the freshly killed beast that filled the air.

Eliza watched as they walked up the cobbled road, all four dressed in their finery, their skirts and mantels made of the finest materials, better than anything she could ever afford. She listened to them talking and discussing what a disgusting place to have to work in, and laughing about the second-hand clothes in the shop. Her heart dropped as she looked around at the small wooden hut and the now bare dolly tub and posser that adorned the window. They might have sold two dresses and made good money but the look on Jessica Bentley's face had told the real tale. That she thought of them as not worthy of their money and custom, that they were just amusing themselves at their father's expense. How Eliza wished she had been born into money! Had she been so she knew she would not waste her time having tea and fancies and gossiping with friends; she would have made her mark on the world. She sighed as she watched the gossiping group go into the tea room further along the street, the one that Mary-Anne and she had only ever dared to look through the window at.

'Eliza, come in. You must be freezing and don't you feel sick with that smell outside?' Mary-Anne called out to her sister from the doorway as she followed her gaze up the road at their departing customers.

'I'm used to it, unlike the Miss Bentleys of the world.' Eliza pulled her shawl around her and climbed the steps back into the workshop.

'Well, didn't you do well? You've sold the dress and we've got an order for another one from Grace Ellershaw, and the price you charged ...! I couldn't believe my ears and they didn't flinch.' Mary-Anne laughed.

'It isn't their money, though, is it? It's their papas; they aren't bothered. I wish we had money, Mary-Anne. I wish we could afford to run a proper shop in a well-to-do area. I'd give anything to know that every morning when I got up I wasn't going to bed hungry or have to worry about how to pay the rent. It's just not fair; we have more brains than the whole of those four put together and yet look at us. Thinking that we have made a fortune selling two dresses made out of stolen material and that we are now able to pay our way for the next month or two, providing we get payment. I hate this place; it's dirty, it smells and we will never come to anything in a place like this.' Eliza slumped down in her chair and stared out of the window. 'I'm fed up of being poor!'

'But an hour ago, we had next to nothing. Eliza, we will do it, we will turn our lives around. You've got to have faith. Grace Ellershaw and Priscilla Eavesham will wear their new dress to whatever balls they attend and their friends will want one just like theirs and they will have to come to you for their fitting, regardless of the building we are in. This is just the start, dear sister, and it's all because of your skills.' Mary-Anne knelt down and hugged her sister tightly as she sobbed.

'I miss Mamma and I miss our father. Can you remember when we were nippers and we used to play around his feet in here?' Eliza looked up at her sister.

'Yes, and you were always in bother because you'd never be quiet. We can't bring back the past, but we can look to the future and there is hope. Besides, just because they have money doesn't mean they are happy. Just think of Grace Ellershaw, her father is nothing more than a bully and a tyrant, not like our dear departed father. Her life cannot be all roses. She'll probably have to marry the man her parents choose for her.' Mary-Anne held her sister tight. 'Think of your Tom, because he is so sweet on you. I swear he is going to burst if he goes any redder in the face when he speaks of you to me. You have a good man there, one that will love you.' Mary-Anne rose to her feet and looked down at her younger sister who was trying to compose herself.

'I know, I'm just a bit jealous, I want so much for the both of us, but we have so little.' Eliza wiped her nose and sighed. 'At least we can pay the rent this month, so that saves you from that bastard Ellershaw. It's ironic that he will be getting his own money back after his daughter pays us. I hope that she doesn't get into trouble if he finds out … Or at least not before we get our money. I quite like her; she's not such a bad soul.' Eliza looked up at Mary-Anne.

'Yes, she does seem to be the best out of that group, her and Priscilla Eavesham. Perhaps it wouldn't hurt if we looked after those two with more care. You never know, something might come of it. Now, am I delivering the dress to Leventhorpe Hall or are you? And let's get the bill written out; the upper classes are notorious for not paying on time and we need that money. We will put a personal note in with the invoice, thanking her for her custom and saying that we hope she will return.' Mary-Anne sat down and started to parcel the dress. 'I don't think she will be returning it. It looked near a perfect fit, so we have no problem with this one.'

'You take it, Mary-Anne. I'd only come away from the hall feeling truly unworthy, after seeing how the other half live.' Eliza sighed and tried to smile at her sister.

'Don't worry, I'm sure it will be a back-door delivery. I can't see the butler opening the entrance door to me in my finery.' Mary-Anne laughed and mocked a curtsy to her sister. '"Good afternoon, sir, got a dress here made out of nicked cloth from Leeds wharf, made by two penniless trollops who are charging the God's earth and Miss Eavesham has just bought it." You got to laugh, Eliza. Things will get better, I promise. Let's face it, they can't get any worse than what we've already been through.' Mary-Anne tied the string tight and pulled her shawl over her shoulders after enclosing the invoice and note giving their thanks for the purchase.

'I'll be back in time for supper, so leave me some of that stew. The walk will do me good and will get me away from the smell of that drain, it is really making me feel quite ill.' Mary-Anne picked up the parcel and invoice and opened the door. 'Cheer up, we've done well today. Get a move on with that dress that you are holding, the dolly tub is looking cold in the window.' Grinning at her own cheek, she walked out of the door and made her way down the street, leaving Eliza looking at the dolly tub display in the window, which she now thought quite frankly looked ridiculous.

Well, you did your job, you sold the dress, she thought, as she moved the posser and the tub. Perhaps we could run to another tailor's dummy for the window, although even the one I use for measurements looks past its best.

Eliza glanced at the moth-eaten dummy in the corner of the room.

If only I had money ... the things I could do, she thought. But I don't think I will, no matter what our Mary-Anne says. My only hope is John Vasey and the material he brings. I hope Mary-Anne keeps him sweet for both our sakes.

'Good afternoon, we meet again.' William Ellershaw stepped down from his carriage just in front of the hurrying Mary-Anne.

'Good afternoon, Mr Ellershaw.' Mary-Anne stopped in her tracks and pulled her shawl tight around her, hoping that the conversation with her attacker's son would not take long.

'In a hurry, I see. May I join you in your walk? A spot of fresh air would serve me well before I join my sister and her group of friends for tea. Any longer than a half hour of their giggling, I'm afraid, makes me weary and as they have been known to spend all the afternoon gossiping over their tea, you would be a welcome diversion.' With his long black cane, top-hat and his elegant dress coat partly hiding the glint of a gold pocket watch hanging from his breast pocket, William Ellershaw was the very image of a well-dressed young gent, just yards away from the small tea-room that his sister was having tea in with her friends.

Mary-Anne watched as the carriage and team of horses pulled away, leaving her alone with the young man that was looking her up and down with some interest.

'If you don't mind, sir, I'm not out for a walk … I have to run an errand.'

'Yes, where are you off to in such a rush? And pray tell what is that package under your arm?'

'I'm off to Leventhorpe Hall, sir. Miss Eavesham, a friend of your sister, has just bought a dress from us and I am about to deliver it, sir.' Mary-Anne hardly dare look at the young man that stood in her way, thinking only of the demeaning manner in which his father had used towards her, at the same time feeling she had to explain her movements to him.

'Has she now? And no doubt my sister did the same and expected you to deliver and wait of your money.' William looked at the beautiful young woman who stood in front of him and saw her trembling either with the cold or fear – which one he wasn't sure.

'Yes, I'm to deliver and invoice Miss Eavesham, but your sister has yet to send her maid with her measurements and then we will deliver and invoice her, once her gown is ready. It really is no problem sir.'

'Ah, but it is a problem, my dear. You will have already paid out good money for the material, not taking into consideration the time that it has taken you to make the garment. Please let me pay you for both gowns now, as I know my sister will definitely want the dress you will make her. As for the Eaveshams … let us say, not everything is always as it seems and you may be waiting a long time for your money. It can be my treat for Priscilla and that headstrong sister of mine, and I will see that this dress gets delivered when I escort Miss Eavesham back in my carriage.' William reached into his pocket and took out his coin holder. 'How much do they owe you?'

'Really, sir, it is not your debt. I feel I cannot accept,' Mary-Anne protested.

'You will be doing me a service if you let me pay. I will win the respect of Miss Eavesham and save her from the embarrassment of her father not being able to pay you at this moment in time. And, as for my sister ... well, what can I say? She's my sister and is always there for me. I'm sure you can understand.' William smiled and waited for Mary-Anne to reply.

'They are a guinea each, sir, and I am much beholden to you for paying for them both.' Mary-Anne looked up at the man who was counting his money out in front of her, without quibbling.

'I do have one stipulation.' William passed the two guineas to Mary-Anne and took the parcel from her.

Mary-Anne turned pale. Was he going to expect the same of her as is father had? 'I beg your pardon, sir?'

'That is you come and join me for tea with these infernal women who think of me as either the target for their quips and japes or some prize to be won. I really don't stand a chance against them. You can be their centre of attention for once.' William laughed mischievously as he closed his money pouch and looked at the face of the girl he was enamoured with. Taking a girl like this to tea would put his sister's friends entirely out of sorts but he also found that he wanted to spend time with her.

'Oh, I couldn't, sir,' Mary-Anne protested. 'It's not right. I'm not dressed ... I wouldn't know what to do ...'

'You are perfect. Come, take my arm and help me survive the afternoon. Mrs Brookes' cream scones are first class, you must have one of those and a slice of her caraway cake. I just can't get enough.'

William held his arm out and linked Mary-Anne's through it. 'Come now, don't let them intimidate you with their noise and looks. They are harmless creatures, believe me.'

Mary-Anne looked up at the handsome dark-haired man on her arm and couldn't quite believe the situation she was in. She breathed in deeply and stepped out hoping that she would not be like Daniel thrown into the lion's den and that she would not be prey for the jabbering women having afternoon tea.

'Well, that didn't take you as long as I feared. You've only been gone a good hour. You can't have delivered it yet. It's quite a walk to the Hall.' Eliza raised her head from her sewing and glanced up at the flushed face of her sister.

'Rest assured it is delivered and I've got the money for both dresses, a full two guineas.' Mary-Anne took the money out of her pocket and placed it on the table in front of Eliza, holding her breath as her sister gasped at the sight of the gold coins.

'How did you manage that? I haven't even started on the second dress yet but you've been paid for it?' Eliza looked from the coins to her sister's face. 'You haven't been up to anything you'll regret, have you? Because there's no need for you to do that.'

'No, I'll never do that again. I was just on my way to deliver the dress when William Ellershaw stopped me. It seems them at Leventhorpe Hall are not as wealthy as we thought and he insisted that he paid for both dresses as a gift to both his sister and for Priscilla, whom I think he must be sweet on. He then asked me to accompany him to tea at Mrs Brookes' tea room where his sister and friends were at. I couldn't say no, he wouldn't let me! You should have seen their faces when I walked in!' Mary-Anne grinned and sat down in her chair. 'I'm so full, I could do with getting out of this corset.'

'You've had tea with all that snobby lot, while I've been sat here my fingers nearly raw from pulling this bloody needle through this thick brocade? I don't suppose you gave me a second thought and brought me back a bit of cake or something.' Eliza looked across at her sister with a smile on her face.

'No, not a thing. It didn't seem proper to ask for seconds for you! But what I do have is an order for a mantle from Jessica Bentley, who, when she realised that William had paid for Priscilla Eavesham's dress, wanted to be part of the spending frenzy. But I rather think William will not be paying for her order – she will have to pay for it herself – as his eyes were on wooing Priscilla. Although I did keep catching him gazing at me, which made me slightly uneasy and I did worry when he first proposed that I joined them for tea, not quite knowing what his motive was.'

'Bloody hell, Mary-Anne! Yesterday we had nowt all on to live, and now we've enough money to get us through to the autumn if we are careful, especially with the sale of the mantle, if she pays for it.' Eliza gazed out of the window.

'She will because they all do as Grace Ellershaws says as they are all desperately trying to catch her brother for a husband.' Mary-Anne sighed.

'But he's so arrogant.' Eliza suddenly looked way concerned. 'He didn't force himself on you in anyway?'

'No, not at all. He was a true gentleman, not at all like his father.' Mary-Anne smiled.

'Oh, lawks, don't you look like that. Remember your place, Mary-Anne. His intentions are not going to be honest, are they? He'll wed one of those simpering girls but he won't be adverse to getting you into bed. Forget him, Mary-Anne, and remember what his father did to you. He can't be all good with a father like that; just enjoy his money and forget about him.' Eliza warned.

'I'll try but he is a gentleman no matter what you say.'

'A wolf in sheep's clothing, more like. And I bet he only took you to tea to cause trouble … I'm willing to bet our two guineas he's a wrong 'un. Stick to John Vasey, he's more our kind.' Eliza tutted.

'You are only jealous.' Mary-Anne laughed.

'Jealous that you've got a full belly of tea and cake and I'm left with mutton stew and nothing to smile about except work,' Eliza grumbled.

Nineteen

Edmund Ellershaw looked up at the most hated man in his employ. 'Well, who owes me this month? I suppose those hussies at Pit Lane haven't managed the rent.' Edmund put his pen down and waited for an answer.

'Aye, they have,' replied Fred Bailey, Edmund Ellershaw's tally-man. 'In fact the eldest one was waiting of me, and she asked me to give you this note.' His hand shook as he passed it across the desk to his employer. He might be fearsome in extracting money from Ellershaw's tenants but in the presence of his employer he was a coward. Besides, a note from a tenant usually meant one of two things: they were either begging for clemency for paying the next month's rent or they were leaving. Either way, Edmund Ellershaw would lose his temper. However, Mary-Anne had handed him this note after paying the rent and with a look of satisfaction on her face that Fred knew did not bode well. He had been sorely tempted to open it and read the contents, especially in view of the gossip about the past history of her late mother and his employer but he'd thought better of it when he noticed it was in a sealed envelope, intent on keeping its contents private.

'Go on, bugger off. You've done your job. Take your pay and leave me be.' Edmund passed over the few coppers he paid the quivering man, and looked at the note in his hands, waiting until Fred had left his office to open it.

'Yes, sir. Thank you, sir.' Fred tugged on his forelock and was thankful to leave the office before the letter was read.

Edmund tore open the envelope and retrieved the note:

By now you will have realised that we have managed to pay this month's rent. So our 'understanding' has come to an end. As long as I have breath in my body, you will never lay another finger on me again. I've also sent the coal you supplied back today. The least I have to do with you the better and unlike my mother I will not be used or belittled by you.

Edmund screwed the note up and swore. Where the hell had the bitch got the money to pay her rent from? He had enjoyed his romp with such a young body under him and looked forward to her next visit where she traded her dignity in lieu of the rent. The bitch had even returned the coal that he'd sent, so she must be sure of her money. Her mother had been easy prey, eager to do anything to keep a roof over the family home and her useless husband in work, but her daughter was stronger willed and headstrong, more of a challenge.

He threw the note and envelope into his waste bin and swore again, and then looked at his rent book. He'd raise the rent on number one Pit Lane. Let's see how she'd like that and see how long she could keep paying her rent then. An extra penny a week would make her worry. Stupid bitch, did she not know he always got what he wanted? Edmund grinned as he altered his rent book; he'd send Fred back with a note of his own about the rent increase and then Mary-Anne would be back in his bed next month, come hell or high water.

'This coal burns better than the last lot we had.' Eliza poked the fire and sat back taking in the warmth of the fire.

'Yes, and it was cheaper.' Mary-Anne sat reading the paper next to the fire and answered Eliza in a bright voice. 'From what I've heard, the new manager at the Nibble and Clink pit is more of a gentleman than Edmund Ellershaw will ever be. His foreman told me a lot of people are turning to him for their coal because they dislike Ellershaw's ways; seemingly he does have a bad reputation.'

'Bill used to be always playing hell about the Rose, but I must admit I never took no notice of his rantings. If it wasn't the Rose he was moaning about it was something else, but it would seem he was right to moan about Ellershaw. I don't know why he didn't go and work for the Nibble and Clink; it's not that far away, just between the canal and railway line. In fact, I think it is even closer than the Rose as the crow flies.' Eliza looked across at her sister.

'Yes, but they don't pay as well, I don't think, and the previous manger didn't look after the safety side. Can't you remember when the pit's cage was brought up too fast, hitting the headstock and making it plummet nearly two hundred yards below, killing the two men within it?'

'I remember, the incident nearly caused a riot.' Mary-Anne looked up from her newspaper. 'Bill hadn't a good word for anyone who worked there. The inquest that followed said that the winding engine man had been drunk and he'd previously been in prison for manslaughter for a similar incident at Glasshoughton. I remember reading it in this very paper and that's why he never worked there.' Mary-Anne put her paper down and looked into the fire.

'Well, Bill was often drunk when he went to work. In fact there would be more days when he was drunk than sober. I don't know how he managed to keep his job.' Eliza sighed. 'Our poor mother, what she had to put up with.'

'What do you mean, Eliza?' Mary-Anne asked her sharply, full of panic. She had taken care to keep her knowledge of the arrangement between her mother and Edmund Ellershaw to herself but could someone else have let something slip?

'Just that Bill was never good with her once he'd had a drink. She must have feared for her life sometimes and always worried that he might come home without a job. Bill couldn't have been that good at his job, else Edmund Ellershaw would have sacked him, and a drunk man is no good down the pit.'

'Just be thankful he didn't, else we would have been out on the streets and Bill wouldn't have cared. I sometimes think he would have been glad to see our mother and us put into the workhouse, once he'd worked his way through Father's savings.' Mary-Anne cast her mind back to the times when they were younger when she and Eliza had laid in their beds listening to Bill ranting and raving in drink and threatening to throw them all out on the street. If Eliza ever knew the sacrifice that their mother had made to keep her husband in work and a roof over their heads, she'd do more than curse Bill; she would probably kill him if she could find him.

'Those days are behind us now; we are women of means. Isn't it good to be able to sit back and enjoy the warmth with a full stomach and our rent paid? I hope that we will always be able to do this.' Eliza curled her toes around the fender, bathing in the warmth.

'Yes, so do I, but it won't always be like this, we won't always be together. Tom, I'm sure, will eventually ask you for your hand, don't think I haven't noticed the correspondence that's been going on between you both. The poor devil must know his way to this door blindfolded. When are you to see him next? I can make myself scarce if you want the house to yourselves, or perhaps you would be better with a chaperone, to keep an eye on you both.' Mary-Anne tried to keep her face straight as Eliza looked horrified.

'He's coming to see me on Friday evening; his mother goes and plays cards with the next-door neighbour on a Friday. So he's going to sneak out for an hour. Can you leave us on our own or at least stay in here while I entertain in the parlour?' Eliza pleaded with her sister.

'Entertain in the parlour! That sounds saucy, I think I'd better sit between you both like a gooseberry,' Mary-Anne teased.

'Oh, Mary-Anne don't be a spoilsport, I wouldn't do that to you. It's bad enough that his mother rules his life without you ruling mine. I don't know why she dislikes me so much, she's never even met me.' Eliza sighed.

'I'm only having you on. You do what you want with Tom the mummy's boy. If he loves you he will have to stand up to his mother sometime; either that or he'll make you wait until you are an old maid and she snuffs it.' Mary-Anne yawned and folded her newspaper away. 'I'll stay in the kitchen on Friday if you stay out of the way next time John Vasey visits. Because I can't see William Ellershaw knocking on our door any time soon. And to be honest the more I think about him, the more I think about what his father did so I don't even want to see him again.'

'It would be nice to have a choice?' Eliza whispered.

'It's not much of a choice, though, is it?' Mary-Anne looked across at her sister. 'A penniless Irishman or the son of my attacker, and I think the latter is only in my dreams, or perhaps I should say my nightmares.'

'Yes, you are better not thinking of him. Let him court the snobby Priscilla and we will move on with our lives. You with John Vasey and me with Tom and we will just take the money that Grace Ellershaw and her friends are willing to send our way.' Eliza looked at the sadness that had suddenly clouded her sister's face. 'Things will get better, believe me. They have already.'

Mary-Anne patted her sister's shoulder. 'I know ... I'm going to bed. I'm tired. Lock up, and I'll wind the clock up.' Mary-Anne kissed her sister gently on the cheek and walked over to the grandfather clock that stood in the hallway. She opened the door on the case and pulled on the chains and weight that operated the cogs that kept the pendulum ticking. She closed the door and looked up at the smiling moon's face that adorned the clock's face. It was the one remaining item that reminded her of better times when their father had been alive; everything else had been pawned or sold to keep the wolf from the door. 'I'm glad you have no worries, because I think mine are just starting,' she whispered to the moon before she climbed up the stairs to bed. If only life would be straightforward and simple for once.

'Not off home, lad?' Bert Simms walked up Pit Lane with his young foreman by his side on his way home from his shift.

'No, I've had a quick wash at the pit and made myself presentable and now I'm going to call on Eliza, so I'm going the same way as you for a change.' Tom walked with a swagger in his step.

'Oh, I see. Are you sweet on the lass? Now, wait, when I think about it, my missus told me she'd seen you walking out with her after chapel one time.' Bert stepped out faster trying to keep up with the eager young man who had his head set on seeing his girl.

'Aye, she's a grand lass, and so bonny. Don't you think so, Mr Simms? You must see a bit of her, with living next door?' Tom turned and looked at the elderly man who he worked with and knew was respected within the colliery.

'Well, we did, but her and the wife fell out a bit over a misunderstanding and she's had nowt to do with us since that. What does your mother think of you setting your cap at her?' Bert couldn't help but ask; he'd heard Tom Thackeray's mother was set in her ways and wouldn't like her son walking out with such a lass as Eliza. She'd want more for her only lad.

'She's not happy, she thinks I could do better for myself. Trouble is she's listened to the gossip about Eliza's mother and Mr Ellershaw, and thinks she will be like her. I've told her it's only gossip!' Tom sighed.

'I don't know, lad, there's usually no smoke without fire and you know and I know her mother was as regular as clockwork visiting that office of Ellershaw, you'll have seen her there more than me what with being the foreman.' Bert slowed down in his walk and caught his breath.

'She preferred to pay her rent in person, so I was told, rather than have Fred knocking on her door. That's why Mr Ellershaw always asked me to leave the office when he saw her coming; she had her pride.' Tom stopped in his tracks and watched as Bert caught his breath.

'Sorry, lad, it's the coal dust. The bloody stuff's got on my lungs and it slows me down nowadays. I think we both know it was more than that. Edmund Ellershaw is a bastard and I think it was more a lack of pride that sent Eliza's mother to see him. Your mother's right, you could do better. We saw Eliza once saying goodbye to a man at dawn on her doorstep. Now I wouldn't have said anything to you, but you are worth more than Eliza Wild. Wild by name and wild by nature; neither lasses have many morals from what I can see.' Bert looked at the deflated youth in front of him, feeling a slight pang of guilt for telling him what he had witnessed, but at the same time the lad had to be saved from a trollop.

Tom was taken aback by Bert's news. 'I think you'll find you are wrong, Mr Simms. My Eliza would never do that to me. She loves me, she's said so in her letters. I think your eyes must have deceived you.'

'Well, make of it what you will, lad. All I'm saying is take care when it comes to the Wild lasses, they aren't as innocent as you think.' Bert set off on the last few yards home and noted that Tom's steps next to him were not as fervent and that he had gone quiet. 'Night, lad, see you in the morning.' Bert left Tom at the gates to the cottages noticing his hesitation as he opened the garden gate of number one. He felt bad telling the lad the truth, but the going on next door didn't sit right with him and his Ada. They'd opened their house to them when they were in need and look how they'd been treated, just because his Ada had commented on Eliza's conduct. Anyway, whatever the lad did, on his own head be it. At least he had been warned.

Tom hesitated before he knocked on Eliza's door. Bert Simms had sowed a seed of doubt and it wasn't the first time Eliza and her sister had been the centre of gossip. It was true that they were tougher than some of the more gentle young women of the district, but that, along with their looks, was the attraction to Tom; he liked their forthright ways.

He stood for a second and then raised the knocker on the cottage door. He'd choose to forget what the old codger said, everyone knew that his wife was a gossip and as straight-laced as one could be. Eliza was true to him of that he was sure. He loved his Eliza and had done for a long time; no gossip was going to put him off from the girl he eventually wanted to marry.

His heart raced when he heard the door being opened and all memories of Bert's conversation was wiped from his head when Eliza welcomed him with a kiss as he passed over the threshold.

No, the old man was wrong; she loved him only and no amount of gossip was going to part them.

Twenty

Mary-Anne was filling the copper boiler with cold water but halfway through had to sit down, resting the empty enamel jug at her feet. She felt faint and sickly and not herself. She breathed in deeply.

The fire beneath the boiler cracked and sparked; it needed further fuelling with coal. Mary-Anne fought the nausea that was building up in her. She stood up and stepped outside the outhouse and breathed in the fresh spring air, trying to quell her natural instincts of expelling her stomach's contents. It was to no avail as she retched and was sick down the drain in the yard.

She wiped her hand across her mouth and breathed in, steadying herself against the red-brick wall of the outhouse and felt like crying. She knew all too well what was wrong with her; she'd seen her mother felled by the same condition and now realised why.

She was with child, fathered by the bastard Edmund Ellershaw, as nobody else had ever touched her. She shook with fear as she remembered her mother's death, looking across at the outside privy, understanding now her mother's desperation. She didn't want the baby that grew in her belly; it was a mistake she could never love.

Life was just beginning to move in the right direction after the year's heartbreak and now her world had been shattered.

'Mary-Anne, what's wrong? Are you not well?' Eliza came out into the backyard after seeing her sister being sick from the kitchen window.

'No, I'm fine.' Mary-Anne, tears in her eyes, shook with the upset of her realisation. 'Really, don't worry.' Looking at her sister, she knew Eliza was sure she was lying.

'I don't think you are. You are never sick.' Eliza returned with the empty enamel jug and filled it with water from the yards pump, swilling the drain free of the contents of Mary-Anne's stomach. She then went back, and added a quick shovelful of coal to the kindling sticks under the boiler that was struggling to keep burning. 'Right, come on, the washing can wait till the water's hot. Come into the kitchen and talk to me, you've looked peaky and have been quiet for a week or two.' Eliza put her arm around her sister and smiled at her ashen-white sister.

'Eliza, I don't know what to do. I've missed a few of my monthlies and just look at my belly! I'm carrying Edmund Ellershaw's baby and I don't want it.' Mary-Anne broke down in tears as she sat down at the kitchen table. 'I can't have the child of a man I don't love! My life was just beginning to look a bit brighter. I hate the bastard for doing this to me.' Mary-Anne sobbed.

Eliza squatted down by the side of her sister and put an arm around her, comforting her by holding her tight and kissing her head. 'Aye, no more tears, we will sort something out. You might be wrong; you might just be tired. I'm not always regular ...' Eliza tried to give her sister hope, but in truth she knew that Mary-Anne would not be wrong in her diagnosis.

'No, I am expecting. I know I am, it's no good ignoring it.' Mary-Anne raised her head and look at her younger sister. 'What a bloody mess. I'll go and confront Edmund Ellershaw with my news; he might have the decency to even pay for me someone to get rid of it, if I'm lucky. Because I don't think I will ever be able to show any love towards this child.'

'Don't go there, Mary-Anne; you know he'll only insult you. He's no heart. Why, he even put our rent up last month because he knew we'd paid it the month before and wanted us to fail so he could either use you or throw us out of our home. He's a heartless bastard and I hate him.' Eliza was furious.

'Well, he didn't get his way, did he? And won't as long as we keep getting the support of his daughter and her followers. But I am going to tackle him; after all this baby is his. It's not like I've lifted my skirts for anybody else. He might do right by us both and actually offer me some means of security for this child of his I'm carrying or at least pay for a backstreet remedy for me.' Mary-Anne lifted her head but knew the words she spoke were empty. She had realised how her mother had been treated by him in the past, and knew exactly what reception she would get if she confronted him, but that she would keep to herself.

'Do you want me to come with you, Mary-Anne? It would be better if we were both together. I could tell him exactly what we think of him, the dirty old bastard.'

'And you'd only rile him into raising our rent more or throwing us out onto the street. No, I'll go on my own and if I don't get anywhere, I'll have to think what to do. There's always Aunt Patsy. She'd be able to help, although I don't want John Vasey to know my predicament.' Mary-Anne hung her head. She'd been waiting for another visit from the quiet-spoken man but he had never shown his face, and she had not seen him on further visits into Leeds, his absence making her realise that she did have feelings for him after all. But now she was ruined.

'Not Aunt Patsy, not since our mother!' Eliza cried. 'I know it was partly our fault, we forgot to tell her the tincture was strong, but I don't trust her potions anymore and I couldn't bear to lose you the same way as her.' Eliza held out her hand and fought back her tears.

'It hasn't come to that.' Mary-Anne squeezed her hand. 'I'll go to the Rose tomorrow and see what Edmund Ellershaw says; surely he should take some responsibility.' Mary-Anne tried to sound positive for the sake of her sister.

'He better had.' Eliza looked unconvinced. 'But my main concern is you my dear sister, you must take care.'

Mary-Anne felt the warmth of the early sun on her face, warming her as she walked along the lane to Rose Pit. It was the beginning of spring and the birds were singing loudly, attracting mates for the nesting season. She looked over at a bank of primroses that were just beginning to show between the brambles that ran the length of the lane. She would have normally stopped to pick a bunch and taken the time to admire the loveliness of the day. However, today, no matter how the sun shone, it could not lift her mood. All she could think about was the child she was carrying, and the predicament she was in, and facing Edmund Ellershaw.

She knew she was dragging her feet as she neared the colliery yard. There she stopped to watch the pithead wheel turning, lowering or returning men to or from the bowels of the earth where the black gold lay. It was responsible for keeping most of the residents of Woodlesford, Rothwell and Oulton in work and their families fed, its dark seams running as far under the ground as Wakefield.

Some of the mines and their owners were well respected, while other ones had bad reputations for unsafe practices or hard, uncaring owners. The later was true of the Rose; the pit was run well, but everyone knew that Ellershaw was a hard, manipulating bastard. A bastard whose child Mary-Anne was now carrying.

She felt her legs nearly buckle from under her as she watched Tom leave the hut that acted as the office and saw Edmund close the door after him. He was on his own; now was the time to confront him.

As she set of across the yard, she wondered how many times her mother had done the same thing as she was doing. Had it been just the once or was it a regular occurrence? How many babies had she disposed of, unwanted and unloved, after the bastard having his way? She caught her breath as she opened the paint-worn door and stepped into the office to tackle the man she hated.

'By hell, you must be eager to see me. You are a week early if you are here to pay this month's rent in kind.' Edmund sat back in his chair and grinned at the lass he'd known would have to return to him at some time.

'I'm not here to pay the rent. Your man will get his money when he calls and always will do as long as we live there, no matter how much you put our rent up.' Mary-Anne looked at the foul man and picked up the courage to tell him the reason for her visit. 'I'm here because I'm carrying your child and I've come to see what you are going to do about it.' Mary-Anne looked at the face that did not flinch an inch.

'Do about it! Why should I do anything about it? Just because you've got caught doesn't mean it's anything to do with me. It could be any Tom, Dick or Harry's from what I hear. You've had a man stopping at your house anyway, go and tell him your sorry tale.' Edmund sat back and laughed. 'By, you've a brass neck, I'll give you that. Accusing me of being the father ... after my money, are you?'

'You know what you did to me. I was an innocent ... I've never ... You know this baby is yours. At least you could pay to get rid of it.' Mary-Anne stood her ground, actually saying the words that she'd been thinking on her walk to confront him.

'I know you're like your bloody whore of a mother. Don't you come wailing to me. You knew what you were doing when you opened your legs, just like she did. I didn't hear you complaining when coal was delivered to your door and you kept your roof over your head. Just get rid of it like your mother did and bugger off.' Edmund stood up and opened the door, grabbing hold of Mary-Anne's arm and shoving her towards the door. 'And hold your tongue, if you know what's good for you, else you will be out on the streets, I'll guarantee you that.'

'But you know it's yours. I was a good girl, I've not been with anyone else.' Mary-Anne clung on to his arm to no avail as he threw her out of his office and down onto the ground.

'Keep your mouth shut, else it will be the worse for you bitch,' Edmund warned again before slamming his door closed, leaving Mary-Anne prostrate on the floor outside.

She lay there for a second or two, reviewing the situation and wondering if she had the nerve to tackle the heartless man again, but she knew her breath would be wasted so she stood herself up and dusted her skirt down from the clinker and dust that littered the yard.

'Mary-Anne, are you all right?' Tom walked around the corner of the office and rushed to her side as he noticed her picking herself up from the floor.

'Yes, I'm fine. I just fell down the steps as I came out from my meeting with Mr Ellershaw. I should have been more careful.' Mary-Anne felt embarrassed that Tom had witnessed her fall and that he had found her visiting the office.

'Are things all right? Have you a problem with the rent?' Tom was racking his head as to why Mary-Anne should be visiting the pithead.

'No, no, I just wanted to leave a message for his daughter, Grace. She was supposed to send Eliza some measurements and she's forgotten.' Mary-Anne lied and smiled as she turned to leave Tom.

'You'll be lucky if he gives that to her, I don't think he's keen on his daughter spending his money at your shop. He's always growling about her expenses.' Tom stood on the steps of the office but couldn't help but notice that while Mary-Anne smiled at him she looked worried and not her usual self. 'Are Eliza and you are all right? Nothing wrong? I'll try and get to see Eliza this Sunday after chapel. Can you tell her?'

'Yes, we are both fine. Still finding it a little hard, now we are on our own, but that is only to be expected. Eliza says she now doesn't want to go to the chapel since we lost our mother and I can take it or leave it; it's a pity because she could meet you there instead of having to sneak behind your mother's back to come to our house.' Mary-Anne felt sorry for Tom; his mother ruled his life and he was torn between doing her wishes and following his heart.

'One day she will understand and come around to my seeing Eliza. She still thinks I'm only young, she forgets that her and Father had been married for three years when she was my age.' Tom sighed. 'I'll have to get a move on. Sorry, Mary-Anne.'

'No, it's fine. I'm just going to make my way home. I might go back along the canal, it's such a grand day.' Mary-Anne picked her skirts up as she picked her way through the yard, leaving Tom to enter into the lair of Edmund Ellershaw.

Mary-Anne walked along the bank of the Leeds to Liverpool canal, lost in her thoughts. Her mind was racing with fear and worry. How was she ever going to cope with bringing a baby into the world with no support from the man who had got her into trouble? She didn't want it, and life was hard enough for her and Eliza without another mouth to feed. Life as she knew it was over and she'd give the gossips like Ada Simms more ammunition to fire at both her and Eliza once her predicament was common knowledge. She might as well end it here and now, because there was nothing left in her life.

How stupid she had been to be used by the bastard Ellershaw; his sort would always win over the likes of her. She stood on the lock that spanned the canal and looked into the depths of the waters below. The wooden, movable bridge felt unsteady under her feet and she thought how easy it would be just to fall into the waters and for some unknown bargehand to fish her out and wonder who she was and how she had ended up there. Was this the way out of her dilemma? Nobody would really miss her. Eliza had Tom; she'd end up wed to him, regardless of his mother's objections.

She breathed in deeply and looked up the canal in the direction of Woodlesford and the railway line, her back towards the pit and Leeds city. She watched as two ducks busily carried reeds and grass to a nest they were making together in readiness of their brood that they were expecting shortly. A true family, something that she would never have. Looking around her at the beautiful spring's day, she took a deep breath before she lay her shawl on to the handle that pushed the lock open, her eyes filled with tears as she made her decision. With her heart beating loudly she asked for forgiveness from the Lord that she didn't really believe in, and looked around at His creation on her last day on his earth. It was better that she ended it this way, her and the baby dead together, instead of the horrible death her mother and the child she'd carried had undergone. She held her breath . . .

'Mary-Anne, Mary-Anne, stop! What are you doing?' John Vasey yelled as he saw Mary-Anne leaning over the wooden bridge, looking like she was about to throw herself into the canal. He dropped the new reams of material he was about to deliver to the sisters and ran to where she stood shaking on the bridge. Tears ran down her face and her body was trembling.

'Tell me I'm wrong? Were you really going to throw yourself in? You'd have gone straight to the bottom with all those layers of skirts and petticoats. Why do such a thing, Mary-Anne? Surely life is not that bad?' John put his arms around her and held her quivering body next to him. Smelling her hair and thinking how wonderful it was to hold her next to him, even as his concern over her state of mind and what had made her take such a terrible decision grew.

'I ... I ... I've just had enough. I can't see any point in carrying on. I miss my mother and life is so hard.' Mary-Anne cried into his shoulder and shook, partly wishing that he had left her to get on with it and partly regretting now she had even thought of taking her own life.

'Mary-Anne, it is the biggest sin of all to take your own life. You'd be burning in the fires of hell if I hadn't have been here to stop you. How can you be so down on life? You are young and beautiful with all your life in front of you. Your mother wouldn't have wanted to see you like this and what would Eliza do without you?' John held her face in his hands and kissed her on the cheek as tears rolled down her face. 'Not to say how much I'd regret your passing. I had a feeling I'd met my match in life and haven't been able to stop thinking about you.' John held her firm as she sobbed on his shoulder.

'I've been a fool; it's just I had a black moment and felt I had no one to turn to. My thoughts had got me into a dark place and I could not escape them.' Mary-Anne held John close and didn't want to leave his arms, not wanting to look into the eyes that seemed to be able to read her soul.

'Well, I'm here for you now, and always will be while you need me. I'd have been here earlier but I've been working nights down at the wharf, so it's been all sleep and work.' John gently held Mary-Anne away from him. 'Now, dry those eyes, give me a smile and we will not talk about what very nearly happened this morning. The least Eliza knows about this the better, she would only be upset and watch your every move and we can't have that as I hope to be seeing a bit more of you – alone. We don't need a chaperone.' John smiled and wiped a tear away for Mary-Anne's cheek.

'No, please don't say anything to Eliza; I wouldn't want her to worry. She can't know how I feel. After all it was just a low moment that over took me.' Mary-Anne coughed, catching her breath, and tried to compose herself.

'Are you sure you're all right now?' John looked at Mary-Anne and stood back, allowing her time to control the sobs that had shook her body.

Mary-Anne sniffed and found her handkerchief, blowing her nose loudly.

'I've got something that will make Eliza's day. One of the fashion houses in Leeds had a delivery, but strangely enough they might find themselves short of a few boards of their material, and I helped myself to a pattern book or two that was bound for the same house. I thought it would give her some ideas and keep her out of mischief. I'll go and pick them up, I dropped them when I saw what you were up to. You'll not do anything stupid while I go and retrieve them?' John looked worriedly at Mary-Anne and held her arm.

Mary-Anne shook her head. 'No, I'm all right now. Like I said, it was just a moment of weakness. I'm better now ... I'll walk to the towpath with you.' Mary-Anne reached for her shawl before walking across the bridge with John who retrieved the stolen boards of material from among the brambles and grasses they had fallen into along the canal's edge.

She felt embarrassed and slightly stupid that she had been found in such a state, but at the same time she felt excited at the words of affection that John Vasey had said to her. However, that did not resolve her predicament of the baby, and it would certainly complicate her friendship with John if she were to tell him the truth about her low spirits. But now she realised that whatever she had to face, suicide was not the answer, and maybe there was a life to look forward to – perhaps even with John Vasey, if she had not misread the feelings between them.

'Oh, these materials are wonderful, I've never seen such fine and delicate fabric.' Eliza was excited as she felt the rich fabrics beneath her fingertips. She turned her attention to one of the purloined pattern books and read the heading: HAUTE COUTURE FROM THE HOUSE OF WORTH. 'What's "Haute Couture"? I've never heard of it ... sounds a bit posh. Just look at some of the dresses in here!'

'I think it's French, but look at this advertisement – it looks like they make lots of dresses in different sizes for people to come and look at, instead of making them to the person's sizing, so they can take them away with them then and there.' Mary-Anne flicked through the pages of the patterns. 'Though don't be thinking that we can go down that route; we haven't the money, and just look at how intricate and decorated these dresses are.'

'I'm sorry if I've put temptation in your path, I didn't mean to,' John said with a smile. 'I just thought that you may appreciate an insight in to how the other half lives. Especially now Mary-Anne has told me that you have some of society's ladies buying from you. Sure, this sort of thing is bound to be up their street.' John sat back and enjoyed the grins on both girls' faces as he supped his tea. Despite Eliza's joy at his offering, he was still worried about her sister. If he'd been a minute or two later along the towpath, it could have been so different. Things did not seem to quite add up as he talked to Mary-Anne on their way back home. She'd less worries financially than she had on his previous visit, and, overall, she and Eliza seemed to have dealt with the death of their mother well. So why contemplate taking her life? Something was not quite right.

'Just listen to this, Mary-Anne.' Eliza giggled and read an extract from the brochure.

'"The perfect dress for the girl trying to win a suitor's hand. The sheer gauze embellished with silk flowers and frills of tulle show how pure the wearer is." What a load of rubbish.'

'If you say so, Eliza.' Mary-Anne blushed and quickly glanced at John, hoping Eliza would say no more about the wearer of such a dress.

'Seemingly they suggest that you replace your gauze dress after two wearings as the material is so sheer and requires a lot of attention. But the wearing of it makes you feel so special it is worth the price. How the other half lives, indeed; my Sunday best dress is at least two years old, and I'll still be wearing it this time next year too.' Eliza put the brochure down and looked across at John, who had not taken his eyes off Mary-Anne since they had arrived together. 'We haven't seen you for a while, Mr Vasey; I swear my sister was wondering where you had got to.' Eliza's eyes shone with mischief as she looked across at the quiet Irish man.

193

'As I explained to Mary-Anne, I've been working nights. I need to make money for my passage to America later in the year. I've also told you both to call me John, let's not be standing on ceremony. Besides, I aim to see more of your sister if she's willing.' John looked across at Mary-Anne and waited for a response.

'That would be most agreeable,' Mary-Anne said quietly, and looked up at her saviour.

'It would. Just so long as you remember to bring more material on your visits,' Eliza agreed cheekily.

'Eliza, stop thinking of your pocket. John will be welcome regardless. Do come, with or without material, John.' Mary-Anne glared at her young sister.

'Well, I'll have to be away now. I need some shut-eye before my next shift. Your Aunt Patsy asks to be remembered, by the way. She says you've to call in next time you are doing business in Leeds.' John reached for his cap from off the back of the chair, placing it on his head as he stood up in front of both women.

'I'll see you out, John.' Mary-Anne bowed her head and walked to the doorway. 'I'll not come outside. When Eliza said goodbye early that morning on your last visit it set tongues wagging – our neighbours misinterpreted her actions and accused her of being too friendly. They are still not talking to us because of it.' Mary-Anne stood in the hallway realising how close to her John was as he looked her up and down.

'Then they've nothing else to think about in their lives, the poor buggers. It was all in innocence that kiss she gave me, although I suppose she should have known better.' John stood across from Mary-Anne in the hallway before leaning over to her. 'Not like this one ... I've been meaning to do this since the first time I met you at your aunt's.' John held Mary-Anne tight in his arms and kissed her softly

194

on the lips, before reluctantly letting her go. 'You'll look after your-self until I return and not do anything stupid?'

Mary-Anne nodded her head, fighting back the tears yet again. Why had he come along at the lowest point of her life and when she was carrying another man's child, a baby that she would never love? 'I promise I will take care. Please keep what you witnessed to yourself, I don't want anyone to ever know ... especially Eliza.'

'Goes without saying, Mary-Anne. You know where I am if you need me before my return.' John held her hand tight and then stepped out into the last of the day's sunshine, looking back as he closed the garden gate and tugging his cap as he made his way back down to the canal side.

She could hear him whistling as he went, slowly disappearing along Pit Lane, her heart going with him with every step. He was going to be the reason she had to keep on going, but he could never find out about the baby she was carrying, else she might lose him forever, and that would never do.

'The bastard!' Eliza sat back and listened to Mary-Anne tell her about how Edmund Ellershaw had wiped his hands of anything to do with her pregnancy. 'He knows it's his baby; he's got to show responsibility.'

'Would you, if you were in his position and you'd taken advantage of me in the way he did? I'm nothing to him and if I told anybody, he's so powerful people would listen to his side and just look at me like a common whore. There's nothing I can do, I've either got to get rid of it, trust in Aunt Patsy and one of her concoctions or have the baby in secret and leave it at the orphanage with a note. I don't want it and never will.' Mary-Anne sighed.

'And how are you going to explain all this to John Vasey? He seems besotted by you. He'll soon lose interest when he finds you're pregnant or if he finds out Aunt Patsy's given you one of her special tonics.'

'She wouldn't say anything and if I decide to have it, I'd just have to disappear for the last month or so, when it's too difficult to hide my shame.' Mary-Anne had thought it through and had covered all options.

'Well, I'm not taking you to Aunt Patsy's; I still blame her on the quiet for the death of our mother. I'm not having your death on my conscience as well. And you think John Vasey will be satisfied with a quick peck on the cheek in the coming months? He looks at you as if he needs more than that already.' Eliza exclaimed in disbelief of her sister's thinking.

'If he's a gentleman he should be prepared to wait. And if I say I'm visiting relations, but still stay here out of sight, it won't even be that I ask him to wait.' Mary-Anne looked across at her sister.

'And who's going to bring this baby into the world? What if anything goes wrong?' Eliza looked hard at her sister.

'We'll manage between us,' Mary-Anne said sharply.

'It sounds as if you've made your mind up.' Eliza sighed. 'But could you really give it up, Mary-Anne? I know who its father is, but even so. Can you turn your back on your own blood once it is born, having carried it that long?'

'I hate it already; it was made out of shame and I wish it was dead.' Mary-Anne patted her stomach and glared at her sister.

'Oh, Mary-Anne, don't say that. The poor soul.' Eliza looked at her sister who usually was the kinder of the two of them.

'If I dared I'd kill it now with one of Patsy's potions and then get on with my life. As it is, I'll have to wait and hope that it doesn't survive birth.' Mary-Anne stared out of the window, fighting back the bitterness and fear that she felt inside her and thinking that if John hadn't found her when he did, then all her troubles would be over by now.

'You'll regret those words, Mary-Anne.' Eliza sighed. She was going to have to be there for her sister.

Twenty One

Eliza stood at the gateway of Highfield House and breathed in deeply as she admired the grandeur of the house. She didn't quite know what to do but she was going to do something. If Ellershaw wouldn't pay outright for the baby that was his, he'd pay indirectly.

In her simple home-made bag she had off-cuts of the fine silks and catalogues that John Vasey had left with her, and it was her intention to show them to Grace Ellershaw and persuade her to order another dress.

So this was where the bastard lived with his little happy family and his many secrets, she thought. He didn't deserve one brick of it with his morals.

She looked at the well-situated double-fronted house with roses growing around the pillars that stood either side of the front entrance. She knew her place and knew full well if she called at the front door it would be slammed in her face. She followed the flagged path around the side of the house and quickly shot a glance through the small-paned tall windows of what looked to be the dining room of the Ellershaw home, noting that it was empty but filled with furniture of quality. Arriving at the kitchen door she hesitated for a moment before lifting the brass knocker and banging it down loudly.

The door opened quickly and what she took to be the under butler stood in the doorway, looking her up and down. 'No, we don't want pegs, ribbons or anything else you've to offer, so bugger off.'

'You can bugger off yourself, I'm no gypsy. I've come to see Miss Grace; she'll be glad to see me. Just be a good man and tell her Miss Eliza is here to see her.' Eliza changed her usually Yorkshire accent to a false posh one as she stared at the young servant in front of her.

'She'll not want to see the likes of you, unless you've come for the scullery maid's job and that went last week, and it's Cook you needed to see for that.' The young man looked at her before trying to close the door, but Eliza put her foot in the way.

'Oi, you sling your hook!' the footman shouted at Eliza.

'Not until I've seen Miss Grace.' Eliza pushed the door open.

'Whatever's going on here? I can hear the racket from inside my kitchen.' Cook came rushing to the back door, wiping her hands on her apron and demanding to know what the fuss was about.

'It's this girl demanding to see Miss Grace. I've told her she'll not want to see her.' The footman scowled at Eliza.

'Now, then, let's see now. You're Eliza Wild; I used to see you with your mother, Sarah. I'm Mrs Bailey – Mary. What are you doing here? Have you come to see Miss Grace? She'll be glad to see you from the noise she makes about your little shop. I'm sorry to hear your mother passed away, lass, she was a good woman.' Mrs Bailey, the cook, had been an old friend of Eliza's mother. Now she gave Eliza a warm smile, looking at the lass she had heard so much of from Miss Grace but hadn't seen since she was a child.

'You knew my mother?' Eliza exclaimed.

'Aye, we were in service together, but then she met your father and I got my post here.' Mary turned to the other servant. 'Well, what are you standing like a big lump for? Shut your gob else you'll catch flies in it open like that, get a move on and get Miss Grace. This lass made that fancy dress she's so keen on. She'll want to see her.'

Eliza grinned at the footman. That had put him in his place.

'I wasn't going to say anything in front of him,' the cook said once the manservant had departed, 'but your mother never came here, that's why you don't know me. She had a strong dislike of Edmund Ellershaw and wouldn't come to the house. I shouldn't say it, but she was right; he's a wrong 'un, even though he pays my wages. Then I heard that folk are talking about her and him. I said to myself that it couldn't be right; the baby she was carrying would never be his. She hated him. So I wouldn't worry your head about that, it's only gossip.' Mary hardly stopped for breath, not noticing the shock on Eliza's face.

'My mother was having Edmund Ellershaw's baby? It was his she lost?' Eliza looked with horror at the gossiping cook.

'I'm sorry, I thought that you'd have heard. I was only trying to assure you not to take any notice of what's being said. I didn't realise you didn't know.' The cook coloured up as she looked at the shocked young girl, realising she'd just ruined her memories of her mother. 'Don't listen to my big mouth, it runs away with itself.'

'You are wrong, my mother would never do that.' Though even as she denied it, Eliza thought about the mornings her mother would disappear for an hour or two and the bottles of 'tonic' that Aunt Patsy supplied to her on a regular basis. And then she thought of Mary-Anne and the baby she was carrying ... had history repeated itself? Was Mary-Anne used by Edmund Ellershaw, just like her mother had been?

'I'm sorry, lass. I really am.' Mary looked at the crestfallen girl standing in her kitchen and wished she had kept her mouth shut.

'Can you give Miss Grace this material and pattern book? Please tell her that she can catch me in the shop if she'd like to know more. I'm going to have to go home, I can't wait any longer.' Eliza passed Mary the samples and pattern book and walked away, leaving the cook in the doorway as she closed the kitchen door, shaking her head.

Eliza walked quickly through the village, not noticing how fast her feet took her, thinking only of what Mary had told her. She had to get back and speak to Mary-Anne, tell her what seemed to be commonly known and see how she felt then about the baby she was carrying. Her heart ached with the thought of what her mother had done. How could she? Had she been forced to do it just like Mary-Anne to keep a roof over their heads, or had it been a sordid affair?

Eliza stood in front of Mary-Anne, her face wet with tears. 'You knew! Why didn't you tell me? It's even worse now that you are carrying his child. How could our mother do it? I thought she loved Bill ... had she no shame?' Eliza sat down, slouching in her chair. She looked up at her secretive sister.

'I only found out when Edmund Ellershaw told me to hurt me and make me know my place in his world. Don't think badly of our mother, she did it because she loved us so much. She did it for the same reason as I did: to pay the rent. Though for her it was also to keep useless Bill in work. He's the one you should blame, spending all his money on drink and going drunk to work. There will always be men like Edmund Ellershaw who take advantage of women like Mother and me. They have power over us and don't give a damn what hurt they do to us, as long as there is something in it for them.

I'm sorry you had to find out in this way. I should have told you. Our mother always said Mary Bailey was an old gossip just like her next door. They are just bitter and twisted old women who haven't got enough in their lives to keep their noses out of others'.' Mary-Anne ran her hand over her sister's shoulders. 'She did it for us, Eliza, just like our mother did everything for us. Don't think badly of her.'

'Did you know Mother was friends with the Ellershaw's cook? That they were in service together? Why didn't I know?' Eliza sobbed.

'I wouldn't say close friends; they had a fall out when our mother married our father. Mary had always had her eye on him and never accepted that Mother won his heart. Can't you remember her coming to tea once? You'd only be five or six, and her and mother had a row because she kept making eyes at Father. I suppose you were too young. She never came back after that. Mother was always polite enough to give her time of day, but other than that I don't think they spent time together, especially with her being cook for Edmund Ellershaw. Surely you heard her whisper, "birds of a feather, stick together" as we passed the gates? It was always aimed at Mary.'

'I just thought she meant the Ellershaw family because they all had money, I didn't realise that Mary Bailey existed.' Eliza wiped her eyes and looked across at her sister. 'Oh, Mary-Anne, what a state we are in! Everything we value has just disappeared, and all because of that family.'

'That is why, dear sister, you have to carry on getting money off Grace Ellershaw. Impress her with your needlework and take her for what you can get out of her and her friends. It's time for them to pay a little, because, let's face it, Grace and her brother will inherit the woollen mills of her grandfather one day and Rose Pit makes a good penny or two for them all to live on at the moment – they've more brass than they know what to do with.' Mary-Anne had lost the feeling of despair, now she just felt angry. As soon as the baby she was carrying was born, she was going to get her revenge. She didn't know how, but get it she would.

'Just look at your baby brother, Grace. Isn't he beautiful? He's walking well now and he's so bright.' Catherine Ellershaw's face beamed with pride as she watched her youngest son toddle across the morning room of Highfield House. 'He's growing up so quickly; before you know it, he'll be going to help your father run the pit. After all, it will be his one day, along with your brother William, of course.'

'Yes, Mother, he is growing quickly. It must be good to have your life planned out for you before you can even walk. I, of course, have not had that, being a girl.' Grace watched her young brother gurgle and stumble to his nanny's arms, to be picked up and shown the garden outside for his amusement.

'Grace, anyone would think you were jealous. Of course your life has been planned out for you. It's just that the right man has not made himself known to you yet. When he does, you'll get married, have a family and be content. Just like I am.' Catherine Ellershaw looked across at her daughter and scowled.

'What if I don't want to be just content? Married with children? What if I want to do and make something of my own? Our William will no doubt get a position in Grandfather's woollen mills, seeing that he is now worming his way into his affections after realising that Priscilla Eavesham is penniless and Father will more than likely leave the Rose entirely to George, after his day. So that leaves me with nothing.' Grace put the catalogue that Eliza had left her down next to her and looked across at her mother.

'Grace, hold your tongue; we all aim to be around for some time yet. You are talking as if we are about to meet our maker. Nothing is certain in this life. You should be grateful for what you've got already; you want for nothing, we have made sure of that. It will be up to your husband to provide for you, although I'm sure your father will make sure you don't leave the family home penniless.'

'What if I wanted to start a business of my own; one I know will succeed?' Eliza fingered the gauze material lightly and thought of the combination of material and patterns, something she knew would have the ladies of the district queuing for fittings.

'Don't be so silly, darling. What on earth would you do? Women like us do not work, that is for our husbands and fathers to do, to supply homes and keep us comfortable. I really don't know what's got into you.' Catherine Ellershaw looked across at her daughter and sighed.

'But a lot of ordinary working-class women work, Mamma.' Grace sat on the edge of her chair and looked at her mother.

'You see, you've said it yourself: "working class" ... those without means. Not like us. Now if you'll excuse me I'm going to join George and his nanny in the garden. I've had enough of this silly talk.' Catherine rose from her chair and her skirts swished as she walked past her daughter into the garden.

Grace looked at the material and patterns. One day she would employ Eliza Wild and set up a fashion business, no matter what her mother said. Women were as clever as men any day, if not more so, it's just that society always kept them in their place, tending to children and running homes. One day things would change, of that she was sure.

*

204

'I've been thinking, Eliza; I think I will go and see Aunt Patsy, ask her for something to get rid of this baby. I can always say I'm helping a friend, she'll not suspect it's for me because she knows I'm not courting anyone. And I'd hope she thinks better of me than to think I'd raise my skirts for anybody.' Mary-Anne tied her boots ready for her trip into Leeds.

'No, don't, you'll regret it. I'm surprised you are even thinking about it, after finding our mother dead. She might even think it's for me and you know how she has a way of quizzing us; she seems to know the answers before we reply anyway.' Eliza stood at the table and looked at her sister. She didn't want her to go to Aunt Patsy for a solution for the problem that was growing daily inside her.

'I'll just try not to look at her, because I know what you mean. It's as if she can read your thoughts. Mother always said she had strange powers and used to tease and call her a witch.' Mary-Anne looked across at her sister.

'She is a bit that way; the house is dark and filled with the smell of herbs and she's always dressed in black. Perhaps Mother was right.' Eliza smiled at her sister. 'If you are going there, I can't let you go on your own. I'm coming with you; besides I know that you are hoping to see John Vasey, either on the wharf or at Aunt Patsy's. And I could do with him being reminded of his promise of more material. Not that I've had any new customers of late.' Eliza looked across at her sister. 'You are playing with fire there, Mary-Anne, he'll drop you for sure when he finds out you are carrying a child or he'll break your heart when he leaves to go to America.'

'He might not do either if I win his heart and ask him to stay, and he need never know about this baby once it's gone.' Mary-Anne picked up her shawl and wrapped it around her. 'Come on then, get a move on if you are joining me; some of us still deal with rags and working folk, not la-di-da toffs.' She grinned and picked up her bag, watching while Eliza banked up the fire.

'La-di-da toffs that you thought you could rely on, but disappear in the blink of an eye. Even your William has not been back to see you.' Eliza grabbed her shawl and linked her arm into her sister's.

'Na, and I'm not bothered. Let someone else have him; he'll only be like his father. You'd never be able to trust him. Upper-class snob.' Mary-Anne smiled at her sister, trying to hide her true feelings about visiting their Aunt Patsy.

She was scared ... scared of what the future held for her.

Twenty Two

'There's no sign of him, Mary-Anne.' Eliza glanced around Calls Wharf, watching the wharf men unload and load the barges but with not a glimpse of John Vasey. Workers knocked her shoulder as she stood in their way and occasionally cursed her.

'Come on, out of the way, we'll look for him on our way back. That load of sacks is going to fall on your head if you don't get out from under them.' Mary-Anne pulled on her sister's arm, moving her out of the way of a board gladden with grain sacks being hauled by chains just over her head. 'We'll probably see him on the way back if he's not at Aunt Patsy's. I need to get to Ma Fletcher and then I thought we could walk over to Park Lane and have a look at the town hall that's being built there. People are saying how grand it looks. Things are changing in Leeds, that's for sure.' Mary-Anne pushed her way through the crowds with her sister in tow, and they darted in and out of the busy wharf side.

'What do you want to go and look at that for? It's costing a small fortune and divided folk in opinion, all that money on a posh town hall, when ordinary folk are living in slums. They want to go and look at Aunt Patsy's square and build new houses for them instead of building something that grand.' Eliza sighed as she caught up with her sister again.

'Leeds is growing, Eliza, it's got wealth and has to move with the times. I like that we're going to have a city to be proud of. After all, we supply nearly all the country with our wool and coal, not to mention the Commonwealth. Also, the local paper says Queen Victoria is rumoured to be opening the hall; we will have to try and get in to see her. I've never seen royalty before. Do you think Prince Albert will be with her? She never seems to go anywhere without him.'

'I just think we have more important things to worry about at the moment and to be quite honest I don't know what she sees in that Albert; he's German for a start, and he's not that handsome. He's not as good-looking as my Tom, and he has strange ways.' Eliza followed in her sister's footsteps up Lower Briggate to the market on Higher Briggate.

'I read that he's heart-broken that his eldest daughter Victoria has gone to live in Prussia, since she got married last month to Prince Frederick. He must love his family and worry about them like any other father, so don't be so hard on him.' Mary-Anne waved at Ma Fletcher as she approached her stall. 'The old bag's waiting of us. Look, she's got something for us. She never fails us, does she?'

Both of them walked quickly towards her, holding their breaths as they made their way past the smells that rose from the butcher's stall at the start of the market. Mary-Anne was conscious of her stomach beginning to erupt.

'I know, girls, the smell's bad today – I've felt bloody sick all morning.' Ma Fletcher watched as Mary-Anne retched and looked for a drain to be sick down. 'Fair turns your stomach, especially if you've a weak belly.'

Eliza watched as her sister made her way as discreetly as she could to the gutter and vomited, knowing that usually she was oblivious to the stench of the market, but not at present.

'You'll feel better for that, although by the looks of your face, you don't.' Ma Fletcher watched as Mary-Anne wiped her mouth along her sleeve and stood in front of her shakily.

'She's not been feeling well for a while. We had some bacon the other night and I think it must have been off. She keeps being sick, thinking about the taste it left behind.' Eliza did her usual of picking through the cart while making an excuse for her sister.

'I'm all right; just the smell reminded me of the bacon, as Eliza says. I should be used to it because our shop's next to the butcher's and we smell it at least twice a week.' Mary-Anne rummaged in the bag and held out her hand with what she thought the lot was worth.

'Maybe something else amiss, you want to take care.' Ma Fletcher counted the money on offer and put up a finger demanding another penny before turning to look at Mary-Anne.

'No, I'm fine. Here take your penny, I'll not argue today.' Mary-Anne picked up the bag of clothes and nodded at Eliza for them both to be on their way.

'Bloody hell, you must be poorly, lass. You are not even haggling today.' Ma Fletcher watched as the usually chatty two wandered away from her stall. Something was wrong with Mary-Anne, and it wasn't anything to do with rancid bacon, if she knew the signs.

'I'm sorry, Eliza. I couldn't stay in Briggate a moment longer. I thought I was going to faint.' Mary-Anne sat down on the steps of the Holy Trinity. 'And she kept on talking and I just couldn't think straight.' She looked up at her sister. 'I hate that I'm in the family way. What have I done to deserve this, apart from keep us safe and dry?'

'It'll get better, Mary-Anne, you'll not always feel like this.' Eliza sat down next to her.

'I won't if I can persuade Aunt Patsy to give me something. That's the best end to what I'm carrying,' Mary-Anne said quietly.

'Ssshh, not on the church steps, that's blasphemy!' Eliza whispered.

'No, what Edmund Ellershaw did was blasphemy but I can't see God striking him down with a thunderbolt from on high.' Mary-Anne leant back and breathed in deeply. 'It's passing now. Let's go as I suggested and look at how fast they are getting on with the town hall, and then we will go to Aunt Patsy's. Heaven only knows what's in this bag this week; I couldn't be bothered to look.' Mary-Anne opened the bag up and pulled a dress and a skirt to the top. 'I think she's pulled a fast one on us, but never mind, it is my fault, I'll just have to make most of a bad lot. She stood up and held onto the iron railings by the church doorway. 'I'll not let that bastard win, Eliza, no matter how bad I feel.'

Eliza stood on the church steps and looked at her sister. 'Please don't go to Aunt Patsy's. I don't want to lose you! What if I find you like you did our mother, dying in the privy. Please, Mary-Anne, I beg you ... don't get rid of it. No matter how it came to be.'

'Oh, Eliza, don't start. I feel so ill at the moment. There's no way out but to get rid of this baby. It's going to ruin our lives. No one will want to know me once the truth gets out and we can't afford another mouth to feed. Don't you think I'm scared too? I remember finding Mother and it was horrific – I'll never forget it. So do you really think I'm going through with this lightly? I just don't know what else to do. I can't have this child.' Mary-Anne wiped back the tears. She felt weak and vulnerable.

'I don't want to lose you, Mary-Anne.' Eliza repeated, pleading. 'I'd be all alone. Aunt Patsy means well and I'm sure she didn't mean to but her potion did kill Mother. A baby should be cherished, it can't help its parentage and it didn't ask to be brought into the world. We'd manage between us, or you just have it and give it up like you thought before.'.

'I don't know, Eliza, I just don't know what to do! I've never felt like this before. I'm expecting a baby, which I don't want. The shop is just starting to be able to keep us and we both have a sweetheart in our lives. It's spoiling everything. All I can do is think about it growing inside of me, making me worry all the time. I even thought of taking my own life the other day and would have done if John Vasey hadn't stopped me in time down by the canal.' Mary-Anne sat back down again on the steps and hid her face in her hands as passers-by looked at her in curiosity.

'Oh my Lord, Mary-Anne!' Eliza reached her arms around her sister, shocked at her confession. 'That was just a moment of weakness. Let's go home ... you know getting rid of the baby is not the answer. You act hard, same as me, but we aren't. I could never kill anything, let alone a baby. Nor would you – you'd not have gone through with it, would you?' Her sister didn't answer but continued to sob into her skirts. 'Lordy, if I'd have known you were that low after visiting Edmund Ellershaw, I'd have not let you out of my sight. I take it you did not tell John Vasey why you were committing such an act of desperation?' Eliza took her sister's hand and squeezed it tight.

'No, and he must never know. I don't feel that way now but you're right, I can't go through with taking away this baby's life. I'll do as I originally planned and have the baby and then leave it on the steps of the orphanage. Are you any good at bringing a baby into the world?

Because I'm going to need help if we are to keep it a secret.' Mary-Anne wiped her tears away and smiled at her sister.

'I don't know, but we will manage between us. This baby's not the end of the world, so don't you think that it is. You've got to remember it is half of you as well; forget that the father is Edmund Ellershaw and just look after yourself.'

'What would I do without you, Eliza? We get our strength through one another, we always have.' Mary-Anne looked at her sister and not for the first time was glad that she was there to talk to, even though she couldn't always tell her everything. 'We'll not bother walking over to Park Lane to look at the town hall or visit Aunt Patsy. Let's just go home and make the best of this bag of rags that Ma Fletcher swindled us with.' She breathed in and smiled warmly at Eliza. 'I'm glad that you stopped me. I couldn't have gone through with it anyway if Aunt Patsy had given me one of her potions. It was terrible finding Mother like that – and the baby ... I wouldn't wish that on any one. It's just that I feel I'm in such a desperate situation. I'm not in control of my life any more.'

'You'll be all right once the baby is born; things will get back to normal. Now, come; let us go and have a proper look for the elusive Mr Vasey. He will cheer you up.' Eliza held her hand out for Mary-Anne to take.

'I doubt that he will look at me the state I'm in.' Mary-Anne rose to her feet.

'What state? You look fine to me and as the months go on ... well, we will just have to disguise your shape under fuller skirts. It's a mercy you have such a talented seamstress for a sister – I can fashion your dresses so no one will never need to know of your predicament.' Eliza linked her arm into her sister's.

Mary-Anne smiled. If only it was to be that simple, she thought. Unwanted babies were born every day to women who had lifted their skirts for pleasure, but she had not even done that. She'd been frightened and felt dirty as Edmund Ellershaw had pushed and thrust himself into her. She would never feel the same again and the next few months were going to be hell, even with her sister's help and support.

'Mr Vasey, I thought you were going to ignore us.' Eliza tapped John on his shoulder, as both of them walked up behind him.

'Eliza, Mary-Anne ... I didn't see you both there. I've been rushed off my feet all morning. I haven't had time to catch my breath, let alone anything else.' John wiped his forehead free of sweat and looked at the two young women fondly, even though he had little time for conversation that morning.

'We can see that the wharf's busy this morning; Eliza nearly got a load dropped on her head when we arrived, and it was so crowded. We'll not keep you, you'll be needed.' Mary-Anne was still aware that she didn't feel well and really hadn't wanted Eliza to find John in the busy throng.

'It's always good to see you two ladies, no matter how busy we are.' John smiled at Mary-Anne while he tucked his shirt in his trousers, knowing that he didn't look at his best covered in coal dust and sweat, with his clothes in disarray.

'Vasey, get your arse moving – that barge from Hull needs emptying. Stop pleasing your cock and get on with some work.'

'Yes, boss,' John answered his ganger as he walked past shouting at him. 'Sorry ladies, I've got to go. The bastard's on my back today.' John looked at Mary-Anne and smiled, wanting to kiss her goodbye but realising he shouldn't.

'Come to tea on Sunday afternoon, John,' Eliza shouted after him as he pushed his way to the wharf side.

'I will, see you then.' John waved his arm at them as he shouted his reply and disappeared through the crowd.

'What did you do that for?' Mary-Anne looked at her sister.

'Because you hardly said a word and it's as obvious as the nose on my face he's besotted by you by the way he looks at you. Besides, I thought I could ask Tom as well, just have the four of us around the tea table. I thought it would be good for both of us.' Eliza grinned.

'Won't his mother have something to say about that? How's he going to explain chapel taking that long?' Mary-Anne pushed her way along the wharf with Eliza by her side.

'I've decided to go and pay Mrs Thackeray a visit, convince her that I'm not as bad as she fears. She never goes out of that house of theirs, so she sits and thinks about things too much and always thinks the worst of people. It's time she met me.'

'Shouldn't Tom introduce you to her?'

'He'll never do that, he's frightened to death of her. No, I'm going on my own. I'll sweeten her up, else I never will get my man.' Eliza took the sack off her sister and swung it over her back as they reached the outskirts of Leeds and Hunslet. 'I'm not going to be bullied by her and it's time she got to know me.'

'He's a mother's boy, Eliza,' Mary-Anne warned, 'you take care, or else he will break your heart as well. His mother will always come first.'

'Not if I have my way, she won't. Now, let's look forward to entertaining on Sunday. It'll give the neighbours something to talk about if nothing else.' Eliza laughed.

'You're a crafty one, Eliza Wild. With no shame.'

Eliza looked at herself in the hall mirror; she'd brushed her hair until it shone and was dressed in her Sunday best. She looked completely respectable in her eyes ... how could old Mrs Thackeray not like her? She'd win her around.

She picked up her basket filled with baking, which she had taken care making earlier in the day, and the bunch of bluebells that she'd picked down by the side of the canal. She picked them up and smelled their sweet smell, looking at the blue hue that matched her eyes. She'd pick another bunch for the tea table on Sunday. She wanted their home to look nice for their gentleman callers and for her sister.

Poor Mary-Anne ... she felt so sorry for her and, although she'd tried to sound positive for her, she didn't honestly know what they were going to do. Grace Ellershaw had not come back after her visit to her home and the money they had made would not last forever. Also, when it came to bringing a baby into the world, Eliza was an innocent and frightened by the very thought that she would have to be the one to help Mary-Anne through it when her time came. Still, something would turn up, it always did.

Months like the last few could not last forever. After Mary-Anne had the baby and they'd given it away to a good home, they could get their lives back on an even keel. She breathed in deeply and smoothed down her dress. Right, Mrs Madge Thackeray was the one to win over today.

'Yes, what do you want?' Madge opened the door slightly to the young lass stood on her doorstep.

'I'm Eliza Wild, Mrs Thackeray. I think Tom might have mentioned me?' Eliza stood on the doorstep of the small double-fronted cottage that stood on the edge of Wood Lane in Rothwell. By its appearance, it had once been part of the nearby estate but now it had been lovingly looked after by Madge and Tom, with the cottage garden just starting to come into bloom with its earliest flowers, while the small-paned windows were well painted and cleaned, sparkling in the sunshine.

'Aye, he's talked of you.' Madge opened the door a little wider and looked Eliza up and down. 'What, tha's only a bit of a thing. How old are you?'

'I'm sixteen, Mrs Thackeray.' Eliza stood on the doorstep and tried to peer in behind Madge. 'I've brought you some baking and picked you these flowers, I thought you might like them.'

'What do I want with any of that? I do my own baking, and my garden's full of flowers. If you think you can charm yourself into my home with them you can think again.' Madge looked at Eliza and was determined to keep her on the step.

'I just thought that you don't know the first thing about me and you must be worried that Tom is showing an interest in me. The baking and flowers are just a small token and I also hoped that I can put your mind to rest if you have thoughts of Tom deserting you for me. I can assure you he loves you deeply and you will always be first in his thoughts.' Eliza smiled.

'He's a good lad, is my Tom. He doesn't want any young hussy that'll lead him astray and just take his money. He belongs with his mother.' Madge stared at Eliza.

'Mrs Thackeray, Tom will always be your son. I've no intention of stealing him from you. We are just friends. It may grow into more than that, but for now we are both happy with how it is. You will always come first, I can assure you, and I respect that. Please accept my gifts, it would be a shame to have to carry them back home. There are some scones and a new loaf of bread; I made them myself first thing this morning. I enjoy baking.' Eliza smiled at the old woman. She'd put up with her insults for the time being, just until she had won her over.

'I suppose you could come in. It wouldn't hurt to get to know you a bit better. His head seems to be set on seeing you, no matter what I think. If nowt else it's good to know what I'm up against.' Madge opened the door wider. 'Go on, sit down, and I'll put the kettle on. You can put your baking on the table. I'll take your flowers and put them in a vase.'

Eliza walked into the low-beamed cottage and looked around her. The house was spotless. The dresser that took pride of place in the kitchen had shelves that were filled with sparkling china, and even the kettle on the hearth shone, the copper gleaming as Madge pulled it onto the coals to boil. She was definitely house proud, and all Eliza could think was what a demanding mother-in-law she would make.

'You've a beautiful house, Mrs Thackeray.' Eliza smiled and sat down at the table while Madge placed a delicately printed cup and saucer next to her.

'Aye, I like me home. I always keep on top of it. Cleanliness is next to godliness, so they say.'

'Indeed. Our mother brought us up the same way.' Eliza sipped the tea that Madge poured from the matching teapot and tried to drink as politely as she could.

'Are you managing without your mother? It was a sad to-do ... losing her. And then Tom tells me your stepfather left you both. He must not have been much of a man, leaving two young girls to look after themselves after just losing their mother.' Madge looked at the young lass over the lip of her teacup and waited for her reply.

'We miss our mother, she meant the world to Mary-Anne and me, and we are still trying to come to terms with her death. My stepfather, we don't miss. I don't want to speak out of turn but he wasn't a good man and we are almost grateful that he's gone.' Eliza bowed her head.

'Liked his drink, I hear. Makes men and women act in strange ways. My old man never touched a drop. He swore he never would; he took the oath and stood by it. How are you two lasses making a living? It'll be hard to going.' Madge was making sure she found out as much as she could while the young lass was under her roof.

'We are both seamstresses and have been managing of late. I've had a few good orders for the dresses I've been making from local gentry, while Mary-Anne deals in repairs and alterations. We haven't done too badly. We watch the pennies and are not frivolous and have no bad habits.' Eliza watched as Madge digested every word said, as she tried to find out if she was suitable material for her son to court, even though it was under the pretence of friendship only.

Finally, at the end of tea and polite conversation, Eliza picked up the courage to ask Madge Thackeray if Tom would be allowed to join her for tea after chapel on the coming Sunday.

'Well, I tell you what, lass … I didn't want him seeing you. From what I'd heard off folk, I'll be honest, I didn't think you were good enough for him. But you seem right enough; he could do worse. So you have my blessing with this so-called friendship. Just as long as he comes home to his mother each night and then I know what he's been up to.'

'Thank you, Mrs Thackeray. I wanted to make myself known, I always think it is better to be straight than sneak about behind folk's backs. Don't you worry, Tom will never be hurt by me and we will always be respectful of your wishes.' Eliza stood in the doorway, empty basket on her arm and looked at the ageing woman who worshiped her son.

'You call in any time, but most of all, you take care of my lad. Else God help you, I might be an old woman, but I've a frightful tongue in my head if riled.' Madge looked at the young lass as she closed the garden gate behind her and waved back to her as she went down the lane. She'd been better than she'd been led to believe, and Tom would need somebody after her day, she thought, as she closed the door behind her unexpected visitor.

Eliza whistled to herself on her way home. Stupid old cow. 'Frightful tongue, my arse,' she whispered to herself. She was all of a quiver with the thought of it, she laughed. Tom had his mother's blessing and that's all that he would be worried about. All for the sake of acting like a timid mouse for an hour and a bit of baking.

She was glad that she'd managed to win the old bag around.

Twenty Three

Mary-Anne sat in the window of the workshop, tacking up the hem of a skirt left by one of their local customers. It was nice and peaceful and the sun shone through the window, warming her, and for the first time in a long time she felt content. Her mind was settled over the baby she was carrying and she now knew which way her life was to take.

Eliza had left her that morning to tackle Tom's mother, intent on winning the old woman over, and Mary-Anne knew that if Eliza turned on her charms she wouldn't stand a chance. She was glad that she thought enough of him to take on his mother and hoped that Tom realised how much her sister thought of him. At least her sister's life was going to plan. She herself would have to be patient, wait until her baby was born, and go through with her plan to leave it on the steps of the orphanage and then carry on with her life.

It wouldn't be the first baby abandoned on St Mary's steps and she was sure it wouldn't be the last. She twined the cotton around her fingers and snapped the thread off, inspecting the neatness of her stitches before going to the back of the room to hang the skirt up to straighten.

'I won't be a minute!' Mary-Anne shouted as she heard the shop's bell ring but didn't bother to turn around.

'That's quite all right, Miss Wild, I'm quite prepared to wait.' The voice of William Ellershaw made her turn around sharply and she quickly composed herself as she looked across at him standing just inside the doorway, smartly dressed with his swagger stick in his hand.

'Mr Ellershaw, I'm sorry. I was just hanging this skirt up, ready for collection.' Mary-Anne glanced up at good-looking man that stood in front of her. She admired him but at the same time could not bear the sight of him, thinking only of what his father had done to her.

'I thought I would just call in and say how much I enjoyed your company the other week. It was quite refreshing not to have a giggling girl sitting next to me, which I'm afraid all my sister's friends are. Although I'd appreciate you don't tell her I said so.' William sighed and tapped his stick on the floor. 'May I?' He pointed to the chair that Mary-Anne had just left and sat down in the sunshine that poured though the shop window.

'I'm sure your sister's friends are lovely people; they seemed to be and I enjoyed their company,' Mary-Anne said tactfully, as she wondered why he had really come to visit her.

'They live in their own little worlds, pampered by their fathers and cossetted by their mothers until a suitable husband is found for them and then they stop giggling and become old women overnight.' William looked across at Mary-Anne and sighed. 'Forgive me, what I am saying is very indiscreet but true. Unfortunately, they all look at me as fair game – especially Priscilla Eavesham, she is desperate to win my heart. More for the security of her home than for the love of me. Her father is in terrible debt through his gambling habit. I fear they will lose everything if she does not find a wealthy suitor to help rescue her home. My grandfather has asked me to show interest in her as he has always coveted Leventhorpe Hall and knows that he could secure it cheaply if we were to marry. But, Miss Wild, my heart is not hers and I am loathe to marry for money not for love.' William stared out into the high street and tapped his stick against the chair leg. 'Though my life, if I did marry her, would be made a lot easier if I knew that somebody else was there to keep me satisfied, kept well and with plenty of my money, just for that person to be there for me go to when needed.' William turned and looked at Mary-Anne. 'I saw how you looked at me; those green eyes of yours seemed to stare into my soul and I knew you could be that woman. I know you find me handsome, Miss Wild, you couldn't take your eyes of me. '

'Sir, you are mistaken. Yes, you are a handsome man, but I'm afraid I have my pride and if you were a married man then I would not be willing to be yours at your convenience, to be used, but never respected. You have read me wrong if you think I'm looking to be your mistress, and if that is what you think of me I wish you good day.' Mary-Anne opened the door and hung her head, not wanting to look at the young man who obviously took after his father. She wanted him out of the shop as fast as she could.

'So, you were playing with me. You women are all the same; you play with us men, lead us on like trained poodles and then cast us aside when you have had enough of us.' William rose from his chair, walked over to Mary-Anne and touched her face with the silver top of his cane. 'You'll regret your hasty words. You could have wanted for nothing, instead of rummaging around in dirty second-hand rags. My father said you were stubborn bitches, but I cared not to listen to him. I hope you stay where you belong, in the gutter just where dirt is always to be found.' William cast one long look at her before stepping out into the sunshine, leaving Mary-Anne shakily closing the shop door behind her.

She breathed in deeply and held back the tears. Thank God he hadn't forced her too; when he'd stood up she thought he had that in mind and she'd felt her legs turning to jelly. Her first thought had been the safety of the baby she carried, even before visions of his father had flashed through her mind. Thank God wounding her with his words had been all he had inflicted on her. Mary-Anne slumped in the chair. She'd not tell Eliza; she'd only worry and hopefully he'd not be returning. Poor Priscilla Eavesham ... she'd rather be penniless than be married to a bastard like William Ellershaw who would never love or respect her. She breathed in again and rethought her fears for the baby ... had she really worried about the baby before herself? Perhaps there was a maternal bond growing between them that was stronger than she had ever imagined.

'Just look at them, Bert! By she has a brass neck, has that'en.' Ada Simms turned around from behind her lace curtains and watched Eliza and Tom walk past their house arm in arm from the chapel. 'They even sat together at chapel, the forward hussy.'

'Well, we did when we were courting, there's nowt wrong with that. And I did warn the lad, so he knows what he's taking on. He must think something of her. Come away and mind your own business, it's nowt to do with us anyway.' Bert folded his newspaper and looked across at his wife who seemed to spend half her life peering from behind her nets.

'They've gone in. I wonder if Mary-Anne is at home. She hasn't been going to chapel of late; at least she's not a hypocrite, and she's not as forthright with her opinions as that Eliza.' Ada reached up to her head and pulled the pin out of her Sunday best hat before having a final look through the window. 'Well, that's going to put the cat among the pigeons. Isn't this the man she was kissing that morning when we spotted her. He's just going through their garden gate? Quick, Bert, come and look.'

'Will you come away from that window and leave them be, woman! No wonder they hardly talk to us any more; they know you watch their every move,' Bert growled.

'I'm going … I'm off to make your tea. I can hear next door better in the kitchen anyway.' Ada put her curtain straight and hung her hat on the hallway stand.

'Mind your own business woman, it's nothing to do with us.' Bert sighed. She'd not listen, and tea would be late as she listened in to next-door's conversation.

'I'm so glad that you've both come; we make a nice foursome.' Mary-Anne poured the tea and looked across at John and then Tom as Eliza passed the sandwiches around. They had been freshly made by Mary-Anne while Eliza attended chapel. 'You don't know one another, do you? Eliza, introduce John to Tom while I refill the teapot.'

'This is the man who is our saviour, Tom. He brings me the material that I make my dresses from and cuts out the middle man, you could say.' Eliza grinned and then sat down quickly as she reached for her brawn sandwich.

'I get it cheap off a man down on the wharf, is what she means.' John gave Eliza a warning glance, not wanting her to say any more in front of a man he'd just met.

'You work on the canal then, down on the wharf side?' Tom looked at the man who had obviously taken Mary-Anne's eye and showed interest in him.

'Aye, for the time being. I aim to get a passage to America later in the year, to join my brother. That's why I'm working all the hours I can get. I can't say my job's ideal, but it'll do for now.' John sipped his tea and looked across at the lad, recognising that he was at least ten years younger than himself.

'America, now that's the place to go. Are you going to join the gold rush? I only read the other day that there had been a huge strike in Kansas and Nebraska at a place called Pike's Peak. Thousands of people are going there, and seemingly gold is as common as coal with us. I wouldn't mind having a go myself. Make my fortune and then come home,' Tom said excitedly, as if he was imagining how he'd spend his gold.

'You hardly dare come here, let alone America. Your mother would have something to say then, Tom Thackeray.' Eliza looked at Tom sternly. 'So you can forget any thoughts of sailing any oceans and leaving us both in tears.'

'John's got a brother in New York, that's why he's going.' Mary-Anne sat down next to John and looked at him with a smile on her face; she felt happy that he was sitting near her and had joined them for tea.

'Oh, I see … makes a lot of difference if you've someone already out there to help you settle into a new life. I hear it can be a bit wild out there. Eliza's right, I'm best stopping home.' Tom went quiet.

'How's the new town hall looking, John? We meant to have a look at it, but didn't get the chance at the beginning of the week.' Mary-Anne changed the subject and looked across at Eliza as she didn't say why they had not made their destination.

'It's going to be a fine building – they have just about finished the clock tower. It looks grand with all the pillars and steps into the main building; I've never seen anything like it built in Leeds. I remember

Liverpool has some magnificent buildings but this can rival them. By the time they've built the new corn exchange and the shopping arcades that they are talking about, Leeds will have changed beyond belief. Sure, it's going to be a bonnier city than my old Dublin town and I don't say that lightly.' John leant back in his chair and looked at the others.

'I can't wait to see Queen Victoria herself open it. Won't that be something? The queen in Leeds!' Eliza exclaimed, noting the excitement on Tom's face.

'I've only dreamt of royalty, I'd love to see her. Not bothered about Prince Albert but definitely the queen.' Mary-Anne cupped her face in her hands and sighed.

'Then why don't we all make a day of it? I think I heard a date in early September ... there's bound to be a fair and side stalls and all sorts if the queen is visiting.' Tom reached for Eliza's hand and smiled.

'What do you think, Mary-Anne? I know it's a while off yet, but it is something to look forward to.' Eliza's face was radiant.

'Yes, that would be good. It is something for you to look forward to and I'm sure it will be a good day.' Mary-Anne put her head down and then lifted it to smile at her sister. Eliza had obviously forgotten that by then she would be as large as a barrel or possibly recovering from childbirth. She hoped it was the latter.

'Well, you can count me out, I'm not going to wave a flag for a woman that knew my people were dying for the sake of a sack or two of grain. We call her the Famine Queen back home; all she gave personally to the whole of Ireland was five pounds, when she spent five thousand holding a so-called banquet for the suffering of the poor in Ireland. Sure, did you not read it in one of your English papers? They said she was illuminating a graveyard. Nah, you'll not get me there. Besides, I hope to be gone by then.' John looked across at Mary-Anne and saw the sorrow in her eyes. 'But nothing's set in stone yet – depends on work and how much my ticket will be.'

'Well, I would still like you to be here and I'm sure Mary-Anne would. We will both miss you when you've gone.' Eliza smiled and then looked across at her sister. 'I think now we've finished tea, Tom and I will take a stroll; it's a lovely afternoon and I feel like a breath of fresh air.'

'Yes, you two go and have a wander. I'll do the washing up. John, are you going with them or will you stay with me?' Mary-Anne rose from her seat and started collecting the dirty side plates and teacups.

Tom and Eliza looked at one another, hoping that the answer from John would be no.

'Now, what kind of question is that to ask of me? Do you want me to get in the way of these two lovebirds and leave you on your own?' John sat back in his chair and laughed.

Mary-Anne looked across at him and smiled as she took the crockery into the kitchen.

'Go on then, bugger off. Don't sit on ceremony … go and do your whispering and wooing down the lane and let me do the same in the kitchen.' John grinned as Eliza and Tom got up immediately, not waiting for Mary-Anne to come back into the room.

John walked through to the kitchen carrying the remains of the cake on a plate and placed it down on the table before walking to where Mary-Anne stood. He slipped his arms around her waist and held her tight to him as he gazed at their reflection in the kitchen window.

'Now doesn't that make a pretty scene? Me and you … a perfect picture of domestic bliss,' John whispered into her ear.

Mary-Anne smiled but felt uncomfortable. Would he be able to feel the baby as he squeezed her to him? She turned and looked at him.

'I can hardly breathe, John, you are holding me so tight.'

'That's because I can't believe what I've found and never want to let it go.' John looked at her, his blue eyes sparkling as he thought about kissing her.

'But you will go, won't you? You'll go and I'll be left broken-hearted,' Mary-Anne whispered. 'I don't think we should get too close.'

'We'll see … things change. As I say, nothing's set in stone.' John held her face in her hands and softly kissed her. 'Don't worry, Mary-Anne, it's just a kiss, nothing more.' He looked into her eyes, realising that she was shaking with fear and sensing her body stiffen with anticipation of his next move. 'Fear not, lass, I'll not take advantage of you. I believe in wooing my women and respecting them.' He loosened his grip from around her waist.

Mary-Anne blushed. 'I'd like to take things slowly. Unlike my sister and her Tom.'

'Then that's exactly what we'll do. You are my sort of a girl, Mary-Anne, and I'll not be rushing doing anything you don't want me to do.'

'Thank you, thank you, and I'm sorry if I lead you to believe anything other.' Mary-Anne bowed her head.

'Now, why would I think that of such a respectable girl like your-self? Was it not that which made me look at you in the first place? You gave the time of day to me and my tales and demanded nothing back. There's not many lasses as bonny and as straight as you and that's why I'm here.' John stepped back and looked at the blushing face of the girl he'd fallen for. 'Now give me the tea towel and let's get these dishes done, and then we might just have time for another quick kiss before the lovebirds return. Let them two make up for us. Lord knows they couldn't take their eyes of one another; we just weren't wanted.'

'Yes, I do believe that they love one another. I'm happy for our Eliza. She deserves some happiness in her life.' Mary-Anne smiled, thankful that John wasn't going to be too demanding.

'You do too, and I will make it my business to bring some happiness into your life. Along with keeping Eliza supplied with material for as long as I can. Life is what you make it, Mary-Anne, so let's enjoy it while we can.'

Mary-Anne looked at the reflection of John in the window and, for the first time in an age, felt cared for. If only she wasn't carrying another man's child, things could be so different. If only she could keep him interested in her and hide the baby from his eyes.

Twenty Four

Edmund Ellershaw paced up and down the parlour of his home, scowling at his son William and wife Catherine as his father-in-law's plans were laid bare for his wastrel son.

'It's a good deal, Edmund. William gets the Hall to live in and a business of his own after taking on their failing woollen mill under father's guidance, as well as Priscilla's hand in marriage. And they in turn get their family debts settled without any disgrace to her family. The Eaveshams have got good connections, William would be moving up in society.' Catherine Ellershaw sighed and glanced across to William who was in the middle of the argument over his grandfather's arrangement to set him up in polite society.

'But, she's no brass, the mill is in disrepair and the Hall is in hock. I've never heard of anybody marrying and worsening their bank balance. He doesn't even know the lass, not properly.' Edmund looked at his son and cursed under his breath.

'Of course he does, he's known her all his life. Grace and she have been friends for years. She's quite pretty and is totally presentable, and with Levensthorpe Hall to live in, and a mill of his own, despite its present state, Father will make it right. William will want for nothing. Not everyone wants to make their living down under the ground digging that black dirt. Besides, you should be welcoming the union and thanking my father for setting our William up in business.' Catherine Ellershaw sipped her sherry and looked at her son for support.

'I quite like her, Father, and I'd rather run a woollen mill than a coal mine. I'll never get an opportunity like this again. Think of it, Levensthorpe Hall is a grand place, much larger than here, and Mother's right, the Eaveshams do have good connections.' William knew there was no way out of marriage if he wanted to escape his father's household and having to marry the empty-headed Priscilla was of little consequence if he was to gain his own business and the Hall. He might not love her, but she needn't know that.

'Like her, lad? You'll need to do more than like her if you are going to live with her. I thought I was a bastard, but I think your father, Catherine, would sell his soul to the devil to get what he wants from folk. William should be first in line for the pit; he's our first-born. I always saw him stepping into my shoes, but he never has taken to it. Too mucky for his namby-pamby life style, which is your doing, woman. You and your bloody father. He'll have to work if he's to make High Watermill work; it's on its last legs. Or is that what your father wants? For it to fail so that it closes and then he is saving money with the Eaveshams not in competition with him.'

'You never think that my father tries to do the best for our family. You always see the bad side of him. He's doing this for William, despite what you think of his plans. You won't move from this squat little house ... well, our son can have something grander and without any help from you.' Catherine finished her sherry and stared at her husband who she knew hated her father with a vengeance.

'I am here, you know.' William interjected. 'You are both talking about me like I have no say in my life, as usual. I am going to do as Grandfather wants: I will marry Priscilla and I will run High Watermill. If only to prove you wrong, Father; you never have any faith in me. You can give baby George my share of Rose Pit when the time comes and he's welcome to it.' William stood up and turned his back on his squabbling parents, fleeing to the quietness of the garden.

Priscilla would make as good a wife as any and anything would be better than remaining at home – at least he would be his own master. It didn't matter that he didn't love Priscilla, he could always find satisfaction somewhere else, even if it wasn't with Mary-Anne Wild.

'Now look what you've done,' he heard his mother say as he made his escape and went to sit on the bench underneath the rambling rose that was just coming into bloom. 'You never do support our William, the marriage will be perfect for him.' He heard his mother shout at his father as the parlour door was slammed shut by his cursing father escaping from her sharp tongue. And then he heard the sobs of his mother, regretting the day she had married such a vulgar, common man and only wanting the best for her son.

'I take it it's you they're arguing over?' Grace appeared from behind the rose tree and sat down next to her brother. 'It's always you. I sometimes think I don't live in this house and George is too young to be part of their schemes yet.'

'Yes, it's me. I'm surprised Priscilla has not spoken to you and that you don't already know, the way you ladies titter and gossip. I am to wed her; her father and Grandfather have come to an arrangement. I am to have her hand in marriage, be master of the Levensthorpe and manage High Watermill so as to clear her father's debts.' William looked at his sister and then put his head down.

'But you don't love her, William! What about the woman you did love in Cambridge? You've pined for her for weeks. No doubt Priscilla will be happy – she has always admired you. Ever since she was young she has said that she loves you. But a marriage cannot be one-sided. Not if it is to work.' Grace took William's hand and comforted him.

'Like our parents' marriage? Mother married beneath her, at least I won't be doing that. Priscilla is over the moon with the news. I met her last night and had dinner with her parents. I know we don't really know one another but we have both flirted together for these last few years. It's just that I never saw her as my wife.' William looked at his sister. 'She was always just one of your empty-headed friends – there to be talked at and flirted with. But, as Grandfather says, it will set me up in society and I will be more than a pit owner's son. So I will make the best of it.' William bowed his head.

'Oh, William, I wish both you and Prissy all my love and best wishes. You will grow to love her, of that I'm sure. She is sweet and tender and has loved you from a distance for years now.' Grace held back a tear.

'And I will grow to love her, or be as bitter and twisted like my father and that I cannot stand.' William sighed. He'd agreed to the deal and now he must stand by it, for the step-up in society it would give him and the freedom to run his own affairs rather than for love.

'Oh, my dear Grace. You've heard the news! What has William told you? Is he excited?' Priscilla Eavesham kissed and hugged her closest friend as she entered into the parlour of Levensthorpe Hall.

'Yes, indeed he is. We all are. How wonderful that you are going to be my sister-in-law. You have finally won the affections of my brother after being besotted with him for all these years.' Grace sat down next to Priscilla and held her hand tightly.

'I couldn't believe it when Father told me that he had come to ask for my hand in marriage, especially when you had said that he was broken-hearted over some girl at college. I had nearly given up all hope of him even looking at me. And then I started thinking that perhaps it was me that he had been broken-hearted over, that he had missed me so much, that he had had to return and ask me to marry him. It all made sense then, especially when he paid for my dress along with yours; he must have been thinking about me then.' Priscilla giggled. Her cheeks were flushed and her blonde ringlets quivered with her excitement and nervousness of the coming marriage. 'Father says that there is no time to waste, that we must go and meet the vicar and get the banns read as soon as possible. The wedding day we have in mind is September the fourth, just into autumn when the days can still be warm and pleasant.'

'That sounds perfect, Prissy, but you have so much to sort and do. Does it give you enough time? What are you going to wear, and am I being presumptuous to think I'm to be a bridesmaid?' Grace had to look excited for the sake of her friend; she had decided to not let her know the truth behind her marriage to William as it would surely break her heart.

'Yes, of course it does. Cook and Mamma are already discussing the wedding banquet, although Father says we have to keep it low-key and not to go mad with the guest list. He says anything too decadent looks vulgar. And I thought of asking those sisters to make my wedding apparel, and, of course, dear Grace, it goes without saying that you will be my bridesmaid. I'm sure it will be what William would expect.' Prissy smiled at her best friend. The wedding could not come quick enough in her eyes and she was just thrilled with whatever arrangements were to be made.

'It is funny that you mention the Wild sisters for your bridal wear. Eliza Wild called on the house a while ago and left me these samples of material and this fashion booklet. It gives all the latest looks from France in it. They call it "Haute Couture", which I think means high fashion, and it does have some stunning ideas in it. The material would also be most sublime for a wedding dress, especially this cream-coloured one.' Grace passed Priscilla over the contents of her posy bag and waited for a response.

'This material is beautiful. It feels like silk and it shines and catches the light so. I remember seeing Princess Victoria's wedding in the newspaper in January this year and the dress was described as having pagoda sleeves and layers of silk with silk roses adorning the bodice and skirts. Do you think Eliza would be able to sew me something along similar lines? And, of course, you something similar. I will only have the one bridesmaid so Papa cannot complain about the price too much. Besides, I would probably pay considerably more if I was take fittings into Leeds itself, and Eliza Wild makes us so welcome in that ramshackle shop of hers.' Prissy beamed at Grace, imagining the dresses that they were both going to be wearing.

'You've just to ask her; I'm sure she will do everything you wish. And she needs our support. If I could I would fund her, and get her a new premises to work in, but my father would only scoff at my intentions. I keep thinking that she has so much potential but because of her being a working-class woman, nothing will become of it as she needs all her money just to keep fed.' Grace sighed.

'I could ask my papa for you,' Priscilla suggested. 'I'm sure he would listen and lend you some money; he knows that I love the dress that she made for me. He even commented on how beautiful it was and that it must have cost William a pretty penny.'

'No, don't do that. I will do it on my own one day hopefully. But shall we go and see if Eliza Wild can make the dress you have your heart set on?' Grace looked at her good friend, knowing that she really did not know the financial predicament her family was in and deciding that she was not about to tell her.

Twenty Five

'Well, what do you think of that?' Eliza turned and looked at Mary-Anne. 'William Ellershaw to marry that empty-headed one. I didn't see that coming.'

'No, neither did I. The poor lass, marrying him. She's no idea what his family is like, not including Grace.' Mary-Anne sat back and pretended she knew nothing of the upcoming wedding.

'He nearly turned your head. I remember that when you came back from having tea with him and his entourage you were full of it.' Eliza grinned.

'Well, I've thought better of it now and she's welcome to him,' Mary-Anne said more sharply than she intended. 'Are you sure you can do all that she's asked for? You are going to be sewing morning, noon and night. Silk roses and pagoda sleeves ... I've never heard of them. Where has she seen them?' Mary-Anne watched Eliza pick up the boards of gauze that had been left untouched until that morning. She wriggled in her chair. She had felt uncomfortable; the baby had been making its presence known all morning beneath her skirts.

'It's a mix up of what she heard Princess Victoria was wearing and what is in the leaflet I left with Grace Ellershaw. I'll be fine.

I might have to put some extra hours in but we are not going to turn that sort of money down. Besides, you can make the roses, they'll be easy enough to do. Once you've fashioned one, the rest will follow. I wonder if your John could get me some Broderie Anglaise; she will need that to attach as a pull-on sleeve underneath the loose pagoda effect. I looked at it and thought, that's going to be a fiddle, but I think I can get it right. When are you next seeing him?' Eliza looked at her quick sketch, which she had pencilled in when her two excited customers had explained what they had wanted, and turned as Mary-Anne gasped.

'It kicked, did you see? It kicked my stomach?' Mary-Anne beamed.

'No, I didn't. Am I supposed to get excited? I swear, you are not going to give that baby away after all. You are too soft. I sometimes think you forget whose baby it is. Which reminds me ... looking at you we had better take that skirt out a little, else everyone will notice your secret.' Eliza looked at her sister, who was rubbing her stomach and smiling down at her unborn child.

'I don't forget how it came about, Eliza, but I can't help but feel something now it is growing and a part of me. It's a baby and the poor soul's not done any wrong. It doesn't know its father is a selfish bastard. As for John, he will be calling on Sunday. We will go for a stroll this time and leave you and Tom in the house, providing the weather is good. But he doesn't order material on demand, you know. Whatever is available that he can steal away is what he brings you, never mind your fancy Broderie Anglaise. Perhaps you'll have to make do with plain cotton.' Not for the first time did Mary-Anne feel defensive towards the life she was carrying; things were changing within her body and it was preparing itself for motherhood ... something she couldn't quite comprehend.

'Your John's not a fool, you know. He may be keeping his distance but I've watched him put his hands on you. He's soon going to suspect that something's not quite right and put two and two together.' Eliza looked at her sister worriedly; she knew she was beginning to love the baby she was carrying as well as the charming Irishman who visited most Sundays.

'I know, but what can I do? He commented that I'd put weight on last week and that it must be because I was content. I don't want to lose him, Eliza. I hate lying to him . . .'

'How about we say you've got to go and see a sick aunt or something and you just hide from Tom when he visits? I could pick up any material John puts his hands on if I walk into Leeds,' Eliza suggested.

'But I'll not see him then and he might go to America without saying goodbye. It's hard enough that he will be leaving before Christmas without spending the rest of summer and early autumn without him. I don't know why I love him like I do; it's a doomed relationship and no matter what happens my heart is going to be broken. Sometimes I think everything will work out fine and then I think, who am I trying to fool? Especially when, as you say, my waistband keeps growing.' Mary-Anne sighed and looked out of the window onto the sunlit streets of Woodlesford. She knew in another few months nature would play its hand and she would become a mother, whether she liked it or not.

'I'll do the best I can. I'll add a line of extra material into that skirt and just keep him at bay for a little longer and try to fashion something to pull your stomach in. Hopefully something will happen and he might never suspect.' Eliza looked away from Mary-Anne; she couldn't help but wish for all their sakes that the baby would come early – healthy but early.

'Perhaps I should tell him I'm with child and explain why. It would show me what sort of man he truly is,' Mary-Anne whispered to her sister.

'I don't know, Mary-Anne ... it is your decision. I do know you don't want to lose him.' Eliza ran her hand around her sister's shoulder. She and Tom had their all lives ahead of them, in love with one another and with no obvious worries, other than what life dealt them, while Mary-Anne worried everyday about where her life and that of her child was going. It just wasn't fair.

Twenty Six

'What's wrong, John?' Mary-Anne asked as they arrived back onto Pit Lane after a Sunday stroll through Woodlesford and neighbouring Oulton. 'You've hardly said a word on our walk. Is something troubling you?' Mary-Anne felt uneasy. Had he guessed the state of her, and was he about to question her regarding it?

'I've been biding my time and have not wanted to tell you this, Mary-Anne, but I've no option. I'm leaving Leeds and am going to be working in Liverpool for a short time before I join my brother.' He took Mary-Anne's hands and looked into her eyes. 'I don't want to go. It's only because of the money; I can earn twice as much on the docks at Liverpool than on that wharf side on the canal. Otherwise I'll still be working there this time next year trying to scrape together enough money to see me straight. And I'll keep in touch and come back to see you from time to time.' John saw the tears in her eyes and knew she was upset.

'Are you sure that's why you are leaving? Perhaps there is no point in us continuing our relationship. After all, it will have to come to an end once you sail for America.' Mary-Anne fought back the tears and secretly cursed her unborn child for not giving her the freedom of what she wanted to say.

'Oh, Mary-Anne, if you only knew how I felt about you. It's because of you that I'm going to Liverpool. I didn't want to have to say this yet because I didn't want to build your hopes up. But if I can earn enough money for us both to seek a passage, I was hoping that you'd join me in my new life. It's time I took a wife, settled down and built a home. To be sure, I'm getting tired of being on my own of an evening, I could do with a good wife to look after me. I wouldn't be looking for a family though, not until we are settled and have a good living. I've seen enough poverty in my life and don't want any bairn of mine lying in its bed with a hungry belly of a night. That's what I'm leaving behind ... this is looking for a better life, hopefully for the both of us, if you'll come with me?' John held his breath; he had been thinking about his plans for both of them for some time and had known Mary-Anne was the girl from him the first day he had set eyes on her in her Aunt Patsy's house.

Mary-Anne looked down and then raised her head to look at him. 'I can't, John; I can't come with you. I'm not what you think I am.' She brushed a tear away and then cried, realising she couldn't keep her secret any longer. 'I am with child ... another two months and it will be born. You won't want me then and I don't blame you. How could you, I'm nothing but a used woman.'

'But you can't be, I've not touched you. If it's not mine, have you been seeing someone else behind my back?' John ran his fingers through his long, black hair and glanced at Mary-Anne and the now-obvious stomach that she had hidden under her skirts. 'How could you lead me on? I've lost my heart to you and you have deceived me.' John grasped Mary-Anne arms and shook her. 'Who's the father? Because by the Lord, I will kill him.'

'I can't say, but the child's not here through love,' Mary-Anne sobbed. 'I too feel the same about you, but it would not be fair for you to pin your hopes on me joining you in America, as I don't know how I will feel once the child is born and you won't want me anyway.'

'Tell me who the father is! When you say you did not love him, why did you let him touch you?' John shouted at Mary-Anne, realising his world with all his dreams for a better life had just fallen apart.

'I thought that I had no option. It was after my mother had died and it was the only way to keep the roof over our heads.' Mary-Anne looked at John and saw the anger on his face.

'You sold yourself! You were no better than the prick-pinchers on the wharf side. My God, have I been blind? Just how long did you think you could hide it from me? And what was to become of the bastard baby that you are carrying?' John shook her again.

'I was going to take it to the poor house or the orphanage, but I'm beginning to realise that I can't be that heartless. That the child is half mine and no matter how it was conceived, I have feelings for it.'

'Well, at least that is to be admired in you. But as for us two, I can't continue with our courtship. You have deceived me, Mary-Anne. You have tricked me into thinking you were someone pure and that I could love, when all the time you were with child. It's best that I leave; this is the last that you will be seeing of me. There's nothing here for me now.' John let go of her arms and stared at her as she shook sobbing and crumpled in the middle of the path to her home. 'I could have loved you, Mary-Anne – a new life waited for us both – but not now.' John straightened his cap, gave her one last glance and then strode off back down the lane.

'John ... don't go! I love you!' Mary-Anne cried. But it was too late. His strides took him quickly down the lane, and he never gave her a backward glance. Tears ran down her face and her body shook as she hugged herself tightly, then she made her way home.

Why had she told him? How had she thought he would take it? She should have said nothing. She should have let him go to Liverpool and by the time he had returned for her, the baby would have been born and a home found for it without his knowing.

Deep down she knew why she'd told him; the life within her might not have been made in love, but it was part of her, her blood, and there was no way she could turn her back on it, no matter how it was conceived. It would be born, she'd raise it the best she could and John Vasey would have to be forgotten. There was nothing else to do.

'What the hell's wrong with you?' Mick watched as his lodger of the last seven months ransacked his basement room, thrusting his few belongings into a bag, which he swung across his back.

Patsy stood next to her husband and watched as John swore, dropping his watch onto the floor as he looked at the time.

'I'm fecking well leaving, that's what's wrong with me. I know I said it would be next week and that I'd pay the rent up to then, but there's nowt here in Leeds for me anymore. I'll not be coming back.' John looked wild-eyed at his old friend, and put his watch back into his waistcoat pocket.

'What's brought this on? Have you and our Mary-Anne had words, or is it the lads down at the quay? Sure they are always gobbing off.' Mick laughed.

'It's bloody Mary-Anne, if you must know. And I'm sorry, Patsy, but your niece is nothing but a slut. She's opened her legs to some bugger and is carrying their child. And I thought she was the one for me, and there she was hiding that growing belly and I just thought how content and well she looked.' John growled at Patsy, and hated himself for telling her, but he wasn't one for not saying it how it was.

'She can't be, she's not like that! Now, young Eliza perhaps, she's got the cheek of the devil, but not Mary-Anne. You are sure it's not yours, John Vasey, and that you are leaving her in such a state?' Patsy stood in the doorway and blocked his way.

'I haven't put a bloody hand on her, she wouldn't let me, and now I know why. Besides, I'd more respect for her to do that, more fool me! I'm not your young buck that just looks at women for one thing.' John cursed as he pushed Patsy aside and Mick caught his arm. 'Let me go, Mick. I'm not stopping a minute longer. My new address and rent money is on the table over there, I was hoping I could leave without seeing you both.'

'You'd better not have disgraced my family, John. If I find out it is yours, I'll not be happy.' Mick held John's arm.

'I'd not be leaving my address if it was mine, now would I? She's broken my heart and shattered my dreams of a new life with her ... now let me be. I've no gripe with you two.' John looked at them both. They'd been good to him and he'd been happy staying with them while courting Mary-Anne.

'Then get away, man. May God be with you and I'm sorry that she's hurt you.' Mick patted John on his back and watched as he went up the cellar steps, listening as he slammed the kitchen door behind him. 'I think you'd better pay your nieces a visit, it sounds as if one of them might be in need of your services.' Mick sat down on the chair next to the table with the rent money and John's forwarding address. 'I thought for the first time in John Vasey's life he was going to be happy. He deserved a good woman in his life and I thought he'd found her in Mary-Anne.'

'She is a good'en, and she wouldn't lead him on. Someone's taken advantage of her, of that I'm sure. I'll go up there at the weekend, see what they are about. In the meantime, you keep in touch with John;

he'll need a friend, and, besides, if he turns out to be the father, we need to know where he is. He can't expect to walk away from his responsibilities.' Patsy sighed. 'I owe it to her mother, God rest her soul, to look after Mary-Anne.'

'It'll not be his, else he wouldn't have left her. I know John.' Mick looked at the hurriedly written address in his hand.

'Aye, well, we will see. Who ever it is, that lass needs help.' Patsy shook her head and sighed as she went up into her kitchen. Her niece needed her, that was for sure.

'What the hell did you tell him for?' Eliza looked at her sister in disbelief as she cried once again over her meagre supper. 'The more I think about it the more I wonder why you opened your gob. Another two months, Mary-Anne ... the baby would have been born, you could have left it in somebody else's care and you could have had a new life with the man with whom there is no doubt you are in love.' Eliza put her hands on her hips and sighed.

'But it wouldn't be cared for, would it? It would just exist, not have a mother or someone to love it ... not like we had. I know I started off hating this baby, but now it's growing I can feel it moving and it's a part of me. It's your kin too, Eliza; I can't just abandon it, no matter how much I love John.' Mary-Anne looked up from her still-full supper dish and across at Eliza. Her eyes were red and swollen and her long auburn hair, which she was so proud of, was tangled about her shoulders.

'But it's Edmund Ellershaw's bastard, and even if you brought him up in front of the parish councillors for the Poor Law, you'd get no money out of him. They are all his cronies and are in league with him. They'll not even listen to you. How are we going to manage to bring it up as well as keep a roof over our heads? The gossip will be fearful, her next door will revel in it for weeks.' Eliza suddenly realised that the plans for the baby had changed, that it was going to be a part of her life as well as Mary-Anne's … something she hadn't seen coming. 'What will Tom think? His mother will definitely not think much of us when she finds out.' Eliza sighed.

'Oh, Eliza, you of all people,' Mary-Anne sobbed. 'This baby could be yours. I've heard you and Tom whispering and carrying on. You are such a hypocrite. I'm in trouble and it was as much to save us both from the poor house as myself. The one time I ask for support and all you can think of is your precious Tom.'

'I just didn't think that you'd be keeping it,' Eliza gasped. 'I didn't think you wanted it. Perhaps I should have taken you to Aunt Patsy's that day and then you wouldn't be here crying broken-hearted.'

'No,' Mary-Anne cried, 'I might have joined my mother and that other lost soul that got buried with her. I'm not the first to have an illegitimate baby and I'll not be the last. But I loved John and I wish I had told him from the start; it just got harder as the weeks went on and I didn't realise how much he thought of me and me of him.'

'Well, he's gone now. We will have to make the best of it. It's a pity because where am I going to get my material from? I was relying on him for future supplies. Did you manage to ask him for some cotton? Do you think he will have hoarded some away for me?' Eliza asked, thinking of the dresses that were taking up most of her time and that would not be completed if she had no material to work with.

'You are unbelievable, Eliza Wild! This dressmaking has gone to your head. I'm broken-hearted and all you can think about is your satins. I couldn't give a damn about the stupid dress. I wish William Ellershaw, his father and his stupid giggling bride would go to hell because that's where they belong. If I can't be happy, why should they?'

Mary-Anne thrust her chair back and ran up to her room, leaving Eliza shocked by her outburst. Perhaps she had been a bit uncaring but the wedding dress would pay for their bread and butter for weeks to come and would be needed, especially if there was to be three of them shortly.

Eliza put her head in her hands and sighed. A baby ... what the hell were they going to do with a baby, and how would she bring it into the world without any help?

Twenty Seven

'Well, this is a nice mess you've got yourself into, Mary-Anne. You, of all folk ... I thought your mother had brought you up correctly and told you not to open your legs for any man.' Patsy sat across the other side of the kitchen table from her niece and scowled at the pale-faced young woman who looked downcast. 'When John Vasey told me, I could hardly believe it. And him there, thinking of wedding you. There isn't a slim chance that it could be his, is there?'

Mary-Anne shook her head.

'Then who's is it? Let's be hearing. The fairies didn't put it there overnight, somebody has had his way with you.' Patsy took off her shawl and looked around the house – the house she hadn't been in for some years as she was never made welcome by Bill Parker. The girls had kept it tidy, she thought, that was something their mother would be proud of.

'I don't want to say. Anyway, it'll make no difference because he denies it being his and he's married.' Mary-Anne looked at Eliza, hoping that she'd keep quiet.

'That's always the way with men ... they like their pleasure but never want to pay for it. But you should have thought, girl. A few minutes' excitement and look what it's done to you ... ruined your life. You should have come to me early on and all this could have been avoided. It's too late now, by the look of that belly that you are trying to hide.' Patsy sighed.

'It wasn't excitement or pleasure, believe me,' Mary-Anne whispered.

'It never is the first time and then you grow to enjoy it and you know their ways. It's a pity your mother isn't here to tell you all this.' Patsy tapped her fingers on the table.

Eliza sprang to her sister's defence.

'She means she didn't want it; she was forced. The dirty old bastard, he knew exactly what he was doing.' How could her aunt think the worse of her sister? They both might be able to give cheek and hold their own, but neither of them were easy.

'You are telling me Mary-Anne was raped? Speak up, child.' Patsy looked at the two sisters exchanging glances at one another. 'Well?'

'Near as damn it, Aunt Patsy. Tell her, Mary-Anne, tell her why you are in this state,' Eliza urged as Mary-Anne scowled and shook her head. 'She did it because we couldn't pay the rent. Edward Ellershaw might as well have raped her as he had his enjoyment, and he wanted it to become a regular understanding rather than find him the rent money. He took her to his club and she came back in the state you find her. And now he won't pay for her trouble.' Eliza wept and hugged her sister as Patsy took it all in.

Mary-Anne hung her head and snivelled. 'It was my fault; I shouldn't have let him touch me. I should have had my pride, but things looked so bleak and we had no money.'

'I should have known. That man will rot in hell one day. He preys on the weak and less fortunate than himself. He's nothing more than a bully; your mother loathed the ground he walked on. I should have been there to warn you.' Patsy wiped a tear from her eye. 'You'll not get any money out of him. It's not the first time he's done something like this; believe me, I know. '

Mary-Anne wanted to say, I know he did it with my mother, but thought better of it.

'Why didn't you tell John all this? He might have understood then and looked differently at the situation. I do believe he loved you, Mary-Anne.'

'I couldn't tell him all of it,' Mary-Anne whispered, 'about what I'd been through. I was too embarrassed.'

'Aye, lass, there's you and Eliza walking about Leeds as if you own the place, and then when it comes to talking about natural things you daren't speak. Sex is what makes the world turn, girls, it just isn't spoken about. It's brushed under the carpet in polite society. But everyone does it behind closed doors, else we wouldn't all be here. Now, what are you going to do about this baby? You are too far gone by the looks of it to get rid of it. The mite will have to be born and that means you need me, because you won't know the first thing about bringing a baby into the world, Eliza, but I'll learn you when the time comes. Are you keeping it or is it to go onto the poorhouse steps? That would be the sensible thing to do. You don't want a burden at your age.' Patsy folded her arms and looked sternly at Mary-Anne.

'I don't know … one minute I want to keep it and then the next it's like you say, it would just be a burden. A burden we could both do without.' Mary-Anne looked at Eliza.

'Well, we will cross that bridge if it's born safely. Now Eliza, you make me a pot of tea while I have a look at Mary-Anne here, just to make sure all's going to plan and see when we can expect this baby to be born.' Patsy got up from the table and waited for Mary-Anne.

251

'Go on lass, get yourself upstairs and let me have a look at you. It's no good being coy now, I'll see it all in another few weeks because this baby is not entering this world without me to help it. I owe that to your mother at least.' Patsy watched as Mary-Anne hesitatingly walked past her.

'She'll be all right, won't she? You won't do anything to make her lose the baby, will you?' Eliza said.

'Heavens, child, do you think me a murderer? She'll be safe in my hands, I've helped bring babies into the world one way or another all my life, depending on the circumstances. I will do my best for Mary-Anne.' Patsy turned and followed Mary-Anne up the stairs and breathed in deeply. A baby in the family was all they needed, but that was what they were going to have and she would have to do her best by her nieces.

'I think you're right – you look to me as if you've got another two months, but it could come early or late, so be careful what you are doing. You'll know when it's due because you'll feel as if you've peed yourself, Mary-Anne; that'll be the water that protects the baby giving way, letting you know it's coming. As soon as you see that or get any sharp pains send for me and I'll come as fast as I can. It's your first, so you'll likely take a while.' Patsy sipped her tea and looked across at the two young women. 'Is there a young lad you can send to get me? You don't want to be left on your own.'

'Aye, there Henry Milburn at the end of the row, he can run like a whippet. We'll send him,' Eliza quickly said. 'I've no intentions of leaving you on your own, Mary-Anne.'

'Well, that's that then. You take it easy these next few weeks, look after yourself and all will be well.' Patsy stood up and patted Mary-Anne on her shoulder. 'I should have known that Edmund Ellershaw had something to do with this. The man is depraved and his wife is such a well-to-do woman. I don't know what she saw in him. I feel guilty that I never came after your mother's death and warned you about him.'

'You weren't to know and you have enough of your own problems. Will you be getting a replacement lodger now that John has gone?' Eliza asked, noticing Mary-Anne's silence.

'I think I'll keep his room empty for a while. See how things pan out. Mick and I like our own company.' Patsy cast her eye on the silk roses that Mary-Anne had been fashioning next to the fire for Priscilla Eavesham's wedding dress; she'd put them to one side when Patsy had knocked on the door. 'They are bonny!' Patsy exclaimed. 'Are they for somebody's dress?'

'They are for William Ellershaw's bride and her bridesmaid. He is to wed Priscilla Eavesham from Levensthorpe Hall on the first Saturday in September,' Mary-Anne said and went to pick them up.

'That'll be Edmund's lad, is it? Aye, lass, you are making his son's intended a wedding dress, while carrying his father's child … I bet with every stitch you are wishing that family ill. He'll only be like his father and be marrying for gain; they'll never be happy. No good ever comes out of a marriage match for brass.' Patsy pulled on her shawl.

'I hate him as much as his father; I pity poor Priscilla. As you say, it will not be a happy marriage.' Mary-Anne sighed.

'Take their brass, lasses. Take as much as you can get out of them and then look after yourselves. And don't worry, this baby will be born safely and then your true worries begin. If you decide to bring it up.' Patsy kissed both girls on the cheek before saying farewell and stepped back into the sunshine on her walk back into Leeds. She'd a letter to write, one that she hoped would change

John Vasey's hasty decision and bring a little pleasure into Mary-Anne's life.

'I thought you had a liking for William Ellershaw?' Eliza said as she cleared the table.

'I hate him. He's just like his father and Aunt Patsy is right, he is just marrying for money. That is all the family thinks about.' Mary-Anne looked down at her stomach and rubbed her hand over it.

'You've certainly changed your tune. Grace is all right, she's put business our way,' Eliza said as she rattled the pots.

'She's just the same, she's using you. She knows that the dresses you make are special and that one day she will gain from it. I hate the whole lot of them. One day Edmund Ellershaw will regret the day he ever lay his hands on me. I don't know how, but I will get my revenge. Mark my words, Eliza, they will hate my name by the time they have all had their day.' Mary-Anne remembered her mother and thought of the heartache that she must have endured. Revenge just wouldn't be for herself but for her mother too; it was time the tables were turned.

Twenty Eight

'Tom's coming this evening. He can't make Sunday, and, besides, I thought you'd probably not want to see him at the moment. I can't wait, I haven't seen him the last few weekends as I've been busy with the dresses and his mother decided he wanted him at home for a few Sundays. Selfish old bat.' Eliza looked across at Mary-Anne. 'He dropped a note in under the shop door to tell me.'

'I'll make myself scarce. You're right, I don't want him to see me in this state. Besides, it is best he doesn't know, just in case I give the baby away. His mother would have a fit if she got wind that I was having a baby, and I'm surprised next door haven't said anything yet.' Mary-Anne looked worried. 'They don't usually miss a thing and would be the first to give my state away.'

'You still don't know what you are going to do, do you? Tom will have to know sometime; I've told him that you've been feeling under the weather and not been going to the shop or into Leeds these past weeks. He was worried about you, so I said it was because you were melancholy over John Vasey leaving for Liverpool, which is partly true; you haven't been yourself since he left.' Eliza glanced at her sister, fearing a backlash for saying the truth.

'I can live without him, I don't miss him that much. He'd only have dragged me over to America with him and what would I have done there? Besides, I couldn't leave you on your own. Tom need not know anything until the baby is born, so don't you go shooting your mouth off.' Mary-Anne went quiet when she heard the knocker on the front door go.

'He's early ... he said he'd be here at seven. It's only six-thirty and he doesn't usually knock nowadays.' Eliza looked at herself in the mirror and pinched her cheeks in readiness to meet her lover. 'Get yourself upstairs, Mary-Anne. I'll wait until you are safely up before I open the door.' She watched has Mary-Anne took herself up the stairs to her bedroom, where she lay silently on her bed.

'I'm coming, Tom, won't be a minute.' She brushed her white apron down and opened the door latch with a wide beam on her face, closing her eyes and puckering her lips up to be kissed by her beau.

'Now, that's some greeting. John didn't warn me of that. Tha's a bit forward for our first meeting.' George Towler stood on the doorstep and grinned, his sack of material down by his side, hastily dropped when confronted by the eager Eliza. 'I'd have been here earlier, if I'd have known that was waiting for me.'

Eliza opened her eyes and looked at the scruffy young man on her doorstep whom she had nearly kissed. 'Who are you?'

'I'm George. I worked down at the quay with John. Before he left he asked if I wanted to keep you supplied with any material I could get my hands on. It was on the understanding that you might give me the odd bob or two if it was to your liking. But I'll not argue if you want to pay me another way ... tha looked fair inviting just then.'

'I think you've got me wrong, George. I'm not that sort of a woman. But I'll have a look at what you've got in your sack. You'd better come in, we don't want to do business in public.' Eliza invited him into the house and took him into the kitchen. She stood by the side of the table and watched as he emptied the contents of his sack.

'John said you wanted some white cotton. My lass says that's what this is when I showed her it. I haven't got a bloody clue myself so I hope this will do. John said you were looking for something white with tiny holes in it, but that sounded bloody wrong. What would you want with material with holes in it for? I asked myself.' George laid his boards of material out upon the table and waited as Eliza looked at them. 'There's some good stuff there, lass; you'd pay a good price anywhere else. I can always lay my hands on more, if we can come to an agreement.' George wiped his nose and waited as Eliza inspected and smiled.

'I don't know; the cotton is not that good in quality and this crepe looks as if it's rolled around a bit. What do you want for it all? I haven't got a lot of money in the house.' Eliza played her usual game of bartering, not used to paying for the material in the past and not wanting to do so now.

'I'd say five shillings for the lot; it's nearly cost me that in boot leather, trailing it here from Leeds.' George stood back and waited, watching Eliza's expression as she pulled a face at his price.

'Three shillings and sixpence,' Eliza offered quickly.

'Four shillings and that kiss you were readily making available to me if I'd been the right man.' George grinned as she looked at him and wondered if she'd dare.

'Right, we have a deal.' Eliza reached for the money box and counted out the four shillings into George's hand and braced herself to kiss a man she hardly knew, knowing she'd only to shout and Mary-Anne would come to her rescue if he got out of hand. She closed her eyes and put her arms around his neck kissing him on the lips quickly. He smelt of sweat and ale and she was glad when he released her. But as she stepped back she realised that the front door had opened and in the doorway of the kitchen stood Tom, who had just witnessed the embrace.

'I'll have another one of them. Take a penny back and give me another, my old lass doesn't do owt like that.' George fumbled in his pocket as a look of sheer panic crossed Eliza's face.

She watched as Tom went down the passage without a word and slammed the front door. Racing after him she shouted, 'Tom, Tom, wait! It isn't what it seems. He'd only come to me with some material. He means nothing to me.'

But Tom didn't wait or reply. He remembered the conversation when Bert Simms had told him about her kissing somebody early morning at the garden gate and the gossip that the Wild girls attracted with their devil-may-care attitude to life. His mother had been right; she'd broken his heart and was nothing more than the hussy his mother had told him she was. That was the last time his feet would take him down Pit Lane, he thought, as he went deaf to the pleas that Eliza shouted at him, and hurried home.

Mary-Anne closed the door behind the visitor that had caused so much upset. She sighed and nodded her head as she walked along the passage and into the kitchen, where her sister sat sobbing.

'I thought that you had learned from the first time, when next door witnessed you with John, that you just can't go kissing folk to get your own way.' Mary-Anne sighed. 'Don't worry, Tom will be back. He thinks too much of you not to be.' She poked the fire and looked at her sister.

'He won't. You didn't see his face and he didn't even turn when I shouted his name. I'm just an idiot, Mary-Anne, all for the sake of sixpence. But we've never paid for the material before and all I could think of was how much money we could make and would we even get paid for the dresses if, as you once said, the Eaveshams have no money.' Eliza sobbed.

'She wouldn't dare not pay for her and Grace's wedding attire, you idiot. You just like getting the cheapest deal you can and now it has backfired upon you. He wasn't even good-looking and he smelt. You'd no reason to kiss him.' Mary-Anne shook her head.

'What am I going to do? Tom will never talk to me again and I've ruined my life.' Eliza looked across at her sister with tears in her eyes.

'When it comes to men, we're not lucky, are we? Don't ask me for advice, I'm not in any position to tell you anything. But if you do love him, go and see him, explain and tell him how much you love him. We both can't be broken-hearted. Surely one of us must deserve the man we love in our lives.' Mary-Anne ran her hand along the back of her sister's shoulders and stood by her as she shook in grief.

'I do love him, I don't want anyone else. I wish I'd never opened the door to that rat and his material.' Eliza looked at the boards of fabric still on the kitchen table. 'You'd think I'd have learnt by your mistake, but no, I just blundered into losing my Tom, all for the sake of a lump of cotton.'

'It's fools that we are, Eliza, and now we are fools without a man in our lives.' Mary-Anne sighed. 'Perhaps it is best that way.'

'No, one of us has to be happy in love; I won't let my Tom go!' Eliza wiped her eyes and lifted her chin firmly as she got angry with herself. 'I'll go and visit him tomorrow evening and explain.'

Mary-Anne looked at her sister. She was determined, but some-how she doubted that Tom's affections would be easy to win back, especially when he told his mother of the circumstances that he had found Eliza in. However, she'd leave her to it and hope that Tom would listen.

'You've got to let me talk to him, Mrs Thackeray. I've got to explain. He's got it all wrong.' Eliza stood on the step of Tom's home and begged his mother to let him come to the door.

'You can just bugger off,' Madge shouted at Eliza as she stood in the doorway. 'I told him what sort of lass you were, but he didn't listen. Well, now he's learnt the hard way. You are not welcome here anymore. He wants nowt to do with you.' Her face was red with anger, and she knew that her neighbours were listening to the ongoing exchange of words. 'Now I'm closing the door and don't come this way again. And don't be thinking of pestering him at work. That would only make you look like a real hussy when them lot hear what you've been about. My Tom is a respectable lad and not for the likes of you.' The door slammed in Eliza's face as she stood her ground, defiant but beside herself with grief over losing the love of her life.

'Well, piss off, you old bitch,' Eliza shouted, and banged on the wooden door, belying her true feelings of who could have been her mother-in-law before she wandered back down Wood Lane sobbing and distraught. Her life in tatters.

'Well, I did warn you, lad. Nowt but trouble, that's what she is … just like their mother. She turned her man to drink, so she did. You heard her calling me an old bitch; no decent lass would come out with that language. Although she nearly had me fooled, coming with her baking and flowers and her sweet words. I should have known better.' Madge Thackeray sat down across from her son and looked at the gloom that had been on his face for over a week now. 'You are best off with your old mother. We want for nothing, and you never know, one day the right lass may come along.'

'I thought Eliza was the right lass. I loved her, Ma, I nearly thought of wedding her. But when I saw that man offering her money for another kiss, I knew what Bert Simms had said was true. You can't be in love with somebody like that, you'd never be able to trust her.' Tom hung his head and ran his fingers through his hair.

'You mean, this isn't the first time she's been seen with another man?' Madge crossed her arms under her ample breasts and went a deeper shade of red.

'Aye, Bert said he'd seen her early one morning with a fella, but I chose not to believe him. He's always gossiping about somebody.' Tom looked up at his mother.

'The dirty little trollop and I've been letting you see her. Not again, do you hear? You have nothing more to do with her.' Madge fumed.

'I know, I should have listened, but I thought she loved me.' Tom sighed. No matter what she had done, a part of his heart would always be hers.

'That's it then, she's gone and things are back to normal.' Madge stood up. 'Now, I'll make you a nice steak and kidney pudding and then you can read me the paper.' Madge smiled; she'd got her precious son back, out of the arms of a wanton hussy, and he was not about to escape again.

Twenty Nine

'Isn't it beautiful, Mama?' Priscilla Eavesham looked at her reflection in the long mirror that stood at the back of Eliza's workshop and admired herself. 'The neckline is just superb and look at the fineness of the flowers that adorn the skirt and finish on the bodice.' Priscilla turned one way and then the other and then looked at Grace as she came from behind a curtain that gave her privacy as she tried on her accompanying dress. 'Grace, you look beautiful!'

'I must agree, the dresses do look fine, but the premises, Priscilla … they are quite unbelievable. Your father would not be impresssed.' Alice Eavesham looked around her with disdain as Eliza pulled the skirt out to the full extent of her daughter's wedding dress. 'And this chair that I'm sitting on … I've seen better in the gardener's potting shed.'

'Mother, do you know how rude you are being? Just look at Grace and myself. Now tell me where else could we have found dresses like these? Forget about where they are made. Eliza here is just starting out; I'm sure better premises will be secured in time.' Priscilla smiled at Eliza as she moved over to Grace, her lack of comment being noted by both Grace and herself.

'I think Eliza here will be a name to be remembered in years to come. I've never worn a more exquisite dress. Everyone will comment about them, Mrs Eavesham ... all our friends are followers of Miss Eliza's work.' Grace smiled down at Eliza as she pinned and tucked her skirt, making the last few adjustments.

'I just think we could have gone to somewhere a little more established. I'm in no doubt that the dresses are well made, it's just they don't have a name behind them, do they?' Alice Eavesham looked at Eliza in her plain clothes and straight, long blonde hair and then gazed out of the window as the girls looked at their reflections together and giggled. 'What does your mother think, Grace? Would she not back me up?'

'I don't think she will be too worried where the dresses come from as long as they fit and look the part, and these certainly do. Besides, she knows I support both Mary-Anne and Eliza, and purchase clothes on a regular basis. I have always found them to be of good quality. My father might complain, but what does he know about ladies' fashion?' Grace smiled at Eliza, noticing the worried look upon her face.

'Oh, I suppose if they are good enough for your mother, then I'm just being a pain. Your mother always shows good taste and is well known in society. You both look beautiful, my dears.' Alice stood up and looked at both radiant girls. 'The trouble is, I can't believe that I am to lose my only daughter so soon. Your brother had better take care of her, Grace.'

'I'm sure he will, Mrs Eavesham, he's counting the days to the wedding now, along with my mother.' Grace smiled.

'And your father?' Alice enquired.

'Father is Father – if it doesn't include coal he is not too bothered. Although I think he is glad that William is to manage High Watermill, as he showed no interest in mining and is thankful that Mr Eavesham and my grandfather have given William the opportunity to prove himself. Everyone has to start somewhere and we all know William truly loves Priscilla.'

'Thank you dear Grace, I cannot wait until we are sisters-in-law.' Priscilla smiled and took a final look at herself in the mirror, as Eliza stood back and admired her handiwork on both.

'Right, girls, if you are happy I will accept them both. Go and get changed behind that dreadful curtain. Hopefully no one will be able to see you.' Alice watched as both young women giggled and followed Eliza to change back to their daywear behind the curtain that saved them from prying eyes. 'Deliver them to Levensthorpe and I will see you get paid,' she told Eliza. 'I want an itemized bill, mind you; nothing else will do. I need to know just exactly what was used in the making of these dresses.' She pulled on her gloves and waited, standing next to the shop window. She turned and looked at the two girls who were flushed with excitement. 'How one could make such a thing of beauty in such squalid conditions I really don't know. But there you go. Perhaps you can make a silk purse out of a sow's ear. Come, girls, we are to have tea with your mother, Grace, at Highfield; she will be waiting and wanting to know our progress. I can tell her now that the dresses are complete at least.'

The Eaveshams stepped gingerly down the steps and past the open gutter and onto the road. Grace held back for a second and whispered her thanks to Eliza and her apologies for any offence that Priscilla's mother may have given as Eliza held the door open for the trio to leave. Grace was aware that that Eliza had bitten back any response, she had not failed to notice the look upon her face as Alice's cutting remarks wounded her. Grace was certain that if she had her way Eliza's name would one day be one of note in the fashion world, despite their humble beginnings.

Eliza sat back in the kitchen chair and looked at Mary-Anne; she'd been telling her about the caustic comments of Alice Eavesham.

"'Perhaps you can make a silk purse out of a sow's ear." Sarcastic old cow.' Eliza growled. 'I'll give her a sow's ear. Does she know that her daughter's about to marry a pig's son and that he probably won't be much better?'

'Don't let it worry you. As long as you get the money, that's all that matters. When are you taking them to the Hall? The sooner you get them delivered the better.' Mary-Anne put a plate full of potato-hash in front of her sister and watched as she picked up her fork to eat.

'Tomorrow, then we will have some good money to go at once they are paid for. That's another thing, she expects an itemized bill. I wrote it out after they had gone. Old cow.'

'I just hope they pay. You never know with their sort and we both know the Eaveshams had no money last time she ordered something.' Mary-Anne looked across at her angry sister.

'They'll pay, because if they don't I'll go in and stop the bloody wedding. If both of us can't be happy, then why should they? Bloody toffs.' Eliza slurped her food and swore under her breath. She was bitter; life was not treating them well but surely it was time for the tables to turn.

John Vasey sat on what in the broadest terms could just be called a bed, its planks covered by a straw-filled mattress and a stained pillow that held the sweat from many a former dockhand's head. He picked up the letter that had found its way to him in the grim surroundings of the boarding house that had been his home for the last seven weeks.

He looked at the handwriting and recognised it to be of his former landlady, Patsy.

He breathed in deeply. He'd hoped to have left any memories of Leeds behind him, but a haunting picture of Mary-Anne possessed him and kept him awake each night, leaving him thinking about her and the life he could have had if it had not been for the unborn child. He played with the letter, not wanting to break the seal and read the contents, as he knew that her name would be mentioned within, probably bringing back more heartache and sadness.

He sighed and ran his thumb under the wax seal, to reveal the contents of the letter that Patsy had felt her duty to write, to reclaim the lives of the two people that she knew deserved happiness. His hands shook as he read the words within, how Edmund Ellershaw had used Mary-Anne's mother and had controlled her for years with the threat of eviction and his hold over her and the useless Bill Parker. He swore as he read that he had continued in the same vein with Mary-Anne, how he had used and abused her, threatened her with the same and for this she had been easy prey for him to do as he liked. Hence the baby she was carrying now – a bastard child, conceived not through love but through greed, rape and manipulation of a young woman.

John looked around the grubby dockside boarding house; another week and he would have enough money and more besides for his passage to America, leaving the hovel he was in behind and the memories of Mary-Anne Wild. He was bound for a new life and he didn't want the ties of another man's bairn to burden him. He was best forgetting her; no matter how the baby had come about, she should have had more pride and respect for herself. She obviously took after her mother, and a woman like that was no good to any man, no matter how good her intentions were towards her family and husband.

Three babies, Patsy had said, three babies her sister had lost to the bastard Ellershaw, and that was only the three she knew about. His mind was filled with mixed emotions. How could any woman go through that? And then for their daughter to fall into the same trap ...

He cast his mind back to the tearful Mary-Anne and how he'd not listened to her pleas. She'd raised her skirts for another man and that was all he'd been able to think about as he had stormed away, and that she had deceived him for all those months while she was carrying the child.

No, no matter what had happened, Mary-Anne was not for him. A new life was calling. Why should he start it with the worries of an old dirty one? Mary-Anne and her baby would have to survive as best they could because it would not be with him, no matter how much Patsy pleaded for the innocence of her niece.

Thirty

'Mary-Anne, I'm home! Put the kettle on, let's celebrate. In fact, do you fancy a drop of gin? I'll go to the Boot and Shoe for a gill. I've never held as much money in my hand.' Eliza slammed the front door shut and yelled along the passage to the back kitchen as she placed her shawl around the banister at the bottom of the stairs. She was grinning widely; the Eavesham's had paid her outright for the wedding garments as she delivered them and now she could have cried with joy at the thought of having security for once in their lives. 'Mary-Anne, where are you?' Eliza quickly hurried into the kitchen, sensing something was wrong as she heard no response from her sister.

'What's wrong, are you ill?' Eliza went over to her sister who was gripping the pot sink with both hands and looked pale. She looked down at the pool of water that lay at her sister's feet and realised at once that the baby was on its way.

'Sorry Eliza, it started as soon as you left the house this morning; the pain is getting stronger every time.' Mary-Anne caught her breath as another bout of pain swept her abdomen and she cringed and bent double as it cut through her speech.

'Here, let's get you upstairs and then I'll go for Henry to get Aunt Patsy.' Eliza gave Mary-Anne her arm and led her up towards the stairs.

'I've managed to fill the boiler outside and it's warming nicely, just like Aunt Patsy instructed us. Please don't be long finding Henry and sending him for her. I think she will be too late in coming anyway, the pains are that bad.' Mary-Anne gripped the baluster rail and stopped in her tracks as another wave of pain hit her, leaving her breathless and panting.

Reaching the top of the stairs, Eliza lead Mary-Anne into her bedroom, and laid a folded old sheet under where Mary-Anne was to lay. 'You'll be all right, I won't be long. It's best we send for her just in case there are any complications.' Eliza helped Mary-Anne out of her dress and into her night shift, fumbling as she undid the buttons and laces of her dress and boots, and conscious that it would not be long before the baby made an appearance into the world.

'I'll not die, will I, Eliza? You'll not let me die. I keep remembering Mother.' Mary-Anne gasped and held onto Eliza's arm, her nails digging into Eliza's skin.

'No, I won't let you. Now I'll only be a second, I saw Henry playing marbles in the lane as I came in home. I'll yell of him to run like the wind and give him threepence for his bother. And then Aunt Patsy will soon be with us.' Eliza stood in the doorway and looked at her sister lying in bed. She knew that the baby would be born long before Aunt Patsy could get to them both. She flew down the stairs and out of the front door, listening to the moans of her sister as she hastily gave Henry the money and a message for Patsy to come quick.

The young lad's eyes shone with the silver threepence in his hand and his marbles scattered in the path as he memorised the address and message that he had been trusted to take.

Eliza watched as the ragged urchin ran down Pit Lane; it would take him at least an hour to reach Leeds, no matter how fast his legs took him. And at least an hour more for Patsy to make the journey back. Two hours or more in which the baby would be born alive or dead; whichever the case, it would be hours that would test her to the limit. She'd never seen a baby enter the world before, but she was all that this one had to help make its appearance. 'God have mercy on their souls,' she whispered to herself, as she poured hot water into an enamel basin from the copper and stood at the bottom of the stairs, as Mary-Anne let out another moan.

'I'm coming, Mary-Anne. Henry's gone for Aunt Patsy. You'll be all right.' Eliza's legs felt like jelly as she climbed the stairs with towels and hot water. She'd do what she could and just hope that neither mother or baby would end up in the graveyard like her mother.

The sweat ran from Mary-Anne's head as she gave a long last push. All she wanted was to be free of the pain and to expel the baby that was causing it.

'That's it, Mary-Anne, it's coming. I can see its head! It's coming ... another one and it's here.' Eliza sat on the side of her sister's bed, holding a towel in one hand and squeezing her sister's hand with the other.

Mary-Anne bore down as her aunt had instructed her previously, her face screwed up in pain and determination. 'You will be born.' She gritted her teeth and pushed.

'It's here, Mary-Anne.' Eliza stood up and pulled on the newborn's head and shoulders as the rest of the body followed, laying squirming, red and crying between Mary-Anne's legs. Eliza looked at the newborn baby and then at Mary-Anne before getting a sheet and wrapping the newborn in it.

She set the child to one side as the pains took hold of Mary-Anne once more. 'I don't know what to do with all this.' She looked at the spluttering red-faced baby and the cord that was still attached to its tiny body and the afterbirth.

'You cut it off and knot it.' Mary-Anne lay back and caught her breath. 'That's what Patsy said. Get Bill's penknife from out of those drawers and use that.' She pointed to the chest of drawers where Bill had left some of his effects and then lay back exhausted.

Eliza left the baby between Mary-Anne's legs and got the penknife. 'What if I hurt you or the baby?' She stood hesitantly over them both.

'You won't ... Aunt Patsy will tidy us both up when she arrives, don't worry. Do I have a boy or a girl, Eliza. Can you tell me?' Mary-Anne lay back and watched as Eliza went about the job of separating the baby from the afterbirth.

'Well, now I know what's what, dear sister, I can tell you that you have a beautiful little girl, although she pulls the most strangest of faces and is just slightly wrinkly.' Eliza wrapped the small gurgling baby up in a blanket and passed it to Mary-Anne. 'Should she look like that? I don't think I've ever seen such a wrinkly prune. And she's so tiny, I don't like holding her in fear that I'll drop her.' She looked at Mary-Anne as she passed her to be held her in her arms and could see the love that automatically comes between mother and baby. 'I'll clear this soiled sheet away. You'll feel better then.' Eliza pulled the under sheet from beneath her sister and looked at Mary-Anne and her daughter, hesitating, before going downstairs with the dirty linen.

'Thank you, Eliza. I couldn't have managed that on my own. I'm sorry I had to put you through it; she came so quickly.' Mary-Anne pulled the blanket away from the baby's face and looked at her with awe. 'She is beautiful, but, as you say, a bit wrinkly, but you would

be if you'd been squashed up inside my belly for nearly nine months.'
Mary-Anne closed her eyes and put her head back on the pillows.
'I'm so tired, and my work has just begun if I choose to keep her.'
Mary-Anne smiled at her baby and then closed her eyes again. She
may have smiled at her baby but inside she was in turmoil, not know-
ing whether to keep her or not.

'I'll leave you to sleep. I'll bring Aunt Patsy up to make sure you
are all right when she comes.' Eliza, with her arms full, struggled to
close the bedroom door, feeling a pang of relief that the baby had
been born safely and that Mary-Anne was still with her. She smiled
as she went down the stairs and into the kitchen. She was an aunt ...
Aunt Eliza to the bit of a thing that was asleep in her mother's arms.
Now what would Mary-Anne call the baby and, more to the point,
would she keep it now it was here and with her? Secretly Eliza hoped
she would. After all, she had brought her into the world and she felt a
bond with the baby already. Although the baby had not initially been
wanted, it was part of them and always would be, no matter what
became of it.

'Well, you've not done a bad job between you.' Patsy looked at
Mary-Anne and the baby. 'The baby is only small but it'll soon
fill out once it's had a feed or two. I think Eliza looks the most
exhausted out of the three of you.' Patsy sat at the bottom of the bed
and watched as the small newborn suckled on Mary-Anne's breast.
'Have you decided what's to become of her? If you are to leave her
at the orphanage or workhouse, you want to do it soon, before you
get too attached.' Patsy watched as Mary-Anne looked down upon
her child.

'I don't know. I don't know how I feel. I'm all confused. Now
she's here it's different ... she's mine. Not just something that is a

nuisance.' Mary-Anne sighed and looked at her aunt. Her heart told her to keep her child but her head told her not too. It would bring hardship into their lives, and the child would grow up with the stigma of being Edmund Ellershaw's bastard.

'Well, child, no matter what you decide, there will be heartache. There always is with offspring. She's got a fine head of dark hair, which must be from her father, because it's not on our side of the family. Every time you look at her, it will remind you of him.' Patsy looked at Mary-Anne; if it had been up to her she'd have done away with it, smothered it at birth and told her that it had been born still. But she'd arrived too late to do as she had planned, so now she had to convince her to abandon her baby. Better that than a life of poverty like her next-door neighbour.

'I've always wanted dark hair. She will be so pretty when she grows up,' Eliza said as she sat on the other side of the bed.

'You've got your mother's looks,' Patsy said, stopping Eliza short. 'You should be proud of those. This'en will always question where hers come from. Poor little bastard. Fancy growing up, not knowing who your father is, because it wouldn't be right to tell her, what with him only living down the road and owner of Rose Pit. And his lad to be wed and become the new master of High Watermill. He'll certainly not want any scandal or to see her face when he walks out through Woodlesford. That's for sure, she'll always have a stigma, no matter where she goes if you keep her.' Patsy tried to influence both girls, just as she had their mother. She couldn't see the point of having unwanted children and had always felt bitter when they were born, more so since she had realised that she could not have a child of her own.

'We will make something up to protect her.' Eliza spouted up. 'There's no need for her to know the truth. Besides, it's up to you,

Mary-Anne, but now she is in the world, I feel different towards her and if she was mine I'd keep her. After all, she is our blood.' Eliza reached out her hand and placed a finger into the minute hand of the baby who automatically grasped it tightly, making both Eliza and Mary-Anne smile.

'Well, I can see which way this argument is going. Think long and hard, Mary-Anne; you could be throwing your life away, and you are both making a rod for your backs. I could take her back into Leeds with me tonight, leave her on the workhouse steps and nobody would know where she came from or who she was. Then you could gain your lives back.' Patsy looked at the three sat on the bed together and she knew she was wasting her breath. They were besotted by the infant.

'I'm going to keep her, Aunt Patsy, to make up for the one that my mother lost. She's my little lost girl, who I will do my best to do right by and will love no matter who her father is.' Mary-Anne looked down at the baby who could hardly open its eyes without squinting because of the strong light, and kissed her on the head. 'She can't help how she came about. She isn't the first and she won't be the last to be brought into the world that way.'

'On your own head be it, lass. I don't doubt you'll regret it; it's no bed of roses bringing up a bairn.' Patsy stood up and went to the bedroom door. 'I'll be off back to my Mick. You know where I'm at if you need me for anything.'

'I'll see you out, Aunt Patsy.' Eliza gave Mary-Anne a quick backward glance as they both left her room.

'We both thank you for coming and we know you mean well,' Eliza whispered as she saw her Aunt to the door. 'Mary-Anne had every intention of not keeping the child at one time. But now it is born, she'll not see it abandoned.'

'Aye, well, she's as soft as her mother. And look where that got her. Take care, Eliza. Call in and see me when you are next up't town. If you can't cope let me know.' Patsy hesitated for a second, wondering whether to convince Eliza to get Mary-Anne to see her point of view, but knew she'd be wasting her breath.

'I will, Aunt Patsy, thank you again.' Eliza watched her aunt trundle down the road and at the same time saw next door's curtains twitch. 'Piss off, you nosy bitch!' she yelled before closing the door on the prevailing evening.

Trust them to be watching the comings and goings of the day, she thought.

'Eliza, these are beautiful.' Mary-Anne looked at the carefully stitched garments that lay on her bed.

'And I've made her some napkins. We can wash them daily until she learns to use a pot. I couldn't have her going without, so I've been making these secretly, when I had time. Even if you had abandoned her, I'd have given her them, just to prove to her when she was older that someone once loved her. It must have been coincidence that there was some flannelette in the batch that was sent with that horrible man by John Vasey; it was just ideal for some clothes for her.'

'Eliza, you are so thoughtful. You've been thinking all this, even though at one time I was intent on not keeping her. Just look at the embroidery and the ribbons you've put on this nightdress.' Mary-Anne picked up the cream-coloured long night dress and looked at it with tears in her eyes.

'I'm on with lining one of the dresser drawers from out of the parlour, I thought it would make a good cot for her for the time being. I'm frightened to death that you'll fall asleep and suffocate the poor little mite while she's in bed with you.' Eliza looked at the tiny face wrapped up warm in blankets next to Mary-Anne and smiled. 'Aye, she's bonny, but will we be able to cope? I'm frightened for us both and her.'

'We'll be all right, I'll take her with me when I walk in to see Ma Fletcher and you can amaze the local gentry with your skills, and I'm sure Tom will return once he's calmed down. He loves you too much. She'll soon get up and make her own way in life.' Mary-Anne looked at her sleeping baby. In truth she was frightened of the future. Would she make a good mother and be able to provide for her child? Life was hard enough without another mouth to feed. 'Did the Eaveshams pay you for the wedding dresses? I've completely forgotten to ask.' Mary-Anne leant back in her pillows and yawned.

'Yes, with this one coming into the world, I forgot to tell you again. And you obviously didn't hear when I returned from delivering them. We will be quite comfortable for the next month or two, providing Ellershaw doesn't put the rent up or decide to evict us.

'He wouldn't dare, would he? Not now that I've had his daughter. And I would tell all the world that she is his, if he did rob us of our home. Besides, he'll be concentrating on the upcoming wedding of his spoilt son.' Mary-Anne yawned again. 'Sorry, I'm still so tired.' She closed her eyes.

'I'll leave you two to sleep. First though … you know she needs a name. What are you going to call our new baby?' Eliza looked at mother and daughter as she went to close the door.

'Victoria, after our queen's visit in a fortnight. She's my Victoria and she will be queen of all she surveys in another few years.' Mary-Anne bent her head down and kissed her before pulling the covers over both of them. 'But now we will sleep just a little while.'

'Victoria, that's perfect. We will always remember when the queen visited Leeds. Perhaps we could go and see her together, now her namesake is born.' But Eliza's words fell on deaf ears as both were asleep. It made no difference, she would go and see her and Prince Albert on her own if she had to, but see her she would because it would be a glorious day.

Thirty One

'Quiet Bert! Was that a baby I could hear crying next door?' Ada Simms listened intently to the noise coming from their neighbours' house. 'There it is again, and I'm sure I heard it yesterday.'

'You are hearing things, woman. Get on with dishing my supper out.' Bert held his plate in mid-air over the kitchen table as Ada stopped as if in a trance, ears pricked and the ladle filled with stew hovering like the latest trick from a magician's bag. 'Am I going to eat tonight or not?' Bert swallowed, his mouth filling with saliva, imagining the beef and dumplings that were so tantalizingly near.

'It is, you know! It's a baby. One of 'em's had a baby!' Ada quickly dolloped a plate full of stew onto Bert's plate and then pressed her ear up to the neighbouring wall. leaving him looking at a half-empty plate.

'For God's sake, woman ... you need to get out more. All you do is bother about next door. What if one of 'em's had a baby? It's nothing to do with us. But that would account for their Aunt Patsy visiting the other day. I just caught a glimpse of her when that foul-mouthed Eliza was saying goodbye to her.' Bert shovelled in his stew and looked at the expression on his wife's face.

'You never told me she was here. How could you forget something like that?' Ada pulled up her chair and looked at her empty supper plate before helping herself to stew.

'I'll have a bit more, if there's any left. You only gave me half a portion.' Bert looked across at his wife.

'You don't deserve any,' Ada growled, 'forgetting to tell me *she* was there. You should have known something was up; she only turns up when folk are in bother.'

'Well, it isn't Eliza, because she swore at me and told me to piss off when she caught me watching them. So if there's a baby in the house it must be Mary-Anne's, but I didn't think she was like that. She always struck me as keeping herself to herself, although she did have that Irishman visiting her for a time.' Bert sighed as Ada held back on the stew; he hadn't been given enough to fill a rat.

'Well, there's definitely a baby, so one of them has been up to no good. I think it's much more likely to be Eliza's, dirty-mouthed little devil she is. It didn't take Tom Thackeray long to realise what sort of lass she was and get himself home to his mother's. Perhaps it's his; perhaps we've not been hearing it for a day or two and Eliza was thanking her aunt for her help with her birth. You said you couldn't make the lad see sense over her. And I've seen both lasses pass the window of late and neither have looked in the family way. His mother won't be happy if it is. Oh! Lordy, old Mrs Thackeray a grandmother and she doesn't know it.' Ada tucked in to her dinner and thought of her latest morsel of gossip, which would be something to share on Sunday.

'You hold your tongue, woman, until I've talked to Tom. He should be the first to know if it's his. I'll have word on the quiet and tell him he should stand by her; I thought better of him than that.' Bert could never quite understand how much delight Ada got out of other folks' hardship. The baby obviously hadn't got a father, whoever its mother was, and if it was Tom's he needed to be told to do the right thing. His father, if he'd been alive, would have done just that, so he would give him some fatherly advice – before the whole village knew, if it was up to his Ada.

'I'm not bloody well responsible, it's nowt to do with me. I didn't even know she was having owt.' Tom looked at the old man who had collared him in a quiet moment when they were on their own. 'I never did owt with her like that, so it can't be mine. Happen a kiss and a squeeze, but nothing else. She must blame the fella I found paying for her services one evening, not me. That'll be the bastard you need to talk to.' Tom looked hurt and shocked. A baby ... Eliza's baby. Everybody would think it was his and look at him and think he hadn't done right by her.

'Aye, lad, was I right? Was she having men at her home? Then it will be his and Eliza the mother! We wondered if it could be Mary-Anne's but she's a decent enough soul and we couldn't see her getting herself in that way.' Bert rubbed his head and knew the young lad in front of him was hurting.

'It won't be Mary-Anne's. Eliza used to always make fun of her sister for being reserved with John Vasey. I think that's why he's left her to go to Liverpool. He couldn't get what he wanted. Obviously the opposite to Eliza.' Tom sighed. A baby ... how had she managed to conceal it so well?

'Aye, that sounds about right. You should have heeded my words those few months back and then it wouldn't have hurt you this bad. Still, she'll be the one who finds out what it's like to be free and easy with her ways. She'll have to bring the bairn up by its bootstraps and perhaps not get another man to look at her but that's not yours to worry about, lad, if your conscience is clear.' Bert patted him on the back and shook his head, as he could see the regret in Tom's eyes.

'Just as she was doing so well with her sewing and business. What a fool.' Tom looked down at his boots and couldn't help but feel turmoil for Eliza whom he still loved.

'Aye, best left alone, lad. Look for a decent lass, someone you can take home to your mother. That's what she would like.' Bert smiled as as he turned to make his way back to work.

'Aye, you are right, and thanks for telling me. I'll steer clear of Pit Lane, I want nowt to do with her from now on.' Tom's heart was broken. How could she? She had better not name him as the father, because it was most definitely not his doing, but that was not for the want of trying.

Thirty Two

Edmund Ellershaw looked at himself in the hallway mirror at Highfield House and didn't like what he saw looking back at him. Time, coal dust and old age was beginning to catch up with him. He fastened his cravat yet again and checked that he looked respectable enough to be the father of the man who was about to marry into the Eavesham family. Not that they had any money, but his wife had been right: they had connections and were respected in the area and now that his father-in-law had taken over High Watermill and put William in charge of running it, he'd better look the part.

His eldest, getting wed ... he wasn't even fit to look after himself, let alone a wife and a few hundred employees. He still thought his son was a useless waste of space, but this was his father-in-law's doing and what he said went if Catherine had anything to do with it.

He sighed and held his stomach in; he could do with losing a few pounds. Nay, better make that a stone, he thought, at he looked at the heavy dark lines under his eyes and expanding waistline ... the darkness under his eyes not made any better by hearing the gossip at the Rose, that there had been a baby born on Pit Lane.

No one was quite sure to which of the Wild girls it had been born to, but he knew all too well and now on his son's wedding day he was hoping that the silly bitch would keep her mouth shut and not name him as the father if she went to the parish or The Friends Society for financial help.

As it was, she and her sister had had enough out of his family already, with his son's bride and his foolish daughter Grace purchasing their wedding attire from them. He'd rather she had got married in rags than give the both of those two money, but he'd not had much say in the matter as it wasn't him paying the bill but his father-in-law as part of the deal he had struck on behalf of William. How they had wheedled their way into supplying the dresses was unbelievable, but he had to admit when he'd seen Grace trying hers on it had looked stunning. Who would have thought that a dress like that could have come out from such a filthy little shop, owned by two whores?

'Edmund, are you ready?' Catherine Ellershaw looked at her husband who seemed to have the worries of the world on his shoulders as she watched him looking at himself for one more time.

'Aye, I'm as right as I'll ever be.' Edmund put on his top hat and reached for his cane. 'Is everybody else waiting on me?'

'Yes, dear, they are all waiting in the carriage. William went a while ago, he's at the church waiting for his Priscilla. It's such a big day for him – I do hope that he'll be happy. Are you not proud to see him striking out on his own? A married man with responsibilities, and who knows … a family of his own soon perhaps.'

'We haven't done raising ours yet. With you being caught with George, we've still a baby in our family, let alone him having any yet. Steady on, woman, don't make me feel older than I am. A grandfather, me … God forgive.' Edmund grunted as he opened the front door to the sound of the chiming church bells. 'Let's be away then to this mockery of a wedding.'

Catherine looked at Edmund. 'Well, didn't you marry me for the same thing as them? Money! If I remember rightly.'

'Aye, happen that, along with the baby you were carrying in your belly and the fact that your father threatened to blow my head off my shoulders if I didn't make you an honest woman.' Edmund held his arm out for her to take.

'But we do love one another now, and I'm sure William will grow to love Priscilla in the same way with time.' Catherine smiled at her husband. He wasn't handsome, he wasn't that rich but he had, as far she was aware, been always true to her.

'Time will tell, lass. Now let's see our lad get wed and get him into that bloody big house that your father now owns.' Edmund stepped out with Catherine on his arm. His lad was going up in society; he only hoped that the scandal of his own doing would never come to the surface and that the brat on Pit Lane would never know its real father. That, he knew, his own marriage would not survive – Catherine could never handle the shame of his secret life. Why had the bitch not got rid of the brat she was carrying and make both their lives easier. It's not as if she didn't have her aunt and all her potions to hand. Instead, the brat would always be there to remind him of his secret, unbeknown to the world.

John Vasey looked around the lodging house that had been his home for nearly three months, glad to be leaving it. The vermin and the fleas and the rough dock workers coming to bed drunk and snoring had taken its toll on him. But now he'd earned enough for his passage to America, he'd done what he'd set out to do.

He lifted his bag over his shoulder and stepped out onto the busy docks. With his cap at an angle and set in his mind of his destination to a new life, he made the first few steps of freedom from a life on the dockside and work in England. He'd done it, and now it was up to him how his life was to continue and with whom.

Thirty Three

'I can't believe how small she is, Mary-Anne. Just look at her tiny feet.' Eliza held the baby on her knee and examined her tiny toes and smiled down at the baby she was proud to be aunt to. 'I'm glad you didn't get rid of her; now she's here I don't know how either of us could even have thought it.'

'I bloody well do ... did you not hear her crying in the middle of the night? I think it's because she was hungry, I don't seem to be giving her enough milk, and, besides, I hate getting my tit out for her to suck. It's just the most embarrassing thing you can think of. That's why I've hunted this old bottle and teat out that our mother must have used for us. I'll fill it with cow's milk, that'll fill the little bugger up.' Mary-Anne lifted the copper pan of the fire and poured it into a jug and then filled the glass bottle half-full with the tepid milk, pulling the rubber teat tightly on and testing it before she held out her arms for baby Victoria to come to her.

'No, I'll feed her, let me. I'd like to try and do it.' Eliza looked down at the little baby that was beginning to get cross with herself as her hands and feet fought with one another in the only way, along with her cries, that she had to express that her stomach was empty.

'Well, you try then. Anything for a bit of of peace. I'm exhausted. I don't think I'm going to be the best mother in the world, I've no patience.' Mary-Anne passed the bottle over to Eliza and watched as her sister smiled down at the little red angry face that was beginning to sob. 'Oh, for God's sake, shut her up. Stick the teat in her mouth and let her suck.'

Eliza gently rubbed the teat over the baby's lips and let a drop of milk flow out into her mouth and almost in the same instance the baby opened its mouth, liking the taste of the milk, and realising to latch onto the rubber teat.

'There you go, my little one. Your ma has no patience, has she? You were just hungry.' Eliza beamed down at the suckling baby and then across at Mary-Anne. 'You worry too much. She's as new to the world as you are to motherhood, you both need time to get to know one another.'

'Do you know, I'm trying to remember when you were a baby. I can't recall you making so much noise, but then I wasn't that old myself. And Mother would know just what to do – she always did, not like me.' Mary-Anne watched Eliza feeding her baby and thought how much more patience she had when it came to the child. In truth she was finding it hard to go near the baby, let alone let her suckle on her breast.

The bond between them, now she was in the world, was not that strong and Mary-Anne was beginning to have doubts about keeping her. She wished she had taken her Aunt Patsy's advice and left her on the poorhouse steps. She did love her in her own way, but was frightened that she could not bring her up in a decent lifestyle.

'There, see, look at her now. She can hardly keep her eyes open. She's even fallen asleep still sucking.' Eliza kissed the small content face as she pulled the teat from Victoria's mouth and wrapped her tightly in a blanket before placing her in the cupboard drawer that was acting as a temporary cot. 'She was only hungry, poor thing. You must not have enough milk,' Eliza suggested gently.

'I don't like her on me.' Mary-Anne pulled a face. 'I think about her bastard father nearly doing the same thing to me and I feel sick with the thought of it.'

'Well, bottle it is then from now on. She'll not take any hurt.' Eliza bent down and stroked the dark-haired baby before she went to the sink to wash the bottle out. 'It'll have been the big day for the Ellershaws, I heard the bells ringing. I hope our dresses looked all right. I nearly thought of going to watch and then I thought better of it.'

'That poor dizzy Priscilla doesn't know what she's marrying into. He'll never be faithful; he'll just be like his father.' Mary-Anne stood next to the sleeping Victoria and looked down at her, thinking that she was part Ellershaw, a part she hoped would never raise its head.

'I don't know, he might just be the opposite – it sometimes works like that. I don't think he takes after his father so much. Can you not remember Bill once saying that Ellershaw was in a mood because his lad wanted nothing to do with the pit, and that he wasn't worth anything?' Eliza sat down next to Mary-Anne and her baby and looked at both of them. 'Perhaps he's different.'

'No, he's not. They are both made of the same stuff.' Mary-Anne had no intention of telling her sister about the younger Ellershaw's offer to her now. 'I only hope this one takes after me.' Mary-Anne gazed into the fire, she was feeling low and could have cried easily if Eliza had not been there She felt used and dirty and there was nobody there to love her.

Eliza leaned back in her chair and looked into the fire. 'I miss my Tom. I wish he'd listen to me, but his mother hates me and he thinks I've been disloyal to him, when I wasn't at all. I suppose next door won't have helped; they are bound to have heard the baby by now and added fuel to the gossip. I bet they think that Victoria is mine, as you have always been sweeter to them. I'm quite surprised they haven't shown their faces by now, especially old bag Ada. She'll be having a great time spreading her venom. Before you know it she'll have turned our house into a brothel, with men coming evening, noon and night.' Eliza looked at her sister who looked pasty and drawn. 'We are a right pair, aren't we? At least we've money in the pot and a roof over our heads. All we have to do is to look to the future for all three of us.'

'I suppose so,' Mary-Anne said. 'I'm glad next door are keeping away. I just couldn't face the look of disgust that she would give me. At least this way I'm not yet condemned in her eyes as a fallen woman.'

'No, but I know I am and always will be.' Eliza sighed, looking quickly across at Mary-Anne as she heard a knock on the front door. 'Who's that, do you think? Speak of the devil, it might be them next door. I knew that they wouldn't be able to keep away.' Eliza got up from her chair and went to answer the late-evening caller.

Mary-Anne looked at her baby fast asleep and sighed. She could do without visitors; she knew she didn't look at her best and she hoped that they would not disturb the sleeping infant. She listened as Eliza opened the door and gasped as she heard a voice she all too well recognised. The soft lilting Irish drawl made her heart beat fast as she hurried to the small mirror near the back door to tidy her hair and pinch her cheeks before he entered the kitchen.

'You've a visitor, Mary-Anne, one I know you'll be glad to see.' Eliza smiled as she opened the kitchen door and revealed John Vasey standing behind her.

John took off his cap and looked across at the woman he loved and had missed so much in his time in Liverpool. He'd regretted every day that he had left her behind and then when Patsy had told him how the baby had been conceived, and the reality of it all had gradually sunk in, he had made his mind up to return and tell her just how he felt. He'd been hurt and hurt badly, but he had mulled the news over and over again in his head and knew that he had to return to his Mary-Anne. He glanced quickly at the sleeping baby in the drawer before stepping forward.

'Mary-Anne, I hope you and the baby are well?' he asked nervously. 'You look a bit pale. Are you eating all right?' John saw the how tired she looked and thought that she needed his care and attention.

'I'm fine, it's just the baby. She's not been sleeping. I thought you'd be long gone by now, across the seas to your brother.' Mary-Anne bowed her head and fought back a tear.

'To be sure, I should have been, but something dragged me back here, or, should I say, someone.' John stood there awkwardly, not wanting to say what he'd been building up to on his journey back into Leeds.

Eliza looked at the two and knew that they needed their privacy. 'I'll take the baby and give you room to talk without me in the way. Mary-Anne, she'll be in my bedroom with me, so she's all right. Besides, she'll sleep for an hour or two now with a full belly.' Eliza went and picked the cot drawer up and carried it past John.

'Here, let me help, I'll carry her upstairs for you. It's a girl that you've had then, Mary-Anne … a bonny one and all.' John looked down on the baby as he took it from the arms of Eliza.

'Yes, I've called her Victoria, after the queen,' Mary-Anne said quickly, regretting her last few words, knowing that John had no great love of the monarch.

'Ah, well, I'll not hold that against the poor wee mite. And I can understand why, seeing she will be in Leeds in a week's time.' John lifted the drawer and baby through the kitchen doorway and followed Eliza up the stairs talking to Eliza as he placed the baby and cot next to her bedside.

Mary-Anne pulled the kettle on to the fire and laid out some cups and waited, heart pounding, as she listened to John's footsteps coming down the stairs.

'Eliza seems smitten with the lil' thing. Quite a mother hen ... you'd think it was hers.' John came back into the kitchen and sat down in what used to be his favourite chair.

'Yes, she makes up for me. I don't seem to be able to bond to her at all.' Mary-Anne sighed as she poured the tea.

'Well, maybe that's because of the way she came into the world. I admire you for carrying her and giving birth. To be sure I'd no idea, else I'd have knocked that Ellershaw man's head off his bloody shoulders. Still will if you want me to.' John screwed his cap up in his hands and then looked up at Mary-Anne.

'You know, then. I guess Aunt Patsy told you? You know what I did and yet you still come back to me? I'd have thought that you would be thankful for your narrow escape. I lead you on and deceived you ... I'm not worth a lot.' Mary-Anne sobbed.

'Oh, Mary-Anne, that's where you are wrong. There's not been a day gone by that I've not thought about you. I went away angry at first, thinking that you had tricked me and that you were carrying a baby by someone you once loved. And then, you are right, Patsy wrote and told me how it had come about. I should have known, because when I held you I knew you felt the same way as I do. I love you, Mary-Anne, and always will. The truth is, I can't live without you.' John got up from his chair and bent down on his knees besides her. He held her hand and softly kissed her lips as she swept away the tears.

'I thought that I'd lost you,' she cried, 'that I'd never see you again. And then the baby came and I've been miserable ever since and I just couldn't see any happiness in my world.'

'You've not lost me. In fact, I'm here to ask you to join me. Come to America with me? I've enough money and tickets for us both. There's a ship sailing next Saturday and it's got our names down for it.' John squeezed her hand tightly and smiled. 'A new life, Mary-Anne, just you and me in a new country away from all this.'

Mary-Ann reached for her handkerchief and blew her nose. 'I don't know, I just can't up and leave. What about Eliza and what about the baby ...? Can I bring her with me?' Thoughts were rushing through her head: she'd never been outside of Leeds and now she was being asked to travel halfway around the world with a baby in her arms.

'Eliza will be fine – she will always make her own way in the world – and when it comes to baby Victoria, I don't think that it's a good thing that she travels with us, not yet, she's too young. But sure, I've been thinking about this. If you take her to the orphanage and leave her there, just for a year or two until we come back for her, she'd be that young she'd never remember it and need be no wiser once she joins us in America.' John looked worried. He didn't mind having a wife that could work with him for the first two or three years but he didn't want to start his new life with a mouth already to feed and one that most of all was not his.

'I couldn't, I couldn't leave her, not now! I know I said we hadn't bonded, but she's still my flesh and blood. The orphanage is a terrible place, she deserves better than that and what if I never returned? She'd be lost without any family.' Mary-Anne looked at John and cried. 'But I love you and don't want you to go without me. Do you have to go?'

'I have to, my love, my only brother is waiting for me. I need to make myself a better life before it's too late. I promise, we would return for her, once we had set up home and she was a little older. I need you, Mary-Anne, and you need me. Please don't say no.' John kissed her on the cheek and held her face in his hands, seeing the hurt in her eyes. 'I promise, she would be back with us once we have made roots. It's no good dragging a child half across the world for it to live in a slum and squalor. This way at least you know she will be fed and dressed.'

'I know, but she's my daughter! I can't abandon her,' Mary-Anne cried.

'I go back to Liverpool day after tomorrow. As I say, the ship sails on Saturday. Think about it tonight and tomorrow, and I'll return tomorrow evening and then you can give me your answer. Either way, I know your decision will be made out of love and I know this sounds hard on the child, but I hope you will be joining me. It will mean a good life for both of us, something we both deserve.' John hugged Mary-Anne next to his chest and whispered, 'Come with me, I'll always love you,' before standing up and making for the kitchen door. 'Tomorrow night I'll need an answer.' Then he quickly turned with Mary-Anne looking after him as he opened the door and left her with one the worst decisions she had ever to make.

Thirty Four

Mary-Anne sat on the edge of Eliza's bed and looked down on her baby daughter fast asleep.

'I can't leave her behind. Especially not in the orphanage or workhouse, no matter how young she is. It's not the best start to life and I just can't do it. What if I never return, what would become of her?' Mary-Anne wiped away the tears. 'But I love John, I don't want him to leave without me. I will never see him again if I say no. That will be it; he will be gone over the seas, forever lost to me.' She sobbed and wrung her hands. 'I don't know what to do. I can't do right for doing wrong.'

'Oh, Mary-Anne, I knew as soon as I opened the door to him that he was up to something. It would have been better if he had stopped out of your life. You were just beginning to forget him.' Eliza looked down at the baby that unknowingly was making all the worry for her sister. She knew Mary-Anne had deep feelings for John Vasey and, unlike her Tom, he must love her with a passion.

Eliza sighed and breathed in deeply. She had to do right by both her sister and her niece. 'You'll only get one chance to make yourself a new life, our Mary-Anne. You take it – go with the man you love.

Don't worry about baby Victoria, I'll look after her until you return. I'll manage; you've said it yourself that I've more patience with her than you.' Eliza couldn't let her niece be abandoned.

'I can't, I can't let you do that. It is far too much to ask of you, my dear sister. You'd be on your own with a child, and still have to make a living. I couldn't leave and see you in such a position.' Mary-Anne looked at her sister and tried to make sense of the offer that she had made. But at the same time she couldn't help but feel her sister had given her a lifeline, to be with the man she loved.

'I can't stand by and watch you turn into a bitter old maid because of losing John Vasey and staying for a baby that was not born out of love. You go with him. Victoria will not want for anything. I'll bring her up in the knowledge that you are her mother but that I equally love her. Perhaps when the right time comes we can tell her about her father, but not until she is old enough to understand.' Eliza understood that the commitment she was showing to the child was to change her life, but she couldn't see her own kith and kin in a place where no love would be shown her.

'Eliza, are you sure? I would be forever in your debt.' Mary-Anne looked at her sister. She was answering all her prayers but was sacrificing her own life.

'I'm sure. Perhaps you could send me some money occasionally to help me bring her up. Besides, it isn't forever. John said you could take her over with you once you were settled. Two or three years will soon fly by. I love her, Mary-Anne. Ever since I saw her come into the world, I knew you did the right thing by keeping her.' Eliza ran her hand over the baby's dark curls and smiled. It was a huge commitment but the right one, everyone had some degree of happiness and she would make sure baby Victoria was loved.

*

'You've got everything that you need?' Eliza looked at Mary-Anne and fought back the tears as she watched Mary-Anne lift her filled carpetbag up from the kitchen floor and smile at John Vasey.

'Yes, I think I've packed everything. I left a lot of my things as I'll be returning once we are settled.' Mary-Anne looked around the kitchen that she'd grown up in for most of her adult life. This was the house she had saved and what for, as she was now deserting it? 'You'll not let Edmund Ellershaw touch you, no matter what. You keep him at arm's-length and pawn any of my things that I've left behind if you need to. Once we are settled, I'll send some cash over to help you.' Mary-Anne looked worriedly at her young sister. 'I can't thank you enough.'

'I'll cut his pudding off along with his balls if he comes near me, don't you worry,' Eliza tried to bluster. 'And you don't worry about baby Victoria here, me and her will get on fine. She's been as quiet as a mouse since her belly's been full of cow's milk.' Eliza looked down at her new ward and smiled. 'Here, you take this.' She reached up to the mantelpiece and opened the cash box, handing over three guineas to her sister. 'You'll need this and it's only fair you have it; it's part of the wedding dress money. Besides I'll be making more shortly. Grace and her friends will not be able to stay away.' Eliza squeezed Mary-Anne's hand tight around the coins. 'Now, get yourselves gone before I start blubbing.' Eliza breathed in deeply and kissed her sister on the cheek. 'You take care of her, John Vasey; you make her a decent woman and get a ring on her finger once you are over there.' Eliza held back the tears.

'To be sure, I will. I love her, Eliza. For the first time in my life, I've found a woman that understands me. She'll be looked after, don't you worry.' John placed his cap on his head and reached over to take Mary-Anne's carpetbag. 'I'll wait outside ... let you say your goodbyes.'

Eliza watched as the quiet man left her sister, her baby and herself alone in the kitchen. 'You'll write, won't you, and you'll take care of yourself.' She hugged Mary-Anne close to her.

'I will, and you take care of yourself and my Victoria. I love you, Eliza, and I can't thank you enough for doing this for me. I'll always be in your debt,' Mary-Anne sobbed. Then she bent down and gently pulled away the blanket from around Victoria's head and kissed her tenderly. 'God take care of you, my little one, I will return for you as soon as I can.' Mary-Anne gazed around her home for the last time and walked down the passage and out of the front door to join her man on their new adventure together. She daren't turn back; she'd decided what to do and now she'd to get on with it. Tears welled up in her throat and her legs shook as John linked his arm through hers and smiled. Was she doing the right thing? Please let it be so, she prayed as she stepped out towards the canal.

'Well, that's it, my little one. It's me and you against the world.' Eliza sat down in her chair and sobbed. She was on her own with a baby that wasn't hers and no man in her life. 'We'll manage ... come hell or high water we will manage, and your mother will return a wealthy lady and take you back with her, if I know Mary-Anne. John Vasey, you had better not let her down, or it will be the worse for you,' she whispered underneath her breath. 'And God protect us from the likes of Edmund Ellershaw, because I think we will need a little of his help to keep us safe.'

Baby Victoria slept on, oblivious to all the commotion that involved her and her birth, content in her own world.

Thirty Five

Mary-Anne had never seen so many people has she climbed out of the barge that had taken them the full length of the Leeds–Liverpool canal. They had passed through numerous locks and docks, calling at wharfs and quays along the way to load and unload goods and now they were finally passing into what John had called the Mann Island Lock in the centre of Liverpool's docklands. It had been a few days gruelling journey, roughing it aboard the small cabined barge with its burly owner, eating at the side of the canal whatever John had poached along its banks, but now she knew it was worth it, as she gazed at the busy dockside and looked with wonder at the tall masts and fully rigged vessels that stood tall and elegant in the water.

'Watch your bags, else the runners will have them,' John said as he helped her off the barge onto the quayside.

'Runners?' Mary-Anne asked.

'Aye, the bastards. They watch for unsuspecting folk, looking for their ship, pinch their bags and then charge a fortune to return them to you. Scum of the earth, they are. Have pinched many a poor man's last possessions and left him on the quayside with nowt.' John grabbed Mary-Anne's arm and hauled her onto the cobbled quay.

'I've never seen as busier place ... is it always like this? There's so many people and everyone in such a hurry.' Mary-Anne looked around her: there was people shouting orders, women with babies crying, men hauling goods, prick-pinchers tallying their trades and the smell of the sea and the goods being unloaded mingled in the air, making her feel quite heady.

'Aye, it's never quiet. Liverpool's one of the main ports in England. You can find anything here: cotton from the Americas; timber from Canada; fruits from the Caribbean; sugar from Jamaica. Anything you want, Liverpool will have it.' John watched as Mary-Anne stared at a dark-skinned gentleman that walked past. 'Aye and not too long ago, it should not have been proud of its past, dealing in slaves from Africa. That's what made the port so wealthy ... money made on the backs of the poor buggers that were sold into slavery, as a rich man's worker to do what he liked with. But enough, we are to make our way to Waterloo Dock. Our ship is called the *Speedwell* and is owned by the Cunard line. It sails at six this evening, so we will just have time to find ourselves a bunk down in steerage and grab something decent to eat before we set sail.' John put his arm through Mary-Anne's and set off at a pace through the crowds.

'What's steerage?' Mary-Anne asked as she tried to keep up with him.

'It's where us poor folk travel. It's two floors down from the top deck, where all the toffs are. We are all in it together, bunks on either side of the boat and a communal table along the middle for us to sit and eat at. Not that you'll be doing much of that on the first day or two, until you get used to the roll of the ship, and by the time we are halfway across the Atlantic, our rations will be cut, fearing that they won't have enough to feed us on before we get to land again.' John pushed his way along the causeway, dragging Mary-Anne behind him.

'You mean I'll be sharing a room with everyone else, that I'll have to dress and do my ablutions in front of everyone!' Mary-Anne exclaimed.

'That you will, but don't be worrying … no one will take a bit of notice, because everyone's the same. You've got to think of the life you are going to, a new one full of hope. If I could have afforded us to be in a better class, I'd have booked it, but as it was it cost me twelve guineas, which includes the bread, potatoes and ships biscuits that they'll give us to live on, so we can't complain. And to be sure, we will have the trip of a lifetime together.' John looked at the worry on her face. 'It'll be fine, my love, and when we reach New York, I'll introduce you to my brother and his family. He's got a job for me already, building, and he says we can live with him until we find somewhere we can afford.'

Mary-Anne listened to all the plans that John had made for their lives together and realised just how much trust she was placing in the man next to her side. Had she done right? Should she have gone with him? She could be safe and sound next to the kitchen fire of number one Pit Lane with baby Victoria on her knee and Eliza making their supper. Instead she was going to be tossed to within an inch of her life on the great waves of the Atlantic for at least thirty-five days with a man she now realised that could be telling her anything.

Deep down inside she felt an unease at the thought of her baby being brought up with Eliza. She should have stayed, not been selfish and abandoned her one commitment in life. She breathed in deeply, closed her eyes and pictured her daughter content and asleep in her home-made cot. It wasn't too late to go home, she thought, as they coursed along the quayside.

John came to a halt as they reached the ship called the *Speedwell*. It was thronged with sailors loading supplies and passengers going up and down the gangway, with cases, hatboxes and their worldly belongings. Sailors were getting ready the sails and singing a shanty as they hauled on the huge ropes that unfurled them.

'Well, this is us. This is what we will be on for over the next month. If you've decided different, now is the time to tell me. I'd have to leave you here, mind, because I'm away with you or without you.' John had sensed her trepidation as he'd told her about their voyage and he could see fear in her eyes. 'I've something here in my pocket that might change your mind; I thought if we travelled as a married couple, you would feel better about the journey. We can always get wed properly once we are in New York.' John reached into his pocket and pulled a thin band of gold from within it. 'It was my mother's, she'd have wanted you to have it, God rest her soul.' He reached out for Mary-Anne's left hand and slipped the wedding ring onto her finger. 'Now, in my eyes, you are Mrs Vasey, who I love with all my heart and I'm hoping that you will join me aboard this good ship to our new life, so that we can make it legally binding.' John watched as Mary-Anne looked at the ring on her finger and then looked at the crowd and the ship awaiting them. He held his breath and just hoped that had swayed her enough after a moment or two of doubt.

'You are asking me to marry you? Here, now, with this ring on my finger?' Mary-Anne looked at John.

'That I am, lass. I promised your Eliza that I would do right by you and as soon as we dock in New York, I'll see to it that we get wed properly.'

'You are not saying it just to get me on this ship are you? You do mean it?' Mary-Anne's eyes filled with tears.

'Why would I come back for you and buy a ticket for your passage if I didn't love you and want to marry you? Now, Mrs Vasey, give me your arm and let us get ourselves settled as the respectable couple we are. Sure, you'd think I'd asked you to shoot yourself, with that look on your face.' John laughed and noticed a smile spreading amongst the tears and doubt.

'I didn't expect you to propose so soon. And should we really act as man and wife? Surely it's sinful.' Mary-Anne looked at John and smiled.

'What other folk don't know won't harm them and you are travelling as Mrs John Vasey on your ticket, so no one will know otherwise.' John showed Mary-Anne her boarding ticket and smiled. 'You see, I knew you'd come with me. Besides, we can get to know one another a little better, with you lying down by my side of a night.'

'You take an awful lot for granted, John Vasey. But doesn't this ring look bonny on my finger? I'll come with you, aye, and I'll marry you, but on one condition, that you let me return in the next five years for my daughter.' Mary-Anne thought about the baby she'd left behind and tried to reassure herself that she would one day return – not just for her, but also to seek revenge on Edmund Ellershaw for the misery he had brought to her and her family.

'You can come back for your Victoria, once we have a roof over our heads and some money in the bank and that won't take long. There's enough work out there to make men millionaires and other ways to make money besides. Come, let's be away, and get a good bunk together in our floating home.' John pulled on her hand and grinned.

Mary-Anne looked around her at the people not thinking twice about boarding the ship, eager to make a new life for themselves. She looked down at the ring of gold on her finger before lifting her carpetbag up. 'To a new life,' she said as she walked up the gangplank. But deep down she thought about her daughter left behind and her beloved devoted sister.

'Too right, Mrs Vasey, one with no worries,' John said as she climbed on board. 'This is just the beginning ... who knows where it will end.'

Mary-Anne stood on the deck and looked around her. She was going to America with the man she loved. Her thoughts veered between regret and the excitement of her new life in front of her. She'd not be sorry to see the back of her little world with the filth and poverty upon the streets of Leeds. No, she'd no regrets. America and John were calling her, and that was where she was bound, whether she could return or not time would tell. She fought tears back as John kissed her on her cheek and breathed in deeply. She had to go, even though deep down her heart was breaking.

Thirty Six

Eliza looked down at baby Victoria. She was a contented child now, only waking for her feeds, and it was as if she had sensed that her mother had secretly despised her being born, despite the love she had tried to give her.

'Well, your mother will have sailed by now. We'll not be seeing her for a while. We are truly on our own, young lady.' Eliza sighed. She had laid awake of a night, staring up at the crack that ran along her bedroom ceiling, wondering if she had done right by offering to bring up her sister's child.

Now that she was on her own, she was frightened. She'd no man to support her and even the neighbours wanted to have nothing to do with her. She managed to smile as she noticed the baby's lips turn upwards and into a cupid's bow as she dreamt. Her skin had turned into beautiful blushed ivory and she looked the picture of health; truly there was not a bonnier baby for miles around, Eliza thought as she watched her sleep. She left her asleep and went to wash her bottle out, glancing at the calendar that hung on the wall next to the sink.

It was finally Tuesday, the seventh of September – the day Queen Victoria was due to visit Leeds, the day all those months ago that

Tom, John, Mary-Anne and herself were going to go into Leeds and see her declare the town hall open. That seemed a lifetime ago now; so much had happened. She looked up at the clock. It was early, only six thirty in the morning. If she re-filled the bottle and wrapped baby Victoria up, she could walk into Leeds and maybe catch a glimpse of the royal party she had set her heart on seeing for so long.

She looked out of the window; the day promised to keep fine by the looks of it. There wasn't a cloud in the sky, even though there was a hint of the coming autumn with a smell of mustiness in the air, she thought as she opened the back kitchen door and breathed in deeply. She could also call and see Ma Fletcher, see what she had and tell her that she'd be down to see her the following week and explain that Mary-Anne had gone to make a new life with John Vasey in America. She'd show her the baby and tell her that she was entrusted with its care until Mary-Anne returned.

Yes, that's what she'd do. It was time to introduce the baby out into the world and what better time than for her to see her namesake Victoria, the queen of England, whom she would never get to see again, unless she was extremely lucky. Eliza looked around her and for the first time in near a fortnight she felt happy. She'd wrap baby Victoria up and go to watch the parade as she had wanted to do. It was time the outside world knew of her birth and on what better day could she announce it.

'Well, look at this'en. Is she yours, Eliza?' Ma Fletcher pulled back the shawl that baby Victoria was tightly wrapped in.

'No, she's our Mary-Anne's, but she couldn't take her with her. John and Mary-Anne have gone to America and want to get settled there before she's sent for.' Eliza held the child tight; the crowds of people buffeted her as they crowded up Briggate awaiting the arrival of the queen.

'So, it's Mary-Anne's, is it? I thought she was in the family way last time I saw her, and the time before that she was as sick as a dog. The smell never usually bothers her, so I thought then what the story was. She's buggered off to America, has she, and left you holding the baby? A fine thing for her to do. That John Vasey wants to keep it in his pocket, until he can look after the consequences.'

'It's not ...' Eliza was about to say that it wasn't John Vasey's but was stopped in her tracks as there was a surge in the crowd as there was rumours that the queen was on her way.

'Here, come behind my cart. You'll be safer. Leeds is no place for a baby today. When she comes nearer, we can stand on it and watch her. They tried to move me from my pitch, but I wasn't having any off it. I've moved to the side as it is. What more do they want? These bloody officials ... they'll be getting paid for today, so why shouldn't I make a living when there's all these folk in Leeds for once.' Ma Fletcher pushed and made room for Eliza to join her in the relative safety that there was between her cart full of rags and the wall of the printer's shop, while the crowds jostled for what space they could get into to watch the procession that was to sweep along Woodhouse Lane, down Upperhead Row and down Briggate, eventually reaching East Parade and the town hall.

'Here, you get on the cart, lass. Pass me the baby and then we'll both stand on it and watch. We'll have one of the best viewing spots above the heads of this lot.' Ma Fletcher held the baby as Eliza hoisted up her skirts and climbed onto the cart, holding her hands out for baby Victoria to be passed to her, and then the elderly woman clambered up beside her.

'Bloody hell, just look at it!' Eliza gasped, holding the baby tightly to her as the crowd jeered and made their noise. 'Look, old Appleby at the florists has littered the street with flowers, silly old fool – they'll only get trampled on. Just look at the flags and banners ... they must be hanging from every rooftop.'

'Half of this lot was here yesterday as well. The queen stopped at Woodsley House last night from what I understand. I have never seen or heard as many people in my life. Hold on to that baby, Eliza. Bless her, she's not got a clue what's happening around her.' Ma Fletcher linked arms with Eliza as they stood on the cart together. Holding one another steady, Eliza keeping baby Victoria safe as she looked around at the wonderful sights of the red, white and blue of the Union Jack being waved and the crowds singing of the National Anthem. Caps and handkerchiefs were waved as the royal procession appeared from off Upperhead Row and made their way down Briggate and the crowd surged and cheered loudly as the carriages containing Queen Victoria, the Prince Consort and Princesses Helena and Alice made their way down the crowded high street. The royal carriages, decked in gold, shone and sparkled in the early autumn light, and Eliza stood entranced as if watching a fairy tale unfold.

'Isn't she beautiful? Just look at the dresses.' Eliza gasped as the queen waved at her subjects. 'She's got the most beautiful mauve dress on and I wish I could see the embroidery work more clearly on her mantle. Although the dress isn't as large as some of the ones worn in the crowd.'

'You hold on to that baby. The queen's nearly drawn level with us now and she's bound to see us as we are a good head and shoulders above this mob below.' Ma Fletcher yelled and waved her hanky, hoping to catch her majesty's eye.

'She's seen us, she's seen us! Look, and she's waving our way!' Eliza shouted excitedly, wishing that she hadn't got a baby in her arms so that she could wave back. 'Look, baby Victoria, your namesake is waving at us! You truly are special.'

The queen smiled and waved directly at Eliza and Ma Fletcher, and the princesses and Prince Albert pointed and waved at the couple holding a baby way above the crowds, smiling in the autumn sunshine, amazed by the reception of the good folk of Leeds.

'Aye, lass, she'll be special. All babies are. I knew that they'd spot us up here. And the queen loves her babies – she's had enough of 'em herself. You hold on to her; we'll climb back down as the crowds follow the parade. I bet there are nearly millions of folk gathered around the town hall. They've erected a huge triumphal arch decorated with loyal inscriptions and flowers, the like of which I've never seen before or never will again in my lifetime.'

'Prince Albert looked so handsome and the princesses' dresses of green and white were beautiful.' Eliza watched as the coach of the royal party and all the following dignitaries made their way down Briggate and then on to Wellington Street, the crowd being held back by the local force and that of the Metropolitan police in order to control them.

'Aye, but if they can't dress well, then who can? She's not exactly short of a bob or two.' Ma Fletcher got down on her knees and gently lowered herself back down onto the cobbled streets of Briggate and held her arms out for the baby again. 'Bless her, she's slept through all that racket and tossing. You must know you've got to be good for your Aunt Eliza. How your mother could bugger off to America and leave you, I don't know.'

Eliza passed Victoria back into safe hands and then climbed down besides the old woman. 'I can't buy anything off you today as I've got to walk back with this one in my arms. But I'll manage another day.'

'Well, I've nowt worth anything to you anyway today. But I was going to suggest that my old man knocks around Woodlesford once a fortnight; it'll not be out of his way to drop you a bag of assortments off when he's your way. It'll save you walking the canal with the baby.' Ma Fletcher looked at the young lass and her ward – they were going to need all the help they could get. 'Just sort through it and pay him for what you want and if you want tick, we can come to some arrangement, seeing Mary-Anne's not here to help you anymore.'

'That would be a real help, because I'll have to get back to mending and re-selling clothes, just to make ends meet.' Eliza was thankful for the old woman's suggestion.

'Aye, well, I'm always here if you want me.' She looked at Eliza and remembered when her mother had visited her with either Mary-Anne or herself in her arms and it seemed like only yesterday.

'The crowd's thinning.' Eliza looked around her and at the baby that was just beginning to stir.

'Aye, they'll be following her or away home. All that fuss for one woman and a second's glance of her.' Ma Fletcher looked around Briggate at the flags flying and the festoons and wreaths hanging from the windows. 'Come next week it will all be back to normal. The tannery will be stinking, there will be pickpockets doing their usual rounds and they'll be complaining on how much brass they've spent on her visiting our great city, for the opening of a town hall that folks are already complaining about, saying that it's too bare.' Ma Fletcher sighed and rearranged her cart.

'I'm going to go. The baby will need a feed and I've a bottle to give her once I'm out of Leeds and following the canal back towards Woodlesford.' Eliza felt in her pocket for the bottle of milk that she had placed within.

'Aye, lass. Well, you take care. That baby will need you and my old man will pass by shortly.' Ma Fletcher looked at the young woman with her worries.

'I will, and thank you for making my life a bit easier.' Eliza smiled and then made her way through the dwindling crowds down to the Calls and along the canal dockside where she and Mary-Anne had walked so many times before, making her way with baby Victoria who was beginning to cry and wail in her arms.

'Shush now, I'm just going to walk a bit further and then you'll be fed.' She pulled the shawl away from the baby and placed her finger into its mouth to quieten the demanding baby for a second or two. 'There now, we'll sit just here. This is where your mother and I used to sit and talk about what we hoped to buy before we entered Leeds.' Eliza sat down on a stone slab that had been left on the side of the towpath from when the canal had been first built, and placed the angry baby on her lap to feed on the bottle of milk that she'd carried with her. 'There now. Yes, I know it's not warm, just for this once, but you'll drink it if you are hungry.' She watched as the tiny mite showed her disgust in the milk not being warm, then realising it was better than nothing as she started to suck greedily.

'So this is the baby we've been hearing!' Ada Simms exclaimed as she and Bert came upon Eliza and her baby at the side of the canal as they walked home from seeing the queen. 'You've kept that quiet. We didn't suspect a thing.'

'Ada, watch that tongue of yours. It's nowt to do with us.' Bert stood by the side of his wife and looked at the young lass with the baby that they had heard but never seen.

'If you will have your fun, this is what becomes of women like you.' Ada looked down her nose at Eliza.

'It's not mine. It's Mary-Anne's. And she's in my care until she returns for her from America.' Eliza looked up at the old nosy couple and resigned herself not to argue with them. 'She's gone there to get married and make a life with John Vasey, leaving me to look after her baby until they are settled.'

'America! She's gone to America, leaving you with all the worry. Aye, lass, you are going to have something on, you just on your own. Ada bent down and looked at the baby now nearly back asleep with the bottle teat still in its mouth. 'Is it a girl or a boy?'

'A girl, Victoria. She's a good one really, doesn't cry that much.' Eliza looked with love at her bundle.

'Victoria, named after our good lady herself. Well, let's see if I've silver threepence with her name on it.' Bert reached into his pocket and placed a silver threepence in the baby's tight gripping pink hand. 'Silver for luck.'

'Thank you. I'll see we spend it wisely.' Eliza looked up at the old couple that had been interfering in her life for as long as she had known them, but knew she felt strangely glad that they were her neighbours. At least she knew they'd be there if ever she really needed them.

'On your way home, are you?' Ada spouted. 'Did you see the queen in all her glory? Wasn't it wonderful?'

'Yes, yes, we did, and yes we are going home. It's been a long day.' Eliza stood up and put the bottle back in her pocket and hugged Victoria tightly to her.

'Then walk back with us. Come in home too. I'll put the kettle on and you have a rest. You know we will always be there for you, especially now with the baby ...' Ada looked at her as she walked along.

'Thank you. I'll go home, but it's good to know I can count on you as neighbours.' Eliza smiled. Home was where she wanted to be, just to be with baby Victoria and her own thoughts. She'd seen the queen, made her peace with Ada and Bert and ensured that she would be supplied with second-hand goods through Ma Fletcher.

Mary-Anne might be travelling halfway around the world but Eliza's heart lay at home with the people that she was just beginning to realise loved her. She'd raise Victoria with the same love that she was shown. A new life was just beginning for Mary-Anne, but for herself it too would be one full of promise and hope, if she had anything to do with it … a good life for her and Victoria until her mother came to claim her. Until then she would be her daughter and be loved by her and her alone.

As for Tom, she hoped that over time he would realise his love for her and understand why the love of her sister had become between them.

Until then she would wait for him.

Don't miss the new heartwarming saga from Gracie Hart

Can she find somewhere to call home?

Victoria Wild is only four years old but already knows about heartbreak, having been abandoned by her unwed mother when she was only a baby. Luckily her Aunt Eliza was there to take her in but times are still hard on Pit Lane and while Eliza does her best to make sure there is always food on the table, Victoria bears the stigma of her illegitimacy. Her aunt also fears the day when Victoria will start to ask about her father...

But even when Eliza is offered a chance to make a better life for herself and her niece, there are sacrifices to be made. And more trouble is around the corner – in the form of Victoria's mother, Mary-Anne Wild, who is finally coming home not to be a proper mother to her daughter but to exact her revenge on the man who ruined her life...

Available to pre-order now.